UNLEASHED

BOOK ONE OF THE SAGA OF RUINATION

RAMÓN TERRELL

TAL PUBLISHING

UNLEASHED
BOOK ONE OF THE SAGA OF RUINATION
RAMÓN TERRELL
Copyright © 2014 Ramon Terrell
3rd Edition 2019
All Rights Reserved
Tal Publishing

ISBN: 978-1-9990903-5-7 (Paperback)

Cover artwork by: Nick Deligaris

Tal Publishing

DEDICATION

This one is for a very special person who touched my heart instantly, but left this world far too soon. To my buddy, Kara-Lunan Mayers. I'm honored to have known you for the brief time I did, and never have I so quickly made a friend. I know that wherever you are, you're having far too much fun.

FOREWORD

This book has sat in an interesting place in my career. When I finished it, I had no doubt that it was the best book I'd written to date, and although I'm proud of everything I've written, I still believe it is my best published full length novel to date.

Many things happened between the release of this book, and the time I'd intended to release all subsequent entries. Multiple publisher rewrites, rebranding, comic convention appearances, acting jobs, and the day job all conspired to delay the sequel to Unleashed in the Saga of Ruination. But it was worth it.

A special, heartfelt thank you goes out to Cat Lee, Karen Pellet, and Flora Samuelson for being fantastic proof and beta readers for the revised version of this book. You have been amazing.

Lastly, I say with all sincerity to you, beloved readers; thank you. The three-year delay has been a long one, but you will receive better books because of it. I truly hope you love this book as much as I enjoyed writing it.

Ramón Terrell

Khatal
Marai
Shetar
Shatteredlands
Sandlands
Shiedra
Mt. Blood
New Dama
Delain Village
Valraga
La'eshma
Jietar
Altarra
Sleeping Morghan
Nassak
Carlayn
Border Highlands
THE RIDGELINE
Desiden Inlet
Port Syara
Terratoma
The Triplets
Barbaros Island
Dokayuk
Werewood
Drylands
Vyne
Frostlands
Glacier Bay
The Black Glacier
Nogth
Port Tryphlan

1

PROLOGUE

The showering rain had been bad enough, but bearable. It was when the raindrops started to freeze, that Dan began to wonder if nature itself was trying to tell them something.

His clothes long ago soaked through, Dan followed behind his fellow diggers, trudging through hail that started as small as rain droplets but were now as large as a child's fist. Was this typical of the trials a digger endured in their endless search for knowledge and discovery? A ball of hail the size of a man's fist smacked Dan in the back of the head, and he pitched forward, stumbling into the man in front of him.

"Hey now!" Jack Hearn shouted over the roar of the hailstorm. "Don't go tripping and falling all over me! You'll get us both on the ground!"

Dan shook away the stars in his vision and with the bigger man's help, regained his balance. It felt like someone had punched him in the back of the head.

"You all right, lad?" Jack asked, scrutinizing the younger man. "You look like you're about to fall over."

Dan shook his head, then regretted it. He swayed and almost fell over, but the big man caught him by the arm and held him upright.

"I'm fine," Dan finally said, steadying himself. "I'm good. Just...got knocked off balance, is all."

"What're you doing back there!" Mick called from up ahead. "Keep moving, we're nearly there!"

Jack waved over his shoulder at the other man, then looked Dan over a little more. Finally, he nodded. "You get yourself between us. I'll take the rear. Don't want you keeling over and being eaten by something before we know you're missing."

Dan couldn't deny the logic. With the noise of this storm, that ball of hail could have knocked him out and some animal might have dragged him away before the other men realized he was missing.

They started out again, leaning forward and using their forearms to protect their faces against the pounding ice. Dan kept his head down, looking up from under his brow to keep the hunched figure of Mick in his sights. The towering evergreens provided some cover from the pounding, but not much. Dan leaned on a thick trunk as he passed, feeling thick vines as large around as his legs that spiraled around it like flames licking their way up a burning pole. Earlier, before this Creator forsaken expedition had turned ugly, Dan had wondered if the vines shared a symbiotic relationship with these massive trees, or consumed them, like other species of vines did in some of the more remote jungles.

He gingerly stepped around the stem of a weather fron jutting up from the muddy ground. He wished he'd seen one of those things sooner. If he'd spotted one like this one, withdrawn inside itself so that nothing but the short green stem was visible, he would have known a major storm was coming.

Dan focused on carefully putting one foot in front of the other without slipping in the thick mud. Falling would be bad enough, but the cursed mud was so thick, it threatened to suck his boots right off his feet. When they'd started out five days ago, Dan had not seen the point of packing mud boots at the height of summer. 'Never know what the world will bring you when you go exploring it, lad,' Jack had said. How right he'd been.

A strong hand grabbed his pack and snatched him back. Dan

gasped, then looked over his shoulder at Jack, who jerked his chin in the direction they had been going.

When Dan looked back, he saw why the other man had grabbed him. So focused was he on his feet, that he'd almost plowed right into Mick, who was standing at the edge of a drop off.

Dan inched his way beside Mick, and leaned forward to peek over the edge. The drop wasn't as steep as it had appeared from further back, but it was far from mild. He looked at Mick, who was already checking the straps of his pack. He noticed Dan's concerned expression but continued his task.

"Ain't turning back now, boy, and we most certainly ain't going to just sit and wait out this storm. The ground would take too long to dry even if it stopped right now. Count us lucky it's let up as much as it has."

Dan looked around. He'd been so focused on being miserable he hadn't noticed the hail was gone. Only normal rain remained of the punishing deluge.

"Not much to hold onto," Jack observed, peering over the edge.

"It's the only way down," Mick replied. "The sooner we get down to the cave, the sooner we can dry off."

Dan squinted, just able to make out what looked like a cave. Tall grass and shrubs had grown over the entrance while moss and vines grew over the arched stone. It looked like the maw of a teliak.

Mick slapped him on the back, almost causing him to stumble over the edge. The old digger laughed at Dan's responding glare. "Can't be a digger if you're gonna be afraid of getting dirty, lad. There's nothin' for it." He nodded his head in the direction of the slope. "Let's get to it."

They started down, Mick and Jack descending the muddy slope at a sideways angle while Dan slowly picked his way down backwards, holding on to roots and vines, anything that looked to have a stronger hold on this slippery slope than he did.

A root snapped under his weight and he slid down. He scrabbled for another handhold, but then his feet struck something hard and he straightened and fell backwards. Mud splashed in his face, ears, and nose as he tumbled end over end, until the ground was flat again.

He rolled to a stop, lying face first on the muddy ground. Somewhere behind him he heard laughter, then a pair of hands grabbed his shoulders and hoisted him to his feet.

"You alright there?" Jack said, looking him over. "Didn't bust up anything important, did you?"

"I'm fine," Dan said, trying to salvage what dignity he had left. "Just lost my footing."

"Now this is interesting," Mick said from the side.

Dan looked at the other digger, then followed his gaze to the sky. The clear sky. "How's that possible?" he asked.

"You're guessing just like me," Mick said.

"Looks like nature's sense of humor, you ask me," Jack grumbled. "We finally make it to the blasted cave and then the weather clears up?" He spat, drawing a grimace from Dan. "Figures."

"Might be us finally finding this cave was a good thing," Mick said, "and the Creator Himself is showing us by lifting the storm."

Or that He was trying to deter us and we were too stubborn, so now it doesn't matter. The thought surprised Dan. It wasn't as if they were grave robbers, looking to loot some king's tomb. They were seekers of ancient knowledge. Digging in the past was fascinating, and the primary reason Dan had sought to become a digger.

"Whatever the cause, we ain't getting anywhere by standing here," Jack said. "Let's move."

Mick used his tinderbox and lit a torch, and the others lit theirs from his. They navigated their way through the tall grass and shrubs until they came to the mouth of the cave.

Mick leaned forward and held his torch out in front of him. "Dark as pitch," he said. "Should be okay as long as the three of us keep our light together. Stay close."

With each step they entered, Dan's anxiety deepened. He almost made himself dizzy as he scanned the tunnel, eyes darting in every direction. He thought he heard a sound and looked over his shoulder.

Nothing. But then, the dark was not far away, like a wraith waiting at the perimeter of the torch's light.

"Calm yourself, lad," he heard Jack say. "We did our studies before coming here. There hasn't been a report of anything larger than a rat living here since anyone could remember."

"When was the last report?" Dan asked.

"'Bout a week ago," Jack said.

Time slipped by and if they'd been traveling an hour or a day, Dan couldn't have said. After stopping for a snack, the trio moved on until they came to a massive cavern.

"By the Creator," Mick whispered. "Never seen anything like this."

Dan's mouth fell open. A soft blue tint with no apparent source floated in the air, illuminating a huge open area with stalactites scattered across the ceiling staring down at a pit of blackness. With more than a little trepidation, he stared at the bridge made of stone, that led to the other side of the pit. Dan felt his stomach lurch at just the thought of it. "We're not crossing that thing, surely."

"Can't be a digger if you're gonna be afraid of a bridge," Mick replied. "Besides, it's made of stone, not even a wood and rope one. Probably much sturdier."

"What I'd like to know," Jack said, "is who could have built it. There's ways to get across a chasm and build a bridge of rope and wood. How in the Creator's own imagination did anyone manage that?"

"Don't matter," Mick said. "There's a tomb not far past the other side of that. I can feel it."

Dan could feel it as well. "I don't like this."

Mick sighed. "Look, lad. I took you on as an apprentice despite your academic nonsense and lack of experience because you seemed enthusiastic about the job. If I'd known you were this skittish about everything I might have reconsidered."

"It's not that I'm afraid," Dan replied. "But don't you feel it? Something isn't right about this place."

"And how would you know what does or doesn't feel right when this is the first dig you've gone on?" Mick countered.

"All right, let's just stop right here," Jack said. "I'm not going to say the boy's wrong, Mick. This place does feel more unwelcoming than usual. Why don't we just go across. When we get to the tomb, we'll call him over when all is well."

"Bah, whatever you wanna do," Mick said. He threw up his hand and continued on.

Jack turned to Dan as Mick started across the bridge, grumbling about babysitting. "You gonna be alright waiting here?"

"This place isn't right, Jack," Dan said. "You feel it too, don't you? Like there's something in here."

Jack smiled. "It's just your nerves, lad. It's your first dig. It's dark in here, and that bridge is mysterious." He looked around the blue-tinged cavern. "And I'll admit that blue haze or whatever it is kind of unnerves me. But this is the job. This is what we do. The knowledge and artifacts of thousands of years past are waiting to be discovered. Learned from."

Dan was about to reply but the big man patted him on the shoulder. "Just wait here and I'll call for you when we get there." He gave Dan's shoulder a squeeze, then turned away. Dan watched the two men slowly cross the stone bridge across that gaping pit until they disappeared in the tunnel on the other side.

Dan looked around. That blue light hung in the air like a fog. But fog didn't emit light. He moved toward the stone wall, thinking to sit down, when the torchlight revealed images carved into it.

"What's this?" He leaned closer.

The entire section of the wall had carvings with glyphs beneath each event. He didn't know how whoever did this managed to get ten feet high to carve the wall, but the light from his torch was not enough to reach it. Instead, Dan focused on the section toward the end that he could see.

They must have been glyphs from the first or second age, as there was no society he knew of that still used this type of writing. His years in academia came to him as he tried to translate the glyphs. Not all were known to him, but he was able to decipher enough to get the idea. He started at the carvings that depicted what was obviously some sort of evil black cloud with slitted eyes and a mouth full of fangs. It looked to be spreading over the land. Underneath it were dead people and animals, lying upon the cracked and charred earth. Trees drooped and plants burned. The glyphs underneath it roughly translated to The Ruination.

Dan felt a shiver. He glanced over his shoulder at the blue tinted cavern, then went back to the carvings. The next row depicted large robed figures standing before the evil cloud. Something seemed to seep from the ground into the robed figures and out in the direction of the cloud. The glyphs underneath this one translated to The Confrontation.

Dan frowned at the final row. The cloud looked to have been destroyed. Not destroyed. It was compressed and forced into what looked like a man. A single man. The last image was of six men holding a large sarcophagus over their heads, leading a long procession of mourners to a cave. The final glyphs under this last row translated to the words Redemption.

Dan's mouth fell open. What did this mean? He looked over the glyphs and carvings again, but there was no mistaking their meaning. And if he hadn't been able to decipher the writing, the depictions on this wall were enough to get an idea of what had happened. Some kind of evil was killing everything, and robed men had gathered to stop it but had succeeded only in trapping it in the body of a man. This man must have been important, judging by the many people who assembled to mourn him.

Dan was well versed in ancient lore, but this was like nothing he'd ever encountered. He would have to research this when he made it back to the university. He looked around the blue tinted darkness and his sense of foreboding deepened. He wasn't given to superstitions, but he was starting to feel an urgent need to be gone from this place. Maybe he should go and get the others; show them what he found.

"Stupid idea," he thought aloud. There was no telling how many tunnels this place had. He'd more likely get lost and die of starvation before they found him.

He looked further to the side and saw a pile of boulders against the wall. He climbed over the smallest of the rocks and shined the light over the top, hoping nothing was sleeping behind it. Dan sighed in relief at the empty spot and made his way down. He'd imagined great underground civilizations and ruins filled with hieroglyphs, artifact, and—when he was honest with himself—corlite.

He sat down and sighed again. He'd heard the stories of diggers stumbling upon veritable treasure troves of the valuable stone. They'd been able to extract enough corlite to live for the rest of their lives in comfort. Dan would use the wealth to buy a home and devote his life to study and digging. He loved what he did, but it would be even more enjoyable without the worry of how he would pay for his monthly taxes and food, not to mention a loan from the crown to buy a home with. Maybe he would move to—

His head snapped up. Was that a scream? Surely not. It was so high-pitched it couldn't have come from Jack or Mick. Dan climbed up and peeked over the top of the cluster of boulders. For a while he stared at the far side of the bridge, then he heard another scream. It wasn't from either of the men, and Dan wasn't even sure it was a human voice.

A claw of fear gripped his chest and his breaths came in short fast huffs. He should find out what was going on, see if the others needed help. His mind told him this, but his body was rooted to the rock he crouched upon.

He nearly dropped his torch when yellow light burst from the tunnel on the other side of the pit. Then he heard Mick's voice, screaming to get the hell out. Then more light burst from the tunnel and the once blue tinted cavern was bathed in red light.

Dan panicked and dropped back down. The light was so bright it was like daylight, but red daylight. On instinct he put out his torch, then climbed up again. He peeked over the top just in time to see Jack sprinting out of the tunnel, Mick not far behind.

"Go, go, GO!" Mick screamed. "It's right behind us!"

"We can't outrun that!" Jack yelled.

"Just keep runni—"

Mick's last words died in his mouth as a black cloud flowed from the tunnel and swept over him. Mick's terror-filled scream nearly made Dan's heart stop. The cloud lifted the poor man into the air, turning him end over end. He continued to scream as the thing consumed him from the inside out. In seconds a rotted corpse fell to the ground, mouth still agape in a silent wail.

Jack was nearly across the bridge by then, and Dan opened his mouth to yell for him when the cloud swept him off his feet. The big man landed flat on his back with a heavy gasp, the wind blasted from his lungs. He turned on his side, trying to catch his breath as the black cloud swirled above him. Then, oddly, it flowed down into the pit and was gone.

Jack coughed, but forced himself to his feet.

Dan started to climb out of his hiding spot when the ground rumbled, and his foot slipped. He held on as the tremor intensified. His legs dangling, all he could do was watch helplessly as the black cloud returned from the pit. Impossible as it seemed, the thing was even darker, as though it simply consumed light.

It burst through the part of the stone bridge that connected to Dan's side of the pit, and seemed to hover there, watching the hopelessness settle over Jack. The big man fell to his knees and clasped his hands before him, his lips moving fast and silent. Tears streamed down Dan's face as he watched the man, clearly praying to the Creator as the cloud hovered in front of him.

The black cloud began to coalesce until it formed into what looked like a black cloud with giant arms ending in claws as long as a man's body. Four red eyes glowed down at Jack, and beneath the fiery orbs opened a maw filled with insubstantial fangs.

It's shoulders bounced as it watched the praying man. Was it laughing? Finally, it flew into Jack, but something odd happened. Jack was thrown to the ground, but not consumed. The cloud screeched in what sounded like irritation, then lifted Jack high into the air and dropped him onto the stone bridge.

He hit the bridge hard, and a trickle of blood flowed from his lips. In the red light that illuminated the cavern, Dan saw Jack's eyes, staring vacantly back at him.

The cavern shook again, and the last thing Dan saw before he lost his grip was the bridge bursting apart and the digger's body falling into the pit of blackness.

Dan tumbled to the ground then curled into a ball as stone debris rained down on him. A sound like breathing and growling echoed throughout the cavern, and it was all he could do to keep from trembling. He cracked an eye open and saw that he was covered in rock and dirt. There was a tiny split at the bottom of the pile of boulders where he could see the evil cloud, hovering over the pit.

The cloud turned left, then right, apparently looking over the cavern. Then, with a great heave, it inhaled. The bright red light was pulled away as the insubstantial creature breathed it in. Several heartbeats later the red light was no more, and even the blue glow was diminished. Lying as still as possible, Dan continued to peer through the hole at the thing. The red light flowed through the blackness of the cloud, which grew before his eyes.

It drew in a long inhale, then shook the cavern with the most awful roar Dan had ever heard. Dan clamped his eyes shut, too afraid to move even enough to cover his ears. When he opened his eyes again, the blue light was gone, leaving the area in darkness. So black was that evil cloud, however, that even in the dark, Dan could still see it swirling around in the air before it shot out of the cavern in the direction they had originally come.

For many heartbeats Dan lay there, afraid to move. Afraid to breathe. When he felt confident the thing had gone, he lifted his head. Dirt and rock streamed from his body and through his matted light brown hair.

He peeked over the top of the rock, then climbed over. He skulked along the wall, passing the hieroglyphs until he came to the tunnel.

Dan pressed his back flat against the wall and leans out for a quick look, bringing his head back too fast and smacking his still sore head against the stone. When the pain subsided, he leaned around the corner again. It was gone, or at least out of sight.

Dan made his way through the tunnels, nearly jumping out of his skin every time he heard a sound. He tried to quell his imagination as it conjured images of that terrible cloud of evil waiting for him around every bend, coming up from behind to devour him.

Finally, he smelled the crisp fresh air from the surface, and it was the sweetest smell in the world. He was alive! His sadness at the loss of his two companions was briefly diminished by the elation of being alive.

The howling wind outside was a warm welcome as Dan ran for the surface. He slowed, then stopped at the sight of the charred black grass and shrubs that had formerly guarded the entrance to the cave. He walked over it, his boots crunching the burned plants.

"What in the name of the Creator ..." Dan looked up from the charred plants at the blackened path leading up the slope from where they had come. It was an easy climb to the top, as the scorched ground hard as a road.

When he made it to the top the strength left his legs and he dropped to his knees. "By the Creator Himself. What have we done?" Tears streamed down his dusty cheeks. A trail as wide as two wagons abreast extended as far as he could see, littered with the corpses of burned and withered vegetation and animals.

Dan knelt there, staring into the distance and repeating the words like a mantra. "What have we done? By the Creator Himself, what have we done?"

2

EMIEL

Cold. That was the only word Emiel could think of as he guided his two horse team up the dirt road. Cold. It was always so cold this time of year in Carlayn. The trees with their bare hanging limbs just sat there, waiting for the cold and dampness to retreat so they could actually bloom a leaf or two. Not that all the trees were like that. Only the seasonal ones. Up in the nearby mountains, the stoutgreens held their green plumage year round.

Emiel snorted. Stoutgreens. More like just plain stubborn. Anything that chose to grow on the side of a freezing wet and hazy mountain and still manage to bloom was more stubborn than anyone ought to be, tree or not. A gust of wind blew across the road causing his scarf to blow across his face. Grumbling, he held the reins with one hand while he reached up to wrap the scarf back around his neck.

Blasted wind. A man could catch death out in something like this. Emiel pulled his hood over his head. The weather was always bad this time of year, but not like this. "Could swear one of the Fallen is walking around, with this land blasted weather."

Emiel smiled despite his grumbling. He would likely have had a scolding by his daughters if they had heard him speak like that. 'Daddy!' Nandi would say. 'You can't talk about the Fallen or they'll come and take you!'

Emiel laughed. Nandi, the more superstitious of the two. Amiya would no doubt take her sister's side while at the same time teasing her twin for being overly superstitious. 'The Fallen won't just come to your house if you speak about them,' she would say. 'But acknowledging them does give them power. You can't talk about them, Dad. It just makes them stronger.'

Not long after the girls had started talking, Emiel had seen that Nandi's personality would be an even balance of his and his wife's, while Amiya was more like her mother. Well, a more extreme version of her mother.

He thought about his wife, and his smile faded. It had been eleven years since Aunya had died giving birth to the twins. Those eleven years had not dulled the pain, but it had given him a tougher hide with which to endure it. So many years that had passed in the blink of an eye.

The road grew less rough as the ruts leveled out, until he finally came to the more well maintained roads that were within the limits of the city of Vyne. The weather lightened, and Emiel looked up at the sky.

"So I get a soaking, and a windburn on the road, but all is nice and calm when I get home?" he drew back his hood and ran a hand over his shaved head. "Surely I must have had one of the cursed Fallen sitting next to me and didn't know it."

The wagon rounded the bend, and the front gates of Vyne came into view. Emiel looked upon the city with a mixture of affection and detachment. The city of Aunya's birth. He had lived here with his wife for four years before the twins had been born.

Vyne was a beautiful place with an ugly heart. That heart was not its people, who were its lifeblood, but archminister Decius. Emiel forced himself not to snarl at the thought of the hated man as he passed through the gate, nodding back at the soldiers who stood guard at the entrance.

Ever since Decius had come to the city and studied under his predecessor, Emiel had kept an eye on things while secretly nurturing a relationship with his contacts from the Barbaros Islands. Something in that man's eyes made Emiel uncomfortable, and the sooner he and the girls could be away from this place, the better.

At the sound of the horses' hooves clip clopping on the cobblestone streets, locals turned and waved. Emiel smiled and waved back, feeling mildly guilty that these fine people would soon have to pay more for his spices once he moved away.

"I'd pack everybody up and move 'em with me if I could," he muttered under his breath.

"Hey Emiel," a nearby man said. "You just missed a nasty storm."

"I assure you I enjoyed every bit of it as much as you," Emiel said. "Though if you've any sense in your head, you would have enjoyed it in your house and not outside like a certain foolish spicetrader." He indicated his soaked clothes with an open hand.

The other man laughed. "You have any luck?"

"A bit," Emiel said as the wagon continued past.

"Well, let me know when you've got another mix of quickburn ready."

Emiel smiled again and waved. Quickburn was his most popular mix of spices.

Many conversations and attempted spice orders later, Emiel finally arrived at his house. Hopefully the girls would have at least started something resembling a meal by now. At only eleven years old, they were already better cooks than he had been his whole life. If not for the kindness of some of his neighbors and longtime customers, he wondered if the girls would have survived his attempts in the kitchen.

He took off his jacket and shook off the excess water, then stomped his feet. "Hey little ladies," he called as he entered. "I'm home and hungry."

Silence.

Emiel frowned. "Girls?"

Strange. The girls would never go outside in the middle of a storm that bad, and he doubted they would have fled the house so soon after it had passed. They knew he would be home by midday and would have had something prepared for him.

"Nandi? Amiya?"

Now his heart pounded in his chest. This was unusual for the normally reliable girls. They'd formed the agreement that when he went out to trade and sell, they would have a meal prepared for when he returned, and then they could spend the remainder of their day as they wished. The girls had never once strayed from the routine.

Emiel was almost running through the house. "Amiya! Nandi!"

He went through all the rooms, not sure what he was looking for but afraid of what he might find. He came to his desk in the living room and sat down, and it was then that he noticed the note.

SPICETRADER:

To my dismay, it has been brought to my attention
that you intend to leave our beloved city of Vyne in
pursuit of ventures in other lands. I find this unfortunate
as well as troublesome. In case you were unaware, the revenue
from your lovely spice making and trading business has brought
remarkable revenue into the city for years. I cannot fathom
why you would wish to leave such a prosperous business
behind. Surely you must reconsider. I have invited your
lovely girls, Nandi and Amiya to enjoy the hospitality
of my personal mansion in an effort to give you plenty
of time to reconsider your course, for surely you must
see that it is a mistake. You needn't worry about your
Precious—and quite adorable—daughters
for I can assure you they aren't going anywhere.
Take all the time you need—but not too much—to rethink
your decision. Young girls develop so quickly and it would be
a shame for you to miss even a moment of it.

*And if I may say, your girls are going to have to beat the
boys away, so beautiful they are!
Perhaps there is something I can
do to make Vyne more attractive to you again?
I look forward to hearing from you very soon, I'm sure.*

SINCERELY,

Archminister Decius

EMIEL STARED AT THE NOTE, then read it again. Cold fear stabbed at his heart. What was going on? Why in the world would the archminister have any reason to detain his girls in an effort to get to him?

He looked around the room, frantic to find an answer, any hint of a clue about what was going on. He slapped his hands on the table and stood, knocking the chair over behind him. He needed to think. He went into his room and sat on the bed, then stood and started pacing. It was too small in there as well. He could practically see the walls closing in. "I need some air."

He crossed through the living room and threw the door open. Emiel leaned against the house and forced himself to take a few long breaths of crisp, post storm air. Gradually, the constriction in his chest eased. He looked in the direction of the archminister's mansion. His girls were in there, probably scared. Well, maybe Nandi was scared. Amiya was probably furious. He hoped they were together, at least.

Emiel went back into the house, grabbed his coat, and was out the door. Friends, neighbors, and customers greeted him as he passed, and he offered distracted replies but never slowed. What was this about? Emiel was hardly the most wealthy man in the city, and although his spice business was lucrative, he doubted he'd be missed by anyone other than his customers.

"Hey! Hey, Emiel!" It was Larren, his next door neighbor. "Emiel!"

"I'm sorry, Larren," Emiel said, lengthening his stride. "Something just came up. I don't have time to talk." Fallen be damned, his heart felt like it was going to pound out of his chest.

"I know!" Larren said, moving in closer. "It's the girls, right?"

Emiel stopped. "What do you know about this?"

"Not much," Larren said, glancing around as if he were afraid someone was watching them. "Just ... keep walking but slow it down and look natural." He led Emiel away from the main street and down a side path between a bakery and tailor shop.

"Look I know you've got to be in a near panic. I know I would be. But listen to me." Larren leaned in close. "Emiel, the city guard came to get Nandi and Amiya." When Emiel didn't react, Larren blinked at him. "I don't think you understand. When I say the city guard, I'm saying twenty of them."

"Twenty?" Emiel frowned. "What? Why? Who would feel it necessary to send twenty guards for two eleven-year-old girls?"

Larren held up his hands. "We could both guess. What I do know is that the looks on those guards faces said they were on dangerous business."

Emiel felt his panic deepening. "What happened? Did they harm Nandi and Amiya?"

Larren patted the air between them. "Keep your voice down, please, Emiel. The guards weren't rough, but they looked like they were escorting two teliak monsters instead of a couple of young girls."

Emiel paced back and forth, running a hand over his head. "This doesn't make any sense. The Fallen curse him. What does he want with my girls?"

Larren held his hands up in a placating gesture. "Don't let anyone hear you saying that. It's the archminister you're talking about."

"I don't care if he's the lord of the underworld," Emiel snapped. "This is outright kidnapping."

"I know, I know." Larren grabbed Emiel's his shoulders. "I agree with you. But you've got to cool your head. If you go to his mansion this, what do you think will happen?"

Emiel looked at his friend and sighed. Larren was right. He'd likely go in there making all sorts of demands to get his daughters back. No matter the fact that he would be justified in doing so, the result would more likely be his imprisonment, or worse.

He took a deep breath and stopped pacing. His heart was still fluttering and he felt cold and hot at the same time. "I'm fine," he finally said.

"What're you gonna do?" Larren asked him.

"Only thing I can do," Emiel replied. "Decius wants to see me, so I've got to go to him and find out what this is all about." He didn't miss how Larren flinched when he spoke the archminister's name without his title, but he didn't care. "I've gotta go."

"I don't like this, Emiel," Larren said. "You want me to come with you?"

Emiel shook his head. "No. All you could do is get yourself into trouble. The best thing anybody can do in this city is to be as indistinguishable as possible. The day you find yourself in that man's sights is the day your troubles begin."

3

EMIEL

Vyne was not a big sprawling city by any standards, but it was not a small town either. Yet when Emiel looked farther up the street at the veritable palace that was the archminister's mansion, he couldn't help but wonder if the man realized the structure looked like it belonged in a kingdom.

The former archminister, Charion, had been a good man. During his tenure, Charion had occupied only a small section of the mansion —which was a great deal smaller at the time—and had insisted that the remaining unused portion be allotted as housing for those less fortunate that worked to improve their lives. The man had been tough, kind, and fair.

This new archminister, Decius, had not only put a swift end to that, but had set about adding on to the mansion before Charion was even cold in the ground.

Emiel came to the iron barred gates and waited while two guards searched him. That an archminister felt he needed to be wary of his fellow residents was odd, given the way Decius ran things, it made sense.

One of the guards, a stocky man with a thick brown beard stepped back and nodded in the direction of the mansion.

Friendly, Emiel thought. Must be a soldier thing.

He tried to hide his disgust as he passed through the halls of the oversized house, ignoring the two 'escorts' that trailed two steps behind him, hands resting on the hilts of the swords at their hips. "Guess spicetraders have a dangerous reputation," he muttered under his breath.

Long red carpets flowed the length of the hallways, muting their footsteps as they walked the polished granite floors. Emiel eyed hand painted portraits and sculptures that sat in semicircular alcoves, then looked up at the ceiling, where depictions of the Illuminarians battled the Fallen in the War of the Immortals.

Emiel frowned at Decius's arrogance. Depictions such as these should only be displayed in the church where they could be discussed with the monks.

The guard escort stopped, and two guards from ahead stepped forward to intercept him. *Am I some deadly animal?* Emiel thought. Given their size difference, he doubted he could overwhelm Decius even if there were two of him.

Emiel had expected to be taken to a grand room with twenty-foot tall doors opening to reveal some great audience hall. Instead, they brought him to a room with a single door, not much larger than the one to his own room.

The guard at the door knocked, then ducked his head in. After a moment, he opened the door and gestured for Emiel to enter.

Emiel passed two more guards on either side as he entered the room. The archminister stood with his hands clasped behind his back, staring up at a life-sized tapestry depicting yet another battle between the Illuminarians and the Fallen.

The guards quickened their pace and crossed their halberds in front of him. *I guess that means stop?*

After a moment, the guards withdrew their weapons, but remained where they were. If the archminister knew Emiel was in the room, he gave no indication as he continued to study the tapestry. Emiel had to admit that it was quite impressive, however wasted it was on this son of a darkwood cat.

To the side of the room stood a figure dressed in a flowing long sleeved cloak. The colors were a beautiful mix of silver and blue, with a darker silver sash tied around the waist. He couldn't tell if the hooded person was male or female, given the volume of the cloak, but something about him or her was unnerving.

The figure looked up, just a bit, and Emiel saw that it was a man. He fixed Emiel with a green-eyed stare that could have frozen his heart. There was no malice or aggression in those eyes, just a cold matter-of-factness that told Emiel that under no uncertain terms, if he stepped wrong in here, he would die. Swiftly.

"Do you ever find yourself wondering what happened to the Illuminarians and the Fallen?"

Emiel blinked, and returned his attention to the archminister. Decius still hadn't looked away from the tapestry. He stared at the back of the man's head, wishing he could ram something heavy across it.

"No?" Decius said, finally turning to face him. He was a six-foot tall, barrel chested man with arms almost as thick as Emiel's legs. He had a puffy black beard that moved with his chin when he spoke, and his hair was tied behind his back with a gold ring. Judging from the excessive opulence surrounding him, Emiel figured the ring was probably some form of rare corlite. "Do you not wonder what happened to the figures of legend?"

"I wonder what happened to my daughters," Emiel replied.

"Yes, of course." Hands still behind his back, the big man made his way toward the side of the room where a set of windowed doors lead to a balcony overlooking the eastern portion of Vyne. He waved for Emiel to join him.

Emiel stared at the man's back, incredulous. The two guards gave him a warning look, and he clenched his jaw and followed. Though he couldn't see them, he felt the cloaked person's eyes on him.

"You wonder why I invited your daughters to enjoy my hospitality, of course."

"I wonder why you abducted them, yes."

Decius huffed in amusement. "You have an interesting way with words."

"I say what it is." Emiel struggled to keep his temper in check. Never mind the guards and that lethal looking cloak standing off to the side, Decius himself could probably overwhelm Emiel and hurl him over the balcony. The archminister may be on the other side of plump, but was nearly twice Emiel's size.

"Your words have a harshness to them, spicetrader."

"Do you have children, archminister?" How it galled him to call the man by a title he didn't deserve.

"The tenets of the church forbid this. It is the masses, the people, who are our children."

"Eloquently put," Emiel replied. *And the mewling of a darkwood cat is enticing until it guts you.* "So by that understanding, you might have a tiny bit of understanding why I'm less than happy at the moment?"

"I assure you they are quite comfortable."

"They were comfortable at home."

"I needed to speak with you."

"An invitation is the usual method."

The man chuckled, his thick shoulders bouncing. "And tell me. Had I sent that invitation, would you have come, or simply put it off until you could be gone from the city?"

"I don't see how it matters what I do or where I go." *Patience. Keep your temper in check.* "I don't believe I've broken any laws, and the law has never had any issue with me. I've lived in Vyne for over fifteen years. I pay my taxes without complaint for the ..." he looked back at the luxurious room, "maintenance, of the city."

"And yet you would leave. You would take your spice trading business and leave the city of Vyne."

Emiel frowned. "What does it matter to you where I go? I'm not some dignitary or anybody important."

"Your business brings a sizable revenue to the city, spicetrader."

"A revenue that is not the lifeblood of the city, archminister." Emiel could feel his temper slipping. "I'm going to have to ask you to excuse my sharpness, given that I'm standing here talking to the man that had my daughters taken from me. I'd like very much to have them back and be gone. You want to know why I'm leaving the city? I want a change of pace. A change of scenery." *I want to put half the world between you and me.*

"That is an unusual thing. I've not met many who would uproot not only their lives, but the lives of their children to live someplace else, simply because they want a change of scenery. Have you no loyalty to this land?"

"With all due respect, archminister, what is it you fear I will do? I know of no secrets to tell anyone. I have not the means to steal the wealth of the city and fly away with it to some distant land. I'm nobody important; just a man living his life."

Decius scrutinized Emiel. "Of course."

What was he looking for? What was this conversation about? "I'd like to have my children back, archminister."

"And of course you will have them back," Decius replied. "But I must ask a favor of you first."

The Creator Himself must have prevented Emiel from jumping on the man right there. "You don't have the right to detain my family, Decius."

"Watch your tone and your words, spicetrader."

"You would have respect from me for abducting two helpless children? *My* children?"

"I would have respect from every person in this city. I would have respect from every single person who crosses the path of the archminister. You are in no position to bargain with me, nor are you in any position to speak to me as though you are my equal."

Fallen take you, Decius! Emiel stood there, staring at the man, meeting those icy blue eyes and determined not to flinch away.

"You have courage in you," the man finally said.

I would cut your heart out of your chest for my girls, he thought, but still he didn't speak. He didn't trust what would come out of his mouth.

"You do not like me, do you?"

Emiel laughed. "Is that a serious question?"

The archminister snapped his fingers, and two guards that he hadn't known were right behind him, grabbed his arms.

"Hey!" He struggled, but the guards held him. "What kind of coward are you?"

"Oh I assure you I'm no coward, spicetrader. I just want to ensure that your temper doesn't make this situation any more complicated than it has to be. You wish your lovely girls back? You will have them. But before that happens, I need a favor from you."

"A favor is asked."

"A favor is whatever I say it will be. Now hold your tongue and listen." He held up a finger in front of Emiel's face. "You have just one task. I need a valuable piece of cargo transported to Altarra. This is a transaction between myself and the magi master that I must see completed within the month. Once you have completed this task, I will see your daughters returned to you."

This had to be a joke. His girls kidnapped because he was moving away, and he had to deliver a package to get them back? What was really going on here?

"You know, I might have done it if you'd just asked me," Emiel replied.

"I prefer a more efficient course."

"Fine. Let's go the efficient route. Give me the package and my daughters, and on my word, I will deliver it for you."

Decius laughed at him. "And why would I trust that you would do this?"

"Because my word is who I am. *I* live with *integrity*, archminister."

"I believe I warned you against your tone."

One of the guards smacked him across the face with an armored hand. The world spun, and Emiel found himself on the ground. After several moments, his vision cleared and the world came back into focus. The pain also came into focus. He placed a hand to his head and cringed. He could feel his pulse in his skull.

"My apologies for that. My elite guard have little tolerance for insubordination."

Emiel said nothing. It would get him nowhere. This man had his girls and there was nothing he could do about it. These guards would kill him right now if Decius gave the order.

"I'd like to see them before I go," he said.

"Excellent." The archminister clapped his hands together. "You see? Why couldn't we have come to this agreement sooner? It would have saved me the proverbial headache, and you the real one.

The Fallen take you.

"Don't look at me in such a way, Emiel. I promise this is very important, and when it is done, your young ladies will be reunited with you." He turned his attention to the guards.

"Take him to see his daughters, then escort him back to his home." The guards grabbed him by the arms and muscled him to his feet. "Now, now," Decius said. "There's no need to continue with the hostilities. This man has just agreed to help me. We must show more gratitude than that."

Emiel forced himself not to touch the side of his face, which was surely bruised, and turned away. He passed the cloaked man, and crossed the room with a determined stride. He stopped at the door and one of the guards opened it and stepped through. Emiel heard Decius's voice as he stepped out.

"No need to worry about your little girls, Emiel. You'll find them quite well cared for, and I am absolutely certain they will remain so."

Emiel left the room without responding and followed the guards down the halls. His mind was racing. What was he going to do about this? This situation was the reason he wanted to leave Vyne in the first place. Archminister Decius held far more power than any one man should be allowed.

They descended a set of spiraling stairs. Were they keeping Amiya and Nandi in some sort of jail cell underground? Emiel wondered if he could find a way to overcome the two men escorting him. And then what? There was a mansion full of armed soldiers that he would have to get past.

The bottom of the stairs ended at another hallway, this one made of stone. Emiel looked around, and his memory was jogged at the sight of a sunken meeting room where monks would gather to discuss scriptures, ancient scrolls, and figures out of legend and what their message was to the world in this age. During Archminister Charion's time, Emiel had been invited to sit in with a discussion. That had been a good time.

Now the room looked as though it hadn't been occupied in years. The other rooms were similarly unkempt or abandoned. When the guards stopped and indicated the room to the right, Emiel took a deep breath and waited for them to unlock the door.

He stepped in and smiled. Amiya and Nandi sat on the floor playing a game of spin-the-chip. It was their favorite game in which both girls would simply hold a piece of a stone they had ground into a flat circular chip. They would place it upright on the ground and hold it up between their thumb and middle finger, and at the same time, flick their fingers and cause the chips to spin. Whomever's chip spun the longest won the game.

Emiel's smile deepened at the sight of them unharmed, playing the game he'd taught them years ago. The trick was focus. The harder one focused, the longer the chips would spin. Despite his objections, the girls had tried to teach other children how to play it, but they were never able to get their chips to spin longer than a few seconds before they would fall over. Emiel had once counted well over a minute before one of Nandi or Amiya's chips fell over.

Amiya noticed him first, and her chip fell. Nandi opened her mouth to shout her victory when she noticed that Amiya was distracted.

"Dad?" they both said in unison.

"Hey ladygirls," Emiel said, using his nickname for them.

He knelt and opened his arms, and they almost knocked him over when they crashed into him with a crushing hug. For several heartbeats they remained there, holding each other. Finally, Emiel patted them on the back and they let go and backed away. He looked over his shoulder at the waiting guards.

"You think you can give me a minute with my daughters, please?"

They stared at him but didn't move.

"I doubt I'm strong enough to knock a hole in that wall, so you don't have to worry about me busting out of here. Okay?"

They continued to stare at him, and when he figured they would just stay where they were, one left the room and the other followed, closing the door. He heard the lock click in place from the other side.

Emiel turned back to the twins. "You two okay?"

"We're fine, Daddy," Nandi said. "But we don't know what's going on."

"The city soldiers just showed up at our home and told us we had to wait for you here," Amiya said. "They wouldn't tell us anything and we've been here for almost the whole day. I'm starting to get irritated they won't let us leave. Can we go now?" That was Amiya. Fiery and short of patience, like her mother. And also like her mother, she was steadfastly courageous and loyal, and particularly protective of her twin sister and even Emiel.

"I don't understand it," Nandi, the more patient of the two, said. Though at times she shared her sister's temper, Nandi was more calculating. "The archminister told us he wanted to have us as guests to wait while you arrived, but I don't believe him. Is he trying to use us against you for some reason, Daddy?"

Emiel grinned. Eleven years old, and not much could get by that one. "We shouldn't speak too loudly or too long, love."

As quickly as he could, he relayed his meeting with the archminister and his impending journey to Altarra. The girls listened quietly until he finished, then Nandi frowned while Amiya fumed.

"This is stupid," the latter snapped. "Does he think we just fell off the red root wagon yesterday?"

Emiel choked back his laughter.

"I don't think he thinks we're stupid," Nandi said. "I think that's just an excuse for something. Maybe he just wants to scare you into not moving away. I heard him talking to one of the other men about it."

Emiel had thought about the same thing on his way down here, but it still didn't make sense. Something didn't add up.

"At the moment it doesn't matter," he said, raising his voice so that the guards could hear. "I'll just have to run his errand. When I get back, I can take you home."

The twins got the message and nodded.

Emiel figured he didn't have much time left, so he bent low and whispered between them. "I'm going to make arrangements for us to get out of the city in the middle of the night. Be ready."

"I'm in!" Amiya whispered, but Nandi was silent.

"What's in your head, little girl?" Emiel asked her.

"Just be careful, Daddy," she said. "I don't like that man, but I think he's smart. That makes me afraid of him."

Amiya snorted, but Emiel thought it a wise way to think. "I will be careful, ladygirl." He heard the key turn in the door and pulled the girls in for another tight hug. "I'll see you in a month, or sooner if I can. Okay?"

"Okay," the girls said in unison, sounding sad and scared. If not for the desperate situation, Emiel might have thought it rather humorous.

"You two be good," he said. They stepped out, and he waved as one of the guards closed the door.

The trip back to the front door of the mansion seemed much shorter, likely because he knew where he was going this time. One of the guards stated that his business was finished, and he was to return home. Unspoken, however, was that he was to be escorted back. The guards followed behind him through the mansion, and into the courtyard.

"You know, I'm pretty confident I can find my way home," Emiel said. He received no response. "Suit yourselves." He picked up his pace, taking long strides and forcing the heavily armored guards to keep pace. By the time his house was in sight, Emiel had broken a sweat despite the cold early evening air.

"Thanks for looking after me," he said, smiling at them.

One of the guards glared at him, but they turned on their heels and strode away. Emiel watched until they disappeared from view, then dashed into his house. He stuffed three packs full of clothes; one for himself, and one for each of the girls. Then he packed some gear for the road, as well as an intimidating hunting knife he'd won in a game of stones. Emiel always had been a good shot at just about anything he had in his hand.

Several minutes later he had the packs ready to go. He went around back to the pasture and stable connected to his house. The smell of rows of vegetables and spice plants greeted him as he passed through and into the barn.

He went into Surefoot's stall first. "Easy, girl," he said when the sleeping roan blinked in his direction. "I'm sorry to get you up but we've got a hard ride ahead." He smiled at the mare, remembering how pointless it had been to explain to the girls how unfitting the name Surefoot was to an animal that had hooves. Amiya and Nandi had both insisted, so Surefoot she was named.

After saddling the horse, he went into the next stall where his buckskin, Nickland, watched. The gelding's ears swiveled in Emiel's direction, and he nickered.

"Sorry, my friend," Emiel whispered. "No treats tonight. Only work."

The horse snorted and swung his head away.

Emiel saddled the horse, strapped the saddlebags and packs in place, and inspected the gear once more to make sure it was secure. He kept the burden as light as possible, with minimal clothes in the packs, and provisions and waterskins in the saddlebags.

He led the horses out of the barn, past his two sleeping mountain moles, and around to the side of the house. He hated the thought of leaving the giant moles behind, but the animals, though able to practically run up the side of a hill or mountain, were no match for the speed of a horse on flat terrain.

Horses in tow, he took to the streets, taking the less populated routes toward the mansion and wincing at the clip clop of the iron shod hooves. By now, daytime activity in the bustling city was replaced by the lights and noise of the local pubs and taverns.

The rain had started up again, and Emiel was soaked through in short order. He took refuge in the awning of a bakery and peered through the curtain of rain. The front of the mansion was just ahead and two streets over. More importantly, though, the side of the mansion where the girls were being held was facing the street he was on.

He started to take the most unused and dark streets, but that might be inviting robbery. Besides, this Creator blasted rain was actually a boon, given that it obscured him in the night, and roared louder than the horses' noisy hooves. Finally, he came to a narrow street that led to the mansion.

He made a roundabout path to the side, tied the horses to a tree, then crept to a nearby window. It was one of the two personal libraries of the archminister. Emiel gazed through the window, remembering a time when Charion had once brought him here to read a passage to him when they'd engaged in a philosophical debate. Emiel missed those conversations.

If he remembered correctly, the girls would be in the room directly below, and there was a set of stairs not far down the hall from the library. He searched the window, hoping it would slide open and was not solidly built into the wall. He sighed in relief when he pushed at the bottom corner and felt it shift.

He reached into his pocket and fished out a finger length pocketknife and wiggled it into the slit between the glass and the wall. It took some patience and a little time, and his wet fingers were growing numb, but he finally got it open enough to slip his hand in. He gritted his teeth and slid the window open as quietly as possible. He didn't know what he would do if he encountered a guard.

Emiel climbed up and swung his foot into the window, half turning. Hopefully he could ...

Something grabbed his ankle and yanked him out of the window. It happened so fast he hadn't even enough time to grab hold of anything.

He fell backward from the window and landed flat on his back. He turned on his side, coughing and wheezing in the cold rain. When he finally opened his eyes, it was just in time to see a thick boned skeleton ram darkness into his face.

4

AMOURA

Amoura Xanna opened her eyes to the feeling of warm sunlight caressing her face. She arched her back and stretched her arms, then slowly uncrossed her legs and stretched them in front of her. She bent forward and touched her toes, then pulled a little farther, grabbing hold of her feet, then her heels, pulling slowly and gently until her chin touched her knees.

For several heartbeats she held the position, then she lay flat on her back and stretched her arms out. She took measured breaths as she lay on her back, allowing her body to come awake. From dusk to dawn, she'd sat in cross-legged meditation, committing her learnings to memory. She was a student of the old ways, though none of her peers knew it.

She rolled onto her stomach then came to her knees. Then, one foot after the other, she placed her feet on the floor and stood. Amoura closed her eyes, allowing her mind to take its time coming into focus. She heard others moving about the grounds, some in conversation, others chanting softly in walking meditation.

She went to the washbasin and rinsed her hands and face, then dipped a piece of tauka root and brushed her teeth. Once finished, she bit off a piece and chewed it, then spat it out in the pail and rinsed her mouth. The refreshing root helped her come more fully awake, and she stretched her arms again, letting out a contented groan.

After slipping on her leggings and boots, Amoura donned a tunic so blue it could have passed for black. Next she slipped on a smoky gray tabard, then her robes that matched the tunic. Lastly she fastened a flat wide belt around her waist, cinching the robe in.

She ran a hand through her thin braids, letting her fingers linger over each of the tiny squares that formed a type of grid on her scalp at the base of the braids. She shook her head, hearing the tinkle of the tiny marble beads as the clanked together. She looked in the long mirror leaned against the wall and saw steely gray eyes staring back at her.

Passing through the dim halls of the fortress of the Order of Magi, Amoura Xanna felt a mix of emotions ranging from pleasure at being surrounded by those who studied the arcane, to disgust at what she saw in many of its members.

Instead of one Order united in its dedicated study of the *essences,* they segregated themselves, forming various sects that catered to the specific strengths of its members. A man dressed in brown flowing robes passed by, offering a nod in greeting.

Amoura returned the gesture. Brown sect. They were the magi that excelled at *earth essence.* She passed members of each of the other three sects as well, receiving greetings that ranged from a friendly smile to a scowl. She received the latter most frequently from the *fire sect,* which was typical.

"Amoura Xanna. My lovely. How go your studies?"

Amoura turned to see solid old Hashma smiling at her. The woman always smiled at Amoura as if she were proud of her. Though Amoura had been the subject of affection by few in any of the sects, Hashma had taken a liking to her when she was but a girl.

Amoura braced herself for the crushing hug that followed, then forced a smile on her face when the woman customarily grabbed her shoulders, and pushed her back to arm's length.

"My, girl! Beauty is supposed to level off in time, but yours continues to glow brighter. Though you have many years yet, for such a thing, your grace extends beyond you years."

"Hardly, Hashma Blue," Amoura said. "I can think of no one who so deftly holds age at bay, while retaining your level of elegance."

Easily past a half century, Hashma's face and body practically radiated power. Her step was as swift and sure as the youngest novices, and even her white hair seemed to glow down her back.

Hashma waved a dismissive hand. "Oh dispense with the formality, girl. You know I don't like it. Hashma Blue, really!" She looked down the hall at a group of *Reds*. "Truth be told, I don't much like this whole *sect* nonsense. I was around long before it came into being, but I was only one voice in but a few that spoke against it. Now we are a divided group of prudes looking down at one another instead sharing our knowledge."

"Would that I could have lived during that time," Amoura said.

"You would have loved it," Hashma replied, starting down the hall.

Amoura fell in step beside her. "Why do you wear the blue robe if you dislike it?"

"I didn't say I disliked the robes," Hashma said. "It is the separatism I care nothing for."

"Are they not one in the same?" Amoura frowned. "By separating into the four *sects*, did we not shun one another?"

"Yes and no," Hashma replied, slipping her hands into the sleeves of her robe. "The forming of the *essence sects* was, like most things touched by the hand of a man, a good idea carried too far. You see, we thought to form *sects* for those who excelled in the various *essences* in an attempt to further nurture our individual strengths while at the same time helping each other strengthen the areas in which we are weak. A strong magi of the *blue* would be an excellent teacher for those who were weaker in the *water essence*."

"But instead, we have become reclusive to each other," Amoura said.

"Instead, we have become egotistical fools," Hashma corrected. "The *blues* think themselves in command of the most powerful *essence,* as do the *silvers, browns,* and *reds.* I cannot tell you how it saddens me to see what we have degenerated into; a gaggle of arguing geese lifting our noses into the air whenever we pass one another."

Amoura hid her smile as they exited the halls and entered the covered courtyard. Hashma had a colorful way of speaking when she grew emotional about a subject. "I see little that can be done about it now," Amoura replied.

"Use yourself as the model," the older woman said. "The fact that you haven't declared any *sect* sets an example for us all."

"Could you not do the same, Hashma?" Amoura asked. "Why not remain neutral?"

"Because my presence is less influential than yours," the other woman said.

Amoura frowned at that comment. "I know few who could project a more imposing presence."

Hashma winked at her. "When it is necessary, perhaps. But I am not the magi master's apprentice."

"Perhaps," Amoura replied, trying to keep the sourness from her voice. Hashma's laughter indicated she hadn't been successful.

"Oh, you are a quite an interesting choice in apprentice, girl. Most would readily amputate any limb the Master chose in order to study directly under him, and here you are his direct student and can barely stand the man."

Amoura felt a spike of alarm but kept her voice steady. "Is it that obvious?"

Hashma regarded her with a chuckle. "It is not obvious when you're in his presence, but I would advise you to remain vigilant against your opinions of him. He may be a detestable old bear, but he is powerful. Very powerful."

"Must you so insult the bears, Hashma?" Amoura asked, grinning. "They are intelligent and powerful animals."

"I'm serious," Hashma said, and Amoura's grin disappeared. When the elder woman took a level tone, it brooked no argument or joking. "Keep your secrets close, and reveal only as much about your-self as you need to, though I suspect I don't need to tell you this." She spared Amoura a sidelong glance. "No. I don't need to tell you that at all."

Amoura felt heat rising to her face at the comment, but it seemed to have more than one meaning. What did the woman know about her? Of everyone in the Order she trusted Hashma the most, but still didn't tell her everything.

"And I believe our conversation must end here," Hashma said. She stopped, and a couple steps later Amoura turned back.

"Is something wrong?" Amoura asked. She followed the other woman's gaze and looked over her shoulder. A young man near to her own age approached. Dust colored hair pulled back into a ponytail, perpetual sneer on his freckled face, and an arrogant slant of his flat red lips. Amoura sighed before she caught herself. Agra.

She turned a questioning look on Hashma. What did the woman care about Agra? He was nowhere near to her level, and she could very likely order him away.

"That snail leaves a trail of slime that leads all the way back to Selvetar," Hashma said. "I have things to be about, in any case, and I would prefer as little interaction with him or any of his lackeys as I can manage."

Amoura didn't blame her. Though it was a mystery why the first magus had taken such an annoying interest in her lately, she would have preferred the distance as well.

"Take care of yourself, child. Keep your secrets close." Hashma spun on her heel, white hair whipping behind her as she departed toward the rose gardens.

"I cannot deny I have oft wondered why you so prefer the company of an ancient companion over those more lively."

The grin on Amoura's face disappeared. She half turned and gave Agra a once-over, then continued on her way. She held back her resigned sigh when the irritating *red* fell in step with her.

"Out for a morning stroll with the flowers, I see."

"Is that where I am," Amoura said, staring straight ahead. "And here I thought I was in the werewood off for a lovely picnic."

"If your tone is any dryer it will catch fire in the morning sun, Amoura."

"I don't know what you mean."

"Of course not," Agra replied. Words seemed to slide off his tongue like oil.

She glanced at him several times in the silence. What did he want?

"Things have been quiet with the wilders lately."

"That's nice."

"Doubtfully." When Amoura didn't offer anything more, he continued. "I don't trust them when they are causing trouble. I trust them even less when they aren't causing trouble."

"Perhaps they've grown tired of dealing with us and have retreated further into the wilds."

"Only to breed and return with larger numbers to harry us." His thin lip curled up in a snarl. "Would that we could eradicate them utterly. So many problems would be solved."

"Now that's a sensible answer to a problem," Amoura said. "Why seek to understand and solve a challenge when you can simply wipe it clean from the world."

Agra frowned at her. "What is there to understand? They are untrained users of the *essences*, they steal corlite at every opportunity, and they cannot be reasoned with. They would have the world ruined in short order if left unchecked."

"You seem to have them figured out," Amoura said.

"It's simple enough to see, 'Moura," he replied.

Amoura narrowed her eyes. "Does your brain have a defect that forces you to omit the 'A' in my name?"

"Agra smirked." She wanted to melt that smirk off his face. "You know it's my little nickname for you. It's a term of endearment to bring us closer."

"It's having the opposite effect."

"Give it time."

Amoura felt her head getting hot and took a quiet deep breath. "Not even the Creator has that much time."

"Such blasphemous words," Agra said with a grin. "Take care or they could land you in the void. You wouldn't want to welcome such endless torment, would you?"

"Only if it would ensure your absence from my life,"

They walked in silence for a while before Agra spoke again. Amoura could feel lines of irritation forming on her forehead.

"What have I done to earn this iciness from you, Amoura?"

"I'd really like to be about my day, Agra," she replied. "My irritation with you would be greatly diminished if you would leave me."

Despite her words, he continued to walk next to her. "First Magus Selvetar thinks we should move further into the field. He thinks we should go and find out what they are about."

"Luck to you in your mission."

Agra laughed. "Nothing has been planned yet, but I think it's only a matter of time."

Amoura stopped and turned her back on him, looking out over the beautiful infusion of colors surrounding them. It seemed every type of flower and plant, bush and tree grew here.

"I have to admit," she heard over her shoulder, "that I find it out of character for one with such an icy heart to so enjoy the gardens."

"You presume to have a good deal of knowledge about me," she said.

Agra shrugged. "I need look no further back than our current conversation."

"I would like you to leave me, Agra. I'm not in the mood to tolerate you today."

Agra didn't leave. "Do you intend to move me, 'Moura?"

She turned a look on him that suggested she would enjoy the prospect.

"Such anger."

Amoura stared into his eyes without blinking. "You have a talent for bringing it out."

"If you could at least try to drop the ice wall for a moment, Amoura," he reached a hand out to touch one of her braids. "You'll find my company much more pleasant."

"If even the tip of your finger touches any part of me," Amoura warned, "I will burn the offending hand away from your arm."

Agra snorted and rolled his eyes, but still withdrew his hand. "Fine, have it your way."

"There was never any question of that."

"Very well, apprentice. Selvetar wishes an audience with you to discuss our next move against the wilders."

"Very well," she said, starting away.

"Immediately," she heard him call from behind. "Not tomorrow or whenever he can track you down, Amoura. He will see you now. Don't think he'll tolerate your little game of avoiding him forever. You may be apprentice to the magi master, but he is first magus, subordinate only to the master himself."

Amoura turned back. "I don't need a reminder of my place in the order, Agra."

"He feels otherwise."

"Then I will hear it from his lips and not your own. And since we have entered into a discussion of rank, perhaps I will remind you of yours. I wish to enjoy these gardens for a bit longer, alone. That means devoid of your company. Leave my presence." She looked at his greasy hair and wondered if it would take more than a spark to light it like a torch.

Agra's thin lips wrinkled. "Watch yourself," he said.

Amoura felt a surge of adrenaline. "If you think to threaten me, Agra, do it openly that I might burn you from existence right here. Right now. It can be made painless, but I'm willing to make an exception for you."

Agra's nostrils flared, and she thought he was about to snort like a horse. Finally, he offered the slightest bow, spun on his heel, and marched away.

I may not have handled that well, she thought, returning her attention to the gardens. Agra may be annoying, but he was still close to Selvetar. A meeting with the first magus was the last thing she wanted, but there was no choice for it. Amoura reminded herself to exercise more discipline when she met with the unpredictable man.

She nodded in greeting at a passing woman wearing the silver robes of the *air sect*. She gave Amoura a polite nod and went back to reading her book. As the woman receded down the hallway, she twirled her index finger in the air, then ended it with a flourish, stabbing her finger toward the sky.

A translucent spear of air shot from her finger into the air, then faded away. A book of *air*, then. The woman continued on, reading the various passages and practicing them as she walked. At the beginning of her tenure with the Order, Amoura had practiced in much the same way. She'd studied the various scrolls and books, honing her skills through hours and hours of practice. That was until she had been in the library and happened upon a book detailing the old ways of controlling the *essences*.

The fragrant roses and endless mixtures of flowers settled her temper and soothed her mind, which was why she always came here. It was the only thing about the grounds that she enjoyed anymore.

She closed her eyes and took a deep breath, then exhaled in huff of surprise when the space around her shifted, and her next step brought her inside Selvetar's personal study.

5

EMIEL

Emiel didn't know if it was the bouncing ride of the horse that had awoken him, or his throbbing left temple. One was uncomfortable, the other a pain that pounded him with each bounce. He groaned.

"And finally you awaken," a voice said from somewhere behind. Emiel tried to lift his head to look at the speaker and immediately regretted it. A wave of pain and dizziness assaulted him, and he let his head hang back down.

Blessedly, the horse stopped. A moment later, he felt hands untying the ropes that held him across the saddle, then he was eased off.

Emiel landed on wobbly legs but was held upright until he was stable. He kept his head down, which helped with the dizziness. He placed a hand on the side of the horse for balance, using the other hand to indicate he could hold himself up.

The pain in his head was like a beating pulse. He closed and opened his eyes a few times. "Thanks."

"You're thanking me?" a male voice said.

Emiel slowly raised his head to see the amused expression of a young man dressed in what looked like a kind of armor of bones.

"You're that skeleton that attacked me," he said weakly, blinking again.

"Heheh. I suppose I must've looked like one to you in the middle of the night. Didn't give you much of a good look at me, did I?"

Everything was starting to come back, now. Creeping along the streets in the rain with the horses and slipping open the window to the archminister's mansion in a failed attempt to rescue his daughters. A very brief and failed attempt. "I'm guessing you were waiting for me to arrive?"

"Sort of," the man said. Barely a man. As his vision came more into focus, Emiel saw a boy who looked to have seen no more than nineteen or twenty years. Above a freckled young face was flaming red hair that hung just above his ears. Those green eyes, however, spoke of a youth that was forced to grow up fast. There was a coldness there. Not necessarily cruel, but hard.

"I was ready, but your archminister had sentries posted to watch for you."

Emiel felt foolish. It had been a predictable move. Of course he would come for Amiya and Nandi. What parent wouldn't try? When he thought about it, it was an impossible situation. If he came for the girls, he would be caught. If he'd waited too long, he would have had to leave to carry out this task. Either way, the odds were rigged.

"No need to look so bitter," the young man said. At least he didn't order me to kill you."

"Hmph." Emiel turned away. "I'm not helpless."

There came a snort in response. "How's your head?"

Snide though the remark was, Emiel couldn't deny the truth of the situation. He was no soldier, and he could think of at least two ways he could have died last night. "So I guess I don't have to ask if we're on our way to Altarra."

"Nope," the boy said.

"Mind if I get your name? Or are we riding the whole way under anonymity?"

"Bone," the boy said. "Call me Bone."

"What kind of a name is Bone?" Emiel asked.

"Didn't say it was a name," Bone replied. "I said it's what you can call me. It's what everyone calls me."

"Nobody knows your real name?"

"If my family hasn't forgotten it, they'd know."

Emiel took a deep breath. "Unless I can talk you into a change of heart about my situation, we're on the road?"

"We're on the road," Bone replied.

***

"Mind if I ask why you're doing this?" Emiel said, breaking a long stretch of silence. The horse-drawn wagon lumbered along at a brisk but comfortable pace, bouncing along the ruts and bumps in the road while trees and hills lazed their way along either side.

"Pay's good," Bone replied.

"So you're holding a man captive whose children were kidnapped, and he's being forced against his will to deliver some package for Decius? I've broken no laws and caused no trouble."

"And none of that means a thing to me," Bone replied. "Your archminister called me in and paid me to escort you to Altarra. He said it was important that you complete your task and that you might try to cheat him. It's your word against his, and his word filled my pouch quite well."

"So morals over money?" Emiel replied.

"Call it what you will. I'll be eating tonight, and many days and nights to come. And under a warm dry roof, I might add."

A mercenary, then. Even if Emiel could afford to bribe the young man over what Decius had paid him—which he couldn't—Bone wouldn't compromise his reputation.

He looked over his shoulder at the wagon, and the crate that held whatever it was the archminister wanted delivered. "Another question."

"If you must."

"Why did you tie me to the horse instead of just laying me in the wagon? There's room enough for me and that crate."

Bone gave him a look. "Well I suppose I could have, but I didn't have the proper pallet and pillows with which to make m'lord comfortable."

Emiel glared at him. Bone didn't seem to care.

"Mind telling me what's in the crate?"

"Yes."

Emiel waited.

"Well?"

Bone frowned. "Well, what?"

"Well what's in the crate?"

"You asked me if I minded telling you, and I said yes, I do mind." He jabbed a thumb back at the large wooden box. "What's in that thing is none of your business."

"I feel like I have a right to know, given all this trouble."

"Because that box back there is the source of your woes?" Bone asked, sarcasm slipping into his voice.

"No, Decius is the source of my woes. I want to know because I'd like to make sense of this stupidity. You could very well have delivered this package without me. You've been paid, and I'm assuming you were doing a fine job while I was unconscious. I could also wager it would be easier for you to complete this task without having to keep an eye on me."

Bone snickered. "You do all that thinking while you were sleeping, or did you drum it up just now?"

"Just now," Emiel snapped, and Bone snickered again.

They rode in silence for a while longer, Emiel secretly hoping the weather might turn for the worst and force them to make camp. He needed some time to figure out how to get away from the mercenary and back to Vyne.

"Expecting rain?" Bone asked. "Or hoping for a storm?"

"What makes you ask that?" Emiel replied.

Bone shook his head. "You keep still enough, but your eyes are practically screaming at me that you're trying to find a way out of this. Let me give you some advice."

Advice from someone who is barely a man, Emiel thought dryly.

"There is no way out of this situation for you. Your archminister wants you to hand deliver his cargo to Altarra, and I'm here to ensure that you do. Yes, I'm young, but I've also been trained by hand and sword for most of my life, so I'd advise you not to try to overwhelm me because you think I may be weaker than you." He looked Emiel over. "You look like a well fit guy, for sure, but you're not a warrior."

"And you are?"

"I'm a mercenary," Bone said. "The nature of my trade demands my proficiency in combat."

"So there's no way I can talk you out of this?"

"I think we've covered that." He looked at Emiel again. "Sorry."

"Yeah, sorry." Emiel gazed out at the open planes. They were nearing some kind of dark wooded area that he didn't much like the looks of. He thought they would surely go around it, but when the dark woods grew closer, he grew less certain.

"You can't intend for us to pass through that," he said, indicating the ominous woods.

"I hadn't intended to, but it's a shortcut, and the weather doesn't look to hold up."

Emiel looked in the direction Bone was pointing and saw thick dark storm clouds stretching across the planes like the shadow of all the Fallen combined.

"Looks like you'll get your wish," the boy said, turning the horses toward the woods.

Emiel looked from the storm clouds to those dark woods, and back. "I think I'd rather gamble on the storm than go in there," he said.

"You don't want to get caught in something like that," Bone said. "It's a cold, windy, and miserable experience. Trust me."

"Cold, windy, and miserable sound a great deal better than death by living consumption," Emiel countered.

"Living consumption?" Bone asked, turning an amused expression on him.

"Eaten alive, yes." Emiel practically shivered at the idea.

"A muscular, fit fellow such as yourself is worried about being eaten alive?"

"I don't think that's a cowardly trait at all," Emiel said. "Humans aren't anywhere near the top of the food chain."

"I doubt there's anything in there big enough to eat you," Bone said as he pulled the team up to the front of those evil-looking woods. For a moment, even the mercenary hesitated. "You won't be eaten, spicetrader."

"Not whole, anyway."

They froze and looked around. That tiny, childlike voice hadn't come from either of them.

"You playing tricks, spicetrader?"

"Do you seriously think I could manage that voice?" Emiel replied.

After several heartbeats, Bone started the wagon forward again.

"Tut tut tut," the tiny voice said again. "Not smart at all."

Bone reached over his shoulder and gripped the hilt of his sword. "Who's there?"

"Sounds like a little girl," Emiel said under his breath. "You gonna cut her down with that?"

"Quiet, old man."

"Quiet?" Emiel snarled. "Old?"

"There are many less gruesome ways to die," the tiny voice said. "Ask, and I can show you."

"Stop making threats from concealment and face me." Bone dismounted and unsheathed his sword.

"I've made no threats."

"You just offered to show me how to die."

"I offered you a less grisly fate than the one you would find in the werewood." This time the voice came from behind a rock the size of a wagon wheel.

Bone turned and leveled his sword in that direction, just as a girl stepped from behind the rock. She placed her hands on her hips and glared up at the mercenary. Despite his amazement, Emiel couldn't help smiling at the sight of the girl, who looked to be no more than a foot and a half tall.

With the mercenary still held in the most obstinate glare, the tiny female actually started tapping her bare foot. Emiel had seen nothing like her before. Her skin was a sandy color that was almost translucent, and her hair was the brownish red color of clay. Those bright, mischievous eyes were as brown as the earth she stood upon.

"Hey Bone," he called out. "Maybe you're not aware, but right now, you don't look very honorable in this face off."

Bone looked from Emiel back to the tiny girl, then growled and sheathed his sword. "Who are you and what do you want?"

The girl arched a little red clay colored eyebrow at him. "You're rude."

Bone opened and closed his mouth several times before deciding on a different version of the same question. "You're too small to be a human girl. So what are you?"

"I'm someone who was trying to be nice by warning you not to go in there." She pointed at the woods ahead. "There's all sorts of things in there only an idiot would want to see."

Bone turned his back on her. "Thanks for the warning, but this'll shave at least three days off our trip."

"Three days of life compared with a few hours of dying," the girl remarked.

Emiel glanced at the woods again, then back at the girl, who was gone. Bone saw his face, then trotted back to the rock and looked behind it. He looked back at Emiel. "You know what in the name of the Creator that was?"

"A really short girl who stopped growing?" Emiel offered.

"That vanishes in the blink of an eye?" Bone replied.

If this had been a conversation between himself and someone friendly, Emiel might have allowed himself to be more shocked by the situation. With Amiya and Nandi's situation in the back of his mind as well as his own, he didn't have anything left. He shrugged. "You could guess as well as I."

"Let's get moving," the mercenary said.

"Still determined to go through there?"

"You're seriously wanting to listen to some little girl that shows up playing games?" Bone asked.

"Every time I look in there, I find it easier to believe her." He looked back in the direction of the storm. Those black clouds were no more than an hour away. "I think I'd prefer roughing it in the storm than going in there." He hopped off the horse and walked closer, peering into the woods.

The trees looked slimy and twisted, and it was so dark, he couldn't see more than a dozen to two dozen feet. It looked like a swamp, but there were none of the typical sounds of frogs, or insects calling to one another. Just dark and quiet.

"Didn't that girl say this was called the werewood?" Emiel asked.

"Yeah, so?"

"Doesn't that raise any warning bells with you?"

"I've had enough of debating this," Bone said. "We're moving."

They hopped back on the wagon and Bone started the two-horse team forward. The horses started to nicker as they drew closer to the woods. Once they were half a dozen feet away, the animals threw their heads back and danced sideways while trying to back away. The nickering grew louder until they were snorting and whinnying.

"I think they know something we don't," Emiel said. His palms were starting to sweat. Something in there would surely hunt them down. Being eaten alive was the worst way to go.

This time, Bone didn't argue. After a few minutes of fighting the horses, he turned them aside and hopped down. "You stay there."

Emiel rolled his eyes, earning a responding scowl.

"There's highwayman all along these country roads, spicetrader," the mercenary warned. "You leave me, I'll eventually find your robbed corpse, or you being robbed just before I kill you myself."

"Love you too, friend," Emiel replied dryly.

Bone unsheathed his sword and carefully made his way to the edge of the woods.

"In all seriousness," Emiel said. "Are you really this stubborn?

That little girl warned us against it. The horses refuse to go in there, and you're still stuck on taking this shortcut?"

Bone ignored him and crept into the woods, sword held before him. Emiel watched as the mercenary disappeared into the darkness. Minutes passed, and Emiel was beginning to wonder if the boy had met his end in there. Despite his lack of manners and judgement in his choice of occupation, Emiel couldn't dislike him. The young man made his living with the skills available to him. As far as mercenaries went, he wasn't half bad.

A nagging feeling pulled at Emiel's stomach, and he was just about to hop down from the wagon when Bone—sword in hand—came crashing out of the woods in a full run.

"Get it moving!" He yelled. "GET IT MOVING!"

Emiel jumped into the driver side and slapped the reins to the horses. "Hyah!"

The animals needed little prodding, and practically leapt into action. Emiel gritted his teeth and pulled back on the reins, lest the desperate animals turn too quickly and topple the wagon.

He looked over his shoulder to see Bone sheathe his sword as he sprinted after them. With an armored hand, had grabbed hold of the rail and pulled himself up. Once he swung his legs over, the mercenary immediately came to his feet and drew his sword again.

"Get those beasts going," he yelled over his shoulder.

"What're you ..." Emiel half turned and yelled back, but then he saw them. Five winged horrors bearing down on them. Emiel clenched his teeth and snapped the reigns again, and the horses lunged forward.

From behind, he heard the sound of flapping wings and Bone cursing. Emiel focused on the road ahead, avoiding holes and ruts while trusting that the mercenary would do his job. "Told the Creator blasted idiot not to go in there," he growled under his breath. The wagon hit a bump, and Emiel nearly lost his seat.

"Keep it steady!"

"Doing the best I can!"

More flapping, then he heard what sounded like a crow, only ten times larger. "Jungle shrike," Emiel muttered. "Great."

The words had barely left his lips when one of the winged beasts flew past his head, its knife-like talons nearly taking his scalp.

Emiel ducked and cursed. "Had to go in there and bring them out, didn't you? Couldn't have just left well enough alone, right?" When Bone didn't answer, he glanced over his shoulder.

The young mercenary was fully engaged with the huge birds, swinging his sword left and right. The shrikes were smart, though. They dove at him, but with a beat of their bat-like wings, kept just out of reach of the weapon.

"Can this thing go any faster?" he yelled over his shoulder.

"Yeah," Emiel shot back, ducking as that same blasted shrike dove at his head again. "I'm just taking it slow so those things can rip us apart. Don't mind, do you?"

He heard Bone growl something in response, then there was a screech. He glanced over his shoulder and saw a line of blood dripping from the ruined leg of one of the shrikes. It flapped unsteadily, snapping its hooked beak at the mercenary.

Emiel looked back to the road just in time to see the large rut. The wagon bounced awkwardly, three of its wheels leaving the road.

He heard Bone yell in surprise, then heard grunting and tumbling. The giant bird turned its attention from Emiel and angled away.

He looked over his shoulder and saw Bone taking a defensive stance as the shrikes converged on him.

Emiel could keep going. There were enough provisions for him to last all the way to Altarra, which meant he could find some local farm and rent a loft in a barn until he figured his situation out. He doubted the mercenary could fend off four jungle shrikes, no matter how good he was.

Emiel sighed, and slowed the horses, then turned them about and snapped the reigns. The horses whinnied, clearly not pleased at the prospect of running in the direction of the danger. "I agree," he said to the animals. "But I'm an idiot who can't just let the kid die. Forgive me."

The horses threw their heads and snorted in disagreement, but they ran on. Much sooner than he'd have liked, the fight came back into view. Two of the shrikes had actually landed on the ground and were snapping at Bone. The birds were as tall as the mercenary!

Emiel snapped the reigns again, and the wagon thundered down the road. The two airborne shrikes gave a great flap of their wings, and lifted higher into the sky. The two on the ground finally saw him and struggled to take off, but it required too much time and effort to get such large bodies into the air. The horses whinnied in protest of the impending collision, but Emiel urged them on. The giant birds had their backs to the speeding wagon as they slowly lifted into the air, and never saw him coming. Horses and wagon slammed right into the birds of prey.

The horses whinnied and the shrikes screeched. Emiel grimaced and spat feathers out of his mouth as he slowed the wagon and turned it around. Having seen the collision, the two airborne shrikes figured it not worth the effort, and angled away.

"Blasted kid's lucky this road is so wide," Emiel grumbled as he watched the huge birds grow smaller as they rose higher into the sky. When he looked down, he saw Bone struggling to rise, and behind the mercenary, the two shrikes he'd plowed into.

One lay dead on the ground, the other near enough. Bone didn't rise when Emiel reached him, and he saw that the boy was panting. He offered a hand which, after staring at it for a few heartbeats, the young man accepted. Emiel hauled him to his feet and Bone practically fell against the wagon.

"You alright?" he asked. "You weren't fighting those things for that long before I came back."

Bone leaned forward and put his hands on his knees. "You ever ... been attacked by ... more than one of those things ... before?" Bone asked in between breaths.

"Never gone into their habitat, so that would be no."

Bone glared up at him. "Yeah well," he swallowed and tried to stand up straight, then groaned and almost fell over again. He held out a hand to forestall another helping hand, and forced himself upright. "They coordinate," he said, holding his free hand against his side. "One comes in close, and when you fend it off, the other one attacks. When you defend against that one, the third moves in. They're one of the few predators that will actually take a chance like that. The third one plowed headfirst right into me, hoping I wouldn't be able to counter. It gambled right."

"So you're telling me that thing took a calculated risk?" Emiel couldn't believe what he was hearing.

"It's a … hard world … spicetrader," Bone said in between careful breaths. "Even for a predator, food can be lethal to catch. You gotta be smart, and the predators are almost always smarter than the prey."

"Does that mean you were almost lunch?"

"You would've liked that, wouldn't you?

Emiel shrugged. "I came back, didn't I?"

"Probably because you figured your chances of surviving out here were a lot slimmer without me."

"So young to be a pessimist," Emiel replied.

"I'll get a lot older because of it," Bone said. "Though what you call a pessimist, I call being pragmatic. People are opportunists, and they do things according to what opportunity it will bring them to further themselves. If it would have been easier for you to leave me to these things," he started toward the twitching shrike, "I have a hard time believing you would have still come back."

He drew a belt knife and knelt next to the dying monster. With a fast cut to the hideous bird's neck, it went still. Emiel moved closer. He'd never seen one this close before. Looking at it now, he imagined the only things that got such an intimate view were likely seeing the last thing they ever would.

The wingspan on it looked to be twelve feet across. Those huge leathery batwings had long hand like bones that were as big around as Emiel's forearm. At the end of its wings were claws as long as fingers. The rest of its body was covered in black feathers, except for its neck, where the feathers were red. Its downward curving bill was also red, while its head was black like the rest of its body.

Emiel looked at its feet, the most dangerous part of any bird other than that sharp beak. Its black, scaly feet had four toes, each ending in dagger-like talons.

Red hair plastered to his face, Bone set about carving the giant bird, not even flinching when a little blood splattered across his face.

"Done this before?" Emiel asked, keeping his distance.

"You take food where it comes," came the reply. There was a squishing sound, as the mercenary cut through sinew and the Creator knew what else. "These birds are strictly predators. They won't eat anything that's already dead unless they're near to starvation."

"What's that mean?" Emiel asked, curious despite his growing nausea.

"It means that the meat will be clean. You don't want to go eating something like a carrion crow, who mostly feed on the dead and rotting."

"I see," Emiel said as the mercenary began on the dead bird's feet. "What are you doing? There's no meat on those."

"But there's weapons on them," came the reply.

The sky rumbled, and Emiel looked up to see a black canopy of storm clouds rolling in. The fresh sweet smell of rain was in the air, and soon enough, the first few drops of water began to fall.

Bone worked fast, probably trying to hurry before they got caught in the open when the storm finally hit. In short order he had two sets of four, finger-length talons that he carefully dropped into a leather sack. He grabbed another empty pouch and packed the meat, then used a little water from his waterskin to rinse off his bloody hands.

There was another crack of thunder, and then the rain came. By the time Bone had packed the wagon, the rain fell in sheets.

Bone looked longingly at the other dead shrike, but shook his head and jumped onto the seat. Emiel climbed up beside him, and the mercenary snapped the reigns.

"I want to get on the other side of that hill," Bone said, nodding ahead where the road inclined. "I'll feel better with that hill between us and that forsaken jungle."

A few quips came to mind, but Emiel kept them to himself.

The horses snorted as they pulled the wagon uphill, struggling against the buffeting wind and rain. Gusts sent stinging raindrops spattering across their faces, and Emiel felt sorry for the laboring animals.

They crested the hill only to find more treeless planes beyond. At least the road leveled off from here.

Bone guided the team into the grass on the side of the road. Their reins jingled as the horses shook their heads and irritably dug their hooves in the ground.

Emiel hopped off the wagon and came alongside one them. "I know, friend," he said, patting the chestnut mare on the neck. It's a bad day, isn't it?" The horse turned her head toward him and looked into his eyes. Despite the water beating down on his clean-shaven head, he forced a smile on his face. The horse blew out through her nostrils and gave him an affectionate head-butt to the chest.

"If you're finished having a moment over there," Bone called from the other side of the wagon, "I need to stake the animals and set up for the night."

Emiel stepped aside as the mercenary unhitched the horses and removed their gear.

"The wagon is big and high enough for us both to shelter under," he said.

"Definitely better than no shelter at all," Emiel agreed.

"And it's low enough to make it difficult for anything that might find us out ..." Bone trailed off at the sound of the horses whickering nervously. They shuffled about, the whites of their eyes showing as they looked around.

"Curse of the Fallen, you are unlucky," Bone spat, looking around.

"I didn't ask for this," Emiel shot back. "And you took this job—"

The young man held up a gloved hand, straining to listen through the roaring storm. After several heartbeats, he swore and stepped away from the wagon, drawing his sword. Emiel remained where he was, listening. Then he heard it. A series of three fast barks. It was answered by another triple bark, then another.

Bone bit his bottom lip. "Jarku."

AMOURA

Amoura's mouth fell open but she snapped it shut, clicking her teeth and wincing at the sound.

"I thought Agra might have had trouble finding you, or that you might have gotten lost on your way to see me. So I offered my assistance."

She turned to see the first magus sitting at his desk, looking over a map. "An offer is something that can be accepted or rejected," Amoura said.

"My apologies for the misunderstanding," Selvetar replied. "You are right. I didn't offer assistance, I simply brought you to me."

Amoura let the jab slide off of her. "For?"

He finally looked up. His eyes were so dark she couldn't tell if they were brown or black. His long black hair and goatee were a stark contrast to his pale skin. He responded by pointing a long thin finger at the map.

Amoura moved closer and leaned over the desk. "The Sleeping Morghan?" She looked up at him, then back down at the map where Selvetar had placed a mark on the largest mountain range in Marai. "What about it?"

"I have strong reasons to believe our enemies have relocated to that region."

"Which is farther away from us," Amoura pointed out. "Why would we be concerned with them from there?"

"I don't know yet, but I intend to find out."

"And if you discover there's nothing to be concerned about?"

"Then we will see what we will see. The one thing that interests me the most is why the wilders would place their backs against the wall. If we came for them in force, they would have no place to retreat."

"Perhaps it is a nonaggressive move. It could be that the Khatala just want to be left alone."

He arched an eyebrow at her. "You believe this?"

"I believe they weren't the instigators in this war."

"They've been hostile toward us from the moment our two peoples met."

"The king of Marai had half a tribe blasted back to the Creator Himself over a misunderstanding."

"They came in aggression."

"It's part of their culture, first magus." Amoura grasped at her waning patience. "The Jahaka Dance is a warrior's dance, and is used to greet outsiders. A warrior's greeting is a show of respect amongst the Khatala."

When Selvetar didn't reply, she realized he'd been toying with her. It was no secret that she was undecided about their lingering conflict with the people of Khatal.

"Did you bring me here to prick my nerves about this situation, or is there more to this?"

"Yes indeed," the first magus replied. "You are about to become a busy young woman."

"Lovely."

He chuckled. The sound was dark and unnerving. "The magi master has an errand for you, and I will have another for you upon your return."

"Has someone neglected to inform me that I've been demoted to the level of page girl?"

"Not that I am aware of," Selvetar replied, returning to his map. "But I suppose it could be arranged if you are unhappy with your current position." When Amoura didn't respond, he looked back up. "Interesting," he said.

"What is?"

He considered her over his steepled fingers. "The prospect of having your rank stripped away doesn't seem to bother you. Do you find being a magus so undesirable? Do you truly covet the position of page girl more than a high ranking member of the Order of Magi?"

"I covet knowledge," Amoura said. All else is illusion."

"That is so?" Selvetar said, indicating she have a seat across the desk from him.

She hesitated, but knew it would be unwise to insult him, so she sat. "All knowledge has value," she continued. "It's how we lead and improve our lives."

"So you place value only in knowledge?" Selvetar replied. "Is there no value in our own personal status based on the accomplishments you've made? Or mine own? Or those of Master Vladrick? Is his status of no value?"

"I see no value in his title," Amoura answered truthfully, "only in his accomplishments. If he were to no longer be magi master of Altarra from this moment forward, his abilities would be no less than they were the moment before his change in status. The title doesn't grant him what he has achieved."

"Is it not a symbol of his achievements?" Selvetar asked.

"Of course it is," Amoura replied. "I don't scorn rank or status simply because it is, first magus. I scorn what people make of it."

"Hmm." The first magus looked into her eyes. She found meeting that gaze difficult, but she forced herself not to look away. "You have power. But more importantly, you understand it."

"I don't follow."

"I suspect you do, apprentice," he said. "You understand a great deal more than most of the instructors under whom you study."

"I still don't follow you line of thought, First Magus." Amoura's palms were starting to sweat. She slid a few braids behind her left ear and glanced down at the map. She needed to get away from this man.

"You make a convincing show of practicing with scrolls and books that have already served your purpose."

"The recordings on the *essences* are always to be studied."

"Well recited," Selvetar said. He tapped a finger on a point on the map. "I need you here."

Amoura looked at the place where the man indicated. The mark at the base of the mountain range known as The Sleeping Morghan.

"And Master Vladrick needs you to ensure the arrival of a precious cargo on the way from Vyne."

"Vyne?" Amoura stared at him. "What could that little out of the way town send that would require my presence?"

"There's been an interesting discovery to come out of the city. Something we haven't seen before."

"A rare species of mountain mole?" she replied. The first magus's features remained perfectly still, those cold green eyes still staring at her. *Not funny, I guess.*

"A hybrid," he finally replied.

"I don't understand ..." she started to say, then her eyes widened when it dawned on her.

Selvetar nodded. "We have reason to believe there are three hybrids in that little city."

"How's that possible?" Amoura asked. "Even if a Marailander and a Khatala were to have a child, it would possess the qualities of one or the other; not both."

"All knowledge has value," Selvetar replied with a wink. "Master Vladrick would like very much to study this hybrid and his offspring. They might be a factor that tilts things to our advantage against the wilders."

"And I'm to babysit him all the way back here so that you can study and use him against his people?"

"That's the interesting part," Selvetar said. "He wasn't born in the lands of Khatal. He was born on a tropical island far from our shores.

His parents, both Barbarosians, came to the land of Marai when he was a child."

"That's odd." Amoura didn't hide her curiosity. "I thought only the Khatala touched the *essence* in the manner they do."

"As did Master Vladrick and myself, Selvetar said. "Apparently the genetics of wilders are not restricted to Khatal."

"And you wish to study this man to see what you might learn from him?" Amoura shifted in her chair. Was this the prelude to another conflict with a people who didn't even live on the continent?

"The potential cannot be ignored, Amoura," Selvetar replied. "Imagine being able to speak with and learn from a Khatala that is not predisposed to kill you first and answer the questions to your corpse." He tapped the map again. "This might be a step in that direction."

"We entered their land and insulted them."

"And they answered that perceived insult with swift action," Selvetar countered.

"They did," Amoura replied, not wanting to continue the conversation further.

The first magus eyed her for a long time, staring right through her with those dark eyes. It took an effort not to fidget. No one relished being in the man's presence; not even Agra, who was his personal sycophant.

"I suppose I should be off to Vyne to collect your specimen, then," she said.

"After you meet with Master Vladrick," Selvetar added.

Of course. "Am I to go to him now?"

"He expressed his wish to see you after you've spoken with me," the first magus replied, still holding her with that piercing gaze.

"Then I'll be gone if there is nothing else you wish of me."

"I believe we are done. Good day, Apprentice Amoura Xanna."

"And you, First Magus." Amoura inclined her head in respect, and let herself out.

She made a brisk trail down the hall and rounded the corner. There, she leaned against the wall and took several breaths to steady herself. Being alone in a room with Selvetar was like holding up a mountain. It felt like there was a steady weight pressing down on her. It took a good deal of energy to not be overwhelmed, not to mention actually trying to keep in step with him during a conversation.

Once she'd gotten her nerves together she made her way toward Vladrick's chamber. The last thing she wanted was to be in the presence of the other of the two people she was the most wary of in the Order, but there was nothing for it.

"I've got to get out of here," she muttered. The words escaped her lips before her mind had the chance to stop them. Was that how she really felt? Perhaps it really was time to go? Could she?"

"You that shaken that you need to get out for fresh air, lovely lady?"

Amoura grimaced. Agra again. "What do you want?"

"So hostile ..."

"I don't have time for you, Agra. What is it?"

"I've got no business with you or that viper tongue of yours," Agra said. "I'm here at the first magus's orders. Unlike some of the magi here, I value any time I'm fortunate enough to have in his presence. His wisdom is a boon to us all."

"Were you born an obsequious beetle or are you honing the trait for your early manhood?"

The smirk on Agra's face dropped away. Behind him, a group of young Seekers giggled as they passed.

Agra rounded on them and the novices scurried away. He turned back to Amoura, and she saw the soft red glow of the *arah* pulsing in his ring. "You must think highly of yourself to insult me in front of a bunch of Seekers."

Amoura rolled her eyes, making a show of indifference though she was quite ready for him. He clenched his fist, and the ring on his finger pulsated with *fire essence*.

"How much *fire* do you have stored in there?" she asked, nodding toward the glowing ring.

"More than enough to burn you clean of this fortress," Agra

replied. "You make a mistake in not wearing yours, Apprentice." His ring flared brighter as his confidence grew.

"Attack me here, and how long do you think you will retain that little bobble on your finger, Agra? You want to establish your manhood, go to the sparring circle and beat on your chest until someone answers your challenge. I don't have the time to waste on you."

Agra growled and leaned forward, and for a moment she seriously thought he would attack her. Then he took a deep breath and the *arah* in his *essence* ring dimmed.

"You're walking a dangerous line, Amoura."

They stared at each other for several heartbeats before the fuming *red* turned his back on her and marched down the hall toward Selvetar's study.

Amoura went on her way. *That was stupid,* she chided herself. If he'd actually attacked her, she would have been forced to defend herself and reveal her secret, and Agra would have wasted no time telling anyone who would listen. What would happen if it was discovered that she was secretly training in the old way. The fact that she was actually able to train in such a way was in itself noteworthy.

Agra's last words to her were more true than he understood. *Watch yourself, Amoura,* she thought. How significant was it that no one else that she knew in the Order was capable of wielding the *essences* without having to re-commit the techniques to memory? And was there anyone else who could wield them simultaneously through the ring and oneself? Hashma had discovered it in Amoura when she was but a child Seeker. The old woman had been quick to insist she keep the ability to herself.

Good, Creator blessed Hashma.

Amoura blew out an irritated breath. She'd had to deal with two of the three men she disliked the most, and now she was on her way to meet with the third.

This day was off to a promising start.

7
____

AMOURA

For the third time that day Amoura considered simply leaving the fortress and fleeing to some distant land. It seemed she was having these thoughts more often, lately. Perhaps she could pack her things and be away in the middle of the night, stopping from town to town, city to city, until she found herself on the other side of the world from the Order of Magi and their complicity in the war with the Khatala. Would that much distance be enough?

Selvetar was the only magus she knew of who could warp space in two places at once and link them, thereby creating a sort of portal. Exactly as he'd done when he brought her to his study earlier. How he'd known her exact location was what disturbed her the most. If he always knew where she was, there was nowhere she could go.

Amoura stopped in front of the door to Magi Master Vladrick's private room. Lately she was starting to feel more trapped than when her parents had sent her to Denneir Academy to learn the arts of seduction. As a child Amoura had been repulsed at the thought of resorting to feminine wiles to advance in life. After several years of somewhat failed training, however, she'd seen its usefulness in the other girls. Some did indeed use their skills in brothels, while others turned to politics, or even the selling of goods. Sex was but one form of seduction amongst many.

Her parents had hoped she would might learn the skills to flourish in the political arena, or at the very least, set up a clothing shop.

Amoura had tried to comply, Madam Lavigne, head mistress of the academy, saw through her efforts as though she were made of glass. That glass had shown an affinity for manipulating the *essences* that even Amoura herself hadn't known she possessed.

When the head mistress had informed her parents of her natural skill in controlling the *essences*, they had hoped the woman might bring about a spark of interest in the arts instead. They saw nothing but danger and death in the pursuit of becoming a magus. Amoura hadn't wanted to disobey her parents, especially after the loss of her older sister. The girl had died three years before Amoura had been born, but her parents had made sure she knew she'd had a sister.

Amoura blinked away the memories and collected her thoughts. She would need a clear head to deal with the magi master.

She knocked on the door.

"Come."

She stepped into a chamber with walls lined not with portraits or canvas paintings, but scrolls. Like any other book or scroll regarding the *essences*, these held power. But unlike most of the body of work the students were supplied with to study, these scrolls were written in *magharthian,* a dead and forgotten language.

The room's only piece of decoration was a three-foot tall oval pot that housed a young peach tree, sitting in front of the room's only window. The pot was glass, but the swirling colors and designs inside the glass could only have been achieved by manipulating a combination of *fire*, *air*, and *water*. It seemed a frivolous use of *essence*.

"Would you like a peach, Amoura?" Vladrick asked, misinterpreting her attention on the tree. "The tree is young, but the fruit is sweet, if a bit small."

Vladrick was just over six feet tall, and solidly built. His long black hair was tied back and hung to his waist.

"No, thank you, Master Vladrick."

"Am I correct to deduce by your sober mood that you've already met with Selvetar?"

"I have, Master."

"Then you're aware of the task I have for you."

"I am, Master."

"What do you think about the prospect of a hybrid?"

"It's an interesting thought, Master. I've never heard of such a thing."

"I cannot deny my curiosity at what it's like to touch the *essences* without the use of corlite and the discipline of study."

Amoura had heard this line of reasoning before. It rang as an old and tired way of thinking from the first time she'd heard it. "I'm sure it is interesting, Master Vladrick."

The magi master regarded her. "You do not approve of our conflict with them, do you?"

"It's not my place to approve or disapprove, Master Vladrick. It is my place to function as apprentice to you, complete those tasks of which you assign me, and strive to serve the world with humility, devotion, and the constant pursuit of knowledge."

Vladrick studied her as she spoke, and his heavy gaze made her feel foolish.

"I sometimes wonder if ever there is a time the Tenets escape your memory even for a moment."

Amoura didn't know how to respond to that, so she waited.

"There are many here who covet the power of becoming a magus, while some covet the luxury of constant study. Then there are others who wish to test themselves in battle. Each person has different motivations, but you intrigue me, Amoura, which is one of the reasons why I made you my apprentice."

"An honor I do not take lightly, Master."

He continued to study her. His gaze wasn't piercing like Selvetar's, but those eyes saw too much. She didn't like it when he looked at her like that; as though reading everything about her.

"In all the years I've served as magi master, I've never met a young woman so guarded as yourself," he finally said. "Usually, young people enter the Order in the hopes of becoming Seekers. It's often the most trying time for instructors, for they must sift through the clutter of romanticized ideas every hopeful has upon arriving at our grounds."

"You were different, though. The day you passed the tests," he offered a little grin, "and quite impressively I might add, you went straight from the tour of the grounds to the central library." His thick shoulders bounced as he chuckled.

"I was informed by your future instructors at the time that there was a new Seeker who was already showing a good deal of promise." He indicated her with an open hand. "And here you are, my personal apprentice and second only to Selvetar in the Order. Besides myself, of course."

He picked an egg-sized peach from the tree and offered it to her. When she politely refused, he took a bite. "Shame," he said after taking a bite. This one is one is sweet." She waited as he finished the fruit and discarded it out the window. "I can practically hear the question in your mind," he said, rinsing his hands in the washbasin.

"I say these things because you are the most gifted magus I've seen in years. Your skills may even match Selvetar's one day, though I wouldn't mention that, were I you."

Amoura didn't know if that was a baited line or not, but she was sure Vladrick didn't think she was so stupid.

"And being the gifted magus you are, it's disappointing that you rarely express an opinion about anything. Our skirmishes with the wilders, the fighting over boarders and their beliefs as opposed to our own. I don't recall you ever expressing so much as a comment about any of it."

"This conflict has been going on long since before I arrived through the gates of Altarra, Master," Amoura said. "What good would come from my commenting on something that precedes my birth? What say would I have in something that others know so much more about than I?"

Vladrick gave her a look that suggested she was a fool if she thought he'd believed a single word. "There is value in the perspective from fresh eyes and ears on an old and stale situation," he replied.

Amoura wanted anything but to travel down this road. She preferred remaining apart from this whole mess, which was why Selvetar's little errand was a particularly sharp thorn in her boot.

"So I ask you plainly, again. What is your opinion on the situation with the Khatala? I've already received Selvetar's position and I would have yours as well."

"I have no position on it, Master," Amoura said.

"You'll have to do better than that, girl," the magi master said.

Amoura repressed her frown. "The Khatala have lived in their lands for well over a thousand years. The king of Marai arrives in their lands with a large contingent of soldiers and makes no move to show them respect." She paused and took a deep breath, then pushed on.

"Despite the insult to them, the Khatala greet King Alyn with a display of spears held high, which signified friendliness since the spear tips were not pointed at the king's entourage. They enter into the Jahaka Dance, which is a warrior's greeting and a great respect among the people of Khatal. A greeting that signifies that you are worthy of the attention of a warrior."

"The king misinterprets the dance as aggression and calls for attack. His magi, obviously ready to strike, wipe out half the clan before they can formulate a response."

She stopped, hoping against hope that Vladrick would be satisfied. He wasn't.

"Go on."

Amoura took another breath. "To King Alyn's surprise, the Khatala recover quickly and despite their devastating loss. They form an effective defense, then begin to push the king's forces back with what looked to be their own use of the *essence*."

"What started as an attack against an inferior tribe of people devolves into an all-out battle against a foe that was underestimated.

The people of Khatal have their own way of touching the *essence* that requires no study of books and scrolls."

"You have my thanks on reciting the inception of our war with the Khatala," Vladrick said. "And your opinion is?"

"That the Khatala are not the savage wilders they are made to be by the people of Marai. They lived for generations in their homeland until King Alyn arrived and waged war over a misunderstanding that could have been avoided if cool heads were present instead of larger than life egos."

Vladrick actually laughed at that. "So you believe this war is not only unnecessary, but our fault?"

"How could I not?" Amoura knew she spoke dangerously, but she push on anyway. "Marai went to Khatal, not the other way around."

"This may be true, but in his ... misunderstanding with the Khatala, King Alyn uncovered a dangerous truth."

Amoura slid her hand through her braids to hide her frustration. "That the people of Khatal are a danger to the world by tapping into a power they do not understand and only have a rudimentary ability to control."

"Your tone suggests you don't agree."

"With all respect due the king, Master, the Khatala seemed to be just fine before he arrived."

"Perhaps it was a matter of time before they affected some sort of catastrophe upon the world."

"That is possible," Master, Amoura replied.

"Your words are diplomatic and hollow, Apprentice," Vladrick said. "You think the king completely responsible for this conflict with the wilders."

"As it is not my place to question the actions of yourself, Magi Master Vladrick, it is even less my place to question the actions of the king."

"A wise response, but your first one was more useful. Your position is shared by some. But it is not our place to oppose the word of our king."

Your king, Amoura thought. "Have you not just repeated my words, Master?"

Vladrick pursed his lips, walking past her with his hands clasped behind his back. "Perhaps. But the purpose of those who protect the king is to see a situation in a way he may not, hmm?"

"But if it is not our place to question—"

"Not our place to question him, no. But it is within our province to bring things to light which may be shrouded in darkness to his eyes. You have a valid observation. To keep that silent would be regrettable, especially if it could affect real change in this situation."

Amoura didn't know whether Vladrick truly believed his own words, or if he was trying to draw more out of her. The fact that she still didn't know why they were having this conversation was motivation enough for her to remain guarded. Not that she would ever let her guard down with this man. That last thought almost made her laugh at herself. Had she not just gushed opinions that bordered on treason to this man? She'd given him the noose to hang her with, should he be inclined, and all because of a moment of frustration.

She looked at him. Had he approached this conversation in such a way to draw that out of her? "Am I here to engage in a philosophical discussion, Master? If so, I fear I am poorly equipped to challenge you."

Vladrick smiled down at her. "You should only speak words that ring true to you, Amoura, and I don't think you believe that claim any more than I do. No. You are not here to engage in a philosophical debate regarding the implications of our difficulties with the wilders."

A tiny frown creased Amoura's brow. Vladrick seemed to at least be partially reasonable regarding the Khatala, yet he still referred to them using that derogatory term.

"Archminister Decius has already dispatched the hybrid with what he assures me is a capable escort. Naturally, I don't leave things to chance, so I would like you to ensure his safe arrival."

"When will I depart, Master?"

"As soon as possible." He looked her over. "Have you been hiding a gift of foresight from me? You seem already dressed for the journey."

"I assure you that is not the case, Master."

He looked at her, frowning.

"Is there something wrong, Master?"

"Not wrong," Vladrick said. "I just find it curious that you walk the halls dressed in your full raiment while your peers move about in more comfortable attire."

"Perhaps I may adopt such habits if ever we enter times of peace," she replied.

"And yet you move about without your ring."

Yet again, reminded of that little mistake. She inclined her head. "You are right, Master. It was a careless omission."

"And one I would find uncharacteristic of one so careful as yourself."

"My days have been long with study, Master. I will rein in my inattentiveness."

"How go your studies?" Vladrick asked.

"Well, Master. Every day yields a bit more improvement in understanding and wielding the *essences*."

Amoura forced herself not to fidget in the lingering silence. While Selvetar made her uncomfortable, Vladrick left her feeling off balance.

"Good," the magi master finally said. "How soon do you expect to leave?"

"I see no reason to delay your lovely apprentice, master."

Amoura narrowed her eyes.

Selvetar's quiet voice practically slithered out of his mouth. Amoura reminded herself that it was a sound of well contained power. She didn't know who made her more ill at ease, Vladrick or the first magus. She did know that she'd rather be anywhere else in the world than standing between these two.

"Please forgive my interruption, Master, but you wished to see me?"

"Of course, First Magus," Vladrick said. "We have things to

discuss that cannot wait." He looked back to Amoura. "There are none other that I would trust with this. I have no doubts you will deliver him to me quickly and unharmed."

"I am honored by your confidence, Master," Amoura replied stiffly.

She bowed her head and turned away, passing Selvetar without looking at him, though she could practically feel those light-swallowing orbs watching her.

"You will find a travel pack ready for your departure," the first magus said. "And fear not for your most fragile privacy. It awaits you outside the door to your room."

"Thank you, First Magus," she replied, and shut the door behind her.

Once outside the magi master's chamber, Amoura ground her teeth. She didn't believe she could best Selvetar in a fight, but oh was she tempted to try.

With an effort, Amoura managed not to stomp through the halls and across the gardens on her way to her room. At least the weather was sunny. She had never been to the distant Vyne, but given the time of year, she couldn't imagine the weather to be much different.

She saw the travel pack sitting beside her door and could practically hear Selvetar's voice mocking her about her unyielding need for privacy.

She snatched the pack from the floor and opened the door. Despite the obvious fact that no one had entered—evidenced by the pack being left outside—she still gave a sigh of relief when she found her *essence ring* in the hidden compartment of her dresser drawer.

She grabbed the ring along with a few other items, then placed them in the pack and went for the door. She took one step out of the room, and into the middle of a soggy road being pounded by a raging storm. In less time than it took her to curse Selvetar to the Fallen, Amoura's robes were soaked through. She looked around in hopes of some kind of shelter, even a single tree. Nothing.

She looked down at her sodden robes. The garments hung heavy on her body. She slowly shook her braided head, making a mental note to repay Selvetar for this. Her anger fell away when she heard three barks in rapid succession, followed by another. Then she heard a man roar, and then the yelp of an animal. Someone was fending off a pack of Jarku, and Amoura was positive it was the men she was sent to babysit all the way back to Altarra.

8

EMIEL

"They usually don't come out till the middle of the night!" Bone yelled over the roaring rain. The shrikes must have attracted them!"

"Wonderful," Emiel muttered, drawing out his hunting knife.

"What do you plan to do with that?" Bone asked, looking like he was on the edge of laughter.

"It's better than nothing," Emiel replied indignantly.

"Do they know that?" Bone asked, turning toward the approaching beasts.

Through the sheets of rain they saw three four-legged animals loping toward them. From what Emiel could make out, they had long skinny muzzles with pointed ears that pressed against their heads. As they drew closer, he saw that they were gray with black spots. Two pairs of curved fangs protruded from the top and bottom of their closed maws.

Emiel looked at his suddenly inadequate knife. He lowered himself into an uncertain stance.

Bone glanced back at him, then took another look. Emiel saw the smirk on is face though the young mercenary tried to hide it.

"Look," he said. "I'm responsible for your safety. You die out here and I don't get paid. Why don't you crawl under the wagon. It's high enough to fit you but too low for one of those things to really get at you. And if they try," he looked back again. "You can just stick them with your knife."

"Cute," Emiel said, not about to hide while this boy defended him. He moved closer to the wagon. Just in case.

The Jarku were nearly on them. Bone gave his head a shake, throwing water from his red locks, then put his helmet on. That armor had the strange effect of a skeleton looking as substantial as a normal person.

One of the gray beasts leaped forward, and Bone dropped to one knee, scoring a long cut along its flank as it passed. The animal gave a high-pitched yelp and tumbled to the ground. Emiel stared in amazement as the beast struggled to rise, despite its lifeblood mixing in the puddle beneath it.

The other two barking animals reached the mercenary, and Bone settled into a defensive stance as they fanned out.

"Predators are smart," Emiel thought aloud, remembering their conversation earlier.

One lunged in and snapped at Bone, and he flipped his wrist and cut downward. The animal recoiled just in time to avoid the counter. While he was occupied with the one on his left, the other Jarku hopped in and snapped at his leg.

Bone had leaned toward the Jarku on his left, but had expected the attack from the other, so he simply continued the motion. The sword went in a downward arc, missing the first beast, but completed the circuit, coming upward and slicing the animal behind him up the middle of its muzzle. It yelped, stumbling away and running it's paw over the injury.

Emiel leaned in that direction, but hesitated. He wanted to help, but on four legs, those things were easily as tall as his waist. He looked down at the hunting knife in his hand. "Ah, Creator blast it all," he growled, running toward the beast, still hopping in a pained circle.

Knife leading, he tackled the animal and drove the blade into its side, then pulled it free and ran it into the neck. He stabbed it repeatedly, drawing the knife free and ramming it home.

"That thing is dead several times over!" Bone yelled. "If you insist on helping, get over here or get under that wagon!"

Heart racing, Emiel stood and turned in the direction of the mercenary, and his spirits sank. Another Jarku had replaced the one he'd just killed, and three more were running in their direction. He heard growling from behind and spun around to see another of the things stalking toward him, green eyes practically glowing.

Emiel settled into a low stance, trying to keep his legs from wobbling. It could probably smell the fear wafting from him. He backed away as the jarku advanced. It's lips quivered and drew back to reveal two sets of curved fangs and tiny sharp teeth lining its maw. Those teeth would easily shred the skin from his arm.

It barked and he flinched, then it lunged. Emiel rolled aside, but the beast was fast. Before he could fully right himself, over two hundred pounds of solid muscle and snapping teeth barreled into him and sent him sprawling.

The impact caused him to drop his knife, and he quickly rolled over and climbed to his hands and knees as he struggled for air, helpless as the jarku came for him. It lunged for his neck, but the ground between Emiel and the beast suddenly rippled and tossed it to the side.

It tumbled, but came back to its feet and shook its head, then snarled at Emiel. He didn't stop to think about his good fortune, but grabbed up the knife and climbed to his feet. It came again, and just before it reached him the ground rippled, this time from the side. A burst of earth slammed into the side of the Jarku's body and threw the animal to the ground.

It struggled to rise on unsteady legs, and Emiel saw his chance. He ran toward the beast, knifed raised. It had enough presence of mind to snap at him, which caused Emiel to skid to a stop, but then the ground beneath it shook, and it stumbled. Emiel circled around behind it and jumped on its back. He wrapped an arm around its neck and drove his knife into its side repeatedly.

The beast let out a high-pitched yelp, and despite the fact that it had tried—and nearly succeeded—to kill him, Emiel felt a pang of remorse. The animal was hungry and saw him as food. There was no malice in its actions, only the need to satisfy its hunger.

When it finally stopped struggling, Emiel stood and wiped his brow with the back of his forearm. He'd never had to kill anything before, and now he'd killed twice. It was a terrible feeling.

"There are more to fight."

The little girl. Emiel looked around, but she was nowhere to be seen.

Bone roared and Emiel looked to see him cut down a jarku that was a little too slow. The action cost him, though, for another had circled behind him and plowed into his back. To his credit, the mercenary dove into a forward role to absorb the impact, coming to a knee and spinning around. He whipped his sword in a horizontal arc as he turned. His instincts saved him.

The Jarku was already in the air, flying toward him, and the horizontal swipe cut it across the face. It yelped and crashed in a heap in front of him, and Bone drove his sword down into the animal's side. With a grunt, he pulled the blade free and stood, at the same time, whipping the sword around and down. Another Jarku had tried to flank him, but the unexpected maneuver cut across the side of its body.

A spray of blood fell over the glistening grass and the pouring rain started to rinse it away. Two more circled around the mercenary, and three more moved in behind them.

Emiel looked around and noted four more of the things moving in from over the hill they had just descended.

"This isn't going to end well," he muttered, trying to figure out how to put his limited skills to best use.

He heard barking from the side, and turned to see yet two more running across the road, nearly on top of him. The wet grass and rain slicked road slowed them not at all. Not until it rippled and sent them tumbling into the grass.

Emiel ran toward the one closest and stabbed out with his knife.

The animal thrashed about and came back to its feet just as Emiel stabbed at it. The jarku was quick, and hopped aside, then bit down on his arm.

Emiel cried out and dropped the knife. He struggled against the large animal, but those sharp teeth tore into his skin and he felt the bone being squeezed. He twisted his body and punched it in the face. It growled and tried to pull at him, but he punched it again. He kept punching and felt the pressure slacken just a bit. It wasn't enough, however, and he knew if he tried to yank his arm free, it would come away missing a great deal of flesh.

He spotted his knife lying a couple feet away, and pounded the beast on the head while trying to force it in a circle. It bit down harder on his arm again, and managed to swipe out one of its forepaws.

A fresh spike of pain shot through his forearm, but Emiel had enough presence of mind to throw his hips out. He ignored the sound of claws tearing through his shirt, leaned out, and snatched up his knife, He used the terrible pain of his arm being torn and compressed as a focus of strength, and drove it into the top of the beast's head. The blade skipped off the hard skull, but still it drew a line of blood that streamed down the jarku's head. Emiel recovered, and this time drove the blade into the top of its neck.

There was a loud yelp as he twisted the knife, and the powerful jaws released his arm. The beast fell to the ground in spasms before finally going still.

Emiel heaved a great breath and looked up just in time to see the second jarku's opened maw, inches from his face. He flinched away at the same time an unseen force slammed into the animal, sending it into a backward somersault. It landed on its side and grunted, coming to a half sitting position. It shook its head and turned an angry gaze at Emiel.

Don't look at me, he thought, holding the dagger in a white-knuckled grip. It growled at him, but hesitated.

Maybe Bone had thrown something at it. He stole a glance over his shoulder, but the mercenary was just felling two more beasts, while four more were surrounding him.

Emiel clenched his teeth against his pain in his torn arm. "Is there an endless supply of these things?" He slowly began backing away from the growling animal.

The ground rumbled, and Emiel looked over his shoulder again to see a wave of muddy earth crash into two of the Jarku farthest away from Bone. The animals fell underneath the assault, and when they righted themselves, the ground burst up from beneath them and sent the jarku spinning through the air to crash to the ground.

The animals hit the ground hard enough to bounce. Their efforts to rise ended in half tumbling over. They shook their heads, but made no move to attack.

Emiel continued to back away from his solitary enemy until he was back to back with the mercenary. "Figured we'd do better closer together," he said over his shoulder.

"More likely you'll get in my way," came the retort.

The jarku encircled them, eight sets of green eyes glaring above snarling muzzles that dripped with saliva.

"Think we'll survive this?" Emiel said, eyes darting this way and that.

"Not really," Bone replied.

"How'd you do that, with the ground?" Emiel asked.

"I don't know what you're talking about," the mercenary replied. "And who's that?"

Bone jerked his chin further along the road, and Emiel saw a solitary figure in soaked, hooded robes approaching. The Jarku took note of the new arrival as well. Seeing an easier kill, three left the two men and went after the lone figure on the road.

The robed person seemed not at all concerned about the fast approaching animals. The closest jarku leaped for the neck, and the person snapped an arm out and sent the three animals—each weighing well over two hundred pounds—flying to the side as if they were no more than children's toys.

The temptation was still too great, and the other animals abandoned Bone and Emiel, and charged.

The robed figure made a gesture of swatting a hand downward. One of the jarku simply crashed to the ground by some invisible force. The others raced past the felled animal, and the figure threw his hand in an upward arc.

As if an unseen hand snatched them from the ground, the five remain jarku lifted into the air, and the figure made a gesture of pushing a hand forward. The airborne beasts flew into the distance to hit the ground, bouncing and skidding in the mud.

They slid to a stop in a tangled heap, and were slow to rise. The beasts were tough and hungry, but not stupid. They shook themselves and glared at the robed figure, who approached Emiel and Bone. They seemed to consider whether the effort was worth it, before one of them, gave a loud bark. All surviving pack members gave up the standoff and loped after the alpha, disappearing into the wall of rain.

Bone held his defensive stance as the hooded figure came to stop in front of them.

Cradling his injured arm, Emiel glanced at him. This person had just saved their lives. He went to offer his hand, but the mercenary held his arm out.

Emiel frowned. "What's wrong with you?" He looked back at the hooded figure. "Our thanks for helping us." He held out his good hand over Bone's extended arm.

The hooded figure regarded the proffered hand, then lowered his hood. Or rather, her hood. The woman stared at Emiel with hard gray eyes the color of steel, then looked Bone over. After assessing the two men, she moved past them to stand beside the wagon where she turned and stared at them.

"I think she wants us to join her," Emiel said after several awkward moments. Bone grumbled but followed him toward the mysterious woman. He still held his sword, which Emiel thought was rude.

As soon as they reached the woman, she raised a fist to the sky and opened it. With that gesture, the deluge no longer touched them. Emiel turned in a circle, looking at the still showering rain that bounced off of an invisible dome that shielded them, the wagon, and the horses.

The horses! Emiel's eyes nearly popped out of his head at the sight of the unharmed animals. Why hadn't the jarku gone for them, since they were staked to the ground and nearly helpless?

Emiel turned back to the woman and swallowed. Her hair was in tiny square plaits, each with a skinny braid hanging down to just above her shoulders and ending in little colored beads. Her smooth dark skin seemed to radiate with an inner light. She was beautiful. Beautiful, but hard, and she studied him with those piercing, steel colored eyes.

After dissecting him fully, those eyes turned to Bone.

"What's your story?" the mercenary demanded. He stood at ease, but still held his sword.

The woman looked down at the weapon, then back up at him. "That won't be necessary."

"I'll be the judge of that," Bone replied.

"You can put that thing away or I can shatter it along with the hand that holds it," the woman said.

Emiel looked from one to the other. For several tense moments, they stared at each other. Then Bone grunted and sheathed his weapon.

"Would I be wrong to guess that Decius sent you," the mercenary asked.

"Yes," the woman answered, leaning against the wagon. She folded her arms and Emiel caught a glimpse of the ring on her finger. He'd seen a ring like that before. And only trouble followed those who wore it.

9

JOGA

"The first step."

Joga lifted his foot and placed it on the ground before him.

"The second step."

Joga took the second step.

Each step called, each step taken. He kept his gaze forward, barely aware of the two rows of men and women of his tribe. They sang in cadence, lunging forward with a stomp of their feet, then settling back.

The sand was warm beneath his bare feet despite the long departed light of *Alyu*. In place of *Alyu's* warmth was the pale cold light of *Salah*.

Joga took another step, the chants of his tribe members muffled to his ears. It was the time of his crossing; his transition from boyhood to manhood.

He took another step, then another. The raised voices of the men penetrated his concentration, and he mentally scrambled to recover it before the first wave hit.

"Wooooooaaaaaaah, HA!"

A heavy force pressed down on Joga's shoulders, forcing him to his knees. He pressed his eyes shut and fought against the pressure, then almost fell over when it suddenly relented. The women of the tribe raised their voices.

"Woooooooaaaaaah, HA!" Another force fell onto his back. He gritted his teeth and willed his wobbling legs and arms to steady, forced himself to stand. The pressure fell away.

The men and women of the tribe stood on either side of him, forming a wide path for him to walk. He continued on, and heard the voices of the men and women from each side.

"Alyu mo Illyu mo Salah mala, HAAA!"

Wind buffeted him from every direction, and Joga crouched, lowering his center of gravity to keep from being swept from the ground. In front of him, the air swirled and grew warm, then humid. A wall of water formed in the air, and crashed into him as though falling horizontally.

The horizontal deluge stung his bare chest and legs and arms, and Joga shielded his eyes with his forearm as he pushed forward.

This was the easy part.

He drew on his power from within, then surrendered it to the earth beneath his feet. He felt the power of Mother *Illyu.* It filled him, swirled around and inside his body.

The cold pelting water grew warmer, then hot. Joga humbled himself and asked for it; asked Sister *Salah* to feed a tiny fleck of Her power to him that he might defend his fragile body.

The power surged into him, and he guided it, forming it into a wall of protective air against the boiling horizontal rain. The rain pushed harder against the wall of air, and Joga pushed back, concentrating on keeping the barrier in tact lest his skin be burned away.

The rain grew more intense, and a chunk of earth broke away from the ground and rose into the air and mixed with the water. It turned in the air as it absorbed the boiling water, and heat wafted from the giant chunk of earth.

Sweat trickled down Joga's brow, but he ignored the hotness, holding the barrier of air between himself and the swirling ball of fiery earth. It grew bigger, pulsating like a molten heart. Such incredible power coalesced before him in a ball of pure magnificent destruction.

The giant ball of magma burst, and every bit of the shrapnel flowed toward him. Joga brought the full force of his concentration into holding the barrier of air up as a steady stream of lava assaulted the wall, splashing against it, passing around the side.

Joga willed the air around him to cool as he summoned water. The water came to him and he guided it into his wall of freezing air, which turned it to ice. The air sizzled as ice formed and instantly melted under the relentless heat of the lava.

The boiling heat retreated little by little. Joga took a deep breath, then let it out in a controlled exhale. He straightened. His focus was solid, Mother *Illyu* had heard him, preserved him.

The horizontal flow of lava diminished, then dissipated.

Joga forced his tired body forward, willing the burning muscles in his legs to carry him forward.

He continued down the pathway until he came to the bonfire where the Ancients stood.

Two men, two women. How long they had walked upon this world, Joga didn't know, but the Ancients were the ones who came before. The four figures looked upon him with hard eyes. Hard, but fair, loving, and compassionate.

"To whom do you belong?" one of the female Ancients asked him.

Joga stared into the flames as he spoke. "I belong to Mother *Illyu*, upon whom I walk."

"Who warms you?"

"Father *Alyu,* whose light gives me life."

"Who watches over you?"

"Sister *Salah*, whose gaze gives me protection."

"To whom does all belong?"

"All belong to *Amyadali*, creator of all things."

The four Ancients spoke as one. "Kneel before the symbol of *Alyu*."

Joga knelt before the bonfire, still staring into its depths. Life and death. Creation and destruction. All existed within the flames that were spawned from Father *Alyu*.

An Ancient came beside him and held out her hand.

Mikuna, Joga's adoptive sister presented a curved knife to the elder woman. Within the blade were four shades of color; blue, red, brown, and a slightly darker silver than the blade itself. The four *aspects* of Mother *Illyu*.

The Ancient lifted the knife with delicate hands and held it before Joga's eyes. He stared in reverence at the blade, reaching out to it, touching the four parts of Mother *Illyu* infused within.

"Learn now, Joga, boy no longer. Learn the purpose for which Creator *Amyadali* in Her infinite wisdom sent you to us."

She lay a warm hand on Joga's shoulder, then let it fall away. As the moments passed, Joga centered his mind, focusing on his purpose, his identity.

He didn't flinch when the tip of the cold blade touched him. The blade pierced the skin just under his collar bone and trailed downward. Joga focused his mind away from the pain, and on the power of *Alyu*, the light of *Salah*, and the love of *Illyu*.

Blood trickled from the cut and flowed downward. Then the blood split into separate lines, like a river dividing at a fork.

The lines of blood separated several times over, some continuing down the left side of his chest, some flowing sideways, while other streams traveled up and over his shoulder.

The Ancients hummed, and Joga felt the four *aspects* of *Illyu* flowing around and through his body. As the power joined with him, Joga felt the blood flowing over his chest and shoulder begin to slow, then go still.

The gathered tribe quieted as the Ancient inspected him. A male Ancient took her place, inspecting Joga's chest, moving around his side to study his shoulder, then his back. "Rise, Joga of the Frostland Khatala."

Joga stood, and kept his eyes fixed the flames as the Ancients studied him. Finally, the weathered face of one of the male Ancients moved in front of him. Endless vitality shined through those green eyes.

"Joga of the southern Frostland Khatala. Joga of the northern Frostland Khatala. Joga, child of *Amyadali*, creator of all that is. Joga, child of Ryin of the Northern Frostlands and Yaila of the Southern Frostlands." He inspected Joga's body again, and the young man saw the tiniest twitch of the Ancient's brow. He fought against the urge to fidget, but the Ancient's next word nearly stilled his heart.

"Mulgin."

10

NANDI

When Amiya's chip fell over after less than half a minute, Nandi knew her sister wasn't concentrating. In truth she felt the same. Dad had promised to get them out of here, but the night had come and gone, and now it was another day. Something had gone wrong. Not that this situation wasn't wrong to begin with, but now it was just more wrong.

After the game was over, they just sat there facing each other, legs crossed, until Amiya finally broke the silence.

"Something happened to Dad," she blurted out. She bent forward and rested her elbows on the floor and cupped her chin in her hands. "He should have come by now."

"I know," was all Nandi could think to say.

"You think they did something to him?"

Nandi shook her head. "I don't think they hurt him. Well, not bad, anyway."

"Why are they doing this to us?" Amiya asked, but it was more a question in general, for Nandi had asked herself the same thing numerous times since their abduction. "We haven't ever caused a problem, and then 'bigbelly' just shows up at our home and makes us come here?"

Despite the situation, Nandi giggled. Amiya had given the archminister that nickname the moment she'd seen him. She leaned forward. "Do you think it has to do with that thing we can do?"

Amiya glanced around the room as if afraid the walls might be listening. "I don't know. Do you think somebody told him?"

"Maybe one of the kids we play the game with. Maybe they were jealous we always win."

Amiya nodded. "That could be it."

Nandi thought about it a moment. "That seems kind of strange, though. Why would it matter to the archminister if we are good at spinning the chips? Why would he care? Why would anyone care?"

"Maybe because only we can do it," Amiya replied. "Maybe he thinks we can do something more for him?"

"I can't think of what that would be," Nandi said.

"What do you think he's going to do to us?" Amiya asked. She looked across the room at the door.

"I don't know," Nandi said. "We have to get out of here though."

"And do what?" Amiya replied. "I don't think Dad's at home any more. I have a feeling the archminister did something to him."

"Don't say that," Nandi replied.

"Don't pretend it's not true, Nandi," Amiya said. "Dad said he was coming for us and he's not here. That means something happened, and 'bigbelly' caused it."

"He might have done something with Dad," Nandi agreed, "but I don't think he hurt him."

"You mean you hope he didn't," Amiya said.

Nandi didn't deny it. "We need to figure out how to get out of this room first."

"Maybe we can lure 'bigbelly' in here with a sandwich," Amiya growled. "I hate that fat son of a darkwood cat."

"Amiya!" Nandi said, fighting back her laughter. "You know better than to talk like that! If Dad heard—"

"Dad's not here," Amiya cut in. "So let's get outta here and find him, then you can be a 'miss-good-girl-Illuminarian' and tell him if you want. I don't care about anything but getting outta here, making sure Dad is alright, then punching 'bigbelly' in one of the flapping hog jowls on his face."

Nandi tried to stop giggling. "Will you stop it? You're gonna get us in more trouble than we already are."

"I heard them talking outside the door last night while you were snoring," Amiya said.

"I do NOT snore!"

"Ya whatever. I heard them saying something about wilders and 'those two little hybrids'. I think they were talking about us." Amiya frowned. "But what do they mean by hybrids?"

"I've heard people talking about men and women from distant lands who can use the power of the earth to do amazing things," Nandi said. "You think that has something to do with us?"

Amiya shrugged. "All we've ever done is spin rock chips for longer than anyone else. I don't think that's the same thing."

"Maybe not exactly the same, but why is it that no one else can do it? And I know you've accidentally made things happen because I do it too, sometimes."

"How would 'bigbelly' know about that?" Amiya asked. "It's not like we run around telling everybody."

"We don't have to," Nandi said. "I think I know why Dad didn't like us playing our game with other kids. Maybe he thought something like this would happen."

"Maybe," Amiya agreed. She leaned in close. "Did you see the way that man in the robes with the hood was staring at us? He made me nervous, Nandi. I don't like that man at all."

"Me either," Nandi said.

"I wish we could just get outta here and find Dad and go to the Barbaros Islands like he promised."

"Me too," Nandi said. "We'll find a way out of here and find Dad and move away."

"Then let's make a plan," Amiya whispered.

"You thinking something?" Nandi leaned in closer until their foreheads were touching.

"Let's try to see what else we can do," Amiya whispered. "If we can make the rock chips spin just by focusing on them, what else can we do?"

Nandi thought about it, but the prospects made her nervous. "What if we hurt someone?"

Her sister snorted. "They kidnapped us and are holding us here for no reason. I don't care if we hurt them."

"Don't talk like that," Nandi said, though looking around at their accommodations, whether comfortable or not, she couldn't wholly disagree with Amiya's sister's assessment. "What do you think we can do?"

"I once made a jar fly off of a table when I got mad about something," Amiya said. "I thought it was a coincidence, but the more I think about it, that jar flew away because I was mad."

"And caused a nice mess on the floor to clean up," Nandi replied, remembering how storming angry Dad had been. "There's no jars to throw at them. You planning on using our two little rock chips here to beat them all?"

"You make jokes if you want to, but I think I can do something to get out of here."

"Okay," Nandi said. "What're you gonna do, Amiya? You gonna ask them to give us water in little jars, then collect them and hurl them at the guards when we've got a bunch?"

Amiya glared at her. "Maybe I'll practice and just hurl *you* at them."

Nandi sighed. "Okay fine. Maybe you're right that we should at least try. It's not like we have anything else to do in here."

"What's weird is that it feels different," Amiya said. "When we're playing the game, I can make the rock spin fast and steady, without wobbling. Sometimes it feels like I'm helping the rock spin. Other times it feels like I'm forcing the rock to spin."

Nandi nodded as her sister spoke. "Yeah. I've done it the same way, and I don't know what it means. When I'm forcing the rock, it's like I'm putting more strength into it, but it takes more energy. When I'm helping it spin, it's still pretty steady, but I can actually move it around a little, and it doesn't take as much energy to do it."

"We could practice on each other," Amiya offered.

"You are NOT going to make me spin around on the floor," Nandi said.

Amiya laughed. "That's not what I meant, but do you think you could stop me anyway?"

"You wanna try and find out?" Nandi replied.

Both girls jumped to their feet at the same time.

"You know I'm better than you," Amiya said, grinning. "You can't beat me."

"The only thing I can't do is stop you from telling yourself lies," Nandi shot back. Now she was grinning. "Let's see who's better."

The two girls stared into each other's eyes. Many heartbeats passed before Amiya snorted, then the girls exploded into laughter.

"As annoying as you are," Nandi said after their laughter had died down, "I can't do it because I don't want to, I think."

"Is it because it's like trying to do something to yourself?" Amiya said, nodding. "And it's not just because you look like me. It's because it really feels like I'm trying to do something to myself, or a part of myself."

Nandi knew exactly what her twin sister meant. They were two parts of a whole. They were their own persons, which was obvious by their contrasting personalities, but they were still each a part of the other. Nandi could feel her sister as a part of herself, and she knew Amiya felt the same.

"Why don't we try it on one of the rocks," Nandi suggested.

"Good idea." Amiya picked up her rock chip and held it in the palm of her hand. She stared hard at it while Nandi tried not to laugh as her sister strained.

"Be careful you don't hurt your brain," Nandi said.

Amiya ignored her and continued to focus. A trickle of sweat ran down the side of her face, but she pressed on.

Nandi sighed and went to the throw rug where they played their game. She looked back, but Amiya hadn't noticed she'd moved. She picked up her rock, turning it over in her hands. Somehow, she had known there was more to their little game than just making the rock chips spin, but she'd never thought much about it. Now the game might be their only means of escape.

"Ah!" Amiya cried.

Nandi's head snapped up and she saw the rock chip hovering above Amiya's hand in front of her astonished expression. Nandi's mouth fell open. "Amiya, how ..." she moved over to stand beside her sister. "Make it do something," she whispered.

Amiya nodded, then squinted at the rock. It quivered and started to move away. A short distance beyond her fingertips, the rock quivered again, then dropped to the floor.

Amiya gave Nandi a triumphant look. "Told you!" she said.

"Yes you did," Nandi agreed. "And I'm sure the entire Vyne city guard will run for their lives as we march out of town, rock shaking above your hand.

That wiped the smugness from Amiya's face. "Think you can do better?"

"Were you forcing the rock or guiding it?" Nandi asked, though she was sure she already knew.

"I think I was forcing it," Amiya said.

"Maybe that's why it fell."

"It definitely took energy to do that. My mind was a little tired after I gave up."

"Maybe we could try guiding it instead?"

Amiya frowned. "But it feels like I have more control if I force it to go the way I want."

Nandi went back to the rug and grabbed her rock. She stood much like her sister had, focusing on the rock, and for a long time nothing happened. She continued to focus, even picturing the rock floating above her hand.

Her mind was beginning to tire, but she shifted her focus away from her fatigue. Nandi felt her energy rapidly depleting, and just as she began to realize she couldn't continue any longer, the rock vibrated. She shoved away her excitement and held her focus. With an effort, the rock lifted from her palm and floated in the air. As it hovered, Nandi felt herself growing more tired. Just making this rock float in the air was draining her. She was forcing it.

She let go and instead, guided the rock through the air. It began to float in a circle above her palm, then moved away.

Nandi's mind gave a jump of excitement and the rock quivered. She tried to regain her focus but it was too late. The rock fell to the floor.

"Same thing happen to you?" Amiya said.

"Yeah," Nandi replied. "But for a moment I felt like I was guiding it instead of forcing it. It feels like forcing it is harder than guiding it."

"Haven't gotten that far yet," Amiya grudgingly admitted.

"We'll get better," Nandi said. "We're gonna practice, and we're gonna get out of here."

11

JOGA

"Mulgin."

Every time Joga said the word, he felt a chill creep down his spine. He looked down at the left side of his chest and shoulder, then pushed his shoulder forward to look down his back. *Amyadali,* the creator of all things, had spoken. But why? Why had She sent him this message? Why had She given him the bloodmark of a Mulgin?

"You are distracted."

He turned to see Ancient Nami standing in the opening to his hut. "I am sorry, Ancient," he said, hurrying to his feet to offer a quick bow.

The woman smiled at him. "Do not apologize for something that cannot be helped." She indicated that he sit, then joined him.

The elder woman's age was indeterminable, though she had the look of someone who had seen more years on this world than anyone should want to. There was strength in her eyes, and her wrinkled and weathered skin emitted a radiance to match Joga's own.

"I have an important task set to me, Ancient," Joga said. "Should I not concentrate on what I must do, and why? Is it not a sign of mental weakness that I would be so distracted?"

"If you can spare an old woman a few minutes of your time?" Ancient Nami asked.

Joga looked stunned. "Of course, Ancient! Never would I think of refusing—"

Ancient Nami looked into his eyes, and Joga fell silent as a sense of calm enveloped him.

"Youth and early middle age are so formal; so stiff. You think that your mind is weak because of fear."

Joga stiffened at the observation but remained quiet.

Ancient Nami chuckled. "I almost forgot. Not just young, but a young warrior. Whatever your lot in life, part of it is to accept truth as it is. You think your mind weak because of your hesitance regarding your bloodmark?"

"I ... yes, Ancient."

"Jista received her bloodmark three years ago. *Amyadali* spoke that she was to use her gifts to help the Frostland tribes better cultivate our crops. Akram received his bloodmark last year, and it spoke of his marriage to a woman of the Dryland tribes, which would bring about a new union between us all. Bazara received his bloodmark three years ago as well, and the Creator spoke of his friendship with a darkwood cat."

Her soft laughter was almost inaudible. "Can you imagine his trepidation at the thought of entering a place where darkwood cats live and actually being close enough to befriend one?"

Joga grinned at that. Even though he was three years his senior, Bazara had seemed like a child when first confronted with his blood-mark task.

"Every bloodmark is unique unto the bearer," Ancient Nami said. "There is a reason for everything, Joga. In Her infinite wisdom, Creator *Amyadali* would never have sent Jista to befriend a darkwood cat, nor would She have given Akram, a young man with a talent for making friends, the destiny of helping to cultivate the Frostland crops."

"So too, is it with you, young warrior. The Creator of all things would not have placed this destiny before you if you were not equal to the task."

"But a Mulgin, Ancient?" Joga shook his head. "I've heard talk of them being near to the size of a teliak lizard." Just thinking of the monstrous lizards, far larger than a great mammoth, was enough to take the heart from him.

"That matters not at all, Joga," the Ancient said. "What matters is what is within you."

"How would I overcome such a beast?"

"That is for you to discover."

Joga's mind was reeling. "There is no weapon I could use. Not by hand or spear or sword could I defeat such a mighty animal?"

"There is a way to accomplish anything, Joga," Nami said.

Joga let his head hang. "Why would the Creator in all Her wisdom, create such a beast that we might need to destroy?"

"Why do you believe you must destroy it?"

"I was not sure at first, Ancient," Joga said. "But while I was in meditation, I saw a vision of the beast. It was the most terrible thing in the world."

"A proclamation from one who has lived so long, hmm." Ancient Nami said. "The mulgin beast has lived on this world for millions of years. It is an ancient species, living in the farthest away places until men built homes near their domains. Even then, they are not hostile. If Creator *Amyadali* sees fit for you to challenge this beast, something is wrong."

The why of it mattered little to Joga, considering his appointed task. "But how am I supposed to do this myself?"

That kind, wrinkled smile returned. "You will find a way."

He thought about that. Every person must carry out their blood-mark's task on their own, without the aid of their tribe members. And if that prospect weren't bad enough, the thought of having to deal with Marailanders along his journey was just as repulsive.

Ancient Nami chuckled. "You look like you've just gotten a mouth full of sour berries, Joga. Not all people from the land of Marai are like those who fight us."

Can the Ancients read minds? "I see none of them rising to stop their leaders who wage their wars on us either," Joga replied. "If some of their people are not bad, then why do they not stop their leaders from trying to take our homes away?"

"Theirs is a different culture," Nami replied. "And cultural differences are what caused this conflict."

"They are quick to fight and take what is not theirs," Joga spat.

"And we were quick to act upon our own customs and beliefs when we met a people who were different from us. Are we without blame, young warrior?"

Joga didn't like that question. The king of Marai had come to their lands already looking down on them. The incident with the jahaka dance was the excuse he needed to take their lands away.

"You will find your own answers," Ancient Nami continued. "You will come to see the different shades of life, and that all are touched by one another."

"I don't understand what you mean, Ancient," Joga said.

"You will," Nami said. She stood, and Joga stood with her. "When will you leave us?"

"Sunrise, Ancient," Joga replied.

The Ancient nodded. "Go then, and enjoy your family."

"Yes, Ancient."

"Yes, Ancient," Nami echoed. "So formal. I suppose I should not gripe. It is a respect you are taught since the moment you could speak. Still, I'm not sure how nice it is to constantly be reminded of one's age." She smiled up at him and lay a hand on his shoulder, then stepped out of the hut.

Joga returned to the circular throw rug in the center of his temporary home and sat back down. The tribe had uprooted the village and come to the Sandlands for his bloodmark ceremony. Joga hadn't understood why everyone had travelled so far at first, but the Ancients had deemed it necessary though even they hadn't known why. Perhaps Creator *Amyadali* had whispered it to them?

Joga looked over the personal items he would carry on his bloodmark journey. His spear, a sack to hold clothes, a waterskin, and a treated sack to carry food. Part of him was excited at the prospects of adventure, but the other part of him wished he'd have been given something smaller, more simple. Less perilous. "Like being chosen to marry a woman from a foreign tribe," he thought aloud.

But he knew the answer. It would have been the most unsatisfying thing that to have happened to him and would have been unfair to the woman he would have been destined to marry. He snorted. How often had he thirsted for adventure as a child; to see the world and make a difference? He thought about how often he declared to his parents that he would be a legendary warrior that would bring his family and tribe honor. All his life he'd desired nothing more.

And now his wish had been granted.

Joga shook his head. He'd barely seen the passing of twenty winters and already he wished he could find his younger self and smack his ears.

He left the hut. "Need to walk." He shielded his eyes in the bright sun of the Sandlands. Sandy wind blew between the huts of the temporary village, and children chased little dirt twisters, laughing and placing leaves in the center to see if they would lift from the ground.

He blew out a labored breath. Out in this land of sand, Father *Alyu* breathed heavily. How anything could—or would want to—live in this harsh heat was beyond him.

Joga gazed at the distant dunes as he made his way toward his adopted sister's hut. They were just like the hills of snow that rippled across the Frostlands, only brown and made of sand. Only *Amyadali* could create such amazing things.

He took a deep breath, filling his lungs with the unfamiliar dry hot air. It was like breathing into a baker's oven.

Joga came to Mikuna's hut and stopped outside the hanging flap. "I come to visit, sister," he said.

"I'll be out in a moment," a woman's voice said from inside.

A few moments later, Mikuna ducked through the flap to her hut and smiled. She was his height, or perhaps a bit taller. To hear her tell it, one would think Mikuna was an entire head taller than he.

She ran a thin-fingered hand through hair that was a mix of white and sandy brown. Everyone's hair in the village was starting to turn this sand color, including his. "You time your visit well, Joga," she said. "I needed some fresh air from that stuffy hut."

"Whatever fresh means to the air here," Joga grumbled, looking around at the endless sand. "How the Ancients did not lose their bearings in this place is something I cannot understand."

"Nor can I," Mikuna replied. "But they say the older you get, the closer to Creator *Amyadali* you become. She is their guide."

"A good thing for us, then," Joga said, "or we would be feeding the buzzards by now." He squinted up at the blazing power of *Alyu*. "Though I think if we remain here much longer we still might."

"Don't complain so much, brother. It isn't a warrior-like trait."

Joga shrugged. "I wish you could come with me," he said as they walked.

"That time may come, but not now."

"How can you be sure?" Joga asked. "Your bloodmark told that you were my sister, not by birth, but that we're given to each other by *Amyadali*. Perhaps we should share this adventure together."

"My bloodmark did not say that I would hover over you like a mother hen," Mikuna said. "You are part of my destiny, but you have your own. In this thing, I cannot help you except to wish you luck and pray to Creator that you return safely."

"I can't imagine anything else to happen in my life after this," Joga said. "A mulgin, Mikuna. They are not evil beasts, but they're as dangerous as their environment."

"There is more to your destiny than the Mulgin," Mikuna said. "I had a dream, Joga."

"A dream?" That caught Joga's attention. Whenever Mikuna had a dream, the events weren't far off from the impending reality.

She nodded. "I saw you confronting your destiny with a ball of fire that split itself in two, then reformed into one. Whether it was in one or two, the ball of fire seemed to be watching over you."

"Strange dream," Joga replied.

"They always are," Mikuna agreed. She stopped, and after a few steps Joga stopped and turned back. "Take care of yourself. I promised your parents I'd look after you, but in this, Creator *Amyadali* has placed you outside of my sight."

"You promised my parents?" Joga said. "When? They died fighting the king of Marai." A bitterness crept into his voice when he spoke of the man. From his luxurious position, the foreign king had ordered the deaths of countless men and women on both sides of the battle, that terrible day.

"That was one of the few clear dreams I've ever had," Mikuna said. They came to me and I promised to look after you."

"It should be me looking after you, sister."

Mikuna snorted. "Barely a man bloodmarked, and already you're ready to protect 'the woman'."

Joga blanched. "I didn't mean—"

"Of course you did," she interrupted. "You're a man, and men can't help but think of women as frail and in need of protecting."

"I'm sorry. I don't mean to think that way."

"Oh quiet with you," Mikuna said. "You have a good heart. You are a protector, and you will defend more than just your tribe against this thing."

Joga frowned. "What thing?" Surely she couldn't be talking about the Mulgin, which rarely ventured from their homes deep inside of volcanoes. And even when they did venture forth, they never went far.

"That was the other part of my dream. The splitting ball of fire was your protector. But I also saw a shadow hanging over a great red lizard. The shadow swallowed the lizard, then swallowed its home, then the lands around it."

Mikuna shivered despite the hot weather. "I don't think it's the Mulgin that threatens us, but something else."

"What else?" Joga asked, desperate to know what he must do.

"I don't know, but the shadow covered everything, Joga." She looked at him with eyes the color of the surrounding sands.

"Everything."

12

EMIEL

Not for the first time, Emiel thanked the Creator for this quiet day of travel following the jarku attack. Bone hadn't been the most companionable of traveling partners, but at least he talked.

Emiel kept his face forward on the infinite road snaking out before them. He stole a glance at the woman sitting to his right. She was undeniably beautiful, but no friend, and surely more dangerous than the mercenary.

"Is there something about me you wish to know?" she asked, still looking forward.

Emiel started. It was the first time she had spoken since they'd "met". "Huh? Is there something I'd like to know?"

She grinned at him. It wasn't friendly. "You can't think fast enough."

"What?" Emiel asked. "What do you mean by that?"

"You were caught off guard because I spoke, and you repeat my question to stall for time while you think of a response that is less embarrassing than the truth."

"Oh?" Emiel said, heart hammering in his chest. "And what is this embarrassing truth, then?"

On his left, Bone sniggered.

The woman's grin crinkled, then disappeared. It happened so fast it might never have been. "You want me to say it here?"

"I've got nothing to be embarrassed about," Emiel lied. "But while we're talking, it would probably be nice to know your name."

She turned her head and gave him a look that said she would play along with his little deflect. "Of what relevance is my name to you?"

"It's generally considered polite, not to mention convenient. Would you rather I say, 'you there!' when I address you? I doubt 'hey woman!' would be any more welcome."

"Silence would be the most welcome," came the reply.

Bone snorted and Emiel tried to ignore him. "Mind simply indulging me, then?"

"You always make a habit of conversing so casually in situations like this?"

"Never been in a situation like this," Emiel replied. "I'm doing the best I can with the jarku dung of a sandwich life just threw me, so I'm trying to make the most of it."

"Eloquent."

"Real. And irritated."

Something in her gray eyes went cold when he said that. "Should I be afraid of your irritation, spicetrader?"

"Not at all," Emiel said. "Should I be afraid of yours?"

"Yes."

Dumbfounded, Emiel just looked at her. After several uncomfortable heartbeats, she looked away.

They rode in silence for a time until the questions just wouldn't allow Emiel to rest. "So how far out are we?"

"You aren't much given to silence, are you?" the woman asked, still gazing out at the rolling planes.

"You aren't much given to friendliness, are you?" Emiel shot back.

"Watch yourself, spicetrader."

Emiel laughed. "What is this 'spicetrader' thing? Are you all constantly calling my by my chosen craft as a way of reminding me that I'm below you?"

"Wherever you feel your trade places you has nothing to do with me."

"Your tone speaks otherwise." Emiel stopped. He was losing his temper, and that would only get him in trouble. "Look, I'm just trying to make the best of a situation I am completely ignorant of and that makes no rational sense to me. I don't know what I could have done in the time between your helping us during the jarku attack, and now, that has earned your irritation. But it's clear you hate me for some reason."

He looked at the road ahead, wishing he was at home with his girls and not between these two hostile people.

Beside him, the woman closed her eyes. "Amoura."

Emiel glanced at her, "my pardon?"

"My name ... is Amoura Xanna."

Emiel held out his hand. "Emiel Dharr."

Amoura looked down at his hand, then at him, then back out at the countryside.

Guess I won't push the subject too far. "Nice to meet you."

"Is it?"

"You saved us from a pack of jarku," Emiel replied.

"Didn't *save* us, Bone mumbled from the other side of the bench. "Just helped out, is all." He gave the reigns a flick, and the team picked up its pace.

Emiel continued to ignore him. "In that light, I'd say it was great to meet you."

"It's what I was tasked to do."

"Doesn't matter. Thank you anyway."

She didn't answer.

"What in the name of the Creator could I have possibly done to make you so angry at me?"

"She's not angry at you," Bone said impatiently. "She's angry at having to babysit while she could be busy doing just about anything else."

Emiel looked from Bone to Amoura and grinned. "So, your sulking, then?"

"I could likely just incinerate you right here and claim you were dead when I arrived," Amoura said. She leaned forward and looked around him at Bone. "Perhaps we could work out an arrangement for your payment? Then I could be done with this chattering jay, and we can both be on with our lives."

Bone seemed actually to consider it, then shook his head. "No, sorry. I gave my word to Decius that he'd survive the trip. Been doing business with him for years. You understand."

"Unfortunately," Amoura replied, leaning back into her seat.

Emiel sighed. "Well anyway, thanks for the help. Can't say I know how you did it from so far away before you reached us, but thanks all the same."

That got her attention. "What do you mean, from so far away?" she asked. "I helped you as soon as I arrived and no time before."

Emiel looked at Bone, who shrugged. "Then what about the little ground ripples you kept throwing at the jarku?"

"I don't know what you're talking about," she replied. "Perhaps it was a fear induced hallucination."

"Perhaps you could be just a little more mannerly and a lot less sour." Emiel thought he heard her teeth grinding. "So, if you didn't help us, I wonder what happened."

A rock flew up between the horses and came straight for Emiel's face. He ducked barely in time, then looked up to see the tiny girl from the forest lounging on one of the horses.

Her nearly translucent skin was difficult to separate from the color of the chestnut mare upon whose back she lay. Her little brown dress rippled in the breeze along with her reddish clay colored hair.

"That's what happened," Amoura said, her tone actually amused.

"Did you just throw a rock at me?" Emiel asked. "What in the name of the Fallen did I do to make so many enemies?"

"You didn't say thank you. It's rude, so I threw a rock at you."

Emiel stared at her. "How could I say thank you if I didn't know it was you?"

She rolled her eyes at him. It was a pet peeve Amiya and Nandi occasionally stroked. Now *he* was grinding his teeth.

"How could you not know? Who else would it have been?"

Beside him, Amoura let out a quiet huff that sounded like half a snicker.

"Well s'cuse me for not knowing everything about the world. I didn't see you anywhere around, so I didn't know you were there. Thank you for helping us, though."

The tiny girl's face brightened. "You're welcome."

"This grows more interesting," Amoura remarked, her tone as dry as the Sandlands. "Mind sharing how you managed to attract an *earth* tinfar?"

"A what?" Emiel responded, looking at Bone, who looked just as surprised.

"An *earth* tinfar," Amoura repeated. "One of the tiny folk. They don't usually bother with humans."

"Because you bring trouble everywhere you go!" the little tinfar declared. "You bring axes and arrows and war. Why would we be around you?"

"You're here," Emiel observed.

"So I am."

"Why so?" Emiel asked, smiling. "Looking to make new friends?"

"Bored," the girl said, and Bone laughed.

"Bored?" Emiel repeated.

The tinfar gasped. "You can imitate like a parrot! Do it again! Do it again!"

"I've had about enough sarcasm to last the rest of my life," Emiel muttered.

The little tinfar tilted her head at him as if she didn't understand, which seemed to be an even more sarcastic gesture.

"My name is Emiel," he said.

"Lief," the tiny girl replied.

"Pretty name," Emiel said. "Are your parents okay with you accompanying us, Lief?"

Amoura snorted.

Lief's smile evaporated. "Why would my parents say anything about me being here?"

"Well," Emiel felt he was on a slippery slope. He looked to Amoura for help.

The woman sighed. "Tinfar look like children to our eyes, but they live longer than we do." She nodded at Lief. "What you see as a little girl could well be older than your parents."

Emiel's mouth fell open and he looked back at Lief, who was now standing on the horse's back, tiny fists on her hips. "She's right, you know. Unless you've seen fifty winters pass, you're too young to go asking me about what my parents think of me traveling where and *when* I please, thank you."

"Alright, alright," Emiel said, holding his hands up in surrender. "I didn't know you were ... more mature than I am. I've never seen one of your kind before. I apologize."

Lief's smile returned. "Apology accepted!"

"Wow," Emiel said. "You don't hold a grudge at all, do you?"

"Um. No, that's a human trait."

"Don't think highly of humans, do you?"

Lief shrugged. "My people don't really think about you at all, except something to avoid, really."

"Ouch," Emiel said. "Are we that bad to you?"

Lief thought about that for a moment. "Well. You all seem to have a hard enough time not killing one another. Why would we talk to you?"

Emiel had no rebut that logic. "So you're here out of boredom. Does that mean you're tagging along with us?"

Again the tinfar shrugged. "For now. If you get boring then maybe I'll leave." She smirked at Bone. "But considering that bone-man over there insisted on passing through the werewood, I might have to stay to keep you from dying."

"You tried to go through there?" Amoura looked around Emiel at Bone. Emiel was happy to have her irritation directed at someone else for a change.

"It was a shorter route than going across these rolling hills and having to pass near the Storm Swirl."

"The Storm Swirl isn't filled with every manner of creature that would make a fast meal of you."

"I'm no fast meal, lady," Bone snapped.

"Oh yes," Emiel said. "Those jungle shrikes back there would attest, I'm sure."

"If they weren't dead," Bone retorted.

"Because I ran two of them over with a wagon," Emiel countered.

"And I ran two of them through with my sword," Bone shot back, fixing him with an angry stare.

"Somewhere in his study, Selvetar is laughing himself dizzy at me," Amoura muttered.

Emiel looked at her. "Pardon? Who's that?"

"Nothing," the woman replied. She looked away.

"See what I mean?" Lief said, waving a hand to encompass them all. "There are only three of you sitting here and none of you can stand the other. That's why we avoid you."

"And yet," Amoura said, turning a sleepy expression on the diminutive tinfar, "here you are."

"Here I am," Lief agreed. "Bored out of my wits, and since my wits have gone due to boredom, I'm inclined to accompany you on your quest!"

"Lovely," Amoura grumbled.

"Who said anything about a quest?" Bone ran a hand through his hair. "Nobody said anything about a quest."

"You're on this road, aren't you?" the tinfar asked. "Of course you're on a quest. All humans are on some kind of quest. It's in your nature! You can't stop yourselves."

"You the resident scholar on humans among your kind?" Bone asked.

"I've spent a good deal of time among you," Lief replied. "More than most. At my home, I'm the one to see for questions about humans."

"Do you have any knowledge regarding our various tolerance level for chatter?" Amoura asked.

"Oh hush, you're just grumpy," Lief said, making a shooing gesture. "You're far too pretty to be such a grumblegen."

Despite her foul mood, Amoura actually chuckled at that.

Emiel's heart lightened a bit. The appearance of this little tinfar—whatever that was—seemed to have lifted the mood. Lief might actually be a light in this dark point in his life. Maybe after he dropped off whatever this nonsense package was in Altarra, the girl/woman might accompany him back. He doubted Bone or this Amoura Xanna woman would wish to be around him any more than need be.

"So where are we going?" Lief hopped from the right horse to the left. A woman she may be, but to Emiel, she seemed so much like a child.

"We?" Bone asked.

"That's what I said."

Bone turned an incredulous look on Amoura, who stared out at the rolling plains with disinterest.

"We're going to a far far away city," Bone said with a broad smile.

"I'll remind you that I'm a fully adult tinfar, whatever I might look like to you, little boy. How many winters have you seen? Nineteen? Twenty?" She made a dismissive gesture. "You're little more than a child yourself, yet I speak to you as an adult. I'll kindly ask the same of you."

"Alright, alright. You pack a mean temper to be so small." He waved a lazy hand out in front of them. "We're headed to Altarra. Okay?"

"Altarra?" Lief replied. "That's a long way from here. Could take you weeks."

"We should get there in seven more days," Bone said.

"Passing through the Storm Swirl?" Lief asked doubtfully. "And what about the Nunorian Marshlands?"

"We'll go around them."

"Ah." Lief tapped a finger to her lips. "That's going to take you awfully close to Carlayn, don't you think?"

"And?" Bone asked.

"You don't travel much, do you, kid?" Amoura asked him.

"Don't ever call me a kid again," Bone said, "and I've traveled plenty. As far as Altarra and its surrounding lands."

Amoura blinked at him. "Okay. Lesson. Between us and Altarra is a city named Carlayn. The prime minister of Carlayn is securely underneath the king's thumb, and suspicious of just about everything. You bring this little group anywhere near those city walls, and we will be standing before the prime minister, answering every question imaginable. Thereafter, we will remain as his 'guests' while he checks and double checks every fact we've stated. Add at least two weeks to our trip if this happens."

"Thanks for the tip," Bone said. "Not planning on going anywhere near that place."

"Good," the magus said. "Then that means we'll be passing through The Triplets."

"The Triplets?" Emiel asked, nervous at Amoura's mock brightness.

"Oh yes, spicetrader. Our good mercenary here plans to ride us straight between a mountain range with three identical peaks, each housing diverse forms of lovely predators who are not particular about what they eat."

"Delightful," Emiel said. "Have I mentioned the most undesirable way I can think of to die is by being made a meal?"

"You should be fine," Lief said. "Just don't do anything foolish."

"I would remind you," Amoura stated, "that you are riding with a comically young mercenary with little traveling experience, and a spicetrader who's never ventured farther than half a day behind us to the outlying villages and towns bordering the province."

Interesting that she knows my business routes, Emiel thought. "So what's next, then?"

"We fight," Bone growled.

Emiel followed the young man's gaze to see two hulking things lumbering toward them. They were too far away for him to make out any distinct features, but it was clear they weren't human. "What ... are those?"

Bone pulled the wagon to a stop while struggling to keep the horses under control.

"Leapers," he growled. "Get away from the wagon."

13

———

AMOURA

Leapers.

Amoura had seen a leaper one other time in her life, and it hadn't been a fun experience. The things had a lumbering gate that belied the power in their misshapen bodies. She knew that as soon as the things got close enough, they would make a mighty leap into the air and crash down on them all. The wagon was the largest target, but as soon as they separated, the leapers would most certainly go for them instead.

"When they jump," she heard the redheaded mercenary say, "keep moving but keep an eye on them. They can change directions in the air. If they land on you, you're done."

Amoura had never battled one, but she had witnessed a single leaper kill four armored men with one stomp.

"Should we spread out or stick together," the spicetrader asked.

"Stay together until we know they're focused on us and not the horses and wagon," Bone answered. "Then we spread out. It'll almost certainly prefer us than the animals."

"You seem pretty worried about the horses," Emiel said. "I like 'em too, but I'm more worried about one of those things getting ahold of me!"

"You want to walk to Altarra, spicetrader?"

"Good point," Emiel conceded. "They'd probably come after us anyway."

"Good thinking," Bone said as they jogged away from the wagon. "You must be a master of the road and its many perils."

"And you're pretty funny. You should be a traveling jokester instead of a mercenary."

"Or I could be both a traveling jokester and a murderer of spice-traders," Bone said, shooting him a warning glance.

"I won't be bored at all being around you three," Lief said, giggling. "If you don't kill each other, this will be fun."

"No guarantees," Bone muttered.

"They're about to jump," Amoura said, eyeing the leapers. They were still approaching, but their legs were a little more bent.

"Try to get as much distance between you and the area of impact."

"Impact?" Emiel said. "That sounds a little dramatic."

Bone snarled at him. "Well then stand right where they land and see what happens."

As one, the leapers jumped. Amoura was reminded of her amazement at just how high the things could leap. They reached a height as high as the top of the magi fortress in one bound. They spread their arms as they descended, and as they drew closer, Amoura saw a web-like membrane that connected the inside of their arms and their torso.

They continued to guide their descent. A direct hit would splatter them across the grassy plane, and the leapers would simply dine on them piece by piece. The thought gave her a shiver.

"They're coming down!" Bone said. "Scatter!"

"No!" Amoura said. "Pair up!" She looked down at the tinfar running beside them, taking three running steps to their one. "Can you fight them with us?"

"Of course I can," Lief replied. "I'm not helpless!"

"Good. Stay with the boy."

"What?" Bone said.

"Quit arguing ..."

Amoura dove to the side in the opposite direction of Emiel just as one of the leapers landed. It hit the ground with a mighty stomp that lifted the ground under them and sent her and the spicetrader into the air.

She hit the ground on her side and tried to roll with the impact, but it still hurt. Amoura ignored the pain in her ribs and twisted around to look over her shoulder. The monster was close enough for her to see its orange eyes glaring at her from deep sockets in a ridged, oval head. Amoura's stomach churned at the sight of that leathery yellow-brown skin. A spike protruded from each of its elbows and knees, and what looked like sharp bone grew from the corner of its shoulders. Its arms were longer than its legs, and each hand ended in long curled nails.

The thing was entirely too close.

She forced herself to her feet, looking past it in the direction of a cursing Bone, who had just hit the ground with a heaving grunt. Lief was the only one of their party that hadn't been affected by the creature's stomp.

Amoura went within, delving the *essences*. The misshapen creature rushed her and she backpedaled, keeping it at a distance long enough to form a counter attack.

It lifted a foot with a somewhat slow and clumsy kick, which Amoura easily avoided. She thought fast. Wind would do nothing to hurt this thing. She could try ice, but combining two *essences* required more time than she had.

It dashed forward with a left-handed slap. Amoura tried to avoid it but the leaper's arms were long. She managed to get her arm up and rolled with the blow, absorbing some of the impact. That had been a mistake. The thing could have broken her arm. The pain in her throbbing arm brought on a spike of anger.

She found *earth* and drew it forth, ripping the ground underneath the leaper. It fell, but was surprisingly quick to regain its feet. Amoura called upon her ring and released a powerful blast of wind to slow the monster. She delved again, and drew upon *air*, not through her ring, but through the actual *essence* itself. She called upon *fire* and heated the air until it was as hot as a furnace.

The leaper made a moaning sound, and stumbled to the side. Amoura followed it, buffeting it with the searing hot wind. She thought she'd it finished it when it dropped to a knee, but then it leaped into the air. Amoura tried to follow it, but the leaper quickly ascended out of reach. As the beast continued its rise into the air, she looked for the others.

A dazed Emiel was just shaking off a blow to the head from when he'd hit the ground, while Bone and Lief battled the other leaper. The mercenary stabbed and retracted, then delivered a downward cut. The leaper was too slow to avoid the attacks, but its tough hide protected it from the blade.

Lief helped by keeping the thing off balance, shifting the ground beneath it, and lifting chunks of earth, condensing it into rock, and hurling it at the monster. Her efforts were not damaging, but it allowed the mercenary to stay on the offensive while figuring out how to inflict damage.

Amoura looked to the sky again, expecting the leaper's descent to be directly on top of her. Her heart practically leapt into her throat when she saw that the monster—likely judging her to be the more dangerous of the two—had decided instead to go after the spicetrader.

Emiel still hadn't looked up yet, and the thing was directly over him. Amoura called upon her ring again, and sent a jet of air into the man. The man tumbled backward in a cloud of curses as he was sent skipping and rolling across the ground before skidding to a stop.

The leaper hit the ground where he had been, just a heartbeat earlier. The ground collapsed into a small crater where it hit, and the shockwave lifted Amoura off the ground.

She landed in a stumble, but kept her feet and once again called upon her ring. The walls of the crater burst apart and pounded into the leaper. She then called upon *fire,* and heated the earth until it was molten, then sent it splashing into the monster. This time, it let out a gurgling howl. Her ring nearly depleted, she went within herself, drawing upon *water* and *air*.

Though it's skin was tough, the molten earth had burned the leaper badly. Though it lay thrashing in agony on the ground, it was still alive. Amoura used that time to combine the *essences* she drew upon *earth*, and also that which was stored within her ring.

Freezing air and jagged shards of ice formed in the air, and she launched them into the leaper. The ice dealt damage to the monster's singed flesh, but the freezing air was worse. Its skin already burning hot, the cold air sent it in to shock while freezing it at the same time. The change from burning hot to freezing cold caused it to crack, then burst into thousands of icy chunks.

The first threat gone, Amoura looked to see Bone and Lief, still struggling against the other leaper. It managed to knock the young mercenary to the ground, but the boy dealt it a strong cut to the side of its knee as he went down. The injury was negligible, and the monster ignored the wound.

Lief spun in a circle, bringing up a spiral of *earth* around her tiny body. She continued to spin, faster and faster, then threw her arm out in the direction of the leaper. The spiraling *earth* assault knocked the leaper into the air. It hit the ground near Emiel, who—to her surprise—drew his hunting knife and stabbed it in the back of the head.

The monster tried to rise, but the spicetrader stabbed it repeatedly, then scrambled away when it finally stood. It advance on the spicetrader, and she heard him let loose a stream of curses as he backpedaled away from its long, swinging arms.

What are you doing? Amoura thought. Emiel held a hunting knife by the blade in his right hand and raised it as if to throw. "Perhaps he learned to throw to fight off highwaymen." She began to draw upon the remaining *essences* stored in her ring.

Emiel let fly, and the dagger spun lazily in the air and bounced hilt-first, off the monster's face.

Amoura sighed. "Perhaps not." Just as she finished formulating her assault, Bone came up behind the monster. He drew a dagger from his belt and leaped on its back, driving the blade home. He then hopped off, and drew his sword, but this time the cutting edge was covered by hard brown plate, similar to his armor.

He spun a circle and swiped the blade around and down into the back of its knees. It fell backwards, and its head hit the ground hard, driving the dagger in further. Bone replaced his sword in its scabbard, then drew it again, this time the cutting edge was naked.

Interesting, she thought as the monster spasmed on the ground a few feet from the mercenary, who had the tip of his sword hovering over its chest. When it finally stopped thrashing and fell still, he relaxed and replaced the sword in its scabbard. After one step, the mercenary thought better of it. In one motion, he turned and drew his sword. He reversed his grip and drove the blade down into the monster's neck.

"I'll be just fine if we don't run into any more of those things," he said, and rolled the heavy thing over. Bone yanked at his embedded dagger until it came away with a squishing sound. He wiped it off on the leathery hide, stabbed it into the dirt, then wiped it off on the monster again. "Nice throw, by the way," he said, smirking up at Emiel as the spicetrader retrieved his hunting knife.

"Funny," Emiel replied. He shoved the knife back into his belt. "I never claimed to be a marksman."

"The truth would certainly have been revealed today if you had," the mercenary replied, chuckling.

"This is strange," Lief said, trotting up to the group. "Leapers don't just come from nowhere and attack people in the open planes like this."

Amoura watched the tinfar, her tiny face scrunched up in a frown. Why was she so worried?

"All manner of monsters travel the plains," Bone said. "Surely you've seen the scattered remains of animals as well as human travelers upon the road from time to time, little one."

"Yes, smart boy. But they're usually attacked by monsters that actually roam the planes. Those things," Lief pointed at the dead leaper, "live in the mountains. I've never seen them lurking any farther than a few miles from their habitat. They would have to be very hungry to do that."

Emiel grimaced at the unsightly corpse. "Then these must have been on the verge of starvation. We're a long way from any mountain."

"I don't like this at all," Lief said. "Leapers only come this far from the mountains during evil times."

Bone gave the tinfar a flat look. "Evil times. I'm so happy to have the resident sprite to share campfire superstitions with us along our harrowing journey."

"You don't have to believe me, bone-boy," Lief said. She pointedly walked past him to stand beside Emiel. Amoura thought it an odd move. The tinfar seemed to have taken a liking to the spicetrader for some reason. "It doesn't change the fact that certain monsters only come around when there is—"

"A great evil in the world," Bone finished.

The tinfar sniffed and looked up at Emiel. "I think it is too dangerous to travel like this. If you're closer to your home than your destination, you should turn back."

"Love to," Emiel said, glaring at Bone. "I would absolutely love to."

Bone eyed the spicetrader, then made for the wagon. "Not an option."

The horses had pulled the wagon farther down the road away from the conflict. That the animals hadn't bolted and injured themselves or destroyed the cart, was a miracle.

"Why not?" Lief asked. She sounded so innocent, that Amoura kept having to remind herself that the tinfar was older than all of them. Perhaps even some of their ages combined.

"Not your concern," Bone replied. "You have my thanks for your help, but we have a destination to reach and turning back is not something we can do."

"You all could die."

"Regardless, we continue on."

The tinfar put her hands on her hips, looking from Bone to

Emiel, then to Amoura. "Understanding humans is impossible," she said.

"How right you are," Emiel muttered, and followed behind the mercenary.

Amoura started after them, and Lief moved up beside her. "Why?" was all she asked.

Amoura glanced down at her. "We have business in Altarra." Lief looked like she wanted to say more, but didn't. To Amoura's relief, the rest of the day was a quiet ride, which left her to gather her thoughts and plan out the rest of their journey. Their options were limited, and the quickest and safest route would take them into the lands surrounding Carlayn. The delay would be undesirable, but it would also allow them to replenish their supplies. But was it worth the risk of drawing the attention of the ever watchful prime minister, in all his paranoia? And there was the possibility that their captive would give them up to the authorities and make a mess of the whole thing.

The other option was The Triplets, which would keep them well out of the Carlayn's watchful gaze, but send them into a place with no shortage of danger. Amoura had her *essence* ring to combine with her innate abilities, but would that see them through?

It was a risk, and one Amoura wasn't inclined to take. She sighed. "There's a fork in the road another half league from here," she said.

"I'm aware," Bone replied.

"Take the right trail."

"The right? But that would take us—"

"To Carlayn, yes." Amoura tried not to growl as she spoke. That Fallen-cursed Selvetar could have had this done in minutes, opening or bending the air, or whatever it was he did, and transported the group to him with little effort. Why send her here and waste time? It was obvious Vladrick wanted the spicetrader as soon as possible. And Amoura was certain the magi master was aware of Selvetar's ability.

Amoura frowned at the rolling plains without seeing them. Something else was going on between Vladrick and the first magus that they hadn't felt necessary to share with her. She would need to be ready when she finally delivered Emiel to Vladrick. The nagging feeling in the back of her mind was never wrong.

Lief suddenly hopped off the wagon.

Emiel turned in his seat and looked back. "Aren't we going to stop for her?" he asked.

"Nope," Bone replied. "She'll catch up. Or not."

Emiel opened his mouth to say more, but Amoura cut him off, not wanting to endure another round between those two. "She needs to touch the earth in order to sense things." Emiel looked at her, and this time she returned his gaze. He had the most sincere eyes she'd seen in a long time. Dark brown pools of a relative innocence of the greater world outside his city.

"Sense things?"

Amoura shrugged. "The weather. Other nearby forms of life. Every type of tinfar needs to have a connection to the *essence* of their particular nature."

"That goes over my head," Emiel said. "Before we started this little trip, I had no idea they existed. And I don't know much about this *essence* you're talking about either. I've got a general idea, but that's about it. Wouldn't mind keeping it that way, too."

Amoura arched an eyebrow at the scorn in the man's tone. He claimed to know almost nothing about the *essences*, yet had such negative feelings about them. What had happened in his life to so color his feelings? Had he met a magus before her?

"Okay, lady," Bone said. "I've gotta ask. Why in the name of the Creator would you want to venture anywhere near Carlayn after what you just told us about the prime minister? By your own words, we'd be at risk of being delayed at best."

"It's a less dangerous route than through The Triplets," Amoura replied. "And if we're discreet, we can pass around the outside of its borders unnoticed."

"But we can still skirt inside the border without being seen," Bone said. "It would take us close to The Triplets, but not into them. If we're swift, we might get through undetected and pass by The Triplets, and even shave off a few days from our trip."

"Or be caught inside Carlayn's domain and delayed weeks," Amoura replied.

"Have you given thought to our supplies?" Bone asked. "That storm delayed us, and the ... encounters ... that we've had up till now have slowed us more. If I'd planned for more than a two week journey, this wagon would be stocked more than it already is, which would have made it heavier, which would have made the horses slower, which would make it more difficult to outrun danger. That means more frequent stops. We need to find one of the outlying farms—"

"Inside the border of Carlayn," Amoura said. "Which means we would still be venturing inside Prime Minister Cravel's domain."

"I don't see how that matters."

Amoura looked at the young mercenary as though he'd lost his mind. "If we're caught riding this wagon to a farm and try to take lodging and replenish supplies, we'll most certainly be taken before Cravel. He will want to know why we attempted a transaction without his knowledge.

Bone's mouth fell open. "This is not unusual or illegal. It's expected that travelers might stop at a local farm of village to rest and replenish."

"You clearly haven't traveled much, boy," Amoura replied, ignoring Bone's glower. "I've already told you the man is suspicious to the point of paranoia. He's also greedy. His farmers pay the same tax whether or not they profit from their goods. If he thinks we're trying to cheat him from his due, he'll go out of his way to make things difficult for us."

"So we go into the city, then," Bone replied. "Closer to the man."

Amoura thought on that. "Travelers come in and out of the city frequently. Nothing unusual about that."

Bone's eyes widened. "You're serious?" When she didn't answer, he threw a hand in the air. "Then all this worrisome conversation was for nothing."

Amoura didn't answer, and the boy made an irritated sound and retuned his attention to the road. She didn't want to verbalize that their captive could most certainly make things problematic for them. Even without trouble from the spicetrader, she didn't like the risk of going into that city. Unfortunately, the fool boy was right, and they needed to restock their provisions.

"A storm is coming."

Emiel made a good show at not being startled by the suddenness of Lief's return, but Amoura wasn't surprised. She'd figured the tinfar had left to get a feeling for the weather.

"You can feel that through the ground?" Emiel asked. "But the weather is in the sky."

Lief shrugged. "The weather affects everything. Only humans can't sense it until it's obvious. The trees can sense the weather, and they're connected to the ground." She flung her little hands into the air. "And so I can speak to them."

"So I'm guessing you can't sense the weather either, since you need to speak to the trees."

The tinfar winked at him. "Oh I can sense the weather just fine, but because I am *et'a* tinfar, I cannot sense the severity of it."

"Ett ... what?"

"Earth," Lief explained. "I am an *earth* tinfar. My nature is tied to *earth essence*."

"The more we talk," Emiel said, "the more I feel like I'm acquiring more questions than answers."

"Then why not talk less?" Amoura asked. "Sound carries far on the planes and I'd like not to happen upon any more horrors this day." That wasn't wholly true, but for a relief the spicetrader heeded her words. The last thing she needed was for the conversation to venture too far in any direction related to his dormant abilities, whatever those might be.

She felt eyes on her and looked down at Lief, who was staring at her. She responded with a warning look, but the tinfar just hopped onto the back of one of the horses. She stretched, then lounged on her back and closed her eyes.

"The world must seem a big place when you're so small," Bone said.

"It's big no matter what size you are," Emiel replied. "A horse might seem bigger to her, but a mountain is the same size to all of us."

"Yeah sure," Bone said, eliciting a scowl from Emiel, which the mercenary ignored. "We need to find a place to camp for the night. We're still more than half a day away from Carlayn."

"I wish we didn't have to camp out in the open like this again," Emiel said. "Especially with another storm coming."

"Better a storm out here than in the middle of the Storm Swirl," Bone replied. He peered into the distance at what looked like a ceiling of dark clouds skulking through the distant mountains. "Can't say I'm disappointed at having avoided that option.

Lief yawned and pointed down the road. "The land gets rocky on the other side of that hill. There's not many trees, but there are some outcroppings. We could shelter there."

"I'm sure whatever lives in those things would welcome us to snuggle in with it," Bone said.

"We'll be fine," the tinfar replied.

"I'm to trust your word, little one?"

"I would," Amoura said.

The boy grumbled but said nothing further.

Sometime later, Lief was proven right when they crested the hill to see several outcroppings scattered across the landscape. She guided them to an uninhabited cluster of boulders some distance from the road, as promised.

"How'd you know there's nothing living in here?" Emiel asked.

Lief responded with a noncommittal shrug. "We should get the horses inside."

To everyone's—except Lief's—surprise, the outcropping was larger than it looked from outside. The opening in the middle was as large as a cave, and had enough space to fit the wagon near the entrance without blocking the opening. It housed the four of them along with the two horses without cramping the space.

Bone started a campfire and went about retrieving food from their supplies.

Lief left while they ate, and returned after they had finished their meal and cleaned up. Emiel unrolled his sleeping pack a little away from the others and slipped inside.

"I'll keep first watch," Bone said to Amoura.

"No," she replied. "I will keep first watch.

"I didn't know you were in charge," the mercenary said.

"I'm not sleepy," Amoura replied. "And I require little of it anyway. You should retain your strength for tomorrow. Sleep. I'll wake you if I tire."

Bone grunted, but offered no argument. He unrolled his pack, but lay on top of it.

Amoura moved closer to the entrance. The wind stirred, howling across the open planes and sneaking through the cracks like a spying wraith.

She took one last glance back at the others, then sat cross-legged, back erect, and drew in a deep breath. She let the air seep between her partially separated lips.

Her heartbeat slowed as she continued her controlled breathing. In time, her body relaxed. Time seemed to slow as she sank deeper into her meditation. Amoura willed her mind to still, only allowing a small part of her conscious mind to recall the various methods of manipulating the *essences* that she had learned over the past four days of study. The knowledge came to her, and her subconscious took control and gathered the experiences, infusing it into her body, her muscles, her being.

She would no longer need to refer to books or scrolls to refill her *essence* ring. They were now as much a part of her as her ability to walk or run.

She closed her eyes and visualized the four *essences* and their attributes. Red, the *essence* of fire. Blue, the *essence* of water. Silver, the *essence* of air. Brown, the *essence*, of earth. She *delved* each of them, feeling them, knowing them. She opened her eyes only a bit, allowing the glowing light of the *arah* in her eyes and her ring to light the darkness in front of her.

She closed her eyes again and *delved* the four *essences*, drawing them forth and funneling them into her *essence* ring. Each in turn, she infused the ring with the four powers, filling it to capacity.

Once the ring was full, she *delved air*, then *fire*. A tiny flame sparked to life, surrounded by a sealed globe of air. She willed it to hover in front of her as she reached into her satchel and withdrew a scroll.

She unrolled it and began to read, glancing up from time to time at the entrance to the cave as she poured over the symbols and text, committing them to memory. She *delved earth*, and allowed herself to feel the ground beneath her, feeling her body grow heavier as she connected with the actual earth itself, through its *essence's* namesake. The power felt solid, and infinitely massive.

Firmly planted within *earth*, Amoura *delved air*, then *fire*, then *water*. She allowed each of the four *essences* to flow around her, through her, filling her. But just a touch. Not more than a flick. Less than a flick. The four *essences* were greater than anything a human could imagine. To allow too much of it to fill her could result in any number of painful ways to die.

A trickle of sweat ran down the side of her face, and she gradually released each of the *essences* until only *earth* remained. She held on to it a while longer, then lowly released it as well.

Amoura let her breath out in a hiss between her parted lips, and blinked at the tiny flame still hovering in front of her. She dismissed it with a gust of air.

For a time, Amoura sat and stared at the opening to the rocky shelter, and the world beyond. The tiny voice in her head telling her to leave was getting louder. She should leave Altarra, and perhaps leave the Order of Magi altogether. But could she? Would Vladrick allow his most prized student to just walk away?

And what of the spicetrader? Her mind said that the best choice was to deliver him to Vladrick as she'd been ordered, and while the magi master was distracted with the man, she could make a discreet exit and be long gone by the time he called upon her. If she was lucky, she could put enough distance between herself and Altarra before the Master discovered her absence. If she made it far enough away, maybe Selvetar wouldn't be able to track her.

She sighed. Her heart spoke differently. Amoura had never met a wilder, only heard stories about them. She'd heard about their fierceness and unpredictability, not to mention their undisciplined use of the *essences*. From her first days of training, it had been vehemently expressed that wilders manipulated a force they did not understand and barely held control over. If too many of them made a big enough mistake, they could break the world.

She thought about the spicetrader again, supposedly a hybrid and just as dangerous as a full blooded Khatala. But also trainable due to his Marailander blood. He didn't seem even remotely as unstable and unpredictable as what the Khatala were supposed to be. He displayed none of their supposed fierceness.

Not fierce at all, but rather gentle. Those sincere brown eyes had no hardness in them. She saw only compassion, warmness, and a repressed despair. She wondered what had happened to him, and why he was so hesitant to leave his home to study with the magi of Altarra. Regardless of what Amoura might think, it was still considered a great honor. Only those with the greatest potential were accepted. She wondered if somehow the spicetrader already knew what she did about the place, and wished to avoid it.

"You don't want him to know, do you?"

Amoura nearly jumped at the sound of Lief's voice beside her. She wondered if all tinfar were adept at sidling up to someone unnoticed.

"Nothing to say?" Lief asked.

Amoura glanced back into the shelter at the others. Still asleep. "What are you talking about?" she whispered back.

"I think you know," Lief replied. "You don't want him to know he can *delve*."

That was a surprise. "You speak our terms?"

"Your people travel a lot, and I listen."

"Why do you find us so interesting, e'ta tinfar? I've never seen any of your kind before and I know of no one who has. Do you not scorn us?"

Lief thought on the question. "We don't scorn you. The best way I can describe it is like how you would avoid a bear. You know that the bear is dangerous, so you avoid it."

"Yet you do not."

"I am like those of your kind that like to study the bear; learn its habits and personality." She shrugged. "I find you interesting. It's also easy to remain unseen. Not many of you have senses sharp enough to know I'm there when I don't want you to."

"Where is your home?" Amoura asked.

"The forests outside that spice-man's city," came the response. "And you're trying to avoid my question."

"I'm not trying to avoid it," Amoura said. "I am avoiding it."

"Why?"

"Because it isn't a question I want to answer."

"To me, or yourself?"

That caught Amoura off guard. "Maybe both."

"You talk in uncertainties. That means you're mind argues with your heart."

"And you're about to tell me to listen to my heart," Amoura replied dryly.

"Nope," Lief said, turning away. "You're already doing that."

14

FREE

*F**ree! After millennia uncountable. After so long trapped in the light.
Free.*

*The ground passed beneath, charred and dead in its wake. Mountains
and hills, oceans, lakes, rivers and streams. Where there was life, now there
was death. Across the edge of the Frostlands, white snow became hard and
black. The black glacier. It still stood, defiant against the light. Protecting
him still. This was good.*

*Across the Sandlands, brown sands became hard and black. The castle
waited. It always waited. Sleeping. A living, vengeful thing. The vast castle
still held her servants, her toys. All slept. She became aware. Through that
awareness was reverence.*

*Trees turned to drooping burned husks. Plant life wilted, water boiled,
fire froze. The land passed beneath, then came the ocean. A path, straight
down, a tunnel of death and blackness in its wake. The ocean life avoided it.
They knew it was death. Down. Ever downward. A cave deep below the
surface. Yes, she still slept with her pet.*

*The lands passed beneath and died. A forest filled with life. No longer.
Twisted and charred. Lucky to die, cursed to live. The lake that was not a
lake. No lake lay on the side of a mountain. No lake was black. Into the
welcome caress of the endless void. The blackness disappeared and then*

there was rock. Ancient rock infused with his malevolence. He still slept. That was good.

The forest; always dark, always resistant to the hated light. There was welcome here. So many pets that could become a different kind of pet. Trees did not wilt, but came alert. Life within the ponds came awake. The tree still stood, the gaping maw at its base still inviting. Down into the darkness where life rotted and waited, dormant. He awoke. Amusement. Anticipation.

The lands charred. The lands burned. The lands dead. The mountain, red as blood. So large. So vast. The highest peak. Above the clouds. Rock exploded and fell as it entered. Tunnels and caverns and chasms. Stalagmites and stalactites. A giant hole of blackness. At the bottom, he slept. At the bottom, he awoke.

The lands charred and burned and died. An angry mountain. Not a mountain, but a churning furnace. In the middle of the molten lake, he slept. Lava bubbled and exploded like a molten geyser. Glowing red eyes opened. He slept no longer.

Light was coming.

The lands charred, burned, twisted, died. Home once more. Home that was once its prison. Prison no longer. The Seven awakened. The seven arisen. The prison destroyed and remade. Now home. They would come. They always came. But they had grown weak, while it had grown strong. Its identity broke through the mindless rage. Yes. He was aware once again. She was aware once again. Humanity would come. They always came. They would fight.

They would die forever.

***

EMIEL WOKE IN A COLD SWEAT. For a moment he didn't know where he was, then he remembered. He lay in a bedroll in the middle of an outcropping with two people 'accompanying' him to deliver some package to Altarra. He wiped sweat from his forehead and looked around the campsite. *What was that dream?*

It felt so real, so clear. It also felt incredibly evil. More like a nightmare. Emiel massaged the back of his neck, glad that horrible night-mare was over. It still gave him a shiver to think of how real it felt, and how the dream hadn't faded even a little upon his waking.

"Sleepy one finally wakes," a tiny voice said from behind.

He looked over his shoulder to see Lief lounging on the ground behind him. She smiled. "Good morning," he said, smiling back. The little tinfar woman was the closest Emiel had to a friend on this journey. He was glad she hadn't simply gotten bored and left him. "How did you sleep? Actually, do you even sleep?"

"Of course, silly. Every living thing sleeps in some way. I just don't need as much of it as you do."

"You know," Emiel said. "I was thinking a few days back. I never got to thank you for saving me when that jarku was about to take a bite out of me."

"It hadn't gotten that close to you yet," Lief replied. "Remember? I stopped it before it could pounce on you."

"I remember," Emiel said. "But before that happened, one of those things had taken me down. If you hadn't knocked it away with that ground thing you do, I'd probably be missing an arm or something."

The one and a half foot tall woman scrunched up her features. It was hard to remind himself that she was a woman and not a very small girl.

"I don't know what you're talking about. I didn't get there until one of them was about to jump you."

"I doubt it was Amoura," he said, lowering his voice to a whisper. Heartbreakingly beautiful, she may be, but the woman was the very definition of uninviting. Half the time she seemed to blame Emiel for her presence on this errand, and other times she seemed to just tolerate him like one would a particularly annoying child.

"You think it was another tinfar like you?"

Lief shook her head. "That's as close to impossible as you could get." She regarded him with those earthy brown eyes. "Someone else helped you."

"There was nobody else there. Amoura hadn't arrived yet and I didn't see anyone else around."

"Then maybe it was you," Lief replied.

"Me?" Emiel laughed. "It wasn't me. I don't have one of those rings like she does." He nodded his head in Amoura's direction.

Lief glanced at the magus, standing at the mouth of the cave with Bone. The two were wrapped in discussion about something Emiel doubted he'd like. The little he could see of the landscape beyond didn't show much promise for good weather. *Gonna be a lovely day.*

"That ring she wears was fashioned by human hands," Lief replied. "The power she brings out of it was made by Creation Itself."

"What does that mean?"

"It means," Lief answered, sounding impatient, "that some don't need a tool to bond with Creation."

Emiel noticed that she kept glancing in Amoura's direction. Did the magus not want the two of them to talk? He couldn't imagine why not. "I have no idea what you're talking about, but I'll keep it in mind."

"Listen to yourself and you will know."

"Myself?"

Lief huffed. "Your body. Your intuition. Your ... whatever it is you listen to! I don't know. Just pay attention to how you feel and what happens when you feel it. Okay?"

"Okay, okay," Emiel patted the air between them. "Didn't mean to get you all in a little huff. Just asking questions."

"You need to understand faster, Emiel," the tinfar said. "There's not a lot of time." And with that, she walked away.

Emiel stared after her, then got up. *Not a lot of time for what?* What was he supposed to understand, and why was time short for it? Her words had planted a nervous seed in his gut.

He rolled and tied his bedroll, then secured it to his pack. When he saw that the other two were still staring outside, now accompanied by Lief, he decided to see what all the fuss was about. As soon as he reached the mouth of the cave, he knew.

The northwestern sky looked to be on fire. "What in the name of the Illuminarians is that?" Emiel whispered.

"The borderland volcano," Bone answered. He seemed just as shaken as Emiel. "It hasn't been active for more than a hundred years."

"Two hundred seventeen," Amoura corrected. "That volcano was the most violent in recorded history."

"So why would it blow its top after so long?" Emiel asked.

"Two hundred seventeen years ago a lavakhan made its home there. Since then it's been dormant, with only the occasional rivers of lava that stream from the top and one of its sides."

"A lavakhan?" Emiel replied. "Those things haven't been seen since the days of the War of the Immortals."

"And the Fallen used them as beasts of war," Amoura said. "Everyone knows that story, and I think it's nonsense."

Both Emiel and Bone turned incredulous looks on her. Lief, however, continued to stare at the red sky coated in a canopy of thick black smoke and ash.

"Lavakhans are animals of this world," the magus said. "They are not creatures of the underworld, which means they're not inherently evil. They would have been corrupted."

"Corrupted ..." Bone gave her a skeptical look. "You ever seen a lavakhan, woman?"

Amoura arched an eyebrow at him. "Have you?"

"I've heard them described and I've seen scrolls from arttellers. All of them look mostly the same. Gigantic and terrifying."

"Fantastical interpretations of an animal that no doubt inspired fear in any who saw it," Amoura agreed. "But there's bound to have been at least a little embellishment, don't you think?"

"If that's the case," Bone replied, "every artteller must have got together to draw the same thing."

"Whether they did or not," Emiel said, "I don't like the looks of that. How far away is it?"

"Probably around five hundred miles from here."

Emiel gaped at him. "Five hundred miles? And we can see it from here?"

"The volcano is big," Amoura said, "and that was a massive explosion, no doubt. What do you say about it, tinfar?" She looked down at Lief, who stood dazed.

"I ... felt it through the ground and through the trees. That eruption was not natural."

"What do you mean, not natural?" Bone asked. "What else could it have been?"

"I don't know." Lief shook her head and snapped out of her stupor. "I have to go."

"Wait, what?" Emiel fought back his panic. "What do you mean? I thought you were in this with us all the way through. Why leave now?" He pointed over his shoulder at the dark red sky in the distance. "That's far away. It won't reach us, not even in Altarra."

She looked up at him with tiny brown eyes filled with fear. "I'll come back, I promise." She ran past him and out of the cave. With every step she seemed to blend with the ground. "You can find it," they heard her say.

Emiel stared at the last spot he'd seen her, then turned and went back toward the camp. The only person resembling a friend had just left. Now it was just him and his two sour escorts.

He took some jerky from his pack and gnawed on a piece as he tied his hunting knife back to his waist and slung his pack over his shoulder.

"We eat and travel," Bone said, rolling up his bedroll. "I think we need to reach our destination as soon as possible."

Since Amoura offered no disagreement, the magus must have agreed. Emiel walked past them both without a word as he exited the outcropping.

"Where you going?" Bone demanded.

Emiel rolled his eyes. "I couldn't likely outrun the wagon even if I didn't have this pack on my shoulder, so I thought I'd just wait outside."

He ignored the grumbling reply and would have continued on had Amoura not stopped him.

"What did she mean?" the woman asked.

"Pardon?" Emiel said. His irritation was starting to show, but he found he didn't much care.

"What did the tinfar mean by what she said to you?"

"What makes you think she was talking to me?"

Amoura gave him a bored look.

Emiel just shrugged and started walking again. "Ask her when she returns."

"I'm asking you."

"That's nice," Emiel replied.

"Did you hit your head when you lay down to sleep last night. In one night you've grown irritatingly willful."

Emiel stopped. "I doubt I could be any more irritating to you than I already am, for some reason." He turned to face her, surprised at how little he tried to hide his anger. "Look. For whatever reason, you either hate or severely dislike me. It seems like if I do little more than breathe, it annoys you. So I'll make this easy for everyone. I'll keep my mouth shut from this point forward. I'll stay out of the way if we run into any trouble, and only get involved if I'm threatened."

To his surprise, the woman's face actually softened a bit. "I don't hate you, spicetrader."

Emiel looked into those steel colored eyes. She was beautiful. Far too beautiful to be so unfriendly. "Alright then. We've settled on severely dislike." He turned away and walked toward the wagon. "And I don't know what Lief was talking about," he said over his shoulder.

He tossed the pack in the empty wagon and leaned against it. Bone could saddle the animals himself, since he'd practically deemed Emiel little more than a liability. The mercenary could bring that fool crate and deposit it back in there by himself, as well.

"What a pleasant little vacation this is turning out to be," he muttered. "I don't want to be out here like some delivery boy, and they don't want to escort someone so 'helpless'." Emiel stared at the angry red sky to the northeast. What was going on over there? He wasn't sure he swallowed Amoura's explanation. How could any animal—even one as horrific as a lavakhan—have an effect one way or another on a volcano?

They rode in silence, which was fine with Emiel. Neither Bone nor Amoura seemed given to conversation of any kind, whether with him or each other. He imagined soldiers on opposing sides of a battle would have been more amicable.

"I wonder where that little sprite went off to," Bone said, staring off into the distance.

When no response came, he looked at Amoura, then at Emiel. "You still sulking over there, spicetrader?"

Emiel favored him with an unfriendly grin. "Sulking?"

"Looks like it to me. You've suddenly felt like sitting on the far end of the wagon, staring off to the side like some pouting kid."

"For someone who's closer to being a kid than anyone else on this cart, you seem to have it all wrong."

Between them, Amoura snorted. It was faint, but he heard it.

"Careful with that tongue of yours," the mercenary warned.

"Yes, yes," Emiel said. "Or you'll cut it out. If you don't like my tone, why did you speak to me? I thought you were more interested in getting on with this without talking?"

"Quiet," Amoura said.

"Who do you ..." Bone cut off the retort when the woman leaned forward and squinted at the distant red sky. "What is it?"

"Stop. Now!"

Bone growled, but complied. As soon as he brought the wagon to a stop, Amoura hopped off and trotted up ahead, continuing to peer into the distance. After a moment, they heard her shout a curse.

"Now that wasn't very ladylike," Bone said.

Despite his irritation, Emiel chuckled. "I don't see anything."

Bone shrugged. "Neither do I ..." His mouth hung open, then he, too growled a curse and hopped off the wagon.

"What?" Emiel looked from Bone to the sky again. A few nervous heartbeats passed before he finally saw them. Tiny dots arcing in the sky. In their direction.

15
____

AMOURA

Amoura thought fast. What to do? Impossible as it was, a shower of debris from a volcano hundreds of leagues away was speeding directly at them. If she used *air* and *water*, that would only make them frozen missiles instead of molten ones.

As the debris grew closer, she could see the sheer size of the molten rock approaching and doubted she was powerful enough to repel them using *air*.

"Is that what I think it is?" Bone said next to her. He had his sword in his hand.

"What do you think to do with that?" she said, indicating the weapon. "Do you plan to stand your ground and cut the molten rock apart as it descends."

The boy seemed to realize the ridiculousness of it and sheathed the blade. "You got any suggestions other than getting away from here, which seems a smarter course?" he asked.

"That burning rock is flying too fast for us to outrun it in any direction. Look how fast it's already traveled." She felt the tingling in her body when it was preparing to touch the *essences*. "Move behind me."

"I hope you've got a lot of juice in that ring of yours," he said.

So do I, she thought.

Once the mercenary had stepped away, Amoura centered her thoughts. She reached into her ring, feeling the four *essences* within. She decided on *air*, and focused on it. At the same time, she began to draw upon *air* from the earth itself.

Behind her, Bone swore. "Whatever you're gonna do, do it fast."

Amoura went deeper, preparing *air,* then *water*. She found the two *essences* within the earth and drew upon them, pulling them forth. The *arah* in her eyes and her corlite ring began to glow, pulsating between silver and blue; *air* and *water*.

The first molten ball of rock reached them and she lashed out with a quick strike of *air*. The rock was small enough to be diverted, and it crashed into the ground several dozen feet away. Another came and she did the same, reserving as much energy as possible. Then the sky seemed to rain red-hot boulders.

Through her corlite ring, Amoura filled herself with the *essences* and exhaled. She lashed out with her right hand, sending forth *air* and *water* in a spiraling jet that froze the molten rock in the air. She then lashed out with *fire* and the ball of ice exploded in a hail of ice. Behind her, Bone and Emiel cursed as they likely were being stung by the tiny ice balls.

More molten rocks fell, and Amoura's arms were a blur as she lashed out with left hand, then right, swiping her arms in wide motions. Left to right. Over her head, or down several dozen paces in front of her. She diverted the fiery boulders or destroyed them.

Another molten rock fell toward her and she diverted it with *air*, sending it crashing to her right. She heard Emiel curse, and Bone rip his sword free. What was happening? She concentrated on repelling the distant volcano's assault.

Another boulder came spinning toward her, and she hit it with *air*, then *water* then *fire*. This time, the rock was merely slowed, but not frozen and not deterred.

Amoura hit it with another blast of *air* as she dove aside. The force of its impact sent her bouncing away, and she was half buried in a shower of dirt. She covered her face with her forearm and scrambled to her feet. This volcanic rain would kill them if she let herself be distracted.

She sent another blast of *air* into a rock the size of her head and sent it falling safely away. It was then that she saw it.

Bone was sorely pressed as he fought against a creature she had never seen before. One of the volcanic rocks had transformed into a two-legged monstrosity with four arms, each holding some sort of crude weapon made of hardened lava rock.

The thing hadn't the skill to match the mercenary, but it didn't need it. The fierceness of its attacks was enough to keep him constantly moving and more often than not, retreating.

Not far from the pressed mercenary, hunting knife in hand, Emiel watched the fight. Amoura could see the man felt helpless. She saw no cowardice in his hesitation, but the realization that his knife was practically useless against that thing.

Amoura turned her attention back to fiery rain. She froze two large rocks at once and shattered them with a blast of fire. Another boulder-sized piece of rock came toward her and she used *air* to divert it.

The giant lava rock hit the ground and bounced, seeming to break apart. As it slid across the ground, the rock didn't break apart, but unfolded itself into another of those four-armed things. It rolled and came to its feet in a charge straight for her.

Amoura's heart skipped a beat when she saw the red and black monstrosity coming her way. In two of its hands it held black and red weapons that looked like swords made of lava rock. One of the lower hands held what looked like a jagged-edged club, and the fourth hand held a wicked-looking axe.

Amoura backpedaled, summoning *water* from her ring. Wind swirled around her, twisting and turning in a spiral, then droplets of water appeared in the air. In ten heartbeats there was a spiraling funnel of water spinning in front of her. She sent it streaming into the monster, and knocked it off its feet.

She summoned *air*, then *water* again, sending spears of ice into it.

As soon as the monster had regained its feet, she knocked it back by the icy assault.

Amoura spun away and swiped first her left arm, then right, left to right. A burst of *air* slammed into several large rocks that were bearing down on her.

The lava rocks hit the ground and rolled, collapsing and opening. Five more four-armed monsters climbed to their feet and charged toward the trio.

Amoura sent a burst of *air* to knock one aside, then sent a stream of *water* into another, and the monster collided with the one behind it.

She turned and dropped to her knee, and sent a blast of *air* and *earth* into another monster.

When she turned again, she ducked and rolled aside just as one of those rock swords came for her head. Amoura rolled to her feet but was forced to dive aside again as the thing attacked. It swung its weapons with more recklessness than tact, while growling and fussing in a language she'd never heard before.

From the corner of her eye she saw the spicetrader jump on the back of a shaken monster she had felled, and drive his knife into the back of its head. He immediately jumped off its back and retreated.

Bone managed to cut away one of the arms of the monster he fought, but suffered some damage to himself as well. He ducked a swipe at his head and rolled backward when the remaining lower limb thrust an axe at him.

He came back up and brought his sword around and up, parrying a right-handed sword. He then brought his sword around and down, slicing through its left leg, then stabbed it through the abdomen. He drew his sword free and retreated several steps to recover. When the monster stumbled after him, he stepped in and drove the tip of his sword into its neck. When it fell to its knees, he stabbed it through the face.

Amoura ducked and rolled to buy herself enough time to formulate an offense. The lava rock monster continued to growl and fuss at her in its angry tongue, hacking and stabbing. It swung with its right sword and continued the movement, spinning around and attacking with each weapon as it turned.

She summoned *air* and *water* from her ring and covered the ground in front of it with ice. When the monster slipped, she sent an arm-sized spear of ice into its chest with enough force to punch through its back.

As it fell to its knees, she turned and sent another spear of ice into a charging monster at her side, then swiped her arms out to the right and sent a blast of *air* into another. She dropped to one knee and thrust her right hand out to the side, fingers curled. Air and water particles formed and thickened as they spiraled away from her.

She touched the ground with her left hand for *earth*. She found the *essence* and willed it forth. Just as hundreds of finger-sized spears of ice flew toward one of the monsters in a horizontal shower, the ground rippled in front of her like waves from the ocean and crashed into the rock monster.

She willed *earth*, and as the monster was knocked backward off its feet, she hit it from behind. The force of the impact shattered it into a spray of rocky pieces that melted and sizzled when they hit the ground.

Bone ran up behind the monster that was still struggling to rise despite dozens of ice spears in its torso. He brought his sword around in a two-handed chop that didn't sever its head, but dug deep enough that the monster collapsed to the ground and began to break apart.

"What in the name of the Fallen are these things?" he yelled, racing toward Amoura.

She looked over her shoulder to tell him to worry about that later when she saw another boulder-sized rock headed toward the mercenary. On instinct she used *air* to divert and freeze it at the same time.

The frozen boulder missed Bone, but crashed into the wagon, reducing it to splinters. She silently thanked the Creator that the horses hadn't been hitched to it yet.

That thanks turned to a scream when she turned to see one of those clubs swinging for her. It hit a wall of *air* next to her head, and she quickly *delved* for *water, air,* and *earth,* and sent all three *essences* flying into the monster.

A spear of ice took it in the face, then a wall of *earth* pounded into it. The plateau burst up beneath it and launched it into the air, and Amoura drew from *air* and *water*. The small plateau fell away at the sides and *air* and *water* smoothed and shaped it into a giant stalagmite made of ice.

The monster fell onto it and was impaled and held aloft. It wailed in that horrible, growling voice, swinging its weapons helplessly before it finally went limp, four arms hanging back toward the ground. As it crumbled apart, Bone rushed past her and slid between the legs of another monster and cut a deep gash in its left ankle.

It stumbled toward Amoura, who summoned *air* and *water* from her ring. Another stalagmite of ice grew from the ground and angled toward the monster's chest. It fell onto the sharp point and impaled itself. While it thrashed, Bone climbed on its back and started chopping at its head.

The monster's thrashing slowed with each stroke, but somehow one of those upper arms stretched around and struck the mercenary in the shoulder with its club. As he tumbled away, the monster rocked left and right, until it broke the ice from the ground.

As it struggled upright, Amoura formed another ice spear, but Emiel was there. He hopped onto the thing's back and drove his hunting knife into the back of its skull, then left it there and hopped off.

The monster dropped to its knees and toppled to the ground. Bone came to his hands and knees and shook his head, then winced and grabbed his left shoulder. Several paces away, Emiel stood panting.

"Okay." Bone groaned as he struggled to his feet. "It's over. Now can someone tell me what those things were?"

Amoura had no answer. She'd never seen or read anything that bore a resemblance to what they were. It was also unnerving that the monsters came from the volcano, which should be too far away.

"We need to get moving," she said. A sense of foreboding crept on her that she couldn't cast aside.

"I'm not gonna argue that," Bone said, starting back toward the outcropping.

"And what about Decius's precious cargo?" Emiel asked, nodding at the remains of the wagon.

"We'll worry about that later," Bone replied. "I just want to be anywhere but out here, preferably in a civilization of some sort. Even Prime Minster Cravel's paranoia is a better trade than those." He pointed at the crumbled remains of a four-armed monster.

They gathered their gear in silence, and soon Bone had the horses prepared. He guided the nervous animals out of the outcropping and looked at Emiel, then Amoura. "Either of you know how to ride?" he asked.

"I ride," Emiel said.

Bone looked at Amoura. "And you?"

Amoura knew what was coming. She would have to ride with the spicetrader because she was the lightest of the three. She sighed. "I've little experience."

"And you're also the lightest," Bone said, and she ground her teeth. "You mind riding behind him?" He jerked his chin in Emiel's direction.

"Is there a choice?" Amoura replied.

"Yes. You could ride with me, and it would be a slower trip out here with who-knows-what else may fall upon us."

Amoura opened her mouth to reply, but Emiel pointed past her.

"Curse our luck! There's more of the things coming!"

Amoura turned and looked toward the distant volcano. Sure enough, more giant lava rocks were in the sky, some arcing toward them, some in other directions.

"Alright, let's get out of here," Bone said, already climbing in the saddle. Amoura waited for Emiel to mount his horse, then she took his offered hand and climbed up behind him. She felt him tense when she wrapped her arms around his waist.

"Relax, spicetrader, or you'll pull us and the horse down."

"I know how to ride," he snapped. His voice cracked as if he were barely into manhood. What was wrong with him?

Bone yelled and gave his horse a kick. The animal whinnied and broke into a run. Emiel did the same and their horse was right behind the boy. The animals must have sensed the danger, as Emiel had to hold the horse back to a manageable pace. Amoura glanced over her shoulder and her heart nearly leapt into her throat. At least a dozen giant lava rocks were falling in their direction.

"Try to stay calm," she yelled into his ear. He nodded.

She looked over at Bone, riding beside them, and jabbed her thumb over her shoulder. The boy looked back and she thought his eyes would pop out of their sockets. He looked back to Amoura and nodded.

"No matter what, just keep going," she said to Emiel.

"Do I even want to know what's behind us?" he yelled over his shoulder.

"No." She wrapped her left arm further around his waist, and turned to summon *air* and *water* through her ring. She hadn't used a great deal of it during the fight earlier. Hopefully there was enough *essence* stored within to get them through this.

The rain of magma wasn't much farther away, so she used the last moments to *delve* from the earth itself. She found *air* and *water* straight from the source, and willed them to be ready for her call.

When she could wait no longer, she brought *air* and *water* forth and blasted boulder after boulder, freezing them into giant balls of ice.

"What good does that do?" Bone shouted.

"They don't form into those things when they're frozen!" Amoura yelled back, having reasoned out why they hadn't been swarmed by the things earlier.

The sky was littered with the things, and though she destroyed many, still more came through.

Giant balls of ice crashed in their midst in a spray of dirt and frozen rock. The horses screamed, and Bone leaned forward and gave his horse its head. Emiel did likewise. Soon boulders of ice and fire crashed around them, pelting them with more dirt and rock. The ice simply shattered, but the lava rocks that made it to the ground rolled and collapsed, and soon well over a dozen four-armed monsters, growling and cursing in their alien tongue, were sprinting after them.

More rocks of fire crashed in front of them, but the horses broke past before the monsters took form. Amoura continued using *water* and *air*, freezing and slowing the things. Some were partially frozen and tumbled to be trampled apart by the others.

Soon, the clump of monsters grew smaller and smaller as the horses outran them. Amoura continued to watch until they were far behind, then turned back.

"Are they strong enough to continue on to Carlayn?" she yelled.

Bone nodded. "They're bred for stamina. We're lucky those things don't run that fast."

Amoura couldn't have agreed more.

After a while, they pulled their tiring mounts back to a moderate pace. Amoura occasionally glanced over her shoulder, but the things were nowhere in sight. She wondered what damage those horrors were doing in their wake. There wasn't a village for at least several leagues or more from where they'd left the monsters behind. Hopefully they wouldn't find their way to any of them.

"We've just crossed the border into Carlayn territory," Bone yelled, slowing his mount further.

"How do you know?" Emiel asked.

The boy pointed to his right, where six mounted soldiers were gaining on them. "Best we stop and get this over with," Bone said, and they slowed their horses to a canter, then a trot, finally bringing them to a walk.

In short order the soldiers had them surrounded.

"We come peacefully," Bone said.

The soldiers responded with swords and halberds leveled at them.

16

───────

AMIYA AND NANDI

Amiya watched her sister focus on the rock. It floated in the air between them, spinning in one direction, then stopped and turned in the other. While Amiya had been able to make her rock spin faster and even zip across the room, it took more energy out of her. Nandi was able to move her rock about for a much longer time, and finished barely tired at all.

She wondered how they could use this. There had to be a way for them to get out of this place and find Dad. Amiya knew he was in trouble and needed their help, and she didn't care that they were just young girls. She would find a way.

"We're getting better," Nandi said, still focused on the rock.

"Yeah we are," Amiya replied. "But what good is it doing us in here? Are we gonna dazzle everyone in this mansion with our floating rocks and then make our escape?"

"It's all we've got right now," Nandi said. "We have to figure out how to use what we've got."

"What we've got is not gonna get us out of here, Nandi."

Her sister sighed and the rock dropped into her waiting palm. "Not yet. But it's better than nothing."

"It might as well be nothing."

"Look at the way you made your rock fly across the room," Nandi said.

Amiya gave her a flat look. "I could throw at someone harder."

"You have to be patient," Nandi said. Amiya always found it irritating when Nandi said that. "A chance will come, and when it does we'll take it."

Amiya looked at her as though she'd lost her mind. "With what?" She giggled, but there was no humor in it. "I can make a rock fly across the room and you can make it float. Really nice. You'll have to help me figure out how that's going to get us out of here, because right now it just seems like a funny way to get us in more trouble than we already are."

"It's not about the stupid rocks, Amiya," Nandi said. "Think! This is something that might help us when an opportunity comes. We just have to be ready for it. That means we keep practicing."

"What makes you think an opportunity is going to come along?" Amiya said. "You keep saying that." She fought down her irritation. As much as she loved her sister, it was maddening how Nandi could refuse to see the reality of a situation and only see what she wanted to see. The girl could see a flower sprouting inside a pile of dung.

"What makes you think this grand opportunity exists?"

"Be patient and we'll find out."

Amiya rolled her eyes and turned her back on her sister. She moved to the far wall and sat down on the throw rug, rolling her flat rock around and around in her hand. Too bad she couldn't force the wall to move like she did with the rock. She could just rip it open and they could escape easily enough. Who would stop them? If she could rip open a wall, she could certainly knock aside a few soldiers.

Amiya crossed her legs and rested her elbows on her knees. She cupped her chin in her hands and thought about what it would be like to be able to move large objects, like a boulder, a house, or even a person. Nandi and Dad were so much alike. The last thing they ever wanted to do was hurt anyone for any reason.

Amiya felt differently. She had no desire to hurt anyone either, but she wouldn't hesitate to do it if the choice was that or harm to herself and her family. Amiya wondered if their mother would have felt the same way. She suspected she would have. The way Dad always said that Amiya was so much like their mother. The mother who had died before they were old enough to know her.

Amiya always heard people talking about the Creator and His great power. If He was so great and so powerful, why did He let their mother die?

She blew out a frustrated breath and pressed the butt of her palms over her eyes. She ran her slender fingers between the rows of tight braids on her scalp. She could feel it. She hadn't spoken to anyone about it, not even Nandi. She didn't have to speak to her twin about it. She knew that Nandi felt it too. A tiny flicker, like a spark, deep inside. She didn't know what it was, but it was there.

On the other side of the room, the door opened. Amiya was instantly on her feet. Nandi moved away from the door and Amiya hurried to her side.

A man in hooded charcoal gray robes stepped into the room. Amiya noticed an odd-looking ring on the finger of his right hand as he reached up to lower the hood.

The shadows underneath the cowl retreated to reveal a man with a black goatee to match inky black hair pulled back and held in place by a corlite ring. The stone used to create that ring could have bought food for a month. How could someone use something that valuable for their hair? Was he rich?

"Good morning," the man said. His deep voice invoked the image of a poisonous mist creeping in the shadows. Amiya didn't like him.

"Now, young ladies. Surely your father has taught you better manners than this. When someone greets you, do you not greet them in turn?"

"We haven't seen our father in so long, maybe we've forgotten what he taught us," Amiya said. Beside her, Nandi stifled a snigger.

"A whip of a tongue for such a young lady."

"Maybe prison makes me impolite."

"Hardly a prison."

Amiya looked around. "There's no bars, no one has tortured us. And we have a window and a bed to sleep on."

She looked back at the creepy man. "That door is the thickest I've ever seen, there are lumps in the bed, we've been out of here only twice, and the window is too high to reach. We can't leave when we want to. Actually, we want to, but we can't leave at all. What would you call this?"

The man seemed amused at her rant, and Amiya felt heat rising to her face. Maybe she should try to be more like Nandi and let other people talk. Her sister had always said she preferred letting other people talk instead of talking about herself. Maybe there was something to that.

"I would call it strict guest arrangements," the man finally said.

"Our Dad also taught us not to talk to people like they're stupid, Mister," Amiya said.

This time the man chuckled. It was a low, ominous sound that made the hairs on the back of her neck stand on end. There was something about this man. Amiya could feel it. Was it that strange ring? Nandi shifted beside her. She'd felt it too.

"I myself would name such arrangements incarceration, yes," the man admitted. "Sadly, it is not within my power to do anything about it."

"I doubt that," Amiya said.

"Oh?"

"I feel like there isn't much that's not in your power to do."

He arched an eyebrow. "And why do you say that?"

Amiya opened her mouth to speak, but a tiny voice in the back of her mind told her to shut up. "Dunno. I just said it. I don't know why."

"Hm." He studied them for several uncomfortable moments. "Would you like to come for a walk with me, young ladies?"

"Do we have a choice?" Nandi asked.

"And so the silent one speaks. I was beginning to worry that lack of exposure to the world outside might have driven you mute."

"I can talk," Nandi replied.

"Very well. Yes, you have a choice. You can come with me," he then indicated the room with an open hand, "or you can remain in your ... room."

Nandi and Amiya looked at each other.

"A walk would be nice," they said in unison.

* * *

THE STATUE GARDENS around the back of the mansion would have been more enjoyable if not for their escort. Nandi tried to keep from stealing glances at the man, but it was hard not to. She found him intimidating, and she didn't know if it was his outward appearance, or that feeling she got from being around him. Whatever it was, it made her nervous.

"I must apologize for archminister Decius's negligence in ensuring your comfort," the man said. "He is quite busy but that doesn't excuse forgetting you."

"He could forget us all the way back to our home and that would be fine," Amiya said.

Nandi gritted her teeth. She understood her sister's anger, but she wished Amiya would stop speaking so sharply to this man. Surely she could feel that energy or whatever it was wafting off of him. Nandi glanced at his ring, wondering if it was coming from there.

"You like my ring?" the man asked.

With an effort she didn't jump at being caught looking. "Um, it's nice."

He smiled. It was unnerving. "I think I should backtrack a little and recover my manners. I haven't told you my name, though I already have yours. My name is Selvetar."

Nandi blinked. Was there anything about this man that wasn't sinister? Even his name made her uncomfortable.

"Are you one of the monks around here?" Amiya asked.

Selvetar chuckled at that. "No, I am not. I am of the Order of Magi, and my particular sect is in the city of Altarra. Do you know of it?"

"We know of the city," Nandi said. "Never heard of a magi."

The smile widened just a bit. "Magi is plural for magus."

"What's a magus, then," Amiya asked. Nandi tried willing her sister to soften her tongue.

"A magus is one who studies the *essences* and how to use them."

"What's an *essence*," Nandi asked, curious despite her apprehension.

"The world has four *essences*," Selvetar said, tucking his hands into his voluminous sleeves. Each *essence* is known to everyone on a fundamental level, and each has its own properties."

They turned down another walkway, passing by detailed painted statues of warriors, and men in robes. One looked like Decius himself, standing tall and arrogant with not nearly enough belly to accurately depict the man. In real life, she'd often wondered if he wore a belt, as his stomach hung over his waist. Nandi figured he had to wear one. How else would his trousers hold up under the weight of that thing?

"The *essence of earth*," Selvetar continued. "Named after the very world upon which we live, comes from the earth itself. Its attributes come from that which is beneath our feet."

"There's cobblestones beneath our feet," Amiya remarked.

"Amiya!" Nandi snapped. "Stop it."

Amiya grinned smugly while Selvetar chuckled. "Quite a witty tongue we have, hmm? And what are the cobblestones made from?"

Amiya didn't answer, and after a moment he continued again. "The *essence* of *air*, deals with just that. What we breathe, the winds that blow. It flows all around us and through us. It is one of the foundations of life itself."

"And then we have *water* and *fire*. Each of the four *essences* are an expression of their namesakes.

"So you study the ground, water, air, and fire?" Amiya asked. "Seems kinda strange to me."

"We do not study them, but the pure *essence* that they are spawned from. These can be understood and with the proper education, manipulated."

"I don't like the way that sounds," Nandi said.

"It is no different than the farmer who manipulates the tools at his disposal. He learns how to use them and puts them to use in his work."

"What is your work?"

"That, I've already told you."

"But why do you study them?" Nandi asked, picking up her sister's thought on it. "What do you study them for?"

"Why does the ranger study the lands?" Selvetar said. "Why does the diver learn to hold his breath for long periods of time that he might spend it under the surface of the ocean, exploring its depths? Why does the gazer study the stars? It is because of what first starts as an interest, then a compulsion, later evolves as we grow older into a calling. It's what we are here to do."

"So that's what you're here to do?" Amiya asked, "study *essences* because you like studying them?"

"In a manner of speaking, yes."

"Sounds interesting," Nandi said.

"A rather conservative response," Selvetar replied.

Doesn't sound interesting at all to me," Amiya said. Nandi knew her sister's offhandedness was an act, but did the magus? What was he after?

"You're quick to judge that which you know nothing about," Selvetar said. They stopped walking and he reached out his right hand, the one with that ring, and turned his palm upward. A gust of wind blew in front of them, then began to spiral in an upright funnel. The funnel continued to turn, forming into a miniature tornado. To her amazement, tiny particles formed in the little tornado, then grew larger.

"Wind," Selvetar said, focused on the funnel. "It comes from the essence, *air*." The translucent particles combined as the funnel turned sideways. The particles continued to spin and merge, until a large funnel of water spun in front of him. Nandi stole a look at his face and took a step back. The magus's face glowed in the blue light of his ring.

"The *essence* of *water* is needed in the creation of the actual water that we drink, and both water and air are needed to form ice." The blue glow in ring faded to be replaced by a silver glow, and the air around the trio grew cold. Nandi and Amiya crossed their arms and hunched over, squinting at the slowly freezing funnel of water.

"And the fire that warms us is created from its namesake."

The ring's silver glow faded to be replaced by a bright red glow as the air around them grew warm, then hot, then unbearably hot. Around the slowly turning funnel of ice, red-yellow particles formed and combined, growing larger and larger till a funnel of fire enveloped and melted the ice. Several heartbeats later the water evaporated and the fire dissipated."

Nandi couldn't deny her amazement at the display, but why was he showing them this?

They walked in silence, passing out of the statue gardens and into the green gardens. It was one of the only things that Decius hadn't changed when he took over the position as archminister. Judging from what she'd seen of the man, Nandi doubted the gardens remained because of his appreciation of them so much as his concern about his image with the resident monks and the general populace were he to dig it up.

"Would you like to learn about the *essences*?" Selvetar asked.

The abruptness of the question startled Nandi, and she glanced at Amiya who she knew was holding back her excitement. No doubt her sister saw this as a way for them to get free.

"You looking for students?" Nandi asked, trying to stay ahead of her sister before she said something rash. "Is that why you came?"

The man turned his dark eyes on her as he considered the question. "Do you ... feel anything while in my presence? Do you feel a force of some sort?"

"A force?" Nandi asked. When Selvetar looked at Amiya, Nandi shook her head vigorously.

"Only thing I felt was the hot and cold from that show you put on," she said, and Nandi sighed in relief. She could have slapped herself when Selvetar arched an eyebrow at her.

"You're sure?" he said. That amused expression returned.

What is he after? The more he talked, the more she wanted to get away from him. "Yes," she said. "I don't know what there is to feel, but I'm not feeling it."

Selvetar held her with that debilitating smile, then nodded and looked away. Nandi felt as if she'd been released from a vise.

"Very well," he said. "And before I've kept you out for too long, I should escort you back to your accommodations."

Nandi fought down her panic at the thought of going back to that cell. "Do you know what we did to be imprisoned like this?" she asked, hoping to get some insight to the situation as well as stall for time out in the open.

"You've done nothing," Selvetar said. "Decius has need of your father's services and he feared for your safety."

"Vyne is a safe city."

He nodded, but said nothing further. For some reason, Nandi felt she shouldn't push the subject, and for a relief, Amiya offered no challenge.

Selvetar saw them to their room and nodded to the guard, who was quick to open the door. Nandi though it interesting that Decius's own guards were more attentive to this *Selvetar* than to himself.

Amiya sniffed and stomped into the room. Nandi stared at the magus for a few heartbeats, then followed. She stood next to her sister and stared out at the guard and the robed man.

"Shall I return to see you again?" Selvetar asked.

Nandi blinked and shared a look with Amiya. That was odd. "Why would you want to come see us again?" she asked.

Amiya elbowed her in the ribs. "Ouch!" she said, leaning away.

"Don't be so rude, Nandi," Amiya said, then to Selvetar, "when can you come see us again?"

"Perhaps in a day or two," the man replied.

"That sounds nice, Mr. Selvetar."

The man chuckled again, and again, there was no humor in it. "Very well. Until then."

"You wanna tell me what your problem is?" Nandi said once they'd moved to the other side of the room. The guard had closed the heavy iron door with a loud crash, and they heard the clicking of metal locks.

"You're the one that seems to have a problem," Amiya said. "He offered to teach us how to do what he did, Nandi. You don't see that as a way out of this whole mess?"

Nandi would have laughed at her if she wasn't busy rubbing her ribs. Amiya had bony elbows. She glanced at her sister's head. "Is your hair braided too tight that you can't think?" She half turned and pointed at the door. "Was there anything about that man that said 'let's be friends'?" Amiya rolled her eyes. Nandi hated when she did that.

"Nandi, I know we've been getting better playing our floating rock game, but I have a feeling he could help us get a little further along with it."

"And I'm sure he doesn't suspect for a moment that when he teaches us more, we would use our newfound powers as a means to get out of here," Nandi said.

"What does it matter?" Amiya countered. "I don't doubt at all that he suspects we might try to use whatever he teaches us to get away. But at the pace we're going right now, we won't be out of here till we're old enough to be sold off somewhere as laborwives."

"Don't joke like that," Nandi said.

"Who said I was joking," Amiya replied. "I don't know what they did with Dad, but I don't want to sit here any longer than we have to. If this Selvetar man can teach us something useful, we can learn from him while we wait for this right time you keep talking about."

"I really don't think he'll teach us anything useful to us getting out of here."

Amiya crossed her arms. "You have anything better?"

Nandi knew arguing was pointless. Whenever Amiya crossed her arms, she was immune to rebuttal of whatever egg she'd hatched in her mind. After she gave it thought, Nandi had to admit to herself that it was the best option they had.

Amiya's face softened. "I know you think I'm hotheaded, sis, but try to trust me. I want to get out of here and find Dad as much as you.

But we're guarded all day and night while sitting in this room with nowhere to go. The only way I see out of this is agreeing to learn from him. Whatever he's got up those giant sleeves of his, we'll have to gamble against it."

Nandi sighed. "You think Decius sent him?"

Amiya thought about it. "Maybe. But I don't think it matters if 'Bigbelly' sent him or not. That Selvetar man doesn't seem like somebody who would be ordered around by him."

"He makes me nervous," Nandi said.

"Me too." Amiya sat down against the wall and wrapped her arms around her knees. "Did you see the way he pulled that *essence* stuff out of his ring and started shaping it? It was like he was molding clay or something."

Nandi frowned. "I barely saw that. But I did see the way all the *essences* started to combine into the ones he wanted when he stopped trying to control them directly."

"What?" Amiya frowned. "What are you talking about?"

"Didn't you see it?" Nandi replied. "At first it was like he was pulling it around and forcing it into what he wanted, like you said. But then, at the right moment, he let go, and those powers combined."

"I kind of saw that, but I guess not as clearly as you."

That was strange. How could she and Amiya watch the same thing yet see something different?

"We already learned something today," Amiya said. "What we've been doing with the rocks, even with the spin game, it's always been with that *air essence* he was talking about."

Nandi nodded. "We'll just be careful and see how we can use this."

"I'm sure you've got enough 'careful' for both of us, sis," Amiya said.

"I'm serious," Nandi snapped, and Amiya raised her hands defensively.

"Okay, so am I. Try not to bite my head off about it."

"Sorry." Nandi sat down next to her twin. "I'm worried about Dad and I'm worried about us."

Amiya leaned her head against Nandi's shoulder. "Me too. But whatever happens, we look out for each other, like always."

"Like always."

Amiya lifted her head away and grinned. It was that devious grin that always preceded some kind of trouble.

"What now?" Nandi asked.

"I know what's going to get us out of here," Amiya said.

"Oh really?" Now Nandi was grinning. "What's that?" Her heart skipped when a red flicker crossed her sister's eyes.

Amiya's grin widened. "*Fire.*"

17
______

JOGA

Only Creator Herself could have understood the depth of Joga's bad luck. Only three days into his travels he was attacked by a pack of jarku that were completely resistant to his efforts to dissuade them. Usually, his people were able to communicate with animals on a rudimentary level. That pack had not only rebuffed his efforts, but they'd responded with a rage that was so primal it felt evil.

He stumbled down a sand dune. How could anything live in this inferno of a place? He wondered if hunger had driven the animals mad and caused them to attack and kill his horse. Jarku were not native to the Sandlands, so it wasn't inconceivable that they would have been so aggressive if they were near to starving.

Once he reached the bottom of the dune, he checked his pack. Seven days left of provisions. It should have been more than enough to see him to the borderland city. Now he wasn't sure if he had enough food and water to last him halfway. A horse's legs moved a great deal faster than his own.

Joga shook his head in disappointment and closed his pack. He slung it back over his shoulder and continued on. He hadn't had the proper time to mourn his horse friend with that pack of angry jarku so near, and the kill would doubtlessly attract a number of other local predators which Joga had no intention of meeting. In the end, he'd been forced to find a shaded place—rare indeed—and meditate to connect with the animal's spirit and apologize for not being able to protect it.

He smiled, remembering the contact he'd made. Though they hadn't been together long enough even for Joga to have named it, they had still bonded. His horse friend had responded with that innocent and unconditional love that only an animal was capable of. It was the way of the world, and its time had come to leave and return to the True Home.

Joga wiped the tears from his cheeks. He wasn't so sure what had happened had been by mother *Illyu's* will, and ultimately, Creator *Amyadali's.*

Joga looked ahead and saw a ray of hope. The last of the sand dunes lay before him, and from there it was mostly hilly terrain. Hills and slopes were more desirable than these cursed sandy mountains shifting beneath his feet, and the relentless heat of Father *Alyu.*

Joga couldn't understand why any sane person would want to live in a place so close to *Alyu's* power. Even the sand baked under it.

Not for the first time, Joga's mind went to temptation. How he wished he could bend the space in front of him, connect it to his destination, and step through the bridge into the place he needed to be. But it was forbidden. The Ancients were uncompromising in this. To travel in such a way was unnatural and out of accord with mother *Illyu*, and it would end with an ... undesirable result. If it was meant for people to travel in such a way, it would not require the methods the outlanders used.

Joga glanced up at the bright burning orb in the sky. Would it not be permissible to use such a method to save his own life?

He unstrapped his waterskin and took a few sips. The water struggled down his dry throat, but it was a relief.

Alyu had begun His descent toward the western sky when Joga heard the most awful explosion. The resulting quake was so violent the ground dropped away from his feet. He hit the ground hard, but the pack on his back cushioned his fall. The shaking continued.

Joga rolled over and stayed low to the ground. When he looked into the distance, his eyes widened. The faraway volcano where the mulgin lived was active! Lava and rock exploded from its peak, arcing across the sky in every direction.

"By the might of *Amyadali* Herself."

The ground finally stopped shaking, but dozens of giant rocks made of liquid fire came arcing in his direction.

Joga looked over his shoulder at the sand dunes behind, then at the lands before him. More of the liquid fire rock exploded into the sky. These went higher than the ones heading in his direction.

"Curse of the Faithless, no!"

The fiery boulders flew high in the sky and soared far beyond him in the direction of his people. His tribe had begun the long trek back to the Frostlands, but at the height and speed those things traveled, they might fall upon them.

Again he thought about warping the space in front of him to warn his people, but then the giant rocks fell around him.

Joga sprinted forward, dodging left and right as rocks the size of his head to three times the size of his body hit the ground in splashes of dirt and sand.

He squinted and shielded his eyes against the rain of dirt and sand, and pressed on. A fiery boulder crashed into the ground several dozen paces in front of him, rolled, then collapsed. Then it stood and started running at him!

"*Amyadali* protect me," he whispered as the four-armed two-legged monster charged, lava dripping from its rocky body.

Joga skidded to a stop and delved *air* and *water*. The *essences* came quickly to his call and the power fill him. He guided it, coaxing the two *essences* to unite as one, then he sent a thick wall of ice into the monster.

It tumbled backward, but was quick to its feet, and came at him again. This time, Joga sent a wave of freezing air at it. The monster slowed, but kept coming, spitting curses in a language he didn't understand.

Joga opened himself more, and the freezing wind blew like a

tempest. He guided it toward the monster until it finally succumbed and fell to the ground and broke apart.

Joga looked behind and saw three more of the things running for him. He broke into a run again, dodging as yet more of the molten rocks fell. The smaller ones simply hit the earth and burst apart, but the larger ones formed into those four-armed monsters.

They quickly outpaced him, and Joga found himself surrounded. He kept running and called *air*, *water*, and *earth* to him. The *essences* heeded his call, and he guided them in every direction, sending waves of freezing air and shards and spears of ice racing through the air.

The monsters were held at bay, some even destroyed, but most kept coming. One came up beside him, growling in that evil language, and swung a sword made of fire and rock.

Joga ducked his head but kept running. Then he dove to the side when another monster came up and brought a club down on him. It broke the ground where he had just been, and Joga rolled back to his feet and sent a spear of ice racing at the beast.

The spear punched through its chest, and Joga didn't bother to wait to see if he'd killed it or not. He sprinted on through the gauntlet of cursing monsters and raining magma rock.

Though he ran as fast as his legs could take him, the things were too big, their strides too long. Several times he was forced to dive into a roll to avoid losing his head, or being pounded into the ground by a giant club.

When he turned to look back, he saw at least fifteen of the things running toward him. Joga gritted his teeth and guided forth *air* and *water*. He sent another small tempest of freezing air and shards of ice biting into the pursuing monsters. Some were small enough that his efforts managed to destroy them, but most were only slowed.

Joga looked over his shoulder. The borderland city was another two to three days away on foot. It had already been questionable whether he could survive the trip in this heat with so few provisions. Now with these evil creatures on him, there was no way he would make it. Though his breathing had become labored, the monsters showed no signs of fatigue.

One of the four-armed monsters made it through his freezing assault, cursing and growling, and swung its sword.

Joga broke off his attack and ducked, then threw his hips back, barely avoiding the swing of an axe by one of the lower limbs. Joga created a solid plank of ice and swiped his right hand in a left hook punch.

The ice pounded into the side of its head, and sent the monster into a sideways roll while Joga ran off. He could hear them catching up to him again. If their steps hadn't been so heavy, he would have heard those infernal voices spewing hate.

He wouldn't make it. He couldn't. Quick as the blink of an eye, Joga thought of his tribe, his people, his bloodmark. He thought of the task the Creator had put to him. He thought of his adoptive sister. Joga didn't fear death, but this was not, could not, be his time to travel to the True Home.

"Ancients forgive me," he panted.

He lowered his head and sprinted as fast as he could. For several heartbeats he managed to keep ahead of the fussing creatures, and he delved *air*. He said a prayer and an apology to Mother *Illyu* and Creator *Amyadali* for what he was about to do. He guided a pocket of air in front of him and held it. Then he tried to envision where he needed to go; the borderland city of New Dama.

The things were getting closer. He could hear them, feel the ground vibrating under their pounding feet. He could feel the heat from them.

He guided *air*, folding it in on itself. That was where he met resistance. Creating fire or air, water or earth from their respective *essences* was within the order of things, for they already existed. To create a pathway by bending air in such a way was not something that naturally occurred. The *essences* themselves were resisting him.

"I am sorry," he said, and subjugated *air* to his will. Instead of guiding the *essence*, he held it and pulled it, pressed it together, folded and bent it, linking it with a space far away. Just as he was about to complete the link, one of the four-armed monsters caught up to him.

Joga dove forward just as a rocky sword came for his head. The connection slipped from his grasp. He scrambled back to his feet and ran, hurriedly grabbing hold of the connection again and creating the bridge. The air in front of him wavered as he dove into it.

Joga gritted his teeth against the pain of rolling onto a hard cobblestone street. He heard frightened murmurs around him and knew he should be up and away, having appeared out of thin air in these people's midst.

He lay there, trying to calm his nerves as he regained his breath. All he wanted to do was lie in this somewhat sitting position, half propped up by the travel pack still strapped to his back. He hung his head back and closed his eyes. *I must be away from here. Get someplace safe ...*

His thoughts were interrupted by a scream, followed by shouts of alarm. Joga's eyes snapped opened and he cried out, rolling aside just as a rocky club crashed into the street where he'd just been. Bits of cobblestone flew into his face but he kept rolling to put some space between himself and the monster.

He came to his feet, but it was there. It raised its club, but then stumbled forward when a city soldier ran the tip of his halberd into its back.

Spitting and cursing, it whirled on the man, at the same time swinging its rock sword. To his credit, the soldier ducked the wild swing and skittered away, then thrust his halberd into its abdomen.

The monster was little affected, and it severed the shaft with a swing of an axe in its lower hand. It swung its sword and the soldier ducked, but the thing continued around, turning a spin while swinging sword and axe and club. The soldier wasn't fast enough and was cut down.

Joga sprang to his feet. How did it get here? How had it followed him? Were those things able to bend space as well?

More soldiers arrived and attacked in a coordinated effort, several stabbing, then others taking their place when they retreated. Archers on the rooftops feathered it with arrows, but despite what would have surely been deadly wounds to a human, the thing barely slowed.

Joga knew that if he delved in the middle of these onlookers, he would be in even more trouble, but he couldn't let this thing kill innocent people; people who had been safe before he'd crashed into their midst with a monster at his back.

Fire would do nothing to it, so Joga delved and found *air* and *water*. He formed a thick spear of solid ice and launched it into the monster's back. It let out a high-pitched growl and stumbled forward, still swinging its weapons, albeit more slowly.

Joga ignored the gasps around him and hoped the creature would fall so that he wouldn't have to use the power again.

It fell to one knee, and two soldiers circled around behind it. One drove his spear into its back and the other hopped onto its back and drove his sword into the back of its head.

The monster toppled over and several heartbeats later, began to crumble. In moments it was reduced to smoking rocky debris.

Joga had started to inch away the moment it was apparent the beast would be defeated. He turned and started down the street, keeping his pace casual. He heard someone bark a command in the Marailander tongue but he pretended not to hear.

The voice barked another command, and though Joga wasn't completely fluent with the language, he understood it well enough. He'd been told to halt. An arrow struck a lamppost beside him and he froze.

Slowly, he turned and held his hands out at his sides in a non-threatening gesture. Archers stood on the rooftops, and every one of them had an arrow trained on him. The five remaining soldiers had swords and halberds leveled at him as well.

Joga's mind raced. This was unusual. As a borderland city, New

Dama saw people from all over the world. His use of the *essences* might have been startling, but he shouldn't be threatened like this.

He heard a voice from behind tell the soldiers to stand down, and as one, they went to attention, swords sheathed and halberds in the vertical position.

The voice then addressed him in his native Khatalese. "This is unexpected. An actual wilder in our midst?"

Wilder. That was a word one didn't expect to hear in New Dama. Which meant that either a sightless was visiting, or Joga had somehow made a mistake and landed himself into a Marailander city.

He turned slowly, still feeling the archers' arrows on him. A man with curly blond hair and somewhat delicate features stood smiling at him. His long red robes were neatly pressed and hung perfectly. Joga doubted the man had seen a day of battle.

On either side of him were two monks dressed in simple white. Their hands were tucked into their sleeves, and their blue eyes held his, unwavering. There was no aggression in their eyes, only confidence.

Joga noted the ring on the central man's finger, glowing with what was no doubt *essence* power trapped within. It was against Mother *Alyu* and Creator *Amyadali* to trap it like that. How could they not know that? Or did they care? This man was one of the sightless. Joga could have spat.

"You look as if you do not know where you are, yet you are practically in the center of the city."

One of the soldiers stepped forward. "Magus." The robed man nodded his head and the soldier continued. "We found him fighting a monster that looked like it could have been sent by one of the Fallen themselves."

The sightless looked from the soldier to Joga. "Even more interesting. Who else saw this?"

The soldier indicated the watching citizens.

The curly-haired man stepped forward and raised his voice to the crowd. "It appears we have a wilder in our midst who brought a monster with him. Through the bravery of our soldiers the monster is no more. Be assured, people of Vyne, that the Order of Magi will dig until we find the root of this matter and tear it free. There will be no evil and no destruction to befall our beloved city.

A series of applause and cheering ensued. Joga continued to look at the man, ignoring the jeers and insults directed at him by the crowd that he had just helped save. They were told that his people were savage, destructive, and wild. Their memories would alter what happened to fit that perception.

The red-robed sightless stepped in front of him. "Let us retreat to the temple, shall we?"

Joga said nothing, only looked the man in the eye.

"Not much for conversation, I see. Well let's become acquainted in a more," he glanced around at the increasingly hostile crowd, "calm setting."

The soldiers fell in behind him, and two men leveled their halberds at his back.

The Ancients had been right. To bend space and bridge it in such a way was unnatural and would result in misfortune. And here Joga was, in a city in the land of Marai, far south of his destination.

18

RAYNA

Rayna giggled, eliciting a good-natured—if inebriated—knuckle to the chin by the man she danced with. "Of course, a man such as yourself is worthy of far more than just the position of a simple assistant advisor, no?"

Davek gave an exaggerated snort. "I'll tell you this much. As long as thoss other foolss sthay wordss that he wanss to hear, mine will be drowned out in the noiss."

Despite his obvious drunkenness, Rayna noted the man still had enough of his wits about him not to mention whom he was talking about. She giggled again, trailing a finger down the middle of his chest. They spun another circle, Rayna practically holding him up.

"We'd better stop spinning like this or your night's partakings are going to make a reappearance."

"Worry not, 'bout my nighss partakings, milady," Davek said. "I hold my drink well enough."

"And well enough for us if you allow me to be the advisor tonight and suggest you have a seat."

Davek winked at her. "Maybe you're right. Bessidss, iss not like it matters much. The ki ... he doessn much lissen to me anyway with them otherss wissprin war in his ears."

That was the most direct he'd spoken about the matter yet. Best she get him to a seat and away from the crowd. His slurred speech and clumsiness would have been noticed by now. The poor man would be the subject of whispered ridicule by dawn. As much as this would ding his reputation, it was necessary.

"I should get you to your room," she said, blinking her long lashes at him. "By now you must be bored with this stuffy ball."

He nodded, then swayed. "Ah, pleass. If you could see me to my room." He winked at her. "I promiss therss more fun up there."

Rayna giggled as the assistant advisor burbled, much of which she barely paid attention to. A couple turned a corner and came in their direction, and Rayna leaned her head against the side of his chest, her shoulder under his. She giggling loudly and draped her arm around his waist. It took considerable strength in her legs and lower back to hold him up while pretending not to.

The passersby sipped glass goblets of wine, and raised their eyebrows at her and Davek. She winked at them and they turned away. She giggled again and guided him around the corner.

"I don't know how I'm going to get you to the advisor's hallway," she said.

"You ssink I live there?" Davek slurred. "Them foolss' rooms are all lined up down the hall from him ... one after another."

"Then might I hope it won't be too difficult getting you home?"

He pointed down the hall. "Lasst one on the left."

She guided him through the door and dumped him on his bed. The room was modestly decorated with only a single painting on the opposite wall from the bed, and a nightstand with a wide-leafed plant atop it.

"Mmm," she murmured. "Comfy." She straddled him and began unfastening the buttons on her dress. He tried to sit up, but she pushed him back. "Ah ah, now. Slowly."

Her dress half unbuttoned and showing more cleavage, she placed a hand on his chest and slid forward, grinding her body against his. She felt his heart beating faster as she moved. Then it slowed.

She watched as his eyes drooped. "You like that?" she whispered in his ear, just as his eyes closed and his body went limp. "Oooh, Davek," she moaned, even though he couldn't have thought of touching her. "Oooh stop that."

This time, she had to repress a genuine giggle, as the man was fast asleep. The corlite beads at the end of her braids clicked as she shook her head. She slid off of him and unfastened the rest of the buttons on her dress.

Tarik weed. When combined with just a little alcohol it had the effect of not only quickly intoxicating the drinker, but also increased in potency the faster the blood rushed through the system, causing lethargy.

Rayna looked him over one last time, glad The Khamra hadn't sent her for him. She closed her eyes and touched the corlite beads with her mind, and they emitted a soft glow.

She finished unfastening her dress and let if fall to the floor. Fortunately her smallclothes covered more of her body after the Nashma fashion than the Marailander type that left a woman virtu-ally naked.

She quietly slid the window open and climbed out onto the balcony, closing it behind her. The King's rooms were at the top floor of course. Five floors up. It was a climb Rayna could make without aid, but she needed to do this quickly.

She concentrated on the corlite beads in her hair and they began to pulsate with a soft silver glow. She looked up again and noted the protrusions in the brick designs, then leapt straight up. She ascended more than ten feet and grabbed hold of a protruding brick, curled her body and planted her feet on the stone. She sprang up again. Stretching, grabbing hold, curling her body and springing up again, like a cat sprinting up the castle wall instead of across the open plains.

With one last jump, she cleared the side of the wall and landed at the base of one of the castle's arched flying buttresses, and ran up the top of it.

Where the buttress and the spine of the building met, there were small rectangular openings. Air vents.

She lay on her stomach, took a deep breath and pushed it all out, then slid through the narrow opening. It was tight, but she managed to squeeze in.

Halfway through, she stopped. It looked to be a thirty-foot drop into an empty circular room, the polished tiles painted with an enormous depiction of a burning light and a bloodied spear. Arrogance.

Rayna slid out of the vent and hung by her hands over the deathly drop. She took another deep breath then blew it out gradually, focusing on the corlite beads. They glowed silver again, and she felt the air lighten her body.

Just then, she heard voices outside the door. She let go and fell the distance, but the corlite beads slowed her descent. She touched the floor without a sound and sprinted into the shadows just as the door opened.

A man in purple velvet pants and jacket stepped into the hall accompanied by two white-robed monks. The man spoke idly as the monks followed silently a step behind. As the door started to close, she slipped out just behind them.

Keeping to the shadows, she crept along the wide open hallways of Castle Jietar. Torchlight from the many sconces lining the walls reflected off of the polished tile floors. The pillars were also made of polished stone, and reached to the ceiling high overhead. Everything about this castle and its King was a paradox. The level of overindulgence and comfort that he lived in was disgusting, yet he went to great efforts to ensure that his subjects had every opportunity to live in comfort relative to their stations in life. He waged war with the Khatala, but it was a small one, and under his rule the land of Marai had never seen such relatively peaceful times.

She continued down the corridors, making her way through the halls. The night's revelries were still going strong, but the King had retired with his personal guard and advisors long before she had gotten poor Davek drunk.

Finally, she turned down a wide hallway with two guards

standing at attention in front of an ornately carved door. Rayna found it gaudy, but a person's tastes were their own.

Across from the two guards the wall was lit by torches. No shadows to hide in that way.

She crossed to the other side of the hall in line with the guards and touched the corlite beads with her mind again. Her body lightened, she sprinted toward the guards, keeping close to the wall. Once she was within two dozen feet from them, she leaped, gliding in an arc high above their heads.

She touched down in the shadows the same distance on the other side and raced silently down the corridor.

Rayna came to a row of three doors and carefully opened the first and slipped in. The room was dark and quiet. And vacant. Rayna held still against the wall, eyes scanning the room. Should she wait for him?

She decided against it and slipped out of the room, and went to next one. Also vacant. As she crept toward the third door she heard voices from inside. She lowered herself beside the door, glanced over her shoulder to make sure no one approached, and listened. The door muffled the voices, but she could hear them clear enough.

One woman's voice, two males.

"In all the wisdom of the Creator, I cannot understand why the three of you can't see reason," the woman's voice said. "King Alyn would listen if the two of you would cease with this warmongering of yours."

Chuckling.

"Warmongering, Demarys?" a male voiced replied. "Warmongering? The savages out west push against our borders and threaten our people. They have sworn to exact what they call a blood retribution, and they wield *essences* to destructive result. Not ever could I think of a more suitable course of action."

"You wish for him to eradicate an entire people," the woman said. Her tone was horrified. "You want to completely destroy them."

"The wilders are beyond dangerous, Demarys," said the other man's voice. "What would you have us do?"

"Talk, Jaksys. You and Jarid have done nothing but advise our King to continue a war that has cost countless lives and not once have you at least suggested he speak with them."

"Talk," said the voice that belonged to Jaksys. "These savage people would kill every man, woman, and child in all of Marai, and you would have him attempt civil conversation? Have you forgotten the events of the first meeting?"

"A misunderstanding and you know it," Demarys snapped. "We both know that you and Jarid see profit in war. So long as the conflict with the Khatala people ensues, commerce will flow more rapidly."

"Nonsense," replied the other voice that belonged to Jarid. "We do nothing of the sort."

Rayna's eyes narrowed. His tone suggested they did exactly that."

"Come, Demarys," Jaksys said. "Are you upset because the King does not heed your advice?"

"With you two always rolling over my words with your propaganda?"

"Perhaps you should form a more convincing argument," Jarid said. His tone was smug; condescending.

Rayna reached behind her lower back and unstrapped her two daggers. She continued to listen, judging their proximity to the door. Finally satisfied she had their location, she opened the door and stepped in.

"What's this?" A man in a yellow shirt and white waistcoat turned toward her. "We're in a meet ..."

Both of Rayna's hands whipped out and at the same time, she sprang forward with a corlite-enhanced leap. Both men on either side of the stunned Demarys clutched at the hilts of the daggers protruding from their abdomens. Just as the woman opened her mouth to scream, Rayna snatched a small hand baton from the side of her left shin and launched it into the woman's abdomen.

The air blasted from her lungs in a pained huff. Still gliding toward the doubled over woman, Rayna twisted and rolled over Demarys's back. She grabbed her throat in a claw grip, forcing the other woman's body to straighten.

"If you attempt to attack me, or scream, or flee, I will kill you. Do you understand?"

Still struggling to breathe, Demarys nodded.

Rayna stared into her eyes until she was convinced the other woman was sufficiently cowed, then released her and moved to one of the men. He'd managed to get the dagger out of his stomach and was trying to stop the bleeding. Rayna retrieved the dagger and opened his throat. Behind her she heard a gasp, and she turned a warning glare at the woman, whose hands snapped to her mouth as she backed away.

The assassin stood and moved to the other man. He was squirming and growling through his teeth, eyes squinted shut. Rayne pulled the dagger free and similarly dispatched him. When she stood and looked over at Demarys, the other woman held her hands up before her.

"Please," she whispered as the assassin approached her. "I don't know what we've done to anger you, but please don't kill me."

"Stop backing away."

Despite her fear, the woman went rigid, then looked around as if surprised she'd complied without thinking about it. Rayne had that kind of effect on people.

She stopped in front of the advisor, fixing the woman with her steel-eyed gaze. Even as a child, people had found the contrast of her eye color and dark skin both beautiful and unnerving. "You advise the one who calls himself King Alyn." It wasn't a question.

The woman gave a shaky nod. "Y ... yes."

"You are the one of three who advises him against the war." Again, not a question, but again the woman answered.

"Yes."

"You sue for peace, for life. You wish to preserve life, and so yours continues."

"Why did you kill them?" the woman asked, her voice soft with fear.

Rayne cleaned her daggers and replaced them behind her lower back. "They sue for death, and so theirs arrived."

"Does that mean you've killed our King?" Now the woman sounded alarmed.

Rayne gave her another warning look, and the woman shook her head, mouth opening and closing like a confused fish.

"No," Rayne finally answered, and she started away. "His intent is unclear. Replace them," she pointed to the two dead advisors lying in pools of their own blood, "with advisors of a mind like your own."

"But even if I do, what if he doesn't listen? What if he continues with this war?"

The assassin stopped in front of the door. "His intent will be clear, and Rayne will come."

"Rain?" the woman asked, mistaking Rayna's Khamra given name for the weather.

The assassin stepped through the door, quietly closed it, and sprinted down the hall. She was well past the King's rooms when the woman finally screamed for help.

The King's guards didn't move from their position, but the assassin knew that there were more patrolling the castle. She melted into the shadows and waited. Soon enough, a pair of guards came jogging down the hall. The armored soldiers passed right by her, and Rayne sped down the hall in the direction they had come.

Now that she knew her destination, she made faster time than before, and reached the large circular room with the painted mural on the floor. She listened at the door but didn't hear any conversation. Either the three men had left, or had heard the guards and gone quiet.

Rayne knew she didn't have much time before a castle-wide alarm was sounded, so she pulled free a small baton from each leg. She held the batons in a reverse grip to hide behind her forearms and opened the door. She stepped in and quietly closed it behind her.

The three men were still there, and were already facing the door. The assassin trotted toward them, half turning to look over her shoulder, her face worried.

"Oh!" she said. "Something has happened and the guards are running the halls. This was the safest place I could think of. Do you know what's happened? What's going on? Do you know if the King is safe?"

The man in the velvet purple affair held up his hands and patted them in the air. "Now, now, my lady, please calm—"

"I fear for his life," Rayne continued. To his sides, she saw the white-robed monks silently assessing her. Both were focused on her hands. Warrior monks, then. The one on the left was smaller. That one had turned his feet into an offensive position while the larger one on the right took a more defensive stance. Both were subtle enough not to be noticed by an untrained eye, but Rayne knew they suspected her. She didn't have time for a drawn out fight. She had to strike fast.

"I hope there aren't assassins about. Do you think we're safe here?" She turned toward the monk on the left. He looked ready to strike. "Can we say a prayer together, good monk? I fear for our lives if there is a killer about ..."

As she said the last word both her hands whipped out. She heard an 'oomph' to her right, indicating her baton had taken the nobleman in the stomach.

Her other baton had been aimed high and the monk caught it out of the air as she knew he would. The assassin had launched herself right behind the weapon, delivering a series of straight-fingered stabs and chops that had the smaller monk backpedaling.

She forced the offensive, knowing the other monk was closing in. She dropped low and struck at the smaller monk's abdomen. He blocked the attack, but by then Rayne was coming back up. She slammed his protecting forearm with a two-handed thrust of her palms that forced him back a few more steps.

She dropped back to the floor in a spin, sweeping her leg out and taking his feet from under him. Still low to the floor, she sprang in the opposite direction and attacked the second monk. He was more prepared and fended her off, but then she sprang back at the smaller monk, who had just recovered. Back and forth she dashed between them, attacking one, then the other.

One of the monks sidestepped her thrusting palm and grabbed

her wrist. He twisted it, attempting to flip her to the floor, but Rayne went into a handless cartwheel. While upside down, she grabbed hold of one of the daggers behind her back and upon landing, slashed down at the monk's arm.

The blade went through the voluminous sleeve and into his flesh. When he recoiled, she kicked first at his face, then when he went to block, she kicked at his abdomen, then face again. The monk managed to block the three kicks, but the fourth connected with his cut arm, then his abdomen, then she brought her foot around in an upward arc, then down on his forehead.

She immediately dropped to the floor and swept her foot out, attempting to trip up the smaller man bearing down on her.

He jumped over her leg and came down with a chop using her own baton. Her hands snapped up, one gripping his wrist and the other under his elbow. With a quick snap, she hyperextended his elbow while at the same time twisting his wrist and forcing his body rigid so that he slammed face first into the tiled floor.

He released the baton into her hand, and on instinct, she turned and launched it at the nobleman. The throw was hurried, but the baton struck his shin just as the man was recovering his breath.

He dropped to the floor, groaning and clutching his shin as Rayne turned back to her adversaries.

The smaller monk had hit the floor but managed to absorb some of the impact with his free hand. Rayne slammed the heel of her foot into the middle of his back, then dropped to the floor and rolled under a horizontal stiff-handed chop by the recovered larger monk. She snapped back to her feet and leapt into a spin, whipping her foot out and connecting the top of it under his arm. She felt the ribs crack, but she'd held enough force back not the break them.

The monk gasped and stumbled to the side, and the assassin was on him. Weakened and struggling for breath, the monk couldn't hold her off for long, and in short order she had him unconscious on the floor.

The smaller monk had just regained his feet and turned when Rayne connected the outside of her foot with his face. His head snapped back and he raised his hand up instinctively. She knelt low and drove her fist into his stomach, then rose with an elbow under his chin.

The monk fell to the floor in a heap, and the assassin was back to the nobleman.

"I have money. Jewels, if you like," the man pleaded.

Rayne retrieved her batons and struck him in the side of the head. She knelt over the unconscious nobleman and felt his pulse just as the sound of booted footsteps and squeaking armor came from outside the door. Satisfied the nobleman was alive, she moved below the opening, thirty feet above.

She focused her mind on the corlite beads in her hair, and felt her body lighten. The muscles in her legs tensed as she crouched and threw her arms back. She swung her arms and gave a great leap up just as the doors banged open.

The ceiling rushed down to her and she stretched for the vent. Her upward momentum began to slow, and she stretched harder. The tips of her fingers on her right hand brushed the bottom of the vent. She gritted her teeth and swung her left arm over. Her body tilted in an angle, giving her that extra couple inches to grab hold of the ledge.

Her body swung forward and she waited for it to swing back, then used the momentum to pull with her left arm, grab hold with her right hand, and pull herself up. She heard shouts from below, but all they would have seen of her was dangling feet that disappeared through the vent.

She raced back down the buttress and climbed over the side. She climbed down as quickly as possible, but she knew time was running short. Again she focused on the corlite beads to lighten her body. She released the handhold and dropped the last several floors, the windows of rooms racing by as she fell.

She hit the balcony of the Davek's room and rolled to absorb the impact. The balcony was not large, and she rolled into the stone rail.

She gritted her teeth through the pain and quietly stepped into the room. With a resigned sigh, she removed her fitted smallclothes and stuffed them inside her dress, then lay it in a pile at the foot of the bed. She slipped into the bed in front of the sleeping assistant advisor, and closed her eyes, willing her heart to slow.

Just as she'd brought her breathing to a steady rhythm, there was a heavy pound on the door, then another, then it burst open to admit four guards.

Davek sat up—perhaps a bit too fast—and grabbed the top of his head. "Ugh. What is the meaning of throwing my privacy to the winds?"

In front of him, Rayna screamed, and sat up, pulling the covers up to her neck. She stared wide-eyed at the guards, pulling the covers up higher until they were under her eyes.

"Look here, men," Davek said, swinging his legs out the other side of the bed. He hopped to his feet, then grabbed his head again and sat back down. "You can't just stomp into my room like this—"

"Please excuse the intrusion, Assistant Advisor," one of the armored soldiers replied. "There has been," he glanced at Rayna who still trembled underneath her covers.

"She is trustworthy, I assure you," Davek said.

The guard gave her one last consideration, then nodded. "There has been a problem of the life-threatening sort."

Sloppy. Rayne thought. *Never discuss something like this in front of anyone.* Did King Alyn know there was incompetence in his midst?

Davek's mouth fell open. "What? The king—"

"The King lives, but two of his advisors were killed."

Rayna whimpered, and Davek touched the bit of her hand that wasn't covered by the blankets. "Nothing to worry about," he said in a soothing voice. "The castle guard is alerted, and I'm here." He turned back to the guard. "Has the assassin been found? And which advisors were killed?"

"The search for the assassin continues," the soldier replied, "and it was his two most senior advisors, Jaksys and Jarid. We've been sent to protect you, as the targets seem to be those who advise the King and possibly the King himself. We had to be sure you weren't killed."

"Well as you can see, I'm fine. My thanks, good soldiers."

"One of us will be stationed on your balcony in case the assassin comes from the outside."

Davek glanced at Rayna. "I doubt that will be necessary, good soldier. We're two floors up and the walls are steep."

"The assassin was last seen climbing through the ceiling vent in the Room of Truth."

"That's impossible," Davek said. "That's almost forty feet high."

"We believe there may have been two, and one waited on the roof of the castle with rope to pull up the other. Either way, they are, or were, on the ceiling and will have to climb down. That makes your balcony and your room a possible contact point."

Davek gave Rayna an apologetic look, but she responded with a nervous smile. "It's okay. I should be going anyway."

"My apologies, milady," the soldier said. "No one enters or leaves the castle until the assassins are either found or we're certain the threat is gone."

Davek sighed. "Very well, then. But might I hope you all are not required to remain in here?"

"Not at all," the soldier replied. He signaled one of his company to the balcony. The others bowed and withdrew.

"Such a regrettable circumstance," Davek said after the remaining soldier had closed the door to the balcony. He sat back on the bed. "I hope this doesn't totally ruin your night with me."

"Oh not at all," Rayna replied. "You must be distraught over the death of your colleagues, for certain."

"I am," Davek said. He pursed his lips then leaned in to whisper, "I would never wish death on anyone, but I can't help but feel that perhaps the world might be better off without them constantly whispering words of war in the King's ear. King Alyn may yet be persuaded to leave off this senseless fighting. Am I a horrible thing for thinking such?"

Rayna smiled at him. "Not at all. Everyone wants peace."

"Not everyone."

"Well, most people," Rayna conceded. I should hope the King's next advisors number those of a mind like yourself. The world would be better for it."

"Your words are too kind," Davek said. "But considering that I was so drunken last night that I don't even remember the lovely events that resulted in your nakedness, I fear my reputation may be tarnished beyond redemption."

"The King did not witness your night revelry," Rayna replied sweetly. "Perhaps he may yet look upon you with favor."

"Perhaps," Davek said.

"Would you be a gentleman and pass me my dress?"

Davek smirked at her. "Would you not rather remind me of all the loveliness I cannot remember?"

Rayna gave him a regretful look. "Sadly, not. This whole assassin business has me as far from the mood as becoming a Contemplative."

"Oh don't say such things," Davek said, his face screwed into a look of fright. "Such a beautiful woman relegating herself to the sterile and frigid life of a Contemplative? A ghastly option for one such as yourself."

"So my worth is relegated to the flesh and not the mind and spirit, good Assistant Advisor?" She blinked her long lashes at him.

"Oh, no of course not!" he said, lunging to his feet and fumbling with her dress. "I meant that not at all." He glanced down at her dress. "I...Would you like my non intimate assistance in donning your clothing, my lady?"

She smiled at him. "I can manage, good sir, if you might spare a bit of consideration for my modesty and turn your back." He did so. "And there's no need for such formality," Rayna continued as she donned her smallclothes while keeping an eye on the soldier. His back was turned. "I only tease you because I know you are a kindly gentleman."

She slipped into her dress and fastened the buttons. Satisfied, she smiled. "You may turn around again. Thank you."

Davek faced her and sighed. "Such beauty I am fortunate to look upon with, or without the benefit of that lovely dress that does little justice to the perfection hidden within."

"Such silky words," Rayna said. "A shame I must leave you now."

"The guards said no one is to leave the castle, little flower. It appears you are stuck with me."

"As much as I would love that, I must return to my own room," Rayna said. "I have things to attend to that cannot wait."

She made for the door and he trotted past her to open it.

The soldier guarding the door stepped in front of them. "You're to stay in your room, milady."

"Of course, sir." She pointed down the hall. "But my room is that way. Should I not be accounted for in my own room? Your superior said that no one was to leave or enter the castle. I seek to enter my room, which his in this castle."

The guard considered her words, then grumbled and stepped aside. "Straight to your room, milady."

"That I shall," Rayna replied.

"Might I at least expect to see you again that we might salvage such a horrible end to a lovely new acquaintance?"

"That's an appealing possibility," Rayna replied, and stepped out of the room. She turned and smiled at the expectant look on his face. He smiled back, looking down at the floor in an attempt not to appear that he was admiring her physical qualities.

"Might a man hope for a kiss goodbye?"

She stepped closer and placed her hand on the side of his face, then let it trail down his chest. She leaned closer, letting her hand slide down his stomach, then the side of his hip. She felt his body go rigid.

"Goodbye, lovely Davek," she whispered, and kissed him on the corner of the lips. She turned away and strode down the hall, leaving the dumbfounded man in her wake.

"Be careful," she said over her shoulder. "I wouldn't want the assassin to get you."

"Maybe you should stay and protect me from him," Davek teased.

"I would love to see you again, but not because you were careless, lovely man. Please be careful."

She looked over her shoulder and smiled at him. He smiled back, oblivious to the double meaning of her words. She rounded the corner and heard him close the door.

Rayna navigated the halls, putting on a nervous smile at any she passed. She hoped Davek would prove to be a better advisor than the two she had just eliminated. He seemed a good man. She was on the brink of giving up hope that good men still existed in this land of Marai. Whether it was stubbornness or naivety, she held on to that flicker of hope.

19

NANDI

Nandi stared down at the book in front of her drooping eyes. No. Book wasn't the right description for this thing. Tome. That was the word.

It had been a little over a week since Selvetar had first come to them with his offer of tutelage in the study of the *essences*. Her head started to slip out of her hand, and she snapped awake. She glanced across the table at Amiya, who was devouring an equally massive book.

Nandi stretched and let out a yawn. She would rather practice the teaching instead of reading the endless texts Selvetar had assigned them. Of course, the rub was that in order to practice, she would need to know what to practice, and expecting the magus to verbally and physically impart all of that knowledge was absurd. So she studied, doing her best to focus on the material as best she could.

"Try not to slobber all over the book when you doze off," Amiya said.

Her sister's voice penetrated the haze in her mind, and Nandi gave her head a little shake. She looked up to see Amiya staring at her. "I do not slobber," she said.

"Right," Amiya replied. "Whatever it is you don't do, don't do it on the book. That thing is old."

"I don't know how you grind through all these books so easily," Nandi said.

"Easy. I just read them."

Nandi rolled her eyes. Her sister loved to read, and she would read almost anything put in front of her. Ironic that Nandi was the more coolheaded of the two, yet Amiya was the bookworm.

"What I don't understand," Nandi said, "is that according to The Book of Essences, the *essences* are actually from the earth itself, and permeate everything, including humans."

"Yeah?" Amiya said, gesturing for her to get to the point.

"Yeah, well what I'm not getting is why the text keeps referring to it as something to be drawn out and used like a tool."

"Because that's what it is," Amiya replied. "It's a tool to be used. It's humans that make the result good or bad."

"That's not what I mean," Nandi said. "The *essences* are in everything, including us. Just like our skin and blood and bones. We don't use any of those as tools, it's a part of us. It's what we are."

"What does that have to do with this?"

"Shouldn't they be guided?" Nandi asked. "Instead of finding and pulling the power out of the earth, shouldn't we guide it to our hand? Channel it, in some way?"

Amiya shrugged and went back to her book. "I don't see much difference whether we do it one way or the other."

"There is a difference." Nandi rested her elbows on the desk and cupped her chin in her hands. The temple library had been filled with people ranging from acolytes to monks to magi, the latter moving about in their various colored robes.

"To me it feels like when we have to wrestle the mountain moles out of their pen. We're forcing them out and making them work. When we ride Surefoot, we guide her out of the stall and on the trails. It's different."

"When have you ever seen a mountain mole willingly come out of its pen?" Amiya said.

"I imagine there's no problem up in the mountains," Nandi said. "And that proves my point. Mountain moles wouldn't live down in the flatlands, but humans brought them here and started breeding them for irrigation and deep underground tunnels beneath the city. We're forcing them to live away from their natural homes."

"I'm going to have to ask you again what this has to do with *essences*," Amiya said.

"Forcing the *essences*, as it says in these books, is one way, but it feels wrong to me."

"So what's the alternative?" Amiya replied. "Ask?"

"In a way," Nandi said. "That's kind of what I do when I make the rock float. Have you noticed how I'm able to make the rock move around for longer than you do?"

"Yeah," Amiya said. "Takes you longer to get started, too."

"It does. But I don't feel as strained or tired as I do when I guide *air* instead of pulling it to my command."

Amiya looked up from her book again. "Pulling it to your command? Pretty dramatic." She held up a hand when Nandi opened her mouth. "No, I get it. I do. I can get going faster, but I can't hold the *essence* as long as you. It takes you longer to get there, but you hold the *essence* longer."

Nandi yawned. "What Selvetar is teaching us through his instructions and these books is that the *essences* are to be pulled from the earth and controlled like a tool."

"He doesn't seem all that fatigued when he instructs us," Amiya said. "Probably because he has all that *essence* stored up in his ring, you think?"

"I think that's exactly what it is. They study the books, like we're doing. Then they learn the basics of how to use the *essences* with an *essence* ring. After some time, they are made into full magi and given a ring of their own. They use the ring and what they've learned to fill it up with the *essences* to use at will. Maybe the ring is like a conduit."

"Sounds like you've got it figured out."

"I'm guessing," Nandi admitted. "But I think that's the idea of it."

"Makes sense."

"But it's only part of it," Nandi continued. "They study all of this and learn how to bring these powers to their command, but the texts say nothing about calling to the *essences* and guiding them through you. When I practiced with the rock, it felt like *air* was passing through me."

"Maybe he's saving that bit for later," Amiya suggested. "We've only been at this a little more than a week. I'm sure there's years of study before we get a solid idea of it."

"That's true," Nandi said. She leaned in and lowered her voice. "But not a single book we've been shown even hints at what I'm talking about. We're only eleven years old and we've already figured this out. Somebody else has to have by now."

"Speak for yourself," Amiya said. "I feel some of what you're talking about, but mostly I feel it the other way. Studying it through books and putting it to use has worked better for me than feeling it through." She nodded toward a cluster of acolytes studying in much the same manner as she and Nandi. "And besides, I haven't seen a single person here using an *essence* without one of those rings on their fingers."

"I've been wondering about that," Nandi said.

"I've been wondering about how long it will be before we can actually practice what's in these books," Amiya replied.

"Wonder no longer," Selvetar's deep voice said from the side of the table.

Both girls nearly jumped from the table.

"Thanks for the sneak-and-startle," Amiya said. The magus arched a questioning eyebrow. "Never mind," she said. "Sorry."

Selvetar replied with one of his half smiles. "Come with me. It's time to put knowledge to hand and see how well you implement what you've learned."

Nandi gladly closed her giant book with a heavy 'thud', and she and Amiya followed him out of the library. Nandi had been increasingly aware of how Selvetar had been more receptive to Amiya than herself. Probably it had to do with the fact that Amiya was more adept at absorbing the information from the books, and the magus saw her as having more potential.

They passed through open halls and out the back of the temple. The grounds were as beautiful as the flower gardens of the archminister's mansion, but there were also several large, fenced circles scattered throughout. Training circles.

Selvetar brought them to one of the circles and opened the gate. The twins stepped in and he closed it behind himself.

"Today you will show me what you've learned. The books you've read speak of the four *essences* and their attributes." The girls nodded. "One must first learn how to feel them in order to utilize them. Once you have achieved this, you draw the *essence* from the earth. It is called delving, and it's done through this." He indicated the ring on the right middle finger of his right hand. "An *essence* ring. It's created from the valuable stone, corlite, which has properties that are tied to the *essences*. Those very properties allow the *essences* to be stored within."

"I thought corlite was money," Nandi said.

"There are many things that can be used as currency," Selvetar said. "There are peoples from distant parts of the world that use labor, or information as currency, while other societies trade." He looked down at her. "Did your father not teach you this?"

"You gonna keep on with the world currency lesson?" Amiya quipped. "We knew all that. We just didn't know about what you said about the corlite."

Nandi held her breath. *Not with him, Amiya.*

Selvetar chuckled. The sound made the hairs on the back of Nandi's neck stand on end. "I fear I ramble like the old man that I am. Please excuse me."

"Um, no, please excuse me." Amiya looked down at her feet. "If Dad knew I spoke like that to you, he wouldn't be happy."

"Such a well-mannered young lady," Selvetar remarked. "Let us continue with your lesson then, shall we?"

"How can we do this without an *essence* ring?" Nandi asked.

"There are ways to channel the power stored in another's ring, if they will it so. I will lend you access to my ring for the purposes of your practice." He looked at Amiya, then at Nandi. "Who would like to proceed first?"

The twins looked at each other. "I'll go first," Nandi said, and she saw the approving look on Amiya's face when Selvetar turned to look at her.

"Very well," the magus said. "Though I am sure your mind is filled with the relentless noise of youth, use the exercises you've learned to clear it."

Nandi stared straight ahead, allowing her eyes to go out of focus as she concentrated on clearing her thoughts. She was aware of Amiya fidgeting on the other side of Selvetar, but after a while she managed to block her out.

She didn't know how much time passed, but as soon as time fell away from her mind, she felt an openness. In that instant, she heard Selvetar's voice.

"Very good, Nandi. Now, extend your awareness to my ring. Feel the stone, connect with it."

She did as instructed, extending her awareness out slowly to remain vigilant against any stray thoughts that threatened to shatter her focus.

It took no more than half a dozen heartbeats before she felt the ring. It was a living thing, a living thing imbued with the properties of the four *essences*. She allowed her mind to touch the ring, and it was like touching it with a finger. The stone from which it was crafted was smooth. There was a heft to it that only partially had to do with its actual weight. The ring was an inanimate object crafted from sentient stone.

"Now," Selvetar said. "Feel the *essences* within, grab hold and bring them to you."

Nandi reached into the ring and felt each of the four *essences*. She didn't grab hold, but touched them, rode them, swam in them, merged with them.

Being more familiar with *air*, she touched it more decisively. She called to it and the *essence* responded like a living thing, drawing nearer.

"Grasp one of the *essences*," Selvetar said, "and draw it to your command."

That felt wrong, but Nandi complied. As soon as the experience changed from interacting to commanding, it started to slip away. The more Nandi tried to grab hold of the *essence*, the more it resisted. She managed to grab hold of it, and she drew it from the ring. Even though the experience was internal, it felt like trying to wrestle a giant fish out of the water. It squirmed and resisted, and was slippery.

Selvetar's ring glowed silver, and then the air around them swirled. Leaves rustled in the wind, and Selvetar's robes stirred. And as quickly as it had started, the wind fell away and all went still again.

The connection slipped from her, and Nandi let it go. Panting, she bent over and put her hands on her knees.

"Not bad," Selvetar said. "Not bad at all. Results usually come with months of training, and even then, they are modest. You have great potential."

"Thank you," Nandi replied between breaths. How could he not feel how wrong it was to draw upon the *essences* that way? When she had simply connected with the *essence* and guided it in the way she wished, it was almost effortless. Grabbing hold of it and pulling it to her command was much more difficult.

"In time, your stamina will grow and you'll be able to longer manipulate them," Selvetar added. He turned to Amiya. "And now you."

Amiya stared straight ahead, much as Nandi had done. Although she didn't know how much time had passed as she focused, she could tell that Amiya had made the connection much sooner.

"Very good," Selvetar said. "You've found the connection quickly. Now, delve and draw forth the *essence* with which you have grasped."

Selvetar had barely finished speaking when a silver spark flashed in Amiya's eyes and the wind picked up again. It swirled and howled as it passed around the trio. Sparks appeared in the air, like tiny flickers of light. The silver light in Amiya's eyes dimmed, and a yellowish red glow replaced it. The sparks combined as they swirled in the air, until a cone of flame stretched from the ring and rotated in front of them.

The flame dissipated almost instantly, and then the ground began to rumble. It wasn't so much a tremble, but a light rumble beneath their feet.

Nandi looked at her sister to see nervousness in her now gray-brown eyes.

The rumbling stopped, and Amiya gasped and fell to her hands and knees.

"Well done," Selvetar said. "You have great potential, Amiya. You lack control, but that is to be expected. With proper training, you could be a powerful magus, should such an endeavor call to you."

"Thank you," Amiya said once she'd caught her breath. "I might like that."

"I suspect you would. Now move beside me." The magus spread his hands open, and the ground rumbled with more force, but more control.

"When you have learned control and developed more stamina, the *essences* come to your command more easily."

The ground stopped shaking at the same time the wind picked up, buffeting his robes and causing the twins to shield their faces against the wind and dirt. Tiny blue particles formed in the air and swirled in the wind.

"There is power within all of us," Selvetar continued. "With experience comes control. That control allows you to tap your inner abilities as well as control the power you access."

The wind intensified, and the blue particles combined and grew larger and larger until the trio stood in the center of a swirling funnel of water. Just outside the funnel they saw yellow-red sparks form. Those sparks combined over and over, growing larger until a funnel of fire swirled outside the water and in the opposite direction. The fire heated the water, and a trickle of sweat fell down the side of Nandi's face.

"Although power and control are essential, experience is the most important. Experience is the path to power. There are no more *essences* available to me than you. It is my experience, and thus my power, that makes the difference."

The air inside the rapidly warming funnel of water began to cool, until it was as comfortable as before the magus had begun his demonstration. Then a large chunk of earth burst from the ground in a wave and fell over the fire and water.

Nandi threw her arms over her face, but didn't feel the rain of filth she was sure would bury her. She peeked over her arms and saw that the flames had been snuffed, the water had fallen away, and the dirt had fallen over what looked to have been an invisible dome. A dome of *air*. She could feel it. She glanced at Amiya, who had the same reaction of wonder that she must surely have.

Selvetar smiled down at them. "You see what is the beginning of possibility. There is more, but you have many years to learn." He moved to the gate and opened it. The girls stepped through and followed a step behind the magus as they made their way around the temple in the direction of the mansion.

Still looking forward, Amiya waggled her fingers to get Nandi's attention. When she looked over, Amiya gave a slight nod of her head farther to the left.

Nandi caught a glimpse of a man in sandy brown pants cut off at the ankles, and a dark brown tunic. He had long black hair mixed with dirt and grime, tangled in the pack strapped to his shoulders and covered with animal skins. He was surrounded by the city guard, but even from that distance, Nandi thought he seemed a gentle soul. He turned sad blue eyes on her and she quickly looked away.

"You will find that you have strengths in some areas more than others," Selvetar said, startling her out of her thoughts. "Every magus finds that they have an affinity for a particular *essence*. This can be due to personality, but not always. If you choose to pursue the study of the *essences* and therefore, study to become magi, you will discover which *essence* you are most strongly connected with."

He looked down at Nandi. "Tell me. When you drew forth *air* from my ring, what was the experience?"

"It was like grabbing hold of a squirming fish and pulling it out of the water," Nandi answered.

"Was there any other sensation?" Selvetar asked.

Nandi made a show of thinking about it, then shook her head. "No," she lied. "I don't think so." She could practically feel Amiya's questioning eyes on her, but she ignored her twin. They had a lot to talk about, but not until they were alone in their room.

20

JOGA

No matter how he wracked his brain, Joga found no solution to this terrible situation. He'd barely escaped being killed by a horrendous explosion of the borderland volcano and those infernal monsters it spawned, only to land into bigger trouble by using the method of travel forbidden by the Ancients of every known tribe in Khatal.

He kept his head down, but stole a glance past his 'escort' at the glares of the less than hospitable onlookers. Why did these people hate him so? He had no personal quarrel with them, and though their two peoples fought, the conflict was between their leaders, not the individuals.

Try as he might, Joga couldn't understand why the people of this city would so hate a person who had not personally declared any kind of blood feud with them. Conflicts were an individual thing to be worked out between the respective parties. If someone wronged one of his people, the tribe would stand in support of the person, but it was up to that person to settle the problem. He did not like the king of Marai, but he held no ill will toward Marailanders. Why would he?

The hostility these people exuded saddened his heart. Such

anger. Were their lives so difficult that they could so readily come to hatred?

He noticed a man in black and red robes practically gliding down the street followed by two identical girls. When he looked at one of them, she quickly looked away. Odd. Magi were the king's weapon against his people, and those girls were obviously in training. But the look that girl had given him was curiosity rather than fear or scorn.

Just before the trio moved out of sight, he caught a trail of *harmony*. Had it come from that girl? But that would be impossible. No sightless would train a child with *harmony*. Such a trait was inherent in his people. In moments it didn't matter, for they turned another corner and the girls were gone.

"Why so forlorn, wilder?" the sightless in front of him said. "I thought you were a fierce folk, yet you surrendered with no fight at all. Are your people so easily conquered?"

Joga said nothing. The level of ignorance of this man who had attained what was obviously some kind of rank, left him stunned. His words were arrogant enough, but even the way he carried himself, with such a strong sense of superiority and entitlement was almost amusing. If the circumstances weren't so dire, Joga would have laughed.

"Still nothing to say, I see."

They reached the temple and the sightless waved the guards away.

"You're sure, magus?" one of the guards asked.

Three monks fell in step on either side and behind the group. "I appreciate your concern, Captain," the sightless replied, "but I assure you that I'm capable of containing him. And in the unlikely event I should falter, help is not far away."

The captain and his soldiers stopped and bowed, and the monks took their place.

Away from the angry eyes of the city, Joga looked around. The walls were hard polished stone, with pillars as large around as a man's body. The floors became hard as well, made out of a different kind of stone. The sun disappeared, blocked away by a ceiling that loomed over his head.

Joga forced his breathing to remain slow and controlled. He squinted his eyes shut, willing his mind to ignore the feeling of the walls and ceiling closing in on him. How could these people stand such a thing? It was so restricting. He actually preferred the angry stares outside.

"I see you admire our grand temple," the sightless said, slipping a hand out of the sleeve of his robe and indicating the detailed carvings and paintings that adorned the walls.

Joga didn't deny that the artwork was beautiful, but it was greatly overshadowed by the sense of confinement.

"And here," the red-robed man said as they passed through a central room. "Even one who lives outside with the animals could appreciate such." He raised his hands to indicate the stained glass dome high overhead. He appreciated the craftsmanship, but why not have it open to the sky? As beautiful as the stained glass was, it paled by comparison to *Amyadali's* own creation; the sky above.

The man looked expectantly at him, and when Joga didn't respond, he sniffed. "Hmph. It's like talking to an animal."

They continued through the halls, then descended several sets of stairs. The halls were darker here, the stone rougher and colder. Torches burned in sconces on the walls, angry shadows dancing in their light.

Joga had to fight down the panic. He felt as though he'd crossed into the maw of some giant beast and was descending into the depths of its stomach. He couldn't feel the earth, and his connection to it flickered inside him, threatening to sever. The four men around him seemed unaffected at all. How could they stand it? His breath started to come out in short bursts.

The sightless looked over his shoulder. "What's your problem?" he asked, his tone irritated rather than concerned.

Joga continued to focus on his breathing to keep from panicking. He shouldn't have fought. He should have let those soldiers fight that monster and run while he had the chance. Maybe he could form another *bridge*. Just one more time to get him out of here. No.

Joga shook his head, squinting his eyes shut. *Bridging* had gotten him into this situation to begin with. Trying it again would likely send him into the lair of a teliak.

"Well no matter," the sightless said. "We've reached your new accommodations."

They stopped at a giant door made of wood so thick, it must have taken the death of an entire tree to fashion it. The entire "accommodation" was surrounded by solid stone that bore no resemblance to the lovely stone one would see in a cave or running stream.

Joga looked at the sightless in confusion. "Done what to deserve prison?" he demanded in his broken version of the Marailander tongue.

"Ah! So our animalistic friend can speak. I was beginning to suspect you were a mute."

"What laws I break?" Joga asked again. "I hurt no one."

"You brought a spawn of evil into our midst and you claim to have broken no laws?" The man stared at him, and Joga found no remorse in those cold blue eyes. "Your presence in our city would be crime enough, but bringing evil in your wake is unforgivable."

"I not bring it here with me."

The sightless signaled down the hall to two guards, who came quickly with a set of keys and manacles. The soldier clamped the chains onto Joga's wrists and ankles, while the monks watched him.

"So you would have me believe the two of you happened here by coincidence?"

The guard unlocked the barred door and stepped aside.

Joga felt his panic rising. "Not my fault," he said, looking around the dank cell. "Not mean to bring it. Not mean to come to your city at all."

"What do your intentions matter?" the sightless said. He pointed. "In you go." When Joga hesitated, he spoke more forcefully. "I'll not say it again. Step into the cell. Now. You will be questioned later."

He couldn't do it. The walls would crush him. He sought *air*. It was like a tiny flicker, that slipped away from the tips of his fingers. Joga's sense of alarm grew. He tried again, but it felt farther away.

A wall of *air* slammed into his back and sent Joga into a headlong dive into the cell. He heard the door slam closed as he crawled to his hands and knees, trying to catch his breath.

"You didn't believe we would have let you walk free in our beloved city, did you?" the sightless asked as the guard locked the door with an audible 'click'. "You may be determined to destroy yourselves and everything around you with your primitive knowledge of the *essences*, but we will not allow you to take us down with you."

The sightless turned, then looked back over his shoulder with open derision. "I'm sure these accommodations are more civilized than the mud and dung dens you're used to, but you won't have long to enjoy it. Someone will arrive to question you soon. I suggest you take this time to decide on the truth. It will go better for you."

Joga remained on his hands and knees, coughing and panting. He heard their footsteps receding and leaned back on his knees to look up at the cold stone ceiling. He quickly looked away, then down at the chains that bound his wrists and ankles. They need not have gone to the trouble. The *essences* fled from him as surely as his freedom the minute he had stumbled upon this city.

He tried again and again, but no matter his efforts, all of the aspects of Mother *Illyu* escaped him.

He curled up in a corner of his dark cell with his knees tucked against his chest, the chains hanging over is shins. Time immeasurable slipped by when the sound of keys rattling caught his attention. He lifted his head and looked in the direction of the barred cell door as it opened to admit a man in flowing black and purple robes. The cowl over his head obscured his features.

Looking at the man, Joga wondered why these monks and sightless preferred to hide themselves even from their own people.

The man walked right up to Joga, and he looked up at the robed figure, but didn't move.

"So it's true that a Khatala has wandered into our midst."

Joga looked back down.

The man stood over him for several silent heartbeats, hands tucked into his robes. *"Would you prefer a conversation in your native tongue, warrior?"* the man said in perfect Khatalese.

"Would prefer to be gone from this place peacefully," Joga replied in Marai, not wanting the man to sully the language of his people.

"Very well," the man said, lowering his cowl. "My name is Selvetar." When Joga didn't respond, he continued. "I believe our cultures have in common what it is considered rude not to offer one's name in response to a greeting."

"Maybe rude in any culture," Joga said. "Do not wish to be rude, but imprisoned in dark stone place for crimes I still don't know."

The sightless named Selvetar signaled to the guard behind him, and a moment later he brought two lit torches into the cell. "Leave the torches and remove his shackles."

"Are you sure, Second Magus?" the guard asked.

Selvetar never took his eyes off of Joga, but a tiny smirk crossed his features. "Trust me when I say that even without use of the *essences*, this man could physically overwhelm you with little effort. Your presence is not required."

Behind him, the guard bristled, but bowed and set about removing the bonds, then set the torches in sconces on the walls and withdrew.

"Might you rise to your feet that we may address one another on equal footing, warrior."

Joga rubbed his wrists, wondering if this man knew he couldn't tap the *essences* in this environment, or if he was simply that powerful that he didn't care. Either way, there was nothing equal about this situation. Joga climbed to his feet. At least this Selvetar offered some respect.

As was the case between most Khatala and Marailanders, Joga was a full head taller than this man and more solidly built. Still, he sensed the power. As with most of his people, Joga knew that sightless held *essence* trapped inside of those horrible rings made of the sacred corlite. This man was no different, but behind those cold dark eyes, there was knowledge; skill. Even if he were able to bring the *essences* to his call, he doubted he could overwhelm this man.

"That's better," Selvetar said, looking up at him. "And now might I have your name, young warrior?"

"Joga of North and South Frostlands."

"And you omit your parentage."

"Is reserved for friendly times," Joga replied, and the sightless nodded.

"Reports have it that you burst into our good city with an infernal creature and caused havoc among the populace."

"Was trying to escape beast and made a mistake. Not trying to come into your city."

"The report stated that you and the beast both caused the deaths of several city guard and injury to others in addition to property destruction."

"Your people bring you lies," Joga said. "Help destroy the monster."

"And yet you were seen trying to flee the scene."

"Knew I would be accused unfairly." Joga indicated the cell. "I stay to help and now am here. Maybe if I left, would still be free."

"Or hunted down and returned to a worse fate."

Joga clenched his teeth. "Am sorry for destroyed property. I can help rebuild."

Selvetar arched an eyebrow. "And the dead soldiers?"

"Not killed by me," Joga replied. "Monster sent them to the true life."

"I doubt their families will agree with your words."

"The truth!" Joga forced down his frustration. "Not my intention to cause hurt. Monster came upon me and I ended up here."

"Where did you encounter this monster?" Selvetar asked. "Surely you did not happen upon it from inside Vyne. From all accounts, it was something that could not have been missed if it were already here."

Joga glanced around the semi-lit cell. He dare not tell this man how he really got here. "Accident. Many of them try to kill me. I destroyed all but that one, which chased me into this place."

"There were no reports of a Khatala man and a particularly large four-armed monster passing through the front gates." Selvetar stared at him. Through him.

Joga hesitated, his mind racing for an answer. "Didn't pass through front gate, but in the confusion, don't know how I came in."

The man named Selvetar thought about this for a moment, then looked back up at Joga and nodded. "Very well."

He spun on his heel and made for the door, robes whipping behind him.

"Can go?" Joga called after him.

"I will see what I can do," the man said, waiting for the guard to open the cell door. "I'm sure I don't have to tell you that the less trouble you make, the easier it will be for me to arrange your ... release."

"Want no trouble here," Joga replied. "Only to leave peacefully."

"I believe you," the man said, stepping out.

Joga watched as the guard slammed the heavy door shut and locked it again. He went back to his corner in the room, slumped against the wall, and slid down to the floor. He halfheartedly reached for an *essence*, any *essence*, but nothing had changed. The stone walls locked him away from it.

Joga closed his eyes and leaned his head back against the wall. He was disconnected from the earth, and if he didn't find a way out of this place he would die here.

Yet again, Joga's thoughts were interrupted by the sound of keys rattling, and the cell door opening. Joga lifted his head. In his windowless cell, the only light came from the two burning torches that illuminated a tall rotund figure flanked by two armed guards.

21

EMIEL

Emiel had traveled a good deal of the southern lands, even slipping past the border on occasion to trade with the neighboring Frostland Khatala. Of all the cities and towns and villages he'd visited, none, not even Vyne, could compare to the sprawling city of Carlayn.

'Accompanied' by the city guard, Emiel strolled the cobblestone streets, perusing the various shops and stands that sold anything from fresh vegetables and meats, to pastries, travel gear, and weapons. They passed stone buildings where tailors had various types of richly dyed garments hanging on display outside their doors, and jewelry shops with open windows showcasing glittering gemstones. He'd passed by the city church, but the monks had looked rather intimidating, so he'd moved on.

Four days they had been waylaid in Carlayn, and despite Amoura's several attempts at an audience with the prime minister, they had been told to wait until he had the time to meet with them.

Emiel glanced at the soldier walking two paces behind and to his right. He supposed it was nice that they weren't confined to their rooms, but the constant presence of a guard was rather annoying. And to top it off, they'd been forced to pay for their lodgings as well!

Emiel sucked at his teeth. At least this Cravel character had had the innkeeper compensated for a bit more than half the cost of their rooms. It was a small courtesy considering the group wouldn't have lingered here long to begin with.

A tall hazel-eyed Nashmarese woman glanced down at him as she passed. Emiel looked over his shoulder at the woman. The coppery skinned folk of the Sandlands were a rare sight in the south. Emiel could only think of seeing a Nashmarese person once or twice in Vyne.

Emiel couldn't imagine why any foreigner would want to come here, given Prime Minister Cravel's reputation for paranoia.

The marketplace proved to be even more diverse, milling with people from all over the land of Marai, mostly, but with sprinkles of more peoples from Nashma, and even the occasional Shetarese with their long raven locks and bright green eyes.

Children chased each other, while older children walked in front of their parents at enough distance to feel independent. The sight brought Nandi and Amiya to his mind, and he felt an ache in his heart. How were his ladygirls fairing without him? Were they being treated well?

Emiel took a deep breath to settle his nerves. Just thinking about how far away he was from them was enough to send him into a panic.

He found himself angry at the prime minister for delaying them. Emiel needed to get this business done as quickly as possible, so that he could get back to the girls and get them away from Decius and that city.

That city. When had Emiel begun to think of Vyne as a place he lived in instead of home? When Aunya had died, Vyne hadn't been the same to him since. Combine that with Decius's rise to power, and Vyne had simply become a place he lived in long enough to find another home.

"Lucky charm for you, Mister?"

Emiel looked down to see a little girl smiling up at him, a polished gray and black sphere held up in both of her tiny hands.

"I'm sorry," he said, smiling back, "but I cannot spare enough coin for such a beautiful and obviously valuable charm."

"It's a charm to keep you safe when evil is near," the girl pressed. "I can sell it to you for less than most."

"Is that so?" Emiel said, squatting in front of the girl. "But if there is evil about, wouldn't you need this for yourself?"

The little girl shook her head and looked into his eyes with a gap-toothed grin.

"My family already has one, Mister," she said. "You are a visitor from far away, I think, so you need this more than we do."

"Ah," Emiel replied. "And for how much 'less' can you sell me this charm?"

"Three pressed silver," the girl said. "Normally sells for much much more."

Emiel nearly choked. "Three pressed silver? I'm afraid that is a good deal outside my budget."

"Two, then."

"How about four coppers and one pressed silver."

The girl made a show of thinking it over, then smiled and handed him the sphere. It was surprisingly heavier than he expected.

"Thank you, Mister," the girl said, still smiling. "Keep it close, and it will protect you from evil."

"I'm sure it will," Emiel said, standing as the girl ran off. He looked at the guard standing not far away. The man shook his head and gave Emiel a look that suggested he'd just been legally robbed.

"How do you say no to a child?" Emiel said.

The guard shrugged. "Keep it up and you'll be 'not saying no' until all the jingle in your pouch is gone."

The guard's words were true enough, for Emiel noticed a good number of children were now moving in his direction.

He hurried through the crowd and came out the back side of the marketplace where he nearly bumped into a man in silver burnished armor. Emiel saw the hand gripping the sword at his hip relax, and the man lifted his visor and addressed the guard following him.

"Soldier."

"Sir!" The guard following Emiel snapped to attention and saluted, fist over heart.

"Take this man back to his room. He and the rest of his party dine with the prime minister at dusk."

"Sir!" the soldier replied, saluting again.

The man in front of Emiel—obviously some kind of ranking soldier—gave him one last look, then moved on, red cape flowing behind him.

The guard stepped up to Emiel as he watched the company of soldiers depart. "Friendly guy."

"Captain of the Carlayn Guard," the soldier said, indicating that Emiel start for the inn. "It is for him to ensure the safety of the city, not be friendly with suspicious visitors."

"And we're back to that again," Emiel said as they moved down the more quiet streets. "What in the name of the Creator Himself makes you think we're suspicious?"

"You came to our borders in a frantic rush."

"We were being chased down by some kind of lava monsters."

The guard gave Emiel a look. "As you say, foreigner. And so the prime minister will judge."

"Over dinner," Emiel said dryly.

The guard didn't reply, and the rest of the walk back to the inn was in silence. Emiel didn't mind, though, as it allowed him to think over his situation while gazing at the tall buildings in the distance and the various streets that led to the housing and commerce districts.

When they reached the Salted Sea Inn—an odd name for an Inn nowhere near the ocean—Emiel stepped up to the door, then looked over his shoulder at the guard, who hadn't followed.

"You not coming in? I might find a way to bolt out a window or something."

The guard stared at him, then moved away to lean against a wall across the street facing the entrance.

Emiel shrugged and went inside. The common room was empty

save two figures sitting at a table in the farthest corner from the door. Amoura and Bone.

Emiel glanced at the mercenary, but lingered on the magus a bit longer. The woman was beautiful; strikingly so. Her smooth dark skin and black braided hair contrasted eerily with those steel gray eyes. Her pale gray dress, which matched her eyes, had a split at both sides, revealing just a bit of the curve of her muscular legs.

Her hand suddenly appeared beside her leg, and made an upward gesture. His head snapped up and he saw those narrowed gray eyes staring directly at him. Those eyes showed annoyance, but the corners of her mouth twitched.

"Gonna stand sentry right there, entranced all day, spicetrader?" Bone said, shattering the moment. "If so, I'll just head on up to relax."

"Didn't want to interrupt," Emiel muttered, pulling up a chair between them.

"Right," the mercenary replied. He glanced at Emiel, then slouched a little further.

A barmaid came to the table, but Emiel smiled and shook his head. When he saw the disappointed look on her face, he called after her.

"I've changed my mind, ma'am. I'll take an ale."

The young woman looked at him with a confused smile, but inclined her head and went to the bar.

Emiel leaned back in his chair, then noticed the others staring at him. "What?"

Bone opened his mouth to speak, then waited until the woman sat the drink down and left. "I swear I've never seen somebody go so far outta his way to be nice to everybody. What's with you?"

"Is it a bad thing to be nice to people?" Emiel asked.

"I'm not saying that," Bone replied, "but why break your neck trying to make a barmaid happy? You didn't want a drink, she goes away."

"A large part of her income is from tips on the drinks and food she sells." Emiel took a sip of the ale, then sat the ghastly thing back down and slid it away.

Bone laughed at him and slid the ale closer to himself. "Ha! See what I mean?" He lifted his mug toward Amoura, who sat quietly watching the two of them. "He doesn't even like it, but he buys one anyway. And all to please a simple barmaid." He took a long draw from the mug, then sat it down and slid it aside.

"It's nice to patronize the establishment you linger in," Emiel said.

"We're already patronizing it with rented rooms and a couple drinks before you got here."

Emiel glanced at the empty space in front of Amoura.

"Well, a couple drinks for me, anyway," the mercenary said.

Emiel shrugged. "Do what you will. That woman is no more simple than I am. She serves food, I make and trade spices."

"Sure thing," Bone scoffed. "Sure thing that serving in a tavern or common room requires more skill than the jobs of you or me," he indicated Amoura, "or the woman here."

Emiel could practically feel the heat off Amoura's glare at being called 'the woman'.

"More skill than you think, mercenary," the magus said, "when having to deal with those lacking couth."

"What's that supposed to mean?" Bone snapped. "He took a long draw from Emiel's mug and slammed it on the table, causing bits of ale to splash over the rim. Amoura's upper lip curled in disgust.

"I think what she means is that it's not as easy as it looks to deal with people who have no respect and look down at you."

"How could I look anywhere but down?" Bone asked. "She's a blasted barmaid."

Emiel patted the air between them. "Mind lowering your voice?"

"You scared of angering the serving girl?"

Emiel rolled his eyes and looked to Amoura for help, but the magus shrugged and looked away.

"So what are we going to do about this prime minister?" Emiel asked, looking from one to the other. "He's kept us here for four days, and finally deigns to grant us an audience."

"I don't see why he'd keep us here any longer," Bone replied, finishing the last of Emiel's ale. "Ain't done nothing wrong to begin with."

"Which is exactly why I'm concerned," Emiel countered. "We haven't done anything wrong, but he's still detained us in his city instead of just letting us be on our way."

"What do you think's gonna happen?" Bone asked, leaning forward. "You think he's gonna throw us in some cell?"

"Seems like we're one step away from it now," Emiel replied. "We can't go anywhere without an escort as it is."

"And there are guards posted around the perimeter of this building," Amoura said. She looked at each of them in turn. "He's kept us here in comfort while he has our backgrounds looked into. If he were to discover that we were bandits or some form of lawless running from one city to the next, he would already have thrown us into the bowels of some prison to await our native city's justice, or his own. Since that hasn't happened, he is likely just curious."

"And this dinner is to sate his curiosity," Emiel said.

The magus shrugged. "More or less, I would think."

Don't know why I'm concerned about this, Emiel thought. *Probably be the best thing for me if they got locked up and I got sent back to Vyne.* He doubted it would happen that way, but it was nice to dream, anyway.

Amoura arched an eyebrow at him.

"What?" he asked.

"Whatever you think of us," she replied, "Cravel is no more your friend."

"What makes you think I was—"

"Your face is an open book," the woman said.

"Don't know how he turns a profit," Bone said. "Man's got a face to tell the story of every thought in his head."

Emiel looked from Bone to Amoura, then looked away. He suddenly missed Lief. The little tinfar had been his only friend in this situation. He hoped she'd return, though he didn't know how she could find them again.

Across the room, the door opened to admit several armed guards.

Like the one accompanying Emiel, they wore burnished gray armor with chain mail underneath.

One of the soldiers came to stand over them. "Prime Minister Cravel is ready to see you."

Emiel and the others stood and followed him back to the door and the other waiting soldiers. The barmaid smiled when Emiel paid for his ale on the way out. Bone shook his head, and Emiel smirked at the faint scowl the woman sent at the back of the mercenary's head.

They stepped out of the inn where a carriage awaited. The driver opened the door.

"A carriage?" Emiel said, staring at the overly elegant affair.

Bone shrugged. "Better than walking, I think." He climbed in after Amoura.

"Do either of you have an idea what those things were?" Emiel asked once the carriage rocked into motion. Outside, the rhythmic 'clip-clop' of the horses' hooves on the stone streets made him feel as if he might actually be a guest of the prime minister, instead of a detainee. "I've never seen or heard of anything like them. And what language were they fussing at us in?"

"That's a good way to put it," Bone said. "It did sound like fussing."

"They spoke the language of Dakorge," Amoura said. "It is an evil language spoken by denizens of the underworld."

"The underworld?" Emiel looked at Bone, who shrugged again.

"You'll have to study ancient history if you want to know more about it," Amoura said. "The last recorded incidents concerning the underworld were during the time of the Illuminarians."

"That makes me very uncomfortable," Emiel said.

"You expected it'd make you all warm inside?" came Bone's reply.

Emiel ignored him. "You can speak this underworld language, then?"

"Speak it? No. But I recognize its sound in the same way you might understand the distinct sounds of a foreign tongue. You may not understand the words, but you know the sound when you hear it."

"So, you've heard it before?"

"It was a brief part of my studies," Amoura replied.

"Your studies to become a magus," Emiel said.

"Is this a life interview?" the woman snapped, but then she softened. "Yes, my studies to become a magus."

Though it had been obvious what she was from the start, the confirmation was still off-putting. The Order of Magi brought nothing but trouble. They toyed with things they shouldn't, and one day nature's force would stamp them down. Emiel wanted nothing to do with them, and certainly wanted to be nowhere near one of them when they pushed nature just a little too far.

"I take it you don't approve."

"It's not my business what you do," Emiel replied.

"But you don't like us?" the woman pressed. "You don't like the Order of Magi."

"Certain things shouldn't be tampered with," Emiel replied. The woman seemed to think on this, but didn't reply further.

"So what're we gonna tell this paranoid man?" Bone asked. "I don't much care for the idea of being detained here while I've got a job to finish."

"How do you plan on finishing this job when the cargo was destroyed?" Emiel asked.

"The truth is good enough," Amoura replied. "We were on our way to Altarra and were chased from our path by those monsters."

Emiel looked from Bone to Amoura. The woman had obviously deflected the conversation. What was going on here? "Sounds like some truth and not all of it," he said.

The mercenary turned a dark look on Emiel. "Be careful," he said.

They stared at each other until Amoura intervened. "Whatever doubt is cast on our errand will ill affect us all."

"I think I'm ill affected either way," Emiel replied, eyes still locked with the Bone's.

"You're playing a dangerous game, spicetrader," Bone said.

"I've been forced away from my kids and into this ridiculous errand that could be done without me," Emiel said. "It's getting tiring."

"I'm sure your endurance is up to the task," the mercenary replied.

"Don't be so sure."

Bone looked like he was on the edge of laughter. "Feeling tough, old man?"

"The fact that you've barely seen enough winters to call yourself a man doesn't make me an old one," Emiel replied.

"Oh really?" the mercenary said.

Emiel saw his sword hand twitch. "If you're going to argue the point," he said, "you have to stop making my point for me."

"What?" Bone snapped.

Emiel shook his head. "No one is doubting your skills with the sword, or survival," he said. "But the fact that you itch to put me in my place by force alone proves you're little more than a child." He spread his hands. "What are you going to do? Run me through right here in the carriage and void your agreement with Decius?"

"I'm starting to think it over."

"This is exactly the type of conversation to have before meeting with Cravel," Amoura said. "I'd advise you against getting one another riled up. The man will see it and question everything that comes out of our mouths."

They continued to stare at one another until Emiel had had enough and looked away. He heard the young mercenary snort, no doubt interpreting the move as him being cowed. Emiel let the boy believe what he would.

The carriage lurched to a stop and soon after, the door opened. Amoura climbed out, followed by Bone. Emiel climbed out to see a mansion easily the size of five or six of the regular homes in the city. He wanted to assume the place housed several families, but Emiel had seen enough greed that accompanied positions of power to be cynical.

Two guards approached and stopped in front of them, while two positioned themselves behind. Emiel looked at their new escort, two with swords strapped to their hips, and two holding pikes. "Is this really necessary?" he asked. "What do you expect we're going to do?"

"This way," one of the front guards nodded toward the mansion.

Once inside, they passed several servants in yellow and white livery, moving about the hallways. One girl who looked to be about the same age as Amiya and Nandi scurried by with a sack of laundry slung over her back.

Emiel half turned to watch her go. The girl looked tired.

One of the guards caught his eye, and nodded his chin forward. Emiel got the hint and turned back.

The more he paid attention, he began to notice that all of the servants were not only young, but female. Emiel didn't think he saw a single girl who looked to have seen more than fifteen years. They passed a large dining room filled with well-dressed men and women sipping wine and conversing about things Emiel was sure would leave him either sleepy or nauseated.

"Mind where your eyes roam," the guard from behind said.

Emiel said nothing and kept his head facing straight. He was starting to wonder if Amoura was telling the truth, and he would be better off on the road with them instead of in this place. The underlying tension in the air was nerve-racking. The magus was right. Best to put on their best face and get out of here as quickly as possible.

They came to an open room with desks covered with books. More books lined the walls in shelves that reached the ceiling. A round table sat at the middle of the room and several rectangular tables surrounded it.

One table was laden with covered platters that failed to hold in the scent of fresh baked pastries and roasted meats. Emiel's stomach rumbled.

A tall thin man stood in front of one of the bookshelves, hands clasped behind his back as he perused the numerous volumes. He turned at the sounds of the soldiers' booted footsteps.

"My guests finally arrive."

"We could have 'finally' arrived sooner," Bone quipped, earning him a warning glance from Amoura.

"We thank you for your hospitality," the magus said.

The prime minister of Carlayn moved closer. He had a short trimmed moustache that matched the sandy brown curls that fell to his ears. He wore a stylish yellow doublet with white stitching, buttons, and collar, which matched his fitted trousers.

Emiel didn't like the man. From the way he sauntered across the room, to the height in which he held his head when speaking. He'd expected a wiry little man, cowering behind a hundred guards. This looked more like arrogance than paranoia.

Cravel nodded. "It was necessary to offer you my hospitality while I researched the necessity of your visit. The border patrol reported that you were approaching this fine city in great haste. Surely you understand that it arouses curiosity when a trio of foreigners comes running toward your home as though they are running from some-thing. Or someone."

"You were wise in your thinking, Prime Minister," Amoura replied. "We were indeed running, not from someone, but from something."

"So the patrol has informed me you've said. Some sort of monster, it was?"

"Several," the magus said. "Large, nearly a man's height twice over."

Cravel's eyebrows rose. "Quite interesting. Do continue."

Amoura studied the man for a moment, then pressed on. "They had four arms, each with a hand clasping a weapon made of hard sharp rock. Cooled lava rock. Their skins were of the same rock, some less cooled than others."

"And these, monsters, came from where, exactly?"

"I cannot say for certain, but we suspect from the borderland volcano."

"The borderland volcano?" Cravel replied with mock incredulity. "That is quite a distance to travel just to attack three travelers."

Emiel could practically feel the heat radiating from the woman's restrained temper.

"I did not say that the things traveled the distance to attack us,

Prime Minister. The volcano erupted, an event we bore witness to. The creatures exploded from the eruption and traveled the distance in the air in the form of giant lava rocks. Upon impact with the ground, they formed into the creatures we encountered."

"That is a compelling story, young lady."

Amoura didn't blink. "If you would define factual events as story, very well. And you may address me as Magus, Prime Minister."

Cravel's eyes widened in amusement. "How rather, formal, of you."

"Master Apprentice would be formal, Prime Minister."

"And you would demand such semi formality of me then? Are we on such stiff terms as this?"

"If you wish to be on relaxed terms, might I refer to you as older gentleman as you refer to me as young lady?"

Cravel laughed, and Emiel let go of a breath he hadn't known he was holding. "Your wit is refreshing, magus." He looked past them to the four guards. "You may take your leave," he said. "Simion will see to my needs."

The guard who had spoken earlier gave the prime minister a doubtful look, but Cravel gestured impatiently, and the soldier bowed and spun on his heel. He remained silent until only himself, and the three visitors remained.

"If you please," he said, indicating the aromatic dining table.

As soon as they were seated, a man in a yellow vest with white stitching and white trousers appeared seemingly from nowhere. He began to remove the lids from platters filled with various types of tropical fruit and berries, as well as carved meats, roasted and grilled.

Hungry as he was, Emiel watched Amoura, figuring the magus would be well versed with the etiquette of this foreign place. Bone grabbed up a pair of tongs and started to reach for a hunk of meat when he gave a subtle hop in his seat and glared at Amoura, who sat erect and looking forward. Bone frowned at the woman, but she continued to look straight ahead.

The man named Simion reached for a pair of tongs and served

Cravel a helping of vegetables and, then a small portion of each type of meat.

Bone made a relieved sound as though he had been released from some sort of clasp, and reached again for the platter of meat in front of him. Emiel followed his instincts and continued to wait.

After he had finished serving Cravel, Simion came around the long table and began to serve Amoura, this time indicating each dish and serving those the woman approved of.

Amoura favored the man with a subtle smile and nod of thanks, and he gently placed the tongs on a platter and withdrew to stand behind them.

Now Emiel picked up a pair of tongs closest to him. He forced himself not to pile his plate high with meat and vegetables despite his hunger. Next to him, Bone had no such modesty. The young mercenary stacked his plate with every type of meat and cheese on the table.

Emiel watched the boy for a moment, then leaned toward him. "Gonna have any kind of vegetable with that?"

The redheaded young man looked at him as though he had lost his wits, then stabbed a sausage with his fork and bit it in half.

Cravel glanced at the mercenary and wrinkled his nose. "Given my reputation, you are curious why a man such as myself would be willing to be in your presence without any guard in attendance." He looked from Emiel to Amoura, then back to his plate. Emiel thought that an interesting admission.

"It seems an unusual choice, Prime Minister," Amoura replied.

Cravel swallowed a bite and nodded. "Am I to assume your companion here is mute?" he asked, indicating Emiel with a glance. "I've not heard a word spoken from him."

Emiel looked from Amoura to Cravel, the latter of whom was now staring at him. "I'm afraid I don't have much to offer, Prime Minister," Emiel said.

"Oh come away from the modesty, good man," Cravel replied. "You've the look of someone who knows what he's about,"—another glance at Bone, who was now savaging a turkey leg—"while some would give the impression of uncouth barbarism. You strike me as a careful, thinking man."

Emiel resisted the urge to shrug. "Guess I'm just out of my element."

"Oh? Do explain."

Emiel had a piece of steaming trout halfway to his mouth when the question came. *I'd like to explain after I eat.* "I've never traveled this far before," he explained. "I've actually never traveled close to Carlayn." He quickly took the bite before another question followed.

"And what do you think of our city?" Cravel asked.

"Easily the biggest city I've ever been in," Emiel answered after swallowing the delectable fish. It tasted like winter trout, but it was seasoned with spices unfamiliar to him. "The tanned brick buildings and red clay-colored homes are beautiful. The marketplace is nice also." He took another bite, still trying to figure out the seasoning.

"Does the fish not please you?" Cravel asked, misreading Emiel's expression.

"Oh no, I mean, yes, it's delicious." He looked at the last few pieces on his plate, black with those amazing spices. "I'm just trying to figure out the spices and seasonings. I think I'm tasting seven or eight different spices, but I'm only familiar with three of them."

The prime minister responded with a surprised smile. "Ah! A connoisseur, then! I should have known." He clapped his hands together.

"Ah ... mmm. No," Emiel stammered. "It's just my trade. I'm a spicetra"—

"Nonsense," Cravel interrupted, waving Emiel's words away. "Enough with the modesty, I insist. I should have seen it from the start. From your inherent skills with etiquette to your silent appraisal of my library and our dining arrangements, it should have been clear to me. You even knew enough about our customs to allow my good Master Servant Simion to serve the lady after myself before partaking of the food. You even knew that I would wait for the lady to eat before taking my first bite! No one could have guessed that little detail."

Amoura's head snapped up at the mention of Simion's title. She glanced back at the man out of the corner of her eye, but he remained passive, as if not hearing any of the conversation.

Emiel's mouth opened and closed several times during the man's outlandish assessment. Amoura leaned forward and reached for her glass of spiced wine, using her left arm that blocked most of her face from the man. She gave Emiel the subtlest of glances. The look suggested he play along with Cravel's observation. If he'd blinked, he would have missed the look, so fleeting was it.

"Well," Emiel said, spreading his hands. "It is not a thing one goes about flaunting. That would be in poor taste, pardon the pun."

Bone snorted, but fortunately Cravel had drowned the sound out with his own laughter.

"It's a rare pleasure to speak with a man of wit and taste who does not go to such lengths to advertise it," Cravel said, pinching the bridge of his nose, his shoulders still bouncing.

Emiel didn't think what he'd said was that funny. "You find yourself in such company often?" he asked.

Cravel sighed. "You've no idea. Even now, I am certain the lords and ladies are all posturing amongst each other while I dine with you." He made a lofty gesture with his left hand. "They await I, the paranoid prime minister of Carlayn who through some freakish fortune has the king's ear, to attend the very fete I've been forced to host."

Amoura's left eyebrow twitched, but her features remained otherwise neutral. Emiel focused on a perfectly seasoned piece of broccoli, and Bone made an openly incredulous sound. Amoura and Emiel both glared at him. Had he not caught Cravel's first comment eluding to his perceived paranoia?

Cravel chuckled at the reaction. "Fear not," he said. "Your boorish friend's reaction is appropriate, for that is what is expected of me and that is what must be."

He looked the trio over with a devious smile. "Underestimation is a more favorable position from which to maneuver."

Emiel did his best to hide his surprise. Was this man really so cleaver as to have people of all of the surrounding lands fooled into thinking him a paranoid coward who only retained his position due to King Alyn's favor?

"Soldiers approach, Prime Minister," Simion announced. "Their pace is brisk."

Several moments later the door opened and the same guard as before stepped in.

"Please excuse the intrusion, Prime Minister, but there is a problem."

"Please don't tell me our four-armed monsters from the children's tales have reached the city gates," Cravel said, returning to his airy persona.

The guard's mouth tightened. "I'm afraid that's exactly what has happened, Prime Minister."

22

——————

AMOURA

Amoura remained seated even as Cravel came to his feet so quickly his chair fell backward. "What?"

"Ten beasts with rocky black and red skin and four arms, each holding a weapon, are nearly to the gates," the guard said.

"And why in the name of the Creator has there been no word before now?" Cravel demanded.

"We have no word from the border patrols, sir," the guard said.

They were dead. Amoura knew it just as she knew that ten of those things could do a good job of destruction if they made it into the city.

Cravel scrambled around the table. "How much time do we have?"

"At the pace those things are running," the guard answered, "not more than twenty minutes."

Cravel threw up his hands, then turned back to the guard. "This is insane. What of the city guard?"

"The captain is formulating the defense as we speak, Prime Minister."

"Well that's something, at least." Cravel turned his back on the guard to look at Amoura and the others. "I would be untruthful if I didn't speak of the possibility that those things followed you here."

"What?" Bone said. He finished the turkey leg and dropped it on his plate, scattering bits of bone and scraps. The spicetrader glared at him in disgust.

"First you don't believe us, now it's our fault?"

Emiel gaped at him. If that boy's head were any more dense it would grow too heavy and snap his neck.

"We will aid your city guard in any way we can, of course," Amoura said to the Prime Minister.

He winked at her, then turned back to the guard. "Take our guests with you. They've already darkened our doorstep. The least they can do is help clean up this mess."

The soldier bowed, then stepped aside for the trio to leave. "See that they are outfitted with the best armor and gear they require," Cravel said from behind.

"Sir," the guard said, fist to chest and bowing again. "Should I have your personal guard remain inside your quarters?"

"That would be best," Cravel said. "Now be off. Tell Captain Narise I hope my confidence in her ability to contain this is well placed."

The lead soldier strode past the trio and indicated for Amoura and the others to follow.

They were fast out of the mansion and jogging toward the barracks that were but a block away. Cravel was good at playing the role of a skittish ruler. Amoura had never been to a city where the barracks were so close to the home of the governing body.

Bone ran up beside the leading soldier. "My armor and sword are back at the inn. I need to get it and I'll meet you at the front gates."

The soldier shook his head. "Not necessary. Have you no idea the worth of your armor?"

They reached the barracks and entered, pressing through a crowd of armored men and women.

"It's of value, yes," Bone answered.

The soldier clapped him on the shoulder. "Son, armor fashioned from the bones of a teliak is some of the most valuable items one could come across, and would fetch enough coin to buy a small home. After the third attempt to break into your room, we confiscated the armor and brought it to the barracks. It is even now being guarded."

In a move that seemed quite uncharacteristic of the mercenary, he smiled and clapped the soldier on the shoulder in kind. "My thanks for that, good man. I know my armor is valuable, but I hadn't known it would cause so much trouble."

The soldier gave a curt nod, the corners of his eyes crinkling. "When this is done I'll want an account on how you came to it." He turned to a nervous soldier that looked to have seen no more than seventeen years.

"Jak. Take this man to his armor. And hurry. We've a city to defend!"

Bone gave the soldier's shoulder another pat, then followed the soldier named Jak around a bend. Amoura stood aside and surveyed the assembling troops. They had formed ranks and were moving outside the building in a lined and orderly fashion. There looked to be at least a hundred. That was good.

"You don't have the look of a soldier about you," their escort said, "but this might help you not to die out there."

She turned to see the man looking Emiel over. While she had been assessing the army, the weathered soldier had sent Emiel away to be fitted for armor and a shortsword. The spicetrader looked out of place in it, but it may well save his life.

"I doubt this would stop a sword or axe from one of those things," he said, holding his arms out at his sides and looking down at himself. It was a true enough assessment. The armor was more like thick, boiled leather.

"No it won't," the old solider said. "But what it will do is protect you from a glancing blow and you'll still be fast enough to avoid an attack. I doubt you've got the conditioning to hold yourself up for long in full armor and mail, correct me if I'm wrong." He stared at Emiel, who offered nothing further.

"You're not a soldier, but you look to be good on your feet. Put that to use. Try to stay out of the way, and don't draw that thing unless running's no option." He patted the sword on Emiel's hip. "I trust you know which end to point where?"

"I think I can figure it out," Emiel said dryly. "Thanks."

The soldier slapped him across the back, causing the spicetrader to stumble forward. "Good." He looked past Emiel. "And our bone-armored lad returns. Let's move."

Bone trotted up to the group and they made their way toward the front gates. The mercenary stood out in stark contrast to the other soldiers in his teliak bone armor. He stopped next to the spicetrader, bone helm tucked under his arm and his teliak bone sword strapped across his back.

Men in brown waistcoats and trousers shouted from street corners for the residents to take to their homes and remain indoors until the threat had passed. Surprisingly, most of the populace moved in a hurried but orderly manner until the streets were empty of all but marching soldiers.

Helm tucked under her arm, a woman in dark green armor directed soldiers into position outside the gates. Her long hair fell in a red cascade down her shoulders and back. She turned as the group approached, and Amoura saw disapproval in the woman's face.

"What've yeh brought me, Erik," the woman demanded. Her accents spoke of the border highlands. "I've not the time fer babyin' this lot."

"They'll be fine enough, Captain Coira," the old soldier named Erik replied. "One's a magus, the other a warrior of some sort." He waved a hand over Emiel. "And, well. He's got enough of a mind about him to stay out of the way."

"I don't care where they've got their skills from," Coira said. "They've not fought with me men."

"We'll find our place on the field, Captain," Bone said.

Amoura arched an eyebrow. The mercenary's accent was as thick as the captain's.

"Ye've got only ta let us play our part and we'll not be gettin' in yer business."

The woman looked Bone over, then nodded and slammed her helm into Erik's chest as a groom brought her horse. The weathered soldier held it while she mounted, then handed it back.

"Verra well. I expect ye ta stay outta the way then."

"Only if ye stay outta our own, lass," Bone replied, and the two shared a devious smirk.

The captain turned her icy blue eyes on Amoura. "And what've yerself, lass? Ye've the look of a power wielder about ye."

Amoura inclined her head. "Be assured that my presence will not hinder your efforts, Captain. And if I may, I would advise putting your pikemen to greatest use as long as possible and try to encircle the monsters. The creatures are erratic in their attacks, but their size, speed, and strength compensate for their lack of skill. Pikes will slow them enough for a sword strike."

"And ye know this how?"

"Personal experience."

The fiery captain nodded and donned her helm, then saw to the rest of the formation.

"When the fun starts, I think we should be able to slip out of here," Bone whispered into Amoura's ear when Erik had moved off a short distance.

She stared at him.

"What?"

"You would leave one of your countrywomen to fight this battle without your assistance?"

Bone considered that. "I can't deny your words, but I'm a mercenary. I'm not getting paid for this."

"There is the possibility of reward when this is done."

"Possibility, yes. But possibility isn't the same as certainty, and I'm certainly getting paid by Decius, not Cravel."

Erik looked over his shoulder and waved for them to follow. They passed through the gates and out into the open fields to see a clump of four-armed figures, fast approaching, axes, swords, and clubs gripped in large rocky hands. The defenders felt the thundering footfalls even from this distance.

"You seem to have forgotten your accent again," Amoura said as she watched the approaching monsters. For a reason she couldn't name, she found the fact that there were only ten of them unsettling.

"Better for business if you sound like the people who hire you," Bone replied.

"Soldier," Amoura said, addressing Erik. The weathered man came up beside her. "Get word to your captain that she will need more soldiers on the field and quickly."

Erik gaped at her. "We're already a hundred strong and they number only ten."

"There will be more," she said.

The soldier pointed at the guard towers to either side of the city wall. "They can see for miles up there. If there was more of those things coming, we'd know about it."

"I advise again to bolster your force," Amoura insisted. "There will be more, and this will end badly."

The old soldier ran his tongue along his teeth as he considered her, then nodded and moved away.

"What do you know?" the spicetrader asked.

"That something foul is upon us," she answered, staring out at the sprinting monsters.

"All the better to be gone," Bone said.

"You didn't strike me as the type to flee from a fight, mercenary," Amoura said.

Bone shrugged. "We've got a lot of ground to cover yet. This isn't our city and we're not in Cravel's employ."

"He offered you the food of his house."

"As forced guests."

"His hospitality could have been less friendly."

Again, the mercenary shrugged, but he offered nothing further when they saw Captain Coira approaching on her tall black gelding.

"What is this about reinforcing me men?" she demanded.

"I cannot tell you what I expect," Amoura answered. "But it will be worse than what we see at the moment."

"And I'm to assemble my army on your hunch?"

Amoura looked up into those icy eyes. "Of course, the decision is yours. I am providing suggestions based on my experience with them and what little knowledge I have of creatures of the underworld."

"Creatures of the what?" Coira said. "I've no games ta play with ye, lass. Out with it now."

Amoura glanced back at the ten creatures that were nearly at the gates. "They are evil from the underworld. I have not the time to explain it, but their presence in this world can actually assist others of their kind to surface if left unchecked. Those ten," she waved a hand at the field beyond, "are enough to challenge your hundred soldiers. Another ten would decimate them."

"Nonsense ye speak," the fiery captain said, but Amoura saw the hesitation in her eyes. She looked out at the field, then back. "Ye'd have me reinforce the troops now."

"I'd have you reinforce your infantry on either side but do not have them engage until the true threat is revealed. I do not pretend to know the scope of their intelligence, but the fewer of your numbers they see, the better."

Coira listened, then nodded and barked orders at one of her runners. "I hope yer right about this, power wielder."

"If I'm not, then you've only wasted time and mobilized troops needlessly."

When the other woman was out of earshot, Bone added, "and caused her no small amount of embarrassment."

"And she would be alive to experience it," Amoura countered.

"So what's the plan?" Emiel asked, walking up beside her. He might not have the make of a warrior, but he was finely built all the same. She could see the nervousness in his face, but he managed it well for someone with no battle experience. His hand rested on the hilt of the shortsword at his waist as though he knew how to wield it.

"Our altruistic mercenary has a point," she replied. "Our situation would be better served if we were to depart and be waylaid no longer."

The man looked at her in shock. Though she kept her features neutral, a part of her felt ashamed at that look. What did she care what he thought? He was a spicetrader who didn't even know what he was.

"I would expect that from him," Emiel pointed at the mercenary's back, "but not you."

"I wasn't aware you were so familiar with my character."

"I don't need to know a person my whole life to have a measure of their character."

"That's a dangerous way to think."

"It's also a survival trait." He glared at Bone's back. "And besides, we have none of our gear. No waterskins, no food, nothing."

Amoura mentally chastised herself for overlooking that little detail. She conceded the point with a nod. "Cravel will not detain us after this. In fact, he may well aid us with mounts and fresh supplies."

Bone turned at that. "What? I thought we spoke about this. We don't have the time to—"

"We don't have much of a choice," Amoura interrupted. "Emiel is right. We have no supplies to continue on. We must stay and fight. Cravel will aid us for aiding him."

"You're so sure?" the mercenary replied.

"Those things are almost on top of us." The spicetrader pointed out at the field, where pikemen were positioned at the front, with the second wave of pikemen at their backs, and swordsmen flanking the vanguard. Archers stood at the city walls, arrows nocked. It would be a waste of resources, but there'd barely been enough time to argue with the captain about reinforcements, let alone the ineffectiveness of the archers against those things.

Once the rocklike creatures were within range, the archers let fly. Arrows flew into the air and arced downward toward the running monsters. Most of the arrows skipped off of hard jagged skin with only some few finding purchase. The monsters ran on as though nothing had happened.

Amoura stepped forward. She had summoned the *essences* during her conversation with Captain Coira, and they were ready for her command.

"So what do I do?" the spicetrader asked.

Amoura continued forward, and surprised herself at how much hope was in her response. "Try not to die."

23

EMIEL

E miel watched the magus slip through the mass of bodies as she made her way to the right side of the formation. Her dark blue robes actually blended well with the smoky gray armor of the soldiers.

"Second volley!" a man's voice shouted, and more arrows soared into the air. The result was the same, and the monsters never slowed. They were so close now that Emiel could hear that hostile cursing language that made his spine go cold.

"Hold fire!" Captain Coira shouted. "Pikes ready." Pikes angled downward toward the approaching monsters. "Draw swords!"

The sound of a field full of swords being drawn from their scabbards rang in Emiel's ears. He drew his shortsword, and glanced around self-consciously. All eyes were focused on the horrors tearing across the field toward them.

"Steady," Coira said. "Steady."

That horrible, evil cursing was loud in his ears now. Emiel gripped his shortsword in both hands, then his right hand. His palms were so sweaty he feared it might slip from his grasp.

A hand grabbed him on the shoulder and he nearly jumped out of his skin.

"Best be a little farther from the action, son." It was the old soldier, Erik. His eyes were hard, but not unkind. He turned Emiel in the direction Amoura had gone. Emiel looked back at the weathered old soldier, and Erik gave him that signature curt nod.

And as if thinking of the mercenary brought him about, Bone moved up behind him. "This way, spicetrader," he said. "If we're sticking this out till the end, we're at least staying to the side and at the back. Unfortunately for me I have to keep you alive through all of this."

"Thanks."

"It's not a favor."

"That wasn't a real thanks."

Bone blinked at him, then laughed, slapping him across the back and shoving him along. "I might just start to like you, old man."

Emiel ground his teeth. Did this boy not know that Emiel wasn't even twice his age?

They made it to the right side of the formation just as the monsters reached the front line. Cursing and growling, the four-armed creatures crashed into the pikemen.

To their credit, the soldiers held formation as long as possible until the unrelenting monsters -almost twice their height- swept them aside and barreled through, chopping and stabbing, kicking and swinging, fussing and cursing.

A row of pikemen went down just as the swordsmen maneuvered around to the rear. Emiel watched the horrible scene unfold as over two dozen soldiers were cut down in less than a minute, while not one of the monsters had yet been killed. Where was Amoura and why hadn't she entered the fight? Surely she saw what was going on.

A soldier ran his pike into the hip of one of the monsters, and it stumbled sideways and into the pike of another. They held it in place while a swordsman circled around behind it and ran his sword through its back. It struggled and thrashed until finally it fell to the ground and began to crumble. One monster dead, and the cost was over twenty dead soldiers.

Emiel held his shortsword in a white-knuckled grip, entranced by the carnage. The pikemen managed to hold the monsters back just long enough for their comrades to retreat out of reach and form up ranks. When the pikemen finally broke away, the things came on, turning circles as they hacked at the smaller humans.

Emiel nearly lost his meal when he saw a soldier's head taken clean from his body. The monster continued its circuit, taking another soldier across the chest and disemboweling a third.

It didn't take a seasoned warrior to see that the battle was turning ugly. The infernal monsters continued their assault, swiping with swords and turning their bodies to take down multiple targets, spinning circles as they swept their large weapons created from the same lava rock in which their bodies were made.

Captain Coira shouted a command, and the soldiers surrounded the monsters, pikemen in front and swordsman at their backs. The strategy was effective and they managed to bring down two more of the creatures, but the sheer size, speed, and reckless power of the things was overwhelming.

Emiel saw a swordsman parry a horizontal chop by one monster's lower arm, but the thing continued the motion, spinning its body and coming back around with a club that connected with the soldier's head. He was knocked off his feet where he was impaled midair by the sword of another lava rock creature that simultaneously buried its axe into another soldier's shoulder.

Two pikemen impaled another monster from both sides while a third leapt onto its back and drove his sword through its neck. It dropped to its knees and crumbled as it fell over.

The remaining monsters continued their tireless spinning flurries. One delivered a backhanded hack of its axe at a soldier in front of it while turning a circuit and slashing its sword at another, then continued its spin, clubbing a soldier on the shoulder, then coming around again and impaling the first soldier with its jagged rocky sword.

Emiel lost track of time as he watched the chaos. The army of one hundred had managed to bring the underworld monsters down to three, and one was nearly finished as three pikemen drove their weapons into its abdomen and forced it onto its back.

Bone grabbed Emiel's arm. "Time to move to the side," he said. "I think this is about done ..." he trailed off when the ground shook. "What ... was that?"

"How would I know?" Emiel replied. "Amoura said something else might—"

An explosion halfway across the field drowned him out. Rocky debris rained down on the army and monsters. The four-armed creatures paid it no heed, and continued their assault. To their credit, Coira's force held their position and remained focused on the immediate threat while she and her lieutenant surveyed the field.

Emiel heard her shouting orders but she was drowned out by the noise of the battle and the cursing monsters. Emiel and Bone looked down at the ground vibrating under their feet, then at each other. He saw the look of concern on the young mercenary's face that matched what he was feeling. Bone looked past him, then cursed and shoved him aside just in time to bring his sword up to parry the horizontal swipe of a rocky sword.

The heavy blow sent him into a sideways roll, but the mercenary came up to one knee and stabbed out with his left hand, driving his sword into the four-armed monster's midsection. He pulled the sword free and rolled between its legs just as it brought its club down. The weapon left an indent in the ground where Bone had just been, but he was now behind the monster, and drove his sword into its lower back.

Emiel backed away, and the ground vibrated again, in a series of heavy 'thuds'. He looked out in the direction of the explosion on the field and saw two extremely large monsters bearing down on the army.

They looked like upside down nautilus shells with long, spear-like appendages digging into the ground as it moved across the field. They were huge, dwarfing the four-armed monsters many times over.

Emiel looked from this new horror, to Bone, still engaged with the cursing and fussing monster that was moving no slower despite its many injuries.

Seven more four-armed monsters broke through the ground and charged in front of the new threat, bearing down on the Carlayn army. Coira shouted a command, and flags rose on either sides of her. The roaring of at least a hundred soldiers on either side of the city gates converged onto the battlefield from the trees.

Bolstered by their newly arrived comrades, Coira's force redoubled their efforts while the new force came at the two giant things that Emiel could only think of as huge mollusks.

The new force tried to engage the shelled monsters, but they were simply tossed aside by the rampaging things. Seven soldiers were knocked into the air by the sweep of one of those long appendages, and one man was trampled over as it continued forward.

The wind howled, and soon Emiel was squinting. He saw Bone parry a thrust, but the lower arm holding the club pounded him in the side and knocked him away. Emiel circled around behind the monster as it bore down on Bone, and leapt onto its back as it reared to spear the mercenary.

It spun in circles as it reached over its shoulder to grab at him, but Emiel held on tight to his sword, which was buried in the center of its back. That cursing and fussing was entirely too close for his comfort, but he resisted the urge to let go of his weapon and run away.

The decision was made for him when the monster lurched forward, then spun again, dislodging the sword, and Emiel with it. He hit the ground in a roll, and stopped beside a dead soldier. He rolled onto his side and coughed up a mouthful of dirt. He felt the ground vibrate as the monster stomped toward him.

It raised its club, and Emiel knew it would crush him before he could stand. He tucked his feet under him and dove to the side as the stroke fell. He felt the heavy impact on the ground, but kept rolling. His instincts saved his life, for a rocky sword stabbed the ground where he had been only an instant earlier.

Emiel tried to keep moving, tried to get back on his feet, but he was still shaken from the fall. He stumbled and fell back, and could only watch as the monster drew its sword back to run him through.

Its back arched and it yelled some kind of curse, rounding on the mercenary who had stabbed it from behind. Emiel forced himself to his feet as the monster engaged Bone again. Emiel stumbled forward and stabbed it in the back of the leg. It lurched sideways, and Bone clenched his teeth as he brought his sword down in a two-handed chop, severing the monster's sword hand.

Emiel yanked at his sword and pulled it free on the second try, then drove it again into the monster's back. It cursed and half turned with a backhanded swing of its thick rocky arm.

Emiel instinctively brought his right arm up to block the blow. He felt the mistake in the form of the butt of his hand smacking him in the side of the face. Stars dotted his vision, and somehow he was on the ground again. He shook his head, which made it worse. He started to reach for his fallen sword but winced at the pain in his right arm.

He looked over his shoulder to see Bone finishing the monster off. Somehow they were farther away from the main fighting.

Once it was no more than crumbling rock, the mercenary scanned their surroundings and sheathed his sword. He walked over to squat next to Emiel, who sat cradling his arm.

"Let me see." As soon as he lifted Emiel's arm, a sharp pain shot through it, and he reflexively snatched it away.

"Your arm'll swell something mighty, and it'll hurt for a while, but it's just really badly bruised. No break."

"You sure?" Emiel said. He kept his arm close to his body as he climbed to his feet.

"If it was broken you wouldn't have been able to pull it away like that," came the reply. The mercenary's red hair whipped about his head as the wind grew more violent.

"Where did this come from?" Emiel shouted over the howling winds. "Feels like we're in the middle of a hurricane."

"How would I know?" Bone yelled back. "Come on. Let's find some higher ground."

They started uphill toward the trees until they had a vantage point to the side and above the battlefield.

All but two of the four-armed monsters were destroyed, but those giant shelled things were mostly unhurt. The violent winds slowed them considerably, and the more Emiel paid attention, it seemed the weather was largely focused on only them.

Amoura.

As soon as the woman's name came to Emiel's mind, the wind increased again, and then thousands of shards of ice descended from the hills farther up from their position. The shards flew downward, then curved just before they came to the ground and flew upward and underneath the protective shells.

The mollusk-like monsters let out a deafening shriek as the razor sharp ice found their softer flesh underneath. Both creatures shrank away, but the assault only intensified. Then the ground rippled in front of them so violently that the monsters fell backward.

The rippling earth scattered some of the nearby soldiers, but they were unharmed. The giant mollusk monsters rolled onto their sides, where their long forelimbs waved in the air in a futile attempt to right themselves. From that angle, Emiel saw that they had rear legs that were less than half the length of their forelimbs.

The soldiers fell upon them immediately, stabbing and chopping. The monsters were practically helpless on their sides and once the more dangerous limbs were severed, the soldiers attacked the area where their heads must be. Soon, both giant creatures lay dead upon the ground.

Emiel looked further back afield to see the last two four-armed monsters being brought down, one still fighting, the other on its knees, crumbling.

An echo of infernal cursing sounded behind them, and Emiel and Bone turned to see two four-armed monsters charging up the hill toward them.

"Where did they come from?" Emiel yelled.

"Time to get moving," Bone said. "Up we go!"

Emiel ran after the mercenary, but his legs were quickly starting to burn from the uphill climb.

Amoura was still gazing down the hill where the battle was finally ended, but the sounds of cursing and fussing drew her attention. "More?" she said, looking past Emiel and Bone.

The magus's ring flared, and she sent another wave of ice spears into the closest monster. It stumbled but pressed on. Amoura pointed toward the woods. "Keep moving!"

"We need to circle around back to the city," Bone said.

Emiel saw two more of the things hacking at the foliage farther to the side. They were drawing closer. "We can't." He pointed.

Bone swore an oath. "Straight on, then."

They pressed on up the ever-inclining terrain. The once sparse woods grew thick with oak and maple trees, dense with green shrubs —some with thorns and burrs that induced misery—pine, and towering redwoods.

Amoura hopped onto a fallen oak and turned to send a blast of freezing air at the closest monster. The air slowed it, and it's steaming rocky skin cracked and fell away. One of its comrades came from behind and stomped right over it, blasting it to pieces.

"Watch out!" Emiel shouted at Bone.

The mercenary ducked just as another monster burst out of the foliage and took a swipe at his head. He rolled and came to one knee while spinning with a horizontal chop of his sword. The sword cleaved right through the rocky leg, and the thing toppled over. Bone was on his feet and running as it flailed.

Emiel heard what sounded like rock being crunched apart and figured the injured monster had been trampled by one of its own. Such loyalty.

His legs felt like hundred pound logs, but he pressed on. "I don't know ... how much longer I can ... keep up."

"There's a drop off!" Bone yelled.

"Keep going!" Amoura replied.

Emiel finally caught up and saw the cliff. "How far is that drop?"

"How hard is the stroke of one of those things?" came the magus's response.

They ran on, and Emiel didn't know which would collapse first, his lungs or his legs.

The two remaining monsters were closing in, he could hear their cursing closer from behind. He forced himself to ignore his protesting legs, lowered his head, and kept going.

Behind him, one of the things gave a shout that sounded like it came from above. Emiel spared a quick glance, just in time to see the thing falling toward him. He tried to dive out of the way but his tired legs only gave him a sideways stumble. It was barely enough, and the monster crashed into the ground beside him and sent him rolling.

Emiel heard Amoura and Bone shouting something, but it was drowned out by the pain that exploded in his right arm, the dirt and leaves in his face and ears, and the cursing that was somewhere nearby.

Emiel felt a kick to his side that sent him into a faster and more painful roll. He clenched his teeth shut to keep from biting his tongue in half. Blinded by the debris in his eyes, Emiel could only hope that his downward roll would put more distance between himself and the pursuing monster.

He rolled and bounced over the declining terrain and then the shouting, along with the ground, fell away.

EMIEL AWOKE to spasms and he coughed up what felt like every ounce of water in his body. Beside him, Bone sat leaning back on his hands.

"You're not getting out of this, spicetrader," the mercenary said. "Not even by drowning."

Emiel coughed again and gasped, once the cold of the water settled in. He caught a fleeting look of concern on Amoura's face, but it was gone in a flash. "I guess ..." he coughed up a bit more water, took a deep breath, then coughed some more. "I guess those things ... are dead," he wheezed.

"Ya," Bone replied. "Bathing doesn't agree with them. Practically broke apart into a steaming mess as soon as they hit the water."

Emiel felt a sudden rush of warm air, and he looked up to see the magus focusing on them. The combination of her dark billowing robes and her glowing ring and eyes was fearsome.

She had them dry in short order, and for a time Emiel lay on his back and stared at the sky. His body ached in a dozen places, and he could practically feel his pulse in his throbbing arm.

Amoura approached and lowered herself beside him. "I can help your arm."

"That would be welcome," Emiel said through clenched teeth.

She sat cross-legged beside him and lay a hand on his arm. Coolness crept into it and steadily grew colder. In a few heartbeats his arm was numb, but the swelling began to diminish.

"There's no need to elevate your hand. The blood will flow properly." She stood. "It should be fine by tomorrow."

Emiel carefully bent and stretched his arm. Only a fraction of the pain remained. "Thanks. That could come in handy, you know?"

"A break would take longer to heal," Amoura said. Her face softened for just a moment before she turned away. "A bruise, even that bad, is easier to deal with."

Even though it came and went in the blink of an eye, Emiel found that he liked that look on her. Quite a bit. "So how far to Altarra?" he asked.

"On foot?" Bone replied. "Depends. If we take the roundabout way, it'll be another week or week and a half."

"Isn't there a village or farm somewhere between us and Altarra that could sell us horses?" Emiel asked.

"On the roundabout route, yes."

Emiel had a feeling he didn't want to ask about the alternate path, but he did anyway. "How long for the more straightforward route?"

"About half to a full week. And time's still moving." He looked up at the sky. "And so's our daylight. Let's get out of here."

Emiel stared at the cliff, some sixty or seventy feet above. There was no going back to Carlayn without tacking on who knew how many days to their trek. Not that he would have minded, but he needed this done as much as the other two. Nandi and Amiya needed him.

They started out again, and the terrain changed several times from grassy fields to woods, then finally to rolling hills with outcroppings and hardy shrubs. They passed through another patch of woods filled with tall redwoods, oaks, and pines. The trees stretched so high that when Emiel looked up, it seemed as though they bent toward the middle of his vision. The rhythmic thumping of a tree-hammer bird pecking on the side of an oak brought a smile to his face. Amiya loved birds. She would likely have squealed in excitement at the sight of the green white-speckled bird. It tilted its orange head and looked down at him, then returned to its work.

"Do I even want to ask why we're considering the roundabout route?" Emiel asked some time later.

"Not really," came the reply, and Bone pointed ahead just as they cleared the last of the trees.

The terrain ended in a steep decline that looked to be forty or fifty feet down where more forestry awaited. They stopped and looked over the vast green carpet of trees that spread below in every direction.

In the direction Bone pointed, Emiel saw small mountains that lay between three enormous rock formations; like sentry towers guarding the land from any would-be intruders. It was both beautiful and ominous, and Emiel had no desire to go that way. But when he looked off to the left or right, he saw nothing but forest.

"We must," Amoura said. "We don't have enough resources to survive the long route."

"What about the farms or villages?" Emiel asked, hoping for a positive answer.

"It has been years since last I travelled these lands. They could be there or not. The land is wild, and it's not unheard of for people to relocate a small dwelling."

Emiel looked at the triple peaks again. He didn't want to go in there. "We don't have any of our provisions, so we can't survive that way either."

The magus shook her head. "There will be plenty of hunting, and there are three rivers and a waterfall to sustain us on our way through."

Emiel did his best to ignore a sinking feeling, and took one last gaze at the imposing rock towers looming over the small mountains between them. "Doom no matter which option."

"No path is certain," Amoura said, starting toward the cliff. Her next words sent a chill through Emiel's body. "But our only viable option is to brave The Triplets."

24

NANDI

Days became a week, a week became two, and for Nandi and Amiya, most of that time was spent under the tutelage of Selvetar. The magus had taken to visiting them frequently of late. In some cases he had come to them one day after the other, taking the girls out of their lonely room for a day of instruction out in the practice yards, and then leaving them with books to study on the *essences*.

Nandi was studying a book that detailed the various attributes of each of the four essences. The information was not as predictable as she would have thought. *Fire*, for instance, was not wholly controlled by aggression, as she'd guessed, but more through calmness and direct purpose. *Water*, on the other hand, was controlled through nonaggressive diversion. *Earth* required strength of will to bring it forth, while *air* required the user to possess a cunning necessary to manipulate it.

As she read through the book, she found herself agreeing and disagreeing with the information therein. During their time under Selvetar's instruction, she'd found that everything the book and the magus taught was true, but not absolutely so. She'd found that if she surrendered control and sought to find the *essences* and draw them to her call, she was more effective.

She looked up from her book at her twin sister, who sat studying a book on combining. Amiya had made much faster progress than Nandi had, and so Selvetar sometimes granted more of his attention to her. At first, Nandi had been jealous, but then she'd realized that the less the magus focused on her, the more she could practice her own way. She didn't know why, but her instincts told her to hide what she felt was her own personal relationship with the *essences*.

"What're you looking at?" Amiya asked.

Nandi blinked. "Oh, nothing. Just thinking."

"Staring at me with that vacant look helps you to think?"

"I don't have a vacant look," Nandi snapped.

Amiya giggled. "Sure." She went back to her book.

"What do you think he's got planned for us?" Nandi asked.

Amiya looked back up from her book. "Dunno. I have to admit I'm a little curious. He's teaching us all this knowing we want to get out of this nice comfy prison cell we're locked in."

"I wonder how he would respond if we just asked him," Nandi said, and Amiya looked at her as if she lost her wits. "What could he do to us, Amiya? He can't take away what we've learned, and he can't take away our abilities."

"I wouldn't be so sure," Amiya said, her tone growing dark. "Something about that man makes me think there's not a lot he can't do."

"There are some things nobody can do. Taking away our ability to touch the *essences* would be like him taking away our ability to breathe."

"That can be done," Amiya replied.

"Only if he was to block off our air," Nandi countered. "He could stop us from breathing, but not our body's innate ability to breathe."

"Okay, fine. He can't take away our ability to delve. Still, I don't know why you would ask him anything. Why make him suspicious?"

"The man is probably one of the smartest people in the city, Amiya." Nandi looked at the door to their cell as if it held the answers. "He knows we want out of here and he knows we want to find Dad. Everything he's giving us is only helping us get a step closer to getting out of here."

Amiya sighed. "I don't know what to think, Nandi. But I'm sure you'll worry over it enough for both of us."

Nandi responded with a smirk, and returned to her book. She would indeed worry over the situation until she had it figured out. Perhaps the magus was sympathetic to their situation. Maybe he was consciously providing them with the tools they needed to escape the prime minister's mansion and find Dad.

As much as Nandi wanted to believe that idea, it didn't ring true. Nothing about Selvetar spoke of trustworthiness. The man was helping them for a reason, and benevolence wasn't it.

She closed the book. The information was useful, but it didn't speak to her sensibilities.

"Any progress?" Amiya asked, not looking up.

"Some. The methods in here don't work as well for me as for you, but I'm making my own progress."

"You mean you're able to hide your progress through our new teacher's interest in me," Amiya said.

Nandi smirked again. As always, she didn't have to say what she was thinking. "Just keep up the star student act. It helps a lot."

"Who said it's an act?" Amiya responded in mock indignation. "I'm just better than you."

"Sure." Nandi stood and stretched her hands over her head and arched her back. She felt heat tingling from her fingertips as warm air swirled around her body, like a warm insubstantial blanket.

"I wish I knew how you do that so easily," Amiya said.

"I wish I could tell you," Nandi replied. "Just like how you can summon an *essence* to you so quickly and with such force."

"I just do it," Amiya said. "I can't explain it."

"Same here," Nandi said.

"I've been thinking about something." Amiya closed the book and leaned back on her hands. "Even if we were to get out of here, where would we go and how would we get there? We'd have a rough time getting out of Vyne once the guard is out looking for us. And even if we made it out, how would we outrun the men Decius would surely send after us?"

"I've been thinking about that, too," Nandi replied. "And even if through some Creator blessed luck we get away from Decius's men and find out where Dad has gone, how far would we make it out there? We're two girls and there's all sorts of predators and monsters roaming."

"Yeah," Amiya agreed. "Predators and monsters of the animal and human sort. And I don't know how confident I am with all this *essence* stuff to rely on it yet."

"We'd be slaughtered in short order, Amiya." Nandi sighed. "Just take a second to think about it. We can summon the power now, but if some monster was charging you, do you think you could do it on the spot when you're about to die?"

Amiya frowned. "I think I could."

Nandi gave her a doubtful look but said nothing. Then a thought came to her. "Hey. You remember that man who was being escorted by the city guards and a group of monks?"

"You mentioned him, but I didn't see him."

"I felt something from him," Nandi said. "It felt like he had some kind of power about him."

"Power?" Amiya replied. "You mean like us?"

"I think so. It was different from Selvetar. His power I can only feel through his *essence* ring. That other man, I felt it from him even from that distance."

"What does it matter?" Amiya asked, her tone growing impatient.

"I'm sure he was being taken to the jails."

"Maybe because he committed some crime?"

"Just like Dad did?" Nandi countered.

"I think your reaching kind of far with this. And what are you getting at, anyway?"

Nandi took a deep breath and blew it out, then sat down in front of her twin. "Maybe we can find a way to help him, and he could help us."

"Being locked in this room has finally cracked your mind, Nandi."

Amiya stood and moved toward the far wall. "We don't know who this man is or what he did to be arrested by the city guard."

With a frustrated growl Nandi followed. "I think he was one of those people the king is fighting. Those people they call the wilders."

Amiya rolled her eyes. "That makes freeing him a *much* more attractive option."

"Don't you remember what Dad says about them?" Nandi replied. "He always talks about how he's traded with them on occasion and that they're good people."

"What does that have to do with this man you saw?" Amiya asked. "There are good and bad people everywhere, Nandi."

"I saw sadness in his eyes."

Her sister snorted. "Sadness because he was caught doing whatever it was he was doing."

"Think about the books we've been reading," Nandi said. "The first books Selvetar gave us talked about how dangerous and unpredictable the *essences* are, and that they can only truly be controlled by use of properly tempered corlite."

"I remember reading that," Amiya said. "But I don't remember reading anything that has to do with why we should go looking for a man who managed to do something to get himself arrested."

Nandi took a deep breath and renewed her patience. "The Order of Magi think that wielding the *essences* without proper training and the use of corlite is dangerous. "They condemn any practice of it outside their order."

"So, what?" Amiya turned back to her. "You think they arrested him because he can wield *essence* without a ring?"

"Yes," Nandi replied. "That's what I think."

Amiya bit her bottom lip. "Okay, still. What does this have to do with us? Let's have it; you're running my patience out."

Nandi sighed. "That man was not evil, or devious, Amiya. I can't explain it, but I feel it. What he can do is delve the *essences* without the need of corlite. And I think that's why they arrested him."

"They can't arrest him just for that?" Amiya said.

"I'm sure they found an excuse," Nandi replied. "He was probably caught delving. Or maybe they made up some other reason. Either way, I think he's in trouble for just that."

Amiya shrugged. "And?"

"And we can do the same thing he can." Nandi hurried along, seeing her sister's patience almost depleted. "If they cooked up some reason to put him in jail, what do you think they would do to us if they found out we can do the same?"

Amiya's expression darkened. "Unless they've already found out."

Nandi felt a chill go through her body. "How could they know that? We didn't even know until recently."

"Just because we didn't know doesn't mean it wasn't a fact that we could delve, Nandi. Maybe someone saw us playing our rock games and told Selvetar or one of the other magi that live in the temple. Maybe one of them could feel it in us like you felt it in that man you saw."

Nandi hadn't thought of that. If that was true, it would make sense of everything that had happened. Them waiting to kidnap her and Amiya until Dad was away, then sending him to some distant place. The visits and subsequent teachings from Selvetar. It all fit. "But why would he train us if they think we're wilders?"

"Don't be so slow," Amiya said. "They can't imprison two young girls because we have the 'ability' to delve. That wouldn't look good. But if they could, maybe, train us ..."

Nandi closed her eyes. "Then they could make us one of them."

"You really think that's what he's doing?" Amiya asked. "Do you think Selvetar is behind all that's happened to us?"

"I can't think of a better reason," Nandi replied.

"So, we place rescuing some stranger on the list with getting out of here," Amiya said in a flat tone.

"I think our chances are better with help," Nandi replied.

"Sounds great," Amiya said. "All we have to do is break out of here, find out where they're keeping this man, break *him* free, then leave. Of course, that's hoping he'll actually help us instead of doing something awful to us or just running off."

"I don't think he'll do either," Nandi said. She couldn't explain why, she just knew it.

Amiya shook her head. "Whatever we're gonna do, we better think of something fast—"

An explosion shook the ground and threw the twins from their feet. Several seconds later, the wall and door to the room exploded.

25
_____

JOGA

In the midst of a restless sleep, Joga awoke in panic to a violent earthquake. His crusted eyes popped open and he looked around the dark cell, seeing nothing out of the ordinary. He remembered his last encounter with the large man that called himself archminister, and hoped it wasn't another visit. That one enjoyed causing other people pain.

He heard scuffling and shouting farther down the corridor, and focused on the voices outside his cell. Something about an attack.

Joga squinted his eyes shut and reached for the *essences*. He strained until a trickle of sweat ran down his temple, but nothing came. He tried again and again, but found only a flicker. It might as well have been nothing.

Joga sighed. He needed the earth beneath his feet; dirt and water, and air. Fresh, clean air. The ground shook again, and Joga climbed to his feet and ran to the door of his cell. His ribs were tender, but fortunately Marailanders weren't particularly strong. He pounded on the door until a guard came.

"What is it, wilder? I don't have time for—"

"What happens?" Joga cut him off.

"We're under attack," the guard replied. "More of them things like the one you brought here."

"Did not bring it," Joga said. "Was chased—"

"I don't care. We've never seen anything like them things till you come running into our city."

The guard ran off, leaving Joga alone again. He looked to the cells to his left and right. There weren't any other prisoners for him to speak with, though he didn't know what he would talk about if there were.

With a growl, he kicked the cell door. If he didn't get out of soon, he would die in here. Whether it be at the end of the rocky blade of one of those monsters, or swinging from a gallows, this Marailander city would be the death of him if he didn't escape. And he had to, if not for himself, then for his people.

The ground shook again, and this time he heard shouts and cries of pain and death. Then he heard an infernal voice that made his blood curdle. It growled and cursed in a language he didn't understand. A language that was evil to his ears.

Joga retreated from the barred door. That thing sounded close.

Ringing steel, shouting, and death filled the air and Joga licked his lips, looking around at his bare cell for something to use as a weapon. Of course, there was nothing.

A guard suddenly crashed into the door with such force, it flew off the hinges. The man tumbled head over heels and skidded to a stop.

Joga ran to the man and knelt beside him, looking into his vacant eyes. He uttered a quick prayer and stood. A few feet away was the soldier's discarded sword. Joga grabbed it just as a large four-armed monster appeared in the broken doorway.

Joga's heart pounded as he strained to touch the *essences*. Nothing. The monster stooped and began to struggle through the too small opening. Seeing his chance, Joga sprinted across the room and drove his sword into its chest.

He pulled away and ducked when the monster spat an infernal curse and swung the club in one of its lower hands at him. The swing was clumsy and inhibited, and Joga waded back in, this time driving the sword into its neck before it could react again.

It shuddered and dropped to its knees, and Joga yanked the sword free and drove the blade into its head. The monster slumped where it was, trapped in the portal and crumbled into a pile of steaming rocks.

Careful not to step on the steaming remains, Joga leaned forward and peeked out. The corridor was lined with twisted bodies lying in pools of blood that mixed together on the cold stone floor.

Joga uttered another prayer. It was a shame that men might meet their final moments surrounded by cold hard stone without the light of Father *Alyu* to light their way to the True Life.

He stepped over the blood, respectful not to touch the bodies. The ground shook again and he leaned against the wall to steady himself. What was causing these tremors?

When the shaking subsided, he raced through the corridors, doing his best to ignore the cold cruel stone closing in on him as he searched for the way to open air. He climbed a spiraling staircase and came to more open halls. He skidded to a stop at the sight of a dozen guards battling three hulking monsters, and the fight was not going well. Joga started to reach for the *essences* again when a bolt of electricity struck one of the monsters. The attack did little damage, but it knocked the four-armed creature off balance and the soldiers fell upon it.

Joga stayed to the side of the open hall. He didn't know if the wielder of that power could sense his ability or not. A man in white robes emerged from a doorway at the far end of the hall. He descended the steps, hand held out before him. Joga saw his ring flair with blue light. The light quickly changed to silver, and a spear of ice formed in the air and flew across the hall.

The force of the racing spear knocked the targeted monster into a tumble across the stone floor. It came to its feet far easier than Joga would have imagined for such hulking beast, however. The monster recovered in a rage of spitting curses, and launched its axe in an overhand throw at the offending human.

To too slow to react, the monk's eyes widened as the spinning weapon buried into his chest and knocked him through the door. Joga felt a pang of guilt at not helping to fight off these monsters, but that would only land him back in another cell to continue his wait for the hangman's noose.

Another monk stepped into the room and launched a ball of fire at the monster. A foolish choice that was likely made in panic. The monster practically stopped fighting to soak in the flames. Then, to all their surprise, it actually grew.

Now double in size, the monster spun a circle as it swung its weapons. The lucky soldiers who were dealt only glancing blows slid into the hard surfaces and lay groaning on the floor with broken bones. Their comrades who'd taken the brunt of those heavy blows, flew overhead into the stone walls and columns, and crumbled to the floor in a lifeless heap.

Two more monks appeared in the doorway the last monk fell through, and assaulted the creature with *air* and *water* just as Joga made his way to the broken doors. He took one last glance over his shoulder to ensure there was no pursuit. The monster struggled under the attack, and looked to be diminishing in size.

Joga ran out of the open hall and down the front steps of the temple into pure chaos. Four-armed monsters cleaved through stone and wood and bone. The city guard had formed ranks and fought valiantly, but for every one of those things they destroyed, several men died.

Despite the horror surrounding him, the Khatala warrior couldn't help but breathe deeply of the brisk fresh air. Air tainted with the coppery smell of blood and the heaviness of death.

Joga moved away from the temple and crouched beside a building to get his bearings. He hadn't come through the front gates so he had no reference points to guide him out.

The ground shook again. What was causing that? Joga looked around, but saw only scattered fighting along the streets. Men and women ran holding children in their arms or pulling them along. The screams and shouts were disorienting. Didn't the citizens know how to form up ranks to bolster their warriors? Even a Khatala tribesman or woman of low skill could be effective enough to give an edge to their warriors.

He moved along the streets where there was no fighting, hoping to come upon a wall to scale or a fence to climb. His efforts were in vain. He needed a higher vantage point.

Joga came to an abandoned blacksmith's shop with wares scattered about the floor where weapons had been snatched up in a hurry. He found a set of battle-axes lying on a table amidst a pile of discarded weaponry. He said private words of apology for the dishonor of the theft but there was no choice. He went into the shop and found the proper torso straps, then returned and strapped the axes over his shoulders. Unlike how he'd seen Marailanders wear the weapons crisscrossed over the back, the Khatala wore them on each side of the back with the handles facing vertical over the shoulders for easy reach.

Thus armed, he climbed onto the display table and jumped, to grab hold of the side of the roof. He pulled himself up and swung his arm over, then a leg, and hoisted himself over the side.

Once he'd regained his feet, Joga looked around. The city was in a state of mayhem. Lava rock monsters cut down panicked civilians that ran too near, and soldiers fought and died to protect them. Four soldiers managed to bring another of the creatures down, but there were at least a dozen remaining that Joga could see.

"Mother *Illyu* bless me with your power." Joga reached for the *essences* and they came readily to his call. He delved deeper into the sweet power, swirling it around his body, filling himself with it. He hadn't realized how much his incarceration had drained him, but now he felt rejuvenated.

The most violent tremor yet shook the roof beneath his feet, and a twenty-foot building toppled over. A giant hooked appendage tore out of the ground, followed by a second. Antennae three times the length of a man twitched in the air, and a giant angular head appeared out of the massive sinkhole. The sudden tremor sent several soldiers and citizens screaming as they tumbled into the sinkhole.

Joga tried not to think about their fate as he gathered himself. He couldn't leave the city to this thing. Even if his actions resulted in capture again, or even death, he would go to the True Life, head held high and honor intact.

The monster climbed out of the ground, fully revealing its red, armor-plated body. It climbed out of the sinkhole on four legs with plate armor growing from the sides. On its back, the armor plates were like diamond-shaped disks that slid over each other, one layer over the other, as it moved.

It opened its angled mouth to let out a deafening shriek that brought Joga to his knees, hands clasped over his ears. When the sound subsided, he called to *air* and *water,* guided as much as he could bear, forming the largest spear of ice he had ever created, and sent it racing across the distance into the giant monster's plated head.

The spear staggered it, and Joga called *earth* and sent a wave of hard rock out of the hole from which the it had come. The hard earth punched the monster's side, keeping it off balance while a group of soldiers formed up ranks and attacked. Their halberds skipped off that plate armor with no effect, and archers let fly and watched as their arrows bouncing away like twigs.

Joga spotted three four-armed monsters closing in on the soldiers, and summoned *air* and *water*. He formed several spears of ice the size of a man's leg and sent the barrage into the monsters. For a relief, all dropped to the cobblestone street and crumbled.

The armored beast gave another deafening shriek, and swung one of the hooked appendages on its head at the foot soldiers. To their credit, they were able to move out of range, then come in to counterattack. Several men found tiny areas between the armor plates and buried their blades in the vulnerable flesh.

The monster shrieked again, this time in pain, and lifted one of its legs and slammed it to the ground. One unfortunate soldier was not fast enough and met a similar end when the exploding cobblestones flew from the impact.

Joga growled and delved again. He found *earth*, and molded it as he sent another barrage of ice spears at the monster. The spears were smaller and more numerous, several finding their marks through spaces between the plates, a few even stinging its eyes.

Joga was beginning to sweat from the exertion of concentrating on more than one thing at a time, but soon a fully formed spear of granite shot away and into the giant beast's head. The granite spear punched a dent into the armor-plated head, and the beast's legs buckled.

Joga delved *earth* once more, again drawing from the hole from where the monster had emerged. Rocks the size of a man pounded into the dented head, and the beast's movements began to slow.

The soldiers saw their opportunity and went in, running their halberds through the gaps in the armor again and through the soft flesh of its neck.

When he was sure the soldiers had the situation in hand, Joga continued his search from the rooftop until he spotted a wall not far away. It was over twelve feet high, but it was his closest way to freedom.

He raced across the rooftops, hearing shouts of recognition in his wake, and leapt from one rooftop to another. The wall and his freedom drew nearer, and when he was but a few rooftops away, he heard a woman scream.

Joga tried to block it out. If he didn't escape soon, he would be tracked down and imprisoned or killed. Just the thought of those looming walls in that cramped cell was enough to speed his steps further.

He heard the scream again, followed by a man crying out in injury. Joga growled a curse and skidded to a stop. After a few frantic heartbeats of looking, he found the source of the distress. A woman was pressed against the wall of a house with two small children behind her. A man stood between her and one of the four-armed lava rock monsters. One of his arms hung limp, while he had a halberd tucked under the other.

The monster swung its sword and the man ducked under the reckless attack, then stepped in and drove the blade into its abdomen.

The man yelled in triumph and pushed harder, driving the weapon in deeper.

Joga saw the mistake, but was too far away yet to help. The monster snapped the shaft of the weapon with one of its lower hands, and delivered a backhanded blow with the other.

There was a loud snap, and the man flew sideways into the wall of a nearby house where he tumbled to the ground, unmoving.

Joga drew his stolen axes and positioned himself in line with the monster's back as it closed in on the sobbing woman. He took a few steps back, then ran and leapt from the roof. At the same time as the jump, he drew his axes back over his head. With a roar to Creator *Amyadali*, he brought the blades down and buried them in the creature's rocky back.

The spitting and cursing monster stumbled forward and the woman and two children scurried away as it fell through the wall of the house. Joga rode it to the ground, and as it started to rise, he yanked an axe free and swung it down, burying it in the monster's back while using the momentum to yank the other weapon free.

He continued the barrage of one-two strikes, pounding the monster in the back and sending chunks of lava rock flying away. Aware of the warmth slowly creeping through his shoes, he struck faster and harder. With each blow, the monster struggled a bit less and a bit slower, until finally it fell flat.

Joga was quick to hop off the beast, lest his feet burn. He dropped his axes and fell to his hands and knees, panting. After finally catching his breath, Joga replaced the axes on his back and stumbled out of the ruined wall.

The woman and her two daughters were crouched over the man, who had apparently survived, but lay on the ground, teeth clinched in a grimace.

Joga crept a little closer, and saw the source of the man's pain. A broken collarbone. They looked over the mother's shoulder at Joga, and he saw hesitation there.

She offered a nervous smile and gave a nod of her head, then returned her attention to the man that must have been her husband.

The two girls simply stared at Joga until he disappeared around the corner.

He found the city wall and moved farther down till he was sure there was no one around, then delved for *air*.

"Stay where you are," a voice said. Joga half turned and looked up to see an archer on the roof behind him, arrow trained on his back. The archer lifted the bow level with Joga's head. "If you flinch, I'll put it through your skull.

"Helped to fight," Joga argued. "Helped to save lives."

"You think I'm stupid? Those things wouldn't be here if not for you."

Joga kept his voice calm. "Did not bring them. Why come alone and bring monsters?"

"That's a good question that I'm sure the first magus would like answered," the archer said.

Joga glanced up and down the street. The man was stalling till help arrived. "Not your enemy," he said, attempting to keep the archer occupied while he delved *air*. He didn't need to kill the man, just get him out of the way.

"I'm sure you're not," came the reply. "You just ..." he made a surprised sound and stumbled as if being pushed off balance.

Joga blinked. The archer was knocked off his feet by an unseen force and tumbled down the slanted roof. He hit the ground and screamed, then rolled onto his side and held his broken leg.

Joga froze. Someone had used *air* to trip the man up. The person also had a true connection to the *essences*; *harmony*. He could sense it from a little farther down the street.

He continued to guide *air* into a defensive swirl, angry at himself for not having thought of that when the archer had first challenged him. He turned back toward the wall when a young girl's voice called out.

"You're not even gonna thank us?"

26

SELVETAR

A meeting with the imbecilic archminister was enough to make anyone wish for the sweet relief of deafness. And so when the first tremor hit, it had come as a shock, but also a welcomed interruption from the large man's incessant and oftentimes repetitive rambling.

"What has happened?" Selvetar asked a monk who had come up beside him.

"We do not yet know, First Magus," the monk replied. "The ground shook, just before ten horrible monsters akin to the one that wilder brought into the city days ago crashed into the ground from the sky."

"Is the city guard so blind?"

The monk hesitated. "Our ... the guards have never had reason to look to the sky for threat of attack, First Magus."

How he hated that title. Of course, the monk was addressing him with the utmost respect, but to Selvetar, it was a constant reminder that he was subordinate to Magi Master Vladrick, a man he didn't particularly like. To the first magus, Vladrick was little different than that narrow-minded king, Alyn. The only thing that made the situation bearable was that Vladrick was at least more intelligent than Alyn.

"No threat has ever come from the sky, so there was no necessity to be mindful of it." Selvetar's expression was neutral, but the monk's responding swallow indicated he caught the tone. "Entire civilizations fall due to such complacency."

They exited the archminister's mansion to chaos. A dozen or more four-armed monsters with skin that looked to be made of lava rock stomped through the city, growling and cursing in a language the first magus didn't understand, but knew to be the infernal language of the underworld. The things swung their weapons all the while spitting that horrible tongue, striking down any who were too slow to get away.

The ground shook again—this time more violently—and an explosion rocked the mansion and sent dust and debris clouding through the main hall. Selvetar and the monk turned toward the commotion, but the threat wasn't yet apparent.

Selvetar pointed at the dust flowing from the main hall. "Deal with that. And see to it that the city watch guards are at the front line to defend against these creatures."

"Yes, First Magus," the monk said in a shaky voice.

Selvetar looked back over his shoulder. The explosion had come from the direction where the spicetrader's twin daughters were being held. The girls were likely in danger, but the resident monks and the guards would have to see to them. What was at work here? Those four-armed creatures were most certainly from the underworld, which meant something had happened to awaken too much evil in the world at once.

He stepped out into the chaos. Spears and arrows flew through the air, snapping against the hard stony bodies of the cursing monsters. One of the creatures cut down three guards at once. It simply spun a circuit and cleaved it's rocky sword through the armor of the soldiers as though it were simple dining garments. It completed its turn to face the first magus, and charged him.

Selvetar continued on his path, only breaking his stride long enough to duck under the swipe of a rocky sword. He avoided the swinging club of its lower arm while summoning *air* and *water* from his ring.

He didn't need to block the arm—which was quite impossible—but instead released the two *essences* into it. The monster's arm slowed as it froze from the inside out.

The first magus then summoned *earth* to strengthen his blow, and struck the monster's arm with a backhanded slap that shattered it.

The creature stumbled back, and Selvetar struck again with a barrage of icy spears into its body. He continued on his way as the ten-foot tall monster fell to its knees and crumbled.

27

____

AMIYA

Pandemonium was the only word to describe what Amiya and Nandi had gone into. The soldier guarding their door had been thrown into the room along with all the debris from the destroyed wall. Nandi had been shaken by the sight of the dead man, but they hadn't time for that. Amiya had grabbed her sister's arm and together they made a run for it.

Now, skulking along the walls, they saw men battling terrifying monsters with four arms, each holding a weapon, and growling in some foul language she couldn't understand. She could feel her sister behind her, filled with the *essences* nearly to bursting. Amiya herself had begun to delve for the power, but couldn't hold nearly as much. She needed a ring.

"That way!" Nandi whispered, pointing toward a break in the wall that led to another hallway.

"You know where that leads?" Amiya whispered back.

"Have you looked ahead?" came the reply.

Amiya looked further down the hall just in time to see the body of a soldier fly through a doorway to crash into the opposite wall. The man crumpled to the floor atop another fallen guard. The screaming came from that direction as well, and they could feel the thud of heavy footsteps on the stone floor. Above the cacophony, they heard more of those strange voices that sounded as if they were arguing. A tremor went down Amiya's spine.

"That way," Amiya said, and they ducked through the broken wall into the adjacent hallway. Luckily there was no danger at the moment, and the girls crept along the wall as quietly as possible. The screams were nerve-wracking.

The ground shook again, and both girls crouched low until the tremor subsided. They waited for a moment, then started forward again. Due to Selvetar's many visits they were able to navigate the expansive mansion easily enough.

They skulked along the walls, stepping over the bodies of dead soldiers while trying not to look at them. Several times Amiya thought Nandi would heave up. For a relief, her twin held her stomach in check, as Amiya herself was on the verge of vomiting.

The ground vibrated from the thuds of more heavy footsteps. The girls froze and crouched even lower to the ground, fear gripping their chests. Amiya kept her eyes fixed on the hallway ahead. Maybe they should turn back?

She looked over her shoulder at the sound of more thudding footsteps behind them, and her eyes widened at the sight of a giant four-armed monster with red and black skin that looked like molten rock. It stepped through another hole in the long hallway and looked down the opposite direction.

Amiya saw the terror in Nandi's face as her sister looked past at what was probably another of those things further down the hall. They were trapped. She gritted her teeth, straining to find the *essences,* pleading for them to come to her call. Nothing happened. They were helpless. She looked at Nandi, whose face surely mirrored her own terror. Her sister gritted her teeth and closed her eyes, and Amiya did the same.

They heard the heavy footsteps grow closer from each end. Closer. Amiya fought to keep her body from shaking. She should look up at the things: look defiantly into their eyes as they killed her, but she could not. So deep in fear's grip was she that Amiya couldn't bring herself to open her eyes, let alone lift her face to look up at those horrible monsters.

The footsteps stopped right beside them, and they heard grunting sounds. Then, after many fluttering heartbeats, the thuds continued on, growing distant.

Once the thudding footsteps were far enough away, Amiya cracked open an eye, and released a breath she hadn't known she was holding. They were gone. How?

She opened her eyes to a strange sight. Everything around them was shrouded in a dark blue color. It was as if the world had gone blue with the arrival of dawn.

"Nandi!" she hissed, and her twin sister slowly opened her eyes. Those eyes widened as well when she looked around.

"What? What did they do to us? Are we dead and in some separate world?"

"I don't know," Amiya said. "But I don't think so. If we're dead, the blow came swift and hard, and we didn't feel ..." she trailed off when she saw Nandi's eyes, glowing silver.

"What is it?" Nandi asked in a shaky voice. She touched her face. "What are you looking at?"

"Your eyes," Amiya said. "They're glowing. They're glowing, and they're silver!"

"Silver?" Nandi repeated, near panic. "My eyes are brown. How could they be silver?"

As she asked the question, the blue tint to their surroundings faded away, and the world reverted to its normal color. They jumped when the sounds of battle and dying assaulted them again. Had that blue colored whatever-it-was actually dulled the sounds as well?

She looked back at Nandi and gasped. The silver glow in her eyes was fading.

"What now?" Nandi demanded. "Are you trying to make my heart stop or something?"

"That silver glow in your eyes is gone, Nandi. It's gone. I think it left when the blue color left."

"And those things didn't kill us." Nandi said, touching her face again. "But why?"

"I think you did it," Amiya said. "I think—"

The floor shook again and threw them off balance. "Forget it," Amiya said. "Let's get out of here first and talk about it later."

She grabbed her sister's wrist and pulled her along. She heard Nandi make an irritated sound, but holding her sister's wrist made Amiya feel safer.

A wall behind them exploded as another of those four-armed monsters crashed through. It whirled in their direction and charged in a fit of shouting and cursing.

"Run!" Nandi yelled.

"You thought I was gonna walk?" Amiya quipped as they sprinted down the hall.

They ran for their lives, feeling those heavy thuds growing closer. The thing was too big, its strides too long.

Farther ahead, a soldier backed into the hallway, battling another of the monsters. He retreated until his back was against the wall, and he leaned aside to avoid being impaled by a rocky sword. He stepped away from the wall, but the monster's swinging club caught him in the head. The heavy blow knocked the helmet from his head, and his feet from the ground.

As the soldier tumbled into the twins' path, Amiya saw the dent in the side of the helm as it bounced past. She looked back in shock. Somehow after that heavy blow, the dazed man was climbing to his feet. The rocky sword pierced his chest, and the man's wail ended in a bloody gurgle as the monster yanked the weapon free and he slumped.

Instinct took over, and the girls sprinted toward the combatants. As the man dropped to his knees, Amiya hopped onto his shoulders and leapt with all her strength.

Fortune was with her, as the monster hadn't noticed them yet. Midair, Amiya thrust her hand out and a freezing cold mist streamed from her hand and into the monster's mouth. She collided sideways into its chest and screamed as parts of the hot rocky flesh burned her right arm and leg.

Nandi landed next to her, and hoisted her up by the arm. Amiya looked over her shoulder to see the red and black monster stumbling sideways, its upper hands gripping its blue neck where pieces of frozen rock crumbled free.

They ran through the gallery where hand-woven portraits and paintings were ripped in half and hanging disheveled from the walls. Broken furniture, pottery, and bodies lay scattered about the floor around the combatants. Three of the hulking nightmares battled more than a dozen soldiers, who's numbers were rapidly declining.

"We can't get through here," Amiya said. "Any chance you can do that thing again with the blue air?"

Nandi shook her head. "I don't know how I did it the first time."

"Figures. Thought I'd ask."

"I don't think anybody's going to be worried about us with those things killing them," Nandi said. Her eyes were partially averted from the fighting. Amiya found herself doing the same. They'd already seen enough blood, stabbings, and dismemberment for a lifetime of nightmares.

Nandi tapped her shoulder and pointed at the door to the far end of the gallery. A monk in white robes came through it and stood at the top of a short row of stairs. He held a rock that began to pulsate between silver and blue. Corlite.

Air blew from the monk, forming into dozens of spears made of ice. The spears feathered the fussing monsters, causing them to slow and stumble, which gave the soldiers a much needed moment of relief.

Amiya nodded her head toward the front doors, and they sprinted from the side of the gallery out of the mansion and into more chaos.

"By the Creator Himself," Nandi breathed. "Is the world ending?"

"It's either ending, or has gone mad," Amiya said. "Either way, we're not getting caught in the middle of it. We need to get out of Vyne."

"Out in the wild?" Nandi replied. "By ourselves?"

The ground shook again, and they nearly fell. Amiya looked at her sister as if that were answer enough.

The twins raced through the streets, dodging monsters and city guard alike. Panicked citizens ran through the streets, screaming and shouting.

Amiya and Nandi skidded to a stop just as a woman was cut down right in front of them. The unfortunate woman was dead the moment she hit the ground, her lifeblood pooling around her.

The girls' hands flew to their mouths in unison, widened eyes staring at the horrible sight. Their trance was broken by the thudding steps of one of those monsters, and a soldier's voice.

"Get away from here!" he shouted at them just as he ran his halberd into the monster's back. It spun around, but the soldier held on. Amiya and Nandi ran for the smaller side streets as more soldiers came to his aid.

The girls ducked in an empty alley and pressed their backs to the wall of a baker's shop. Nandi forced herself to slow her breathing, and peeked around the building. "Dad isn't here, so we don't have to find him." She looked at Amiya.

"You're right," Amiya said. "Let's get out of here and figure out the rest later. We can always hide outside the city till things are safe again, and—"

The ground shook violently, and Amiya fell on her side. It took everything she had not to scream when she landed on her burned leg. In all the chaos she had been able to somewhat forget the injury.

"You alright?" Nandi asked, gingerly grabbing Amiya's uninjured arm.

"Yeah. Not as bad as it looks, just hurts." She grabbed Nandi's hand and her sister pulled her back to her feet. The tremors continued, and then they saw rock and debris flying from around the wall. Both girls peeked around the building again and saw what looked like a giant tentacle burst from the ground, sending cobblestones and debris flying everywhere.

"Have the Fallen themselves returned?" Nandi breathed.

"Whether they have or not," Amiya replied. "We're not going to be here to greet them."

The ground shook again, and they heard an unearthly sound that could only have come from the monster digging itself out of the ground.

They peeked around the corner again and saw a huge beast with red plated scales climb out of a massive hole, destroying a nearby building in the process.

"By the Creator!" Nandi said.

"He had nothing to do with that," Amiya said, watching as soldiers gather around the thing in some form of attack pattern. Four died with the sweep of an appendage.

Amiya had no doubts that all of those men would be dead in short order, when a giant rock burst from the hole in which the beast had come, and crashed into its armored head. Then a stream of ice spears flew into it.

The twins stepped out of the alley and looked in the direction the spears had come, and saw a lone man in animal furs standing on the roof of a house. He was focused on the giant beast, and another barrage of icy spears formed in front of him and shot across the distance into the giant beast.

"That our guy?" Amiya asked.

"Yes it is," Nandi said. "We've got to get to him."

"I think he's doing fine," Amiya replied.

"Yeah but we're not. He's helping the people who imprisoned him, and he seems pretty powerful."

Amiya was about to ask Nandi what she was expecting from the guy when she spotted another of those four-armed monsters heading their way. "Fine. Let's go!"

They ran from the alley, but stayed along the front of the houses and buildings, out of the way of the general fighting. A group of soldiers battling a fussing lava rock monster blocked their path, so they ducked down another street, went to its end and turned right.

A deafening screech split the air, and they stopped and clamped their hands to their ears. When it stopped, Amiya looked at Nandi, who nodded for them to continue.

Ducking flying debris and dodging pockets of fighting, the twins finally came to the house on which the man was standing. He'd stopped attacking the monster and was talking to someone. They crept forward and saw a bowman on the roof of another house. He had an arrow trained on the man in the furs.

Amiya looked at Nandi, then jerked her head in the direction of the bowman. Her sister was a better shot when it came to delving the *essences* without a ring.

Nandi crept past her, and Amiya felt *air* gathering around and within her sister as that silver glow came into her eyes again. Nandi drew her arm back, then swung it out in what looked like a left-handed slap.

The man gave a cry of surprise that was cut short when he fell from the roof and hit the ground. Nandi gasped, but Amiya grabbed her arm and nodded for her to follow. They stood over the man and saw that he was unconscious, but alive. Behind her, Nandi breathed a relieved sigh.

Amiya turned to see the man in the furs turning toward the city wall.

"Hey!" she yelled. "You're not even gonna thank us?"

28

JOGA

Jogging beside the two identical twin girls, Joga didn't know if his luck came from the Creator or the Fallen. He had felt one of them use *air* to knock that archer off the rooftop and that puzzled him. These girls obviously were not blood of the Khatala, but he could sense their ability to delve.

"Where are we going?" one of them asked.

"Woods," he answered. "Harder to follow us."

"Sounds like we're trading capture for being eaten," the other girl said. She was the one that had yelled at him about thanking them. Joga hid is amusement. That one was the more fiery of the two.

When they finally reached the relative shelter of the nearby tree line, he trotted to a stop to allow the girls to catch their breath. When he turned back, however, they were staring at him with what looked like irritation.

"What're we stopping for?" the fiery one asked, hands on her hips. Both girls wore their hair in tight rows of braids from the front to the back of their heads. Their tiny arms had hints of muscle, and they were barely breathing heavy.

"I know we're city folk and all, Mister," the calmer girl said, "but

I'll feel better with more distance between us and all that." She waved her hand in the direction behind them.

The side of Joga's mouth twitched. Even that one had some spark. "Then we go," he replied.

"What's your name?" the fiery one asked as they jogged through the woods.

"Joga, of the Frostlands." He leapt over a fallen log without missing a step. He glanced over his shoulder to see the two girls jump side by side. They each placed a hand on the trunk, and up and over they went, still matching his pace. Impressive. He had only encountered Marailanders on one other occasion, and they didn't seem particularly athletic.

"He thought we were soft," he heard one of the girls say to the other, and they giggled. That prejudice was long gone. Though he did run a bit slower to compensate for their shorter legs, their endurance was a surprise.

He led them north, in the direction of the volcano where all this trouble began. He still had to fulfill the task given him by his blood-mark, but what of these two?

The terrain started to incline, and they navigated up and around as many boulders as trees. Once they came to a clearing at the top of a grassy knoll, he stopped. This time, no protests came, and the girls plopped down on a half exposed boulder.

Joga climbed atop a cluster of boulders nearby and looked back to the southeast. Smoke rose from the direction of the Marailander city, but that was all he could see. He hoped the soldiers had managed to destroy all the monsters, and felt a pang of guilt at leaving. He reminded himself that there was nothing for it. His staying to help would have landed him back in that cell.

"Where to now?" the feisty one asked.

Joga wasn't sure how to answer the question. He was bound for the borderland volcano and his confrontation with the mulgin. He had no intention of bringing two young girls with him to what could likely be a one-way journey. And where were their parents?

The other twin stared right into his eyes. "Trying to decide how to tell us we can't come with you, or something? If you must know, we think our dad has been kidnapped, or in some other kind of trouble that has taken him to Altarra. Do you know that place?"

"I know it," Joga replied. "Very big city." The girls laughed at that, and heat rose to Joga's face. "What is funny?"

"Nothing," the calmer girl said.

"But you laugh ..."

"It's just the way you put it," the feisty girl said. "To say that Altarra is 'big', is a really modest way to describe it."

"You would say what?" Joga asked.

The girls looked at each other. "The place is huge. Bigger than any other city in Marai."

"You've been to this place?" Joga asked.

"Well, we haven't actually been there," the calmer girl said, "but we've heard the stories."

Joga sat down on his boulder and stared down at the two. "Have my name and homeland," he said, indicating the girls with an open hand. Then he stared at them expectantly. After an extended silence where the three of them stared at each other, the calmer girl looked at her sister.

"I think he means it's rude for him to tell us his name and where he's from and for us not to return the favor."

"Oh," said the other girl, a hint of annoyance in her voice. "Then why didn't he just ask?"

"Everybody's not the same, Amiya." She turned to Joga. "My name is Nandi, from the city of Vyne, though my ancestry is actually Barbarosian."

"And you just heard my name," the other girl said, "and since I'm sure you figured out that we're related, you know all my other stuff, too."

The corner of Joga's mouth twitched again. Twins tended to be similar or completely different. These two were definitely the latter.

"I say something funny?" the girl named Amiya asked, misreading his expression.

"Why you want to come with me?" he asked.

"We were in the same situation," Nandi replied. "You were imprisoned, and we were as well, in a way."

Joga thought that was the shallowest reason to join a stranger that he'd ever heard, so he waited for more.

"Look," Nandi continued. "When I saw you being taken by that monk and those soldiers, I felt your ability to do that thing. You know; delving? Is that what you're people call it too?" When Joga nodded, she went on.

"I had a feeling that's why you'd been arrested, and we were hoping we could help each other."

"Trust me, but don't know me," Joga responded. "Dangerous. You are young girls."

Amiya snorted. "Yeah I told her the same thing, but she's hard-headed like that."

The girl named Nandi glared at her twin. "Thank you, Amiya. Anyway, I could feel your ability and you didn't feel hostile. I can't explain why, but I knew you were a gentle person. Plus, you don't have mean eyes."

Mean eyes? Joga nearly laughed. He leaned back and let the sun warm his face. There were clouds coming in from the distant south, but they wouldn't arrive till nightfall. What would he do with them? These two weren't his responsibility. Or where they? He couldn't simply leave them in the wild, yet their home city was no safer. Given what he knew about Marailanders' feelings toward those who could delve without the use of those horrible rings, he figured that was the reason for their incarceration.

He lay flat on his back and enjoyed the sun for a while longer, leaving the girls to talk amongst themselves.

JOGA'S EYES popped open and he scrambled to his feet. He crouched on the top of his boulder and scanned the area.

"Whoa, calm down mountain man!"

Still crouched, Joga spun in the direction of the voice. The feisty girl named Amiya was smirking up at him.

"You always wake up in a fluster like that?" Nandi asked.

Joga stood. "Did not realize I slept," he replied.

"Yeah, you dozed almost as soon as you stretched out on your rock," Amiya said. "We figured you were tired, so we let you sleep."

How long had he slept? Joga looked to the west, where Father *Alyu* had partially dipped below the horizon. He'd slept a quarter of the day away.

Joga sighed and looked to the south—where the storm clouds were significantly closer—then to the southeast. No more smoke rose from the direction of Vyne, so he guessed, hoped, that the people had succeeded in quelling the attack.

He took in a slow, deep breath, then let it out and delved *air*. He opened himself to the essence, allowing his senses to drift on the wind. Several moments passed when he caught a whiff of horse perspiration. He sniffed. At least ten horses, and heavily perspiring.

That was worrisome. The animals wouldn't drive themselves to such a degree unless by threat or rider upon their backs. He sniffed again, and caught the scent of dogs. Several dogs! He let out the breath in a huff, then delved *earth*, though he already knew.

"What's the deal?" Amiya asked.

"And why are you delving," asked the other girl.

Joga listened to the earth, the trees, the birds, the fleeing animals. Two-leggeds rode astride horses, following their vicious dog servants.

Joga hopped off of his boulder. "We go, now."

"What?" Amiya said. "Are we being followed?"

"No. He just wants to go climb trees," Nandi quipped.

"Watch it," the other girl warned.

After a while of running in silence, Joga checked over his shoulder.

"Still back here, mountain man," Amiya said. "You'll not lose us that easily."

Why did she keep calling him 'mountain man'? He'd told them he was from the Frostlands. There were few mountains there.

"How far away are they?" Nandi asked.

"Don't know," Joga replied. "Far but not that far. Have dogs and horses."

"Well they'll at least be delayed when they get to the rocks," Amiya said.

"And what do we do about those bloodhounds?" Nandi asked.

"You wanna sit down and figure it out now?" Amiya replied.

"Save air for running," Joga snapped. To ensure the girls complied, he increased his pace. It worked, for he could hear their heavier breathing, though they still kept up.

The trio ran well after the sun dipped below the horizon, only stopping occasionally to catch their breath.

"Do we know where we're going, or are we just running?" Amiya asked.

"North," Joga replied. "Borderlands."

"Borderlands?" both girls repeated in unison.

Joga looked from one to the other. "Where I must go."

The twins looked at each other, seeming at a loss. "How far are the borderlands from Altarra?"

"Three day's ride. Maybe four." Joga turned away. "A river not far north and east. We stop there."

"Three or four day's ride," Amiya said. "Yup. That is, if you've got something to ride, or money to acquire something to ride. We don't have either."

"We'll figure something out," Nandi said.

"That'll be interesting."

"Just as interesting as what happened that got us out of Vyne to catch up with him," Nandi countered.

Joga felt those two sets of brown eyes boring into his back.

"What are we going to do with this situation?" Amiya asked. "It's not like he's promised to take us anywhere. We just happened to be going the same direction as him."

"All people from Marai talk about someone as if they are not there?" Joga asked over his shoulder.

"Sorry," Amiya replied. "Didn't mean to be rude, but we've got this little problem to figure out."

"Caravans in and out of borderlands all the time," Joga suggested.

"And I'm sure more than a few of them would gladly provide passage for two girls to Altarra for no money instead of selling us off as laborwives or something," Amiya replied.

"Laborwives if we're lucky," Nandi added.

What did they want from him? It wasn't Joga's responsibility to see these girls off to a distant land. For all he knew, they were runaways rebelling from their parents. The more he thought about it, the more Joga wondered if it had been a wise choice to allow the girls to accompany him. Maybe he should have watched over them until the trouble in their city was over, then sent them back home.

"I bet he's wishing he'd sent us back home," Nandi remarked.

Joga stopped and turned on her. "How you do that?"

"Do what?" the girl asked.

Joga looked into her eyes. She genuinely seemed not to know what he was talking about. "You read my mind. Twice you do this."

"I *have*?" Nandi replied. "You've just told me something new, because I'm not aware I've done any such thing."

Joga stared hard at her.

"I'm serious!" she said. "When we were walking just now, I got the feeling you didn't know what to do with us. Seemed like you wish you'd just sent us home, or something like that."

That was exactly how he felt. Joga shook his head, still looking into her eyes. The girl wasn't lying. Could this be some manifestation of her ability to delve? It was different in everyone. Some could survive in intense heat or cold without the need of a shield of *air* to protect them. Others could project their voices in different directions on a whim. And there were still others who had no such extra abilities at all. Could this girl be some sort of mind reader?

"You know. When you stand there staring at me like that, it makes me a little uneasy," the girl said. Her sister came to stand beside her, and both girls wore an identical look of preparedness. They were delving, he could feel it, though the one named Nandi was quicker and stronger at it than her sister.

Joga laughed and held up his hands, palms together in a gesture of peace. "You have ability, that is all. Unusual for Marailander."

"You do as well," the girl said.

"Not same as you," he replied. "You sense that others can delve. You feel other's thoughts, or maybe feelings, yes?"

"Yes."

"You do that?" he asked the other girl.

Amiya grunted. "No need to rub it in."

Joga frowned. That was interesting. Twins usually shared attributes, even being able to read each other's minds on some level.

He turned away. "I think maybe one day you find you can do something." He smiled over his shoulder.

"Right," the girl said. "So we gonna camp out in the rain or press on, drinking the rain as we run until starvation has its say?"

"You have tongue of a Jarku," Joga said.

"Why do you say that?"

"Rude."

"I wouldn't say that," Amiya replied.

"Then you would say what?" Joga asked.

The girl put her hands on her hips. "Witty."

"Rude."

"Maybe a little sarcastic."

Joga raised his eyebrows. "Sarcastic is rude."

"Sarcastic is witty," came the snappy reply.

"Or rude," Joga countered.

"Or not," the girl said.

Joga sighed. "River is near. Water is fresh and fish are many."

"Sounds good," Nandi said. "And don't mind my recalcitrant sister. She appreciates you as much as I do."

"There's a big word, Nandi," Amiya teased. "And come on already. Both of you. We're on the run and out in the wild with who-knows-who chasing us. Let's loosen up a little." There was a pause and Joga thought that was the end of it. Then the girl spoke again.

"And I'm not trying to be rude. I appreciate you helping us out, mountain man."

Joga tried to be annoyed. Instead he laughed.

29

SELVETAR

"Please be at ease and assured that they are being tracked down as I speak and you bellow, Archminister."

The bloated man glared at Selvetar, but the first magus hardly cared. This man's farcical tirade only served to make it more challenging not to laugh at him, not that Selvetar was given to laughter.

"I still cannot understand how this could have happened in the first place!" the man shouted, though careful to direct his ire at the attending captain of the city guard, or one of the representing monks. Whenever he met Selvetar's gaze, his tone was more ... controlled. Bloated, dramatic, but not stupid.

"If you cannot understand how your two prisoners escaped the mansion, Archminister," the captain responded, "then perhaps you were not properly briefed of the situation." The man stood tall in his scratched and bloody armor, dented helm tucked under his arm. His tone was neutral despite the stupidity of the man attempting to loom over him.

"What did you say, Captain?" Decius asked, his tone warning.

"That whoever briefed you of the situation did a poor job of it, Archminister," Captain Joniver Task replied without flinching. "A man as firm yet reasonable as yourself would surely be less disturbed by these events if you were properly informed that the city was nearly destroyed by monsters the like we have never seen."

Selvetar smirked inwardly. That may be true to Captain Joniver, but it wasn't reality. The monsters had never been seen before, true. Not by people of this age.

Decius looked on the edge of an explosion, then to Selvetar and Joniver's surprise, he calmed. "You are right, of course, Captain," Decius replied, cupping his chin in his hand. It gave the impression of a stupefied ape trying to think. "I am a reasonable man, and had I known the city was in such a dire situation, of course I would not have been so angry. You and your men have done a fine job defending our beloved Vyne. Withdraw and bolster the defenses. See to it that every available soldier patrols the city perimeters as well as the streets. I'll not have our precious home attacked again."

Captain Joniver's left eye twitched, the only indication that he shared Selvetar's feeling that this man knew nothing of what he was talking about. The thought of the entire two thousand soldiers that made up the city garrison patrolling the streets and perimeter was comical.

"Of course, Archminister," Joniver replied precisely. His departing bow was equally precise, and he spun on his heel and exited the room, leaving Selvetar with Decius and Brother Amerus Layun, of the Vyne sect of the Brotherhood of the Source.

"And what say you, Brother Amerus," Decius asked, his voice going low. "How do you explain this attack upon our unwitting city?" He looked from the monk to Selvetar, then turned away, hands clasped behind his back as he paced the room.

"I have in my city, four members of the Order of Magi," he looked at Selvetar, "five, counting yourself, First Magus." Decius then looked back at Amerus. "I also have an entire temple full of monks of the Brotherhood of the Source. Your warrior monks are legendary, Brother Amerus, and some are even acolytes to the Order of Magi."

He turned away again, then turned back. Selvetar wondered if the man would break into dance with all the turning he was doing.

"So how can I not ask myself, how? How is it that my fine city was caught completely unawares by those ... things," he pointed at the far wall, in the direction most of the fighting had happened.

"It looks as though you are asking me instead of yourself, Archminister," Amerus replied. Selvetar's respect for the man instantly grew. "And whether you ask myself, or yourself, your answer will be the same. I do not know. I am not capable of detecting threats that come from underground, nor am I capable detecting threats that come seemingly from nowhere, or falling from the sky."

Decius looked like he wanted to throttle the man. That would be interesting to witness, especially given that the calm monk could do more damage to the archminister before he could fully extend one of his corpulent arms. "So you're telling me there is no way to know whether or not this attack was an anomaly, or the first of more to come?"

"I am telling you that you could conjure any number of scenarios and they would be just as valid as my own, Archminister. Whatever those things were, I believe they are straight from the underworld."

Decius snorted and turned away. Again. He walked over to his plush armchair and settled into it, invoking the image in Selvetar's mind of pudding flowing into a bowl. His stomach gave a tiny complaint.

"And what say you, First Magus?" Decius asked, raising his hand to indicate Selvetar, then letting it drop to the armrest. Such dramatic exasperation was worthy of the theater. "Surely you don't believe these things are from the 'underworld'." The archminister's tongue in cheek tone caused Brother Amerus's face to harden.

"I believe we must look further into the matter before we come to any hard conclusions," Selvetar said.

"Ah. But you at least agree that these things aren't from some fictitious hellish realm, yes?"

Selvetar let the question hang in the air for several heartbeats before responding. "I did not say that, Archminister."

From the corner of his eye, he saw Amerus blink. The man likely hadn't expected Selvetar to agree with him. He took a mental note of that. Whether Amerus believed his own words or not, they were more true than he understood.

Decius opened and closed his mouth several times, a giant beached catfish struggling to breathe.

"I will need to refer to my library in Altarra," Selvetar interrupted before a bird mistakenly flew into that cavernous hole under the archminister's nose.

"Brother Amerus," Decius said. "I would have a word with the first magus in confidence, if you please."

Amerus arched an eyebrow. "I should hope that you know by now that I am not of the fanatical zealot type that would go screaming through the streets proclaiming that the end is nigh, Archminister. Though I find your request insulting, I will of course heed it."

"I would prefer that Brother Amerus remain," Selvetar said as the monk turned to leave. Amerus stopped mid-step, turning a surprised look on him. "The monks of the Brotherhood were instrumental in preventing Vyne's demise this day, and it would be a boon for him to remain apprised of the situation.

Decius looked from one man to the other and grumbled. "Very well." He at least had the grace to give the monk an apologetic nod. "You are saying this is possible, then?"

"I am saying this is very possible, Archminister," Selvetar replied. "Those creatures were like nothing I've seen in the world, and my travels are extensive."

"The world is a big place," Decius said.

"And I assure you that in no corner of this 'big place' is such an infernal language spoken." Beside him, Brother Amerus stiffened.

"What are you saying?" Decius asked. "From the reports given me, they spoke in a most horrible, blood chilling tongue. It was said that no one understood it, but all felt that same cursing, hate-filled tone within. Are you saying you understand this?"

"I do not understand their words, Archminister, but I do know the sounds; the intonations. I assure you it is the tongue of the under-world that they spoke."

"Then the world over is in grave danger," Amerus said.

Decius gave the monk a skeptical look, but it was halfhearted.

"Brother Amerus's words are not be unfounded," Selvetar said.

"Then we must find out what needs be done," Decius said.

Obviously. "You are correct, Archminister," Selvetar replied. "And therefore, I must return to Altarra and consult my library."

"When will you depart?"

"Posthaste."

Decius looked like he wanted to say more. He glanced at Amerus, who smirked. "If matters regarding the attack are finished, Archminister, I would excuse myself. The Brotherhood must be properly and discretely informed, that we may prepare for what, if anything, is to come."

"Very well, Brother," Decius replied. "The work you monks have done has not gone unnoticed."

"My ... thanks, Archminister." The monk was quick to the door and gone.

"That one has a fair amount of insolence in him," Decius said, staring at the closed door through which Amerus had departed.

"You speak to him in a manner that does not befit his station, Archminister," Selvetar replied. "The man has served under King Alyn himself, as well as the chief of the northwest Sandland Khatala."

Decius snorted yet again. Selvetar was certain that somewhere, a boar thought it was hearing a mating call.

"Why Amerus would play consultant to a savage tribe that is at war with us, I cannot fathom."

"Perhaps to know the enemy."

Decius nodded. "There is that."

"Or perhaps to know whether there is the possibility of diplomacy with the enemy," Selvetar added, and again, Decius nodded. "Or, perhaps to attempt to understand a people that may not at all be an enemy, but simply a misunderstood people."

Decius frowned at him. "Is this a philosophical discussion? I was not aware."

"You posed a question to which I provided several possible answers."

"Answers that do not concern me, First Magus. War with the wilders is not my province."

Selvetar couldn't have disagreed more. This war was everyone's concern. The first magus nodded silently, then said, "you wish to speak with me about your ... guests, I presume?"

The man's face gave a twinge of irritation at the mention of the escaped girls. "Yes. I'm told they may have escaped the city during the fighting. I was also informed that they accompanied some wilder who had been imprisoned for bringing one of those hellish beasts here to cause havoc."

The man's doubtful tone showed he possessed at least some degree of intelligence. Decius might not be the wittiest of men, but he was no fool. Not a complete fool, at least. Selvetar reminded himself not to take him for granted. No man could attain any level of power without some form of intelligence that got him there.

"That is a doubtful scenario," Selvetar replied. "More likely, he was trying to escape the thing and ended up here."

"In the middle of the city? How could that have happened? Reports said that he and that beast simply fell into the middle of the street from thin air. Is such a form of travel possible?"

"Would that it was," Selvetar replied. "I would love to enjoy such a convenience."

"Wouldn't we all?" Decius agreed. "Can you track the girls?"

"No better than your soldiers, unfortunately. My skills do not include those of a ranger."

Decius slammed a plump fist on the armrest. "I had a sizable profit hanging on those two. Your own Master Vladrick would pay well for them, if they proved to have the same potential as their father. Those trackers had better bring them back."

"You sent the most capable trackers in the city, Archminister," Selvetar assured him. "It is simply a matter of finding them before something higher on the food chain does."

"That's a worry," the man said. "What of your assessment of

them?" he asked. "You apparently gained enough of their trust to test their aptitude?"

Selvetar nodded. "They exhibited a good degree of potential, but only in channeling through conventional means."

"So they are not hybrids, then?" Decius asked, disappointed.

"I would like the opportunity to test them further, but it seems unlikely. Perhaps whatever attribute the father possesses is a random mutation, or skips generations. There is no way to know without further testing."

Decius let out a heavy sigh. "They *must* be found. I want this transaction completed soon so that I might be done with it."

So that he might receive the generous payment Vladrick had promised him. "I am sure your trackers will return them."

"Even if they do," Decius said, "if they aren't anything special, it's a moot point anyway."

"I believe that whether or not the girls share their father's attributes, Magi Master Vladrick will still pay handsomely for them." That brought a smile to the man's puffy face.

"And now I must be off to Altarra."

"I will have a horse prepared for your departure."

Selvetar gave a slight bow. "I appreciate it, Archminister, but I have already taken the liberty. After the attack was quelled, I saw the necessity to return to my library."

"And to your esteemed magi master," Decius added with a note of sarcasm. "Do keep me informed of his thoughts. The man thinks to extend his reach. I think to delay that indefinitely."

"As do I," Selvetar agreed. "There is no reason for his hand to grasp a hold in this fine city."

"I'm glad we continue to agree on this," Decius said.

"As am I," Selvetar replied.

SELVETAR RODE his chestnut gelding until the city of Vyne was well out of sight. Through his *essence* ring, he grasped *air*. As soon as he was on the other side of one of the many hills in the road, he manipulated *air*. The horse continued to walk even as the space about them rippled.

A few heartbeats later, the great city of Altarra was in sight. He slapped the reins to the gelding's rump and the horse broke into a gallop.

A short time later, the first magus strode the halls of the fortress of the Altarra Order of Magi, his many subordinates inclining their heads in deference as they passed. Soon, he sat opposite magi master Vladrick in his private study.

"You've returned early," Vladrick said. "Pressing news, I presume?"

"That would be a mild statement," Selvetar replied, and the master raised his eyebrows.

"Oh?"

"Vyne was attacked by warriors of the underworld."

Vladrick leaned forward in his chair. "What?"

"Drauk," Selvetar continued. "At least a score of them. And a tunneler."

Vladrick swore. "You're sure of this?"

"I've no doubt, Master."

Vladrick leaned back and tucked his hands in his sleeves. "Something has happened and we must find out what that is. If the underworld has become emboldened, something has happened." When Selvetar didn't speak, he asked, "there is more?"

"A lone Khatala entered the city with a drauk at his back."

"And this is noteworthy because?"

"It was several days before the attack on the city. He escaped during the excitement, the spicetrader's daughters in tow."

Vladrick nodded thoughtfully. "Have they been found?"

"No, Master."

"What are their chances of survival until they are found?"

"I would say they are quite good, Master."

"Why so?"

"Every Marailander knows of the conflict with Khatal. One would at least think twice before interacting with one from the tribes west of our borders. The girls actually sought him out. I believe it was their plan from the beginning."

"Oh? How so?"

"They had been scheming on a way to escape days before I first came to visit them," Selvetar said. "They're smart. They knew there was no way for them to escape the mansion and leave the city unassisted, so they waited."

"Did you not try to coax them into believing you might be that aid they sought?"

Selvetar chuckled mirthlessly. "They're too smart to trust me. Even when I began their informal instruction, both held back their potential, though the more levelheaded one named Nandi went to great pains to ensure I did not detect her ability to summon without the aid of a ring."

"So they're hybrids like their father, then," Vladrick said.

"Each with their own way of wielding the *essences*," Selvetar replied. "The other twin, Amiya, has more affinity with the use of the ring, while Nandi has more affinity with summoning the *essences* directly."

"And Decius ..."

"Knows nothing for sure. He only has his hopes. The girls would have me believe as little as possible regarding their potential, and Decius is none the wiser. I'm content to let the matter remain so, if it pleases you, of course."

Vladrick pressed the tips of his fingers together and touched his lips. "And they latch themselves onto another who is able to summon as they do, and escape the city."

"Possibly on their way here."

"They know of their father's destination?"

"Through his own words," Selvetar said. It was the primary reason I convinced Decius to allow the spicetrader a reunion with them before he left."

Vladrick barked a laugh. "And the attack provides their means to escape. What world is it we live in, when the underworld commits an act that actually aids our intentions?"

"I cannot say I have ever witnessed a more amusing irony," Selvetar lied.

"The wilders have begun moving from Mt. Blood," Vladrick said. "King Alyn's settlement there is in danger of being overrun."

"Amoura should arrive with the twins' father soon."

"We have heard no word of that," Vladrick said. "And this situation is time sensitive."

"As is this new development concerning the underworld, Master."

"Be that as it may, we must handle our battles as they come."

Selvetar remained silent.

Magi Master Vladrick smiled. "I do not discount the severity of this new development, Selvetar. If Amoura Xanna was here, I wouldn't hesitate to send her in your stead."

"When must I depart for Mt. Blood, Master?"

"I can spare you one full day of study before you are needed there. King Alyn grows nervous about the wilders, as well he should be."

"Very well." Selvetar stood.

"Have messengers dispatched to the other temples across Marai," Vladrick said as Selvetar reached the door. "If the underworld stirs, we must be prepared."

"Of course, Master Vladrick," Selvetar replied.

He closed the door and walked quickly down the halls, speeding past the many magi and acolytes and students who made way for him.

He nearly ran up the spiraling stairs of the fortress tower, and started across the walkway connecting the two towers at either end of the massive structure. Robes wrapped closely around his body against the cold wind, he stopped in the middle, and looked west. Far in the distance, a black fog billowed from the borderland volcano.

He then looked to the northeast, in the direction of Mt. Blood. The mountain sat quiet and formidable. No, foreboding. Selvetar could practically feel the threat building. Something was happening, and finding the answer was more important than playing in King Alyn's foolish war.

He looked to the south, in the direction from which the apprentice was traveling. Barring any unforeseen difficulties, the woman should be in Altarra to deliver her living cargo within a day. Selvetar had a feeling Amoura had met with trouble on the road, which would only delay her arrival and delay Selvetar in being able to put any solid effort into discerning the cause of the underworld's rumblings.

The first magus's eyes narrowed as he scanned the surrounding lands as far as he could see. If his suspicions had merit, trouble would come from everywhere.

30

EMIEL

Emiel hopped over a fallen tree and landed in a patch of mud. His feet slipped out from under him and he landed flat on his back. Again.

"Up spicetrader." Bone grabbed him by the shoulder and hoisting him to his feet. "You can lie on your back later."

Emiel thought he heard a flicker of affection in the young man's tone. Behind them Amoura Xanna skidded to a stop and turned to send a spray of fire at the pursuing morgs. Two of the brown wolfish beasts went down thrashing in flames.

"How's it look back there?" Bone yelled over his shoulder.

"Three more behind," Amoura answered.

"Two at the top of the hill on the left," Bone replied. "Two up front."

"They can't jump down on us from up there," Emiel said between breaths. "That's got to be a thirty-foot drop."

"You'll lose your life on that bet," came the reply.

At that statement, Emiel looked up the side of the hill and saw the two morgs pacing them. He felt his heart flutter.

Just in front of him Bone ran on, ignoring the steady rain that spattered off of his armor. The mercenary also kept an eye on the pursuing predators up the hill.

Emiel wiped his face. He was soaked through, as was Amoura who followed a dozen paces behind. Emiel paid little heed to his heavy and sodden clothes. The threat of being eaten by one of those horrid things overrode his discomfort and complaining muscles.

Running from being eaten alive. Again.

Emiel nearly slipped in another patch of mud, but managed to keep his balance. Of all the fears a man could have, being eaten was one he rarely considered, since he didn't live out in the wild. Yet here he was, running from a pack of monsters straight out of a nightmare, and much higher in the food chain than himself. Emiel could think of more than a few ways he would rather die than being eaten, though given the choice, he'd rather not die at all.

He squeezed his eyes shut at a blinding flash of light from behind, followed by an agonized howl. Amoura. Further ahead Emiel saw two morgs charging them, muzzles curled back in a snarl that displayed two rows of yellow teeth fronted by a set of fangs protruding the top of the mouth. Those things looked as long as Emiel's forearm.

"Blast the light," Bone cursed, and he gripped his sword in two hands at his side. "Just ... try to keep moving. You've still got that toothpick, right?"

Emiel would have been indignant, where his heart not hammering in his chest. "Yeah I got it."

"Keep moving and don't worry about us," Bone said.

"Continue on by myself so that I can get ripped apart by anything else up there?"

Bone frowned, then nodded. "Good point ..." He dropped to one knee, sliding on the wet ground just as the closest morg leapt at him.

The mercenary bent low while at the same time bringing his sword up and over. He cut the monster through from front to back, and it hit the ground, spasming in its death throes as its insides spilled out.

Emiel's stomach lurched at the sight.

"Watch where you're going!" Bone shouted at him, and Emiel

looked forward just in time to see the second morg spring at him. He threw himself to the side, feeling the hot breath of the animal as its slavering jaws snapped inches beside his face. The side of the morg's body clipped Emiel in the shoulder and sent him in a sideways spin to the ground.

He rolled into a puddle of muddy water and came back to his feet, or tried to. He blinked, trying to steady his throbbing head when from the corner of his eye he spotted the monster barreling toward him, Bone sprinting not far behind. The mercenary was shouting, but in the fog of his mind, Emiel couldn't hear.

He tried to turn and run but succeeded only in stumbling sideways and falling over. The morg crashed into him and sent Emiel tumbling away to crash into the side of the mountain. He groaned through the pain in his head. Even his eyes were throbbing. Emiel slid down on his side, staring up as the heavy drops of water fell from the sky and spattered on his face. The pain in his arm flared again.

The rain suddenly stopped, and a large, furry brown head appeared over his face. It's lips curled back to reveal those awful teeth. It growled and opened its jaws wider. There was a flash of light, and all was warmth and blackness.

CALM AND GENTLE, Nandi's warm and healing hands hovered over his wounds while the more hard Amiya watched. They'd been in danger and he hadn't able to get them out. They had come for him instead. Such good girls. Aunya would be proud of them.

"I love you, my ladygirls," he croaked. "I wish I could have saved you two, but I'm glad you found you're ole man."

Nandi didn't respond, but kept hovering her hands over his body, stopping over a painful area in his shoulder. He flinched, and Nandi placed a gentle hand on him.

"Think you can get him patched up a little quicker?" he heard Amiya say from a little farther off. "We need to be gone from here."

That was unusual. Amiya wasn't the most affectionate person for sure, but she was never this cold.

"Not much longer," Nandi said, still holding Emiel's shoulder. Warmth flowed from her hand and he could feel his flesh knitting back together. Wherever there was more pain, she sent more warmth in that spot. "Almost done," she said in a much more mature voice than when he'd last seen them. How long had it been?

Her hands went down his arm, then over his chest and abdomen. They weren't hovering anymore, but sliding across his body; almost caressing.

Emiel frowned. "Nandi," he groaned. His head was still so foggy. "What are you doing?" The hands hesitated. What was wrong with her, and why in the world was she touching him this way? He almost thought he felt more than daughterly affection in her touch. He must be mistaken.

"Just remain still a little longer. I'm almost done."

She continued to run her hands over his body, hovering over him at first, then settling on wounds and a few bruises. Then came that caressing touch again. Her touch was warm and gentle and soothing, and very, very wrong. His hand snapped up and grabbed her wrist.

"That's enough young lady," he said, sitting up. He regretted the movement almost immediately, and his head went spinning again. He pressed the butt of his other hand in the space between his forehead and his nose and pressed. A low groan escaped his throat. When he removed his hand, he saw the blurred image of Nandi staring back at him, a look of veiled amusement on her face. And her hair was no longer in the front-to-back rows, braided tightly to her scalp, but free hanging braids that hung to her shoulders. How long had it been since he'd seen them?

"Just ... sit for a moment," she said. "You're disoriented from getting knocked around."

The girl's voice was like steel. Feminine steel with a touch of affection she seemed to be trying to hide. What was wrong with her?

"I don't know what you did, ladygirl, but it worked." He ran a hand over his face. "Still. I think you and I need to have a little talk."

He looked up again, and as his vision started to clear, he saw not his little girl, but a woman fully grown. A heartbreakingly beautiful woman.

Amoura Xanna.

Emiel looked around, and everything came back to him. The look on the magus's face sent plenty of heat to his own. He opened and closed his mouth several times before he finally managed a sound.

"I'm ... I thought—"

"If you can stand," Amoura interrupted, "we should be moving."

Emiel glanced over her shoulder at the impatiently waiting mercenary, who most certainly was not Amiya. Even though he realized where he was, he couldn't help feeling disappointed that it wasn't his daughters here.

Amoura was still crouched over him. Her face was neutral as usual, but he saw a hint of affection in her steel colored eyes. "Come." She offered him a hand. He took it and she helped him to his feet. She was stronger than she looked. "Let's be away from here."

"Yeah," Emiel said.

Amoura reached up and gave his good arm a squeeze. The gesture seemed to surprise them both, and she quickly withdrew her hand and turned away.

Emiel frowned. What was that about? He thought about that caressing touch moments earlier. He hadn't enjoyed it because he had thought it was his daughter at the time. Now that he thought back, there was clearly affection in the touch. Or was that just his head fog distorting the reality?

"You coming, spicetrader?" Bone asked from up ahead, "or were you planning to set up camp and wait for more of those things to come and make a meal of you?"

Emiel checked himself. His belt knife was still there but his short sword was missing. "Must have lost it in the mud." He trotted after the others. Shame. It was a good sword, even if he didn't know how to use it.

"Is there any other kind of danger in this place besides those things?" Emiel asked, looking up at the towering peaks on either side.

Their path snaked its way between the middle and left two peaks of The Triplets. They encountered sparse plant life beyond the occasional tumbleweeds and barbed brush.

"Plenty," answered a tiny female voice.

Bone rolled his eyes. "Thought we were done with that one."

They heard a sniff. "I would think it's a testament to my affection that I'm willing to endure your personal scent."

"No one asked you to."

"Lick a raspweed!"

This time, Lief's voice came from slightly behind and to Emiel's right. He looked over his shoulder to see the two-foot-tall tinfar behind him, her simple brown dress blowing in the wind.

Bone actually chuckled. "Little vermin," he said under his breath, but there was no hostility in his words. Not much, at least.

"I wouldn't say *all* humans are vermin," Lief replied. "And you're certainly not little."

Amoura snorted.

"So where did you go?" Emiel asked. "I thought you'd abandoned us?"

"No, silly. I told you I would come back."

"Well you certainly took your time."

"It wasn't that long," Lief said.

Her tiny voice sounded almost plaintive, like a guilty child. Again Emiel had to remind himself she was older than he was. "You were gone over a week." When she just looked up at him with that innocent expression that seemed to say, "and?", he let it go.

"Good to have you back," he said instead. "Where did you go?"

"I already told you."

Emiel frowned. "No you didn't."

"Oh." Lief tilted her head in thought. "I had things to do. I had some matters I needed to look into."

Emiel waited, but the tiny woman didn't offer anything else. "Like?" he prodded.

Lief frowned up at him. He was sure it was supposed to be an annoyed expression, but it came off as a pouty child. "Do you always ask after somebody else's business?" she asked. "And what are you smirking at?"

Emiel's smile fell away. Up ahead, he heard sniggering.

"Sounds like he upset his little girlfriend," Bone said in a low voice that was meant to be heard. Amoura actually chuckled at that.

Emiel glared at the mercenary's back as he replied. "Sorry. Just missed you, is all."

Lief smiled up at him. "I guess I missed you too."

Up ahead, Bone tripped over a rough patch of ground that hadn't been there a second before. The mercenary cursed as he struggled not to fall flat on his face. Beside Emiel, Lief smiled deviously.

For a mercy, the rain finally abated, and the clouds parted just enough for the sun to stare down on them. It took only moments for the rain to be replaced with humidity.

"We're near the halfway point," Amoura said, seeming not at all bothered by the thick moist air. Did anything bother her? "From what I remember of maps of the area, there should be rough terrain ahead that ends in a climb. The hills aren't steep, but they're difficult for anything on four legs to manage. We'll make our camp there."

"Then we'd better get there fast," Bone said. He pointed a gloved hand up and to the left.

Emiel squinted in the direction the mercenary was pointing. It was nothing but the rocky wall of the mountain. He started to say as much, when a piece detached from the wall and started climbing toward them.

31

AMOURA

Amoura Xanna tapped into her *essence* ring while at the same time drawing upon the earth. First it was four-armed monsters, then giant terrestrial mollusks and leapers. Now, rocklords.

The magus narrowed her gray eyes. Like leapers, those things were inherently evil. If ever there was an environment these things loved, it would be The Triplets. Still, seeing them out in the open day like this was disconcerting. Amoura had a bad feeling about all of this. She needed to get back to Altarra. As much as she hated to admit to herself, Selvetar would probably know what was going on. And if he didn't, his personal library held the answers.

A second rocklord detached itself from the mountain wall and the two dropped to the ground ahead. A third was beginning to form just as Amoura had gathered enough power to attack. She threw her hand out and sent a funnel of wind at the half-formed rocklord. Tiny blue particles appeared and grew larger, combining with each other until a long column of water streamed through the air from the magus to her target.

The stream was powerful, and in seconds the monster was eroded to nothing. What was left slid down the mountain wall in a wet sludge.

"Think you can do that again?" Emiel pulled out his belt knife.

Amoura glanced him. He was going to get himself killed trying to rely on such a small weapon. "Not fast enough."

Bone unsheathed his sword. "Come now, spicetrader. It would be too easy otherwise."

"I've got a name, you know," the man snapped. "Would you prefer me to just call you 'mercenary'?"

"Don't matter what you call me," Bone replied. "No sweat off my back."

"Kids," Emiel said.

"I've not been a kid for years," Bone said as he approached the rocklords.

"Almost two decades to your name makes you little more," the spicetrader quipped.

"You both argue like children," Amoura said.

"He started it," Bone muttered.

"Not a child at all," Emiel muttered."

Behind them, Lief giggled.

At that moment Amoura felt like the only adult in the group. *Somewhere Vladrick, Selvetar, and the Creator Himself are laughing at me.*

One of the rocklords dashed forward and simply fell into the ground.

"Should we be happy about that?" Emiel asked.

"No." Bone had barely uttered the reply before the thing burst from the ground in front of him and slammed its shoulder into his chest. Emiel dove aside to avoid the flying mercenary.

Amoura loosed a blast of water at it. Though not as powerful as her initial assault, it was enough to dampen the monster and slow its movements. She looked back ahead and saw the second rocklord dive into the ground. "Other one coming!" she shouted.

It burst out of the ground between the group and whipped its arm backward. Amoura ducked under a hand almost as large as her body, though the thing was no bigger than an average sized human.

It turned toward Emiel and brought its other hand down in a clap. She didn't see the spicetrader appear on either side of it, and

Amoura thought that was the end of him. Her heart fluttered and the pit of her stomach went cold. "NO!" she shouted, and she whipped her ring hand in a left hook, fingers curled as though scratching the air.

Several shards of ice formed in the air and sliced the rocklord across its body. She raked her hand back and forth, up and down, until the monster simply fell apart. Then she thrust her hand forward and sent another blast of wind that formed into a funnel of water that disintegrated what was left of it.

The remaining rocklord slapped its massive hand down on Bone, and it looked as if he too might be crushed, but the mercenary's amazing armor protected him from the worst of it. Amoura curled her fingers as though holding a cylindrical object, and made stabbing motion. A large spear of ice formed in the air and stabbed into the monster's back.

The attack dealt little damage, but the monster did stumble. Bone climbed to his feet and brought his sword around in a low slice. The blade bit deep into the monster's leg. He pulled it free and swung again, this time cleaving straight through.

It's leg gone, the rocklord fell on its side, and Bone came to his feet and chopped down, severing its head.

He stepped back and breathed a sigh that came out as a gasp when his feet were suddenly snatched out from under him. Bone lost his grip on his sword as the monster, head reattaching to its body, picked him up by both legs as if he weighed nothing. It lifted him over its head and slammed him on the ground.

Reflexes taking over, Amoura sent a barrage of icy spears into the rocklord while summoning *water* again. She sent another devastating funnel at the monster, and in seconds reduced it to muddy remains on the damp earth.

Bone lay on his side, groaning but alive. Amoura trotted to where the other monster had slammed its hand down on Emiel. The spice-trader was lying on the ground unharmed.

"How?" Amoura stared at the man, who climbed to his feet.

"Well," he said. "That was close ..."

She nearly knocked him over with a crushing hug. "I thought ... I thought you were ..." she realized what she was doing and shoved him away. "I'm sorry." She needlessly straightened her soaked robes. "I just thought that you were killed. You're under my protection."

"You always this protective?" he asked.

She turned her back. "Yes, of course. All life is valuable." She walked over to where the redheaded mercenary knelt, holding his head. He shook it slowly, squinting his eyes open and close.

"That hurt," Bone said. "What? No big hug for me?"

"We need to get moving, now." Amoura offered him a hand, but he waved her away, pushing off of his knee to stand. "Don't worry about it, lass," he said, some of his highlander accent slipping through. "Save all that stony efficiency for the rest of this fool's errand."

"As you wish." She withdrew her hand and started back on the trail. She gave Emiel a quick once-over. The man was totally unharmed. Odd. "If you're alright, we really must keep moving. Everything about this region is dangerous."

"That's fine with me," he replied. "Let's go."

"I think you're growing on her," Lief whispered. The tinfar had conveniently reappeared once the battle was over, offering not the slightest explanation for her disappearance. They were a dozen paces behind the magus, who took the lead down the path that had grown too narrow for them to walk together.

"Eh," Emiel replied. "Spending so much time surviving in the wild tends to bring people together. Even he is less irritating." Emiel nodded his head back at the mercenary, who was several paces behind, watching the rear.

"You don't believe that any more than I do," Lief said. She crossed her tiny arms and glared up at him. "And if you do, you are a fool, Emiel Dharr."

"Alright, little Miss." Emiel patted the air between them. "I hear you. Whatever the situation is, she's still not trying to help me get back home, is she?"

"What would she do?" Lief countered. "Fight that mercenary and rescue you from him? Take you all the way back to Vyne? And, what about the ones who sent her to see you to Altarra?"

Emiel wanted to refute the argument with some kind of logic, but he couldn't. The truth was, Amoura hadn't been cruel toward him, just irritated. And the more time he spent in her company, the more he suspected her irritation might not be directed at him. Well, not *all* of her irritation, anyway.

Emiel sighed. This whole situation was impersonal. The young mercenary from the Highlands had been the primary force at his back on the path to Altarra, and aside from their first meeting outside Decius's mansion, the young man had become somewhat of a companion. A gruff companion.

"Whether she's friendly or not, it still doesn't change my situation. All that matters to me right now is getting my girls back from that bloated slug." The more he thought about what Decius had done, the angrier he became. What right did the man have to keep him from his daughters?

"It doesn't help your situation at the moment," Lief agreed. Emiel waited, but the tinfar said no more on the subject.

"So what's life like for you, anyway?" He looked down at her. "Do you all live in villages or cities of some sort?" I admit I haven't traveled much of the world, but I've never come across anything like you."

"We've already talked about this. It's because my people avoid you." She smiled up at him. "Though I find you interesting enough to be around.

"But most of your people don't?"

"Oh we do," Lief replied. "Tinfar consider humans very interesting, just like an earthquake or a storm or fire is interesting."

Emiel looked up at the walls of the mountain on either side of them. Though they were not visible in the haze, he could practically feel the peaks known as The Triplets, looming over them like dark sentries glaring down at four tiny intruders. The weight of their gaze was an almost palpable thing.

"Why do I feel so uneasy about this place?" he asked, as much to himself as anyone else.

"Because evil has a home here," the tinfar replied. She looked up at the mountain peaks, then turned worried dark brown eyes on him. "I don't like this place. I wish you hadn't come this way."

"So do I," he said. "But I didn't have a choice in the matter. We're doing pretty well, though. I think we might just get out of here alive." He smiled. "And thanks for helping me back there."

"Helping you?" She looked confused. "Helping you when?"

"Do you tiny folk have memories to match your size?" He jabbed a thumb in the direction they'd come. "Back when that thing nearly flattened me. You stopped it. Thanks."

"I didn't do that, Emiel," Lief said. She actually looked a bit guilty. "I wish I could have helped, but those things manifested from the earth, and I'm e'ta tinfar; earth tinfar. Nothing I could do would have any effect on them."

Emiel frowned. "But I felt something protecting me. It was almost like some kind of air, only solid. I know that doesn't make sense, but that's what it felt like. Maybe she did it." He nodded toward Amoura."

"And that's why she was so relieved to see you alive?"

Emiel frowned at the magus's back. What had happened? "Well maybe the Creator was looking after me, then."

Lief nodded. "By giving you the means to protect yourself, if you would only use them."

"What? Use what, myself? All I have is this knife," he patted the hilt at his waist, "and I'm not really what you'd call a master of the blade."

"What you have inside is worth more than any of those tools you humans use to cut each other with."

"So you're saying I did whatever it was back there to shield myself from that thing?" Emiel shook his head. "I can't do that, Lief. It was probably the magus. She's powerful enough."

"What did it feel like when you were shielded?" Lief asked in a tone that suggested she was talking to a child.

Emiel thought back to the moment he was sure was his last. He'd reflexively curled in a ball and thrown his arms over his head. He'd squinted his eyes shut, and felt a rush of air swirl around him. Then there was stillness. When he'd opened his eyes, he's seen the monster, face consisting of only glowing red slits, pressing its massive hand down on an invisible barrier. Only one or two fluttering heartbeats had passed before Amoura had blasted the thing apart.

"I felt what I can only describe as a shield of air," he finally said.

Lief nodded. "That's because the essence, *air*, came to your call."

"I didn't call anything," Emiel said. "I didn't have enough time to think about anything."

"It's called reflex, human. I'm sure you've heard of it."

"Thanks for the attitude," Emiel replied. "Yes I've heard of it, and I have them. But I can't reflexively do something that I'm unable to do."

Lief shrugged. "Where's your stone?"

Emiel's hand went to the sack at his waist. "How do you know about that?"

"Who do you think got it to you?"

"I bought it from a little girl ..." he stared at her. "Was that you?"

The tinfar gave him a dry look. "Do I look like the little girl that gave that to you?"

"Well, you could have disguised yourself ..."

"I'm not quite two feet tall, you know."

"You can't make yourself look different?" Emiel asked. "Larger or something."

"What would make you think I could do that?"

"Well, you can make yourself disappear." The tiny woman just glared up at him as though one thing had absolutely nothing to do with the other.

"I told that girl to sell it to you, fool man."

Emiel's mouth fell open. "Why would you do that? Why didn't you just give it to me yourself instead of making me part with money I would rather have kept?"

Now she looked disappointed in him. He wondered if he would ever understand this tinfar woman. Were they all like this?

"The little girl was from a poor family. Selling you that piece of corlite helped her a great deal, and you did a good deed to boot!"

"How do you know all that?"

Lief rolled her eyes. "She told me, obviously."

"I thought you didn't normally associate with humans."

"We don't associate with adult humans," Lief corrected. "Some of your offspring can be just as cruel, but they're generally more kind and accepting of the world around them. The little girl had gone with friends to collect fruit and berries just outside the walls. I found her alone and talked her into selling you the corlite."

"That was trusting of you," he said. "Corlite is extremely valuable."

"Why do you think I chose her and not one of the other children?"

Emiel didn't know how he could possibly answer that question, but fortunately she continued talking.

"And you're changing the subject. No tinfar would set a foot inside a human city, well, no tinfar other than an *air*, that is."

Emiel started to ask why that was, but thought better of it. He nodded for her to continue.

"That piece of corlite will help you learn how to delve, if you use it properly." She huffed at his confused expression. "Delve; meaning access the earth's *essences*. And I don't mean reach in and grab hold and wrench them out to do your bidding like those humans you call magi do. Corlite is part of the earth, and can be used as a tool to link you with the *essences*. After a while, you might not even need the stone. It's an aid. Nothing more."

"I don't know anything about any of that," Emiel said. "And I'm fine not knowing, either. Best to leave nature's power alone."

Lief gave him a look that suggested an adult patting a child on the head.

"So you don't approve of the way she uses it?" He indicated

Amoura, wondering if she was hearing all this despite their low voices.

"She uses the corlite the way it is supposed to be used," Lief said. "Though I don't think she realizes it. I think she should wean herself off of that ring. It's becoming less of an aid and more of a dependence."

"Don't tell her that," Emiel said. "If there is one thing I know about magi, it's that they believe use of the *essences* without the proper tool to channel it is dangerous and should be outlawed. In fact, in some places it is."

Lief sniffed. "Human nonsense. And you're changing the subject again! Use the corlite as an aid. It will help you understand the earth's power; its magic. It is in every living thing. We are made up of every one of the *essences*.

"That's a scary thought," Emiel said, feeling an involuntary shiver.

"What are you so afraid of?"

Emiel thought on that for a while as raindrops started to fall from the once again gathering clouds. It kept to a drizzle for a time, but as if in indecision, the light rain let up again and settled for the thick textured humid air they labored to breathe. The humidity gave way to chill as they traveled upward, and soon they were navigating through fog. A wet mist fell over them from the low-hanging clouds.

"Maybe burning myself to cinders, or drowning myself," Emiel finally answered.

"That's ridiculous," Lief said. She sounded on the verge of laughter. "Always fearing what you don't understand." She pointed at the pouch tied to his waist. "Use it. It will help you understand."

Emiel looked down at the pouch. The tinfar's words made him feel like he had a poisonous snake in there. "I don't know how."

"If you try, you will learn."

"I'm not sure if I want to."

Lief gave him a long, hard look, then shrugged. "Too bad, but it's your decision."

They crossed over rocky terrain and through wetlands, and Bone hunted and killed a few rabbits, much to Lief's displeasure. The tinfar left them while they ate, and returned only after they had departed their camp, and thus the remains of their meal.

"We'll reach the first river before nightfall," Amoura said. "We can camp there, then start before dawn."

"Won't it be dangerous trying to sleep at night here?" Emiel asked.

"Probably," Bone replied. "But I'd rather be on familiar ground if something does come, rather than while I'm stumbling around in the dark."

"Good point." Emiel looked up at the gray sky. "I'll be glad to be out of here. This gloom is depressing."

"Be thankful for it," Amoura said, gazing at the land ahead. "The clouds do not sap the moisture from our bodies. We can travel longer without water."

The magus's words were true enough, but Emiel hadn't realized how thirsty he was until they finally reached the river. He cupped his hands in the clear cold water and took a sip. The water was sweet and refreshing, and he gulped down as much as his stomach could hold. "Never had mountain fresh water before. Only from wells. As far as water goes, I have to say this is delicious."

"I'll keep first watch," Bone said. "I've got a good ear and a good nose."

"So do I take second or third watch?" Emiel asked.

Bone gave him a blank look. "Why would you take a shift?"

Emiel was getting tired of this. "Look, kid. I may not be able to whip a sword around like you, or hurl *essence* around either, but I still know how to keep an eye out for danger. Last I was aware, it doesn't take a lot of skill to open my mouth and tell everyone there's danger."

"I'm not going to tell you again to stop calling me a kid," Bone said.

"That's fine," Emiel shot back. "Stop treating me like some helpless liability and we've got a deal."

"How helpful can you truly be out here?" Bone said, his voice growing louder. "What have you killed? Have you hunted any food? Or are you only able to hunt down the shrubs and bushes that supply your spice recipes?"

Emiel laughed, which angered the young mercenary further. He thought Bone's face would explode, so red was it.

"You can throw insults all you like. Everyone has a slot to fill in the world. Mine is to help people add flavor to their food, which makes them happy. Yours is transporting people places against their will, and inserting that sword into living bodies to make them not living. I may not be as skilled at the blade and surviving in such a hostile environment as you, but I also wouldn't normally be out here. I'm out of my element as much as you would be in mine."

He saw Amoura walking off down the river, Lief in tow. He turned back to the fuming mercenary.

"We really don't need to go back and forth like this, Bone. You're good at fighting and survival out in the wild. I'm a simple spicetrader. I didn't ask for this little adventure, yet you took the pay to see that I complete it. So why not stop with trying to belittle me, and let's concentrate on surviving."

"What do you think this argument is about?" Bone snapped. "Are you truly thinking I would entrust my life to the watchful eyes of a spicetrader? I think not."

Emiel turned his back on the younger man and walked away. "Do as you will. I extended my hand to help and you spat in it. Fair enough. I'll offer nothing more."

"That's all I've needed from you from the start," he heard the young man say, but in a quieter voice. "Just shut your mouth so I can deliver you to the Creator blasted city and be done with it."

Fortunately, Emiel's back was turned so that the mercenary couldn't see his confused expression. Had it been a simple error of words when Bone had said he was 'delivering' Emiel to Altarra, or a slip of the tongue?

32

RAYNE

Perched on a beam high above the bed of the Royain of the city of Shiedra, Rayna questioned not for the first time the wisdom of this move. Royain Dimitri of the land of Nashma had sided with King Alyn against the Khatala from the start, and the foolish king was only gaining ground in his war against what the eastern lands referred to as the wild folk, or Wilders. That was why The Khamra had sent her, Rayne, for him.

Rayna thought of her lost family, and about how his family might grieve him. Her mother and father, who no doubt thought her dead upon that battlefield, more than two decades past. She wondered if they felt the same ache at the thought of her like she did them. Those first years had been the hardest. She'd been a child, darting through the horror of a battle where the earth's power had been used to devastating effect.

Every time she thought about that day, she could still smell the death and blood. The resonance of the use of the *essences* still hung strong in her nostrils. The blast of earth that had struck between herself and her parents, and had sent her flying away still caused her nightmares. She'd been within a hairsbreadth of being blasted into nothing.

Air, water, fire, and *earth.* All around her, death and destruction, and suffering. To her young sensibilities it had been the end of the world. And when the world didn't end, it had been the end of her world when she'd realized her parents were dead. For three days after the fighting had ended, young Rayna had searched among the bodies of the dead, searching for some clue to her parent's fate. She'd only found pieces of her mother's necklace lying in the middle of gruesome and unidentifiable remains.

Gone. In the blink of an eye her family was torn asunder and she was alone in the world. Now all that remained to her, Rayna Myss, sole child to Jorban and Liran—whose surname she couldn't even remember—was a burning hatred for the king of Marai. Every day she wished for and at the same time dreaded the message that would tell her it must Rayne upon King Alyn.

Rayna shook off the thought and looked down at the sleeping Royain below her. He was the monarch of an entire kingdom, and his death would leave chaos and speculation in its wake. The people would blame the Khatala, of course, despite the fact that such an act is not in their culture. By their regards, Rayna's occupation was a cowardly one. The Khatala saw honor in facing one's foe straight, with head held high, in open challenge.

The assassin shook her head. She wasn't well versed in every world culture, but she knew that in most of the eastern lands, the noble and honorable were the easiest to bring down for those attributes alone.

She flexed her fingers and slowly arched her hand back, stretching her wrists and feeling the slow pull of the spring-loaded mechanism that would launch the concealed flat blade from her sleeve with but a quick flick of her wrist. The device was genius. Similar to that of a crossbow, only miniaturized and modified to fit around the forearm. The equipment served the double function of shooting the blade as a projectile from beneath the wrist, and was also a vambrace.

She drew two daggers strapped to the sides of her legs and focused on the corlite beads in her braided hair. The beads made from her dead mother's necklace. What would her mother think of her now, about to take the life of a man with a family? She dropped away from the beam, calling upon *air* through her beads to slow her descent just enough that she could withstand the forty-foot fall.

In the first moment of her descent, doubt struck her. What if this man could be reasoned with? What if he wasn't aiding in this war just for financial benefit and to share in the spoils of claiming a land that didn't belong to him? What if he was misguided by that foolish king —whom she would love nothing more than to gut alive—and thought he was doing good for his people?

The assassin drew up short just as she landed in a crouch over the man's body. Her daggers flicked into her hands the instant she landed, and she pressed them against the hollow of Royain Dimitri's throat.

Dimitri's eyes and mouth popped open, but one look into those steel gray eyes silenced him. The assassin named Rayne watched his eyes as the realization came that she could have had him dead the instant her feet touched the bed.

"I held my stroke for a single reason, Royain," she whispered, staring into his terrified eyes. "What is that reason?"

The Royain's mouth quivered as he struggled to speak. "B ... balance," he managed. His voice was barely a whisper.

That was good. Few other than rulers knew of the existence of The Khamra.

"You are correct."

"But why me?" he whispered. "The Wilders ..." his eyes widened when hers narrowed. "The ... Khatala wage this war, not I. King Alyn was nearly killed by them, surely you must know this."

"Have you not heard any other perspectives of that encounter?"

Dimitri's mouth bobbed open and closed several times. He was searching for an answer he thought she would want to hear. "The only news that came to me was of his attempted assassination by those wild folk to the west. King Alyn is my good friend, and I came to his aid when he was in need."

"Is he still in need?"

The Royain looked confused. "Y ... yes."

A lie. She could see it in his eyes, the way his throat moved when he spoke it, as if his body squirmed against the untruth. She could practically smell it in his breath.

"What is your gain?"

"My gain?"

He was preparing a lie. Rayne sheathed one of her blades.

"My gain." His eyes flicked down, then up again. Searching. "I seek only to help defend the lands of a good man and a good fr—"

His words ended in a gurgle.

Rayne held the dagger in his neck and a her free hand over his mouth until his body stopped convulsing. She pulled the bloody weapon free and wiped it on the dead Royain's sheets. The Khamra had been right. The man was not misguided, but hoped to profit upon the annihilation of an entire people.

She had one task left.

Rayne sheathed her blade and called upon her corlite beads again and summoned *air*. With a great leap, she ascended to the beam she'd previously occupied, forty feet overhead. She stretched her arm out and caught hold, then hoisted herself up.

She ran across the beams along the ceiling, coming back to the window she'd entered from. The assassin ran across the roof of the Royain's house, which was modest in comparison to King Alyn's castle, but still easily larger than any three homes in this land. She leaped from the rooftop and glided across the street to the next rooftop, stopping just long enough to see a carriage pulled by a team of horses making its way to Dimitri's house. Royana Lindra.

Rayne had studied her target for two days, learning his and his family's patterns. Unlike her opportunistic husband, Lindra spent her days feeding the hungry, visiting the surrounding farmlands to ensure their needs met, and every other night in prayer at the monastery. This was the second night of the week, and she and their two sons would be in that carriage, on the way home to discover the death of their father and husband.

Rayna felt a pang of guilt, but Rayne forced it down. She did what must be done, and it would be one grieving family in exchange for the survival of many. If it took the death of these powerful men and Rayne's tarnished soul to stop a war with ramifications these people didn't fathom, so be it.

The assassin ran, leaping the rooftops, making her way to one more house. This one was situated dangerously close to the Royain's residence, but this last bit of business must be done.

Rayne hopped off of the roof and picked the lock on the door. In several heartbeats she was in the house, navigating its dark hallways until she came to a bedroom. She listened at the door, hearing rhythmic breathing. Rhythmic, but light breathing. A child.

She took a step away from the door, then her instincts screamed at her, and she ducked just in time to avoid a wooden pole swinging for her head. The pole struck the door where her head had been, causing a loud crash. On the other side of the door, there was a gasp, then screaming.

Rayne dropped to one knee and punched the attacker in the groin. He grunted a curse and doubled over, and the assassin came up to her feet, shoving the top of her head into his nose in the motion.

His head snapped back and he staggered away, and Rayne grabbed him by his nightshirt and yanked him toward her. She gripped him by the throat with her other hand, ignoring the blood that flowed from his nose and dripped onto her wrist.

"You might die right now," she said. This needed to be quick.

"Lyle?" they heard from the other bedroom.

"Answer her," the assassin ordered, and slightly loosened her grip.

"Just stumbled, dear," Lyle answered, his voice nasal due to his injured nose. Don't worry about it."

"Check on Dava."

"Doing it now," he called back.

Rayne kept an iron grip on his throat, but allowed him to wipe his nose on his shirt as she walked him to the door. The muffled sound of a little girl whimpering and calling for her parents came from within. Rayne looked him in the eye, then nodded her head toward the door and slowly released his throat. Her other hand rested conspicuously on the visible dagger of the many about her person.

Eyeing her, the man cracked the door open and peeked in, speaking soothing words to his daughter. A moment later, the girl quieted and he closed the door. He turned back to face the assassin, fear, but also desperation in his face. Desperation for his family more than himself. This one had a good heart.

"I beg you," he whispered, "leave my family out of this—"

"You're work is good, but it is run over by those with more power," Rayne interrupted. "You clean the mess of those more powerful than you. You act for life, and so yours continues."

Ambassador Lyle Tobain of Nashma stared at her, dumbfounded. "You're—"

"The result of the actions that have brought me here," Rayne interrupted again. "Walk the right path."

His eyes widened in alarm. "The Royain?"

"Has been visited by his actions and intentions this night."

"You killed him!" he hissed, glancing at the door to his daughter's room, then his own bedroom."

She saw the alarm in his eyes, but not sadness, or regret. This one knew the heart of the man he served.

"What have you done to this land and its people?"

"Given it an option," Rayne answered. "Walk the right path." She darted across the room and was out the front door. As soon as she was back in the night air, she bolted around the side of the house and pressed her back against the wall. Odd that there was no alarm sounded. Surely Royana Lindra had discovered her husband by now.

Rayne climbed atop a stack of crates and quietly pulled herself up to the roof of the neighboring house. She kept low and moved up the slope and down the other side, then leaped across to the next house.

She made her way toward the gates of the central portion of the city, where the Royain and his closest associates resided. From her perch, she saw that what had been four guards at the iron gates, was now eight. She looked beyond to see the city being more vigilantly patrolled. More soldiers roved the streets, and they were looking for something.

The assassin gave a mental nod of appreciation for the Royana's discretion. Instead of sounding an alarm and sending the city into chaos over the assassination of their leader, she had quickly and quietly sent word, and was having the city combed for the culprit. Information and results first.

Rayne sighed. The exit to the city would be heavily watched, and even if she managed to escape, pursuit would be swift and untiring. Leaving now would be difficult, but if she dared to stay, she would be easily recognized as a foreigner.

Still atop the roof, she lowered herself to her stomach and scanned the city. There was no apparent way out, but she might be able to continue along the rooftops.

She had to get out. Her horse grazed a mile outside of town. Hopefully the border patrols wouldn't take notice, since it roamed freely and was ladened with no gear.

Rayna navigated the rooftops, coming to the last house of the inner circle of the city that was surrounded by the iron barred fence. She summoned *air* through her corlite beads and raced across the roof. With all the strength in her legs, she gave a great leap, gliding forty feet through the air, past the fence, and into the street beyond.

She landed in a roll and sprinted down a dark street. In one leap, she was back to the rooftops and making her way to the edge of the city. There was no wall to either side of Shiedra, for the city ended in a steep drop on both sides. The only way out was through those front gates.

She drew nearer, taking a roundabout path to avoid the watchful eyes of the patrol. She leaped to another rooftop then skidded to a stop and dropped onto her stomach. Across the street on the next rooftop was an archer.

She heard a whistle, and the man nocked an arrow and swung toward her. The keen vision of an archer. Of course.

Rayna came to her feet and raced across the roof. The archer spat out his whistle and leaned his head to the side, taking a bead on her.

She looked in the general direction of the archer, but not at him. He let fly, and Rayna's hand snapped up in an outward chop. The arrow fell away in two pieces and the archer quickly drew another.

Rayna leaped from the roof and reached behind her back, drawing her twin batons. The archer drew back. Her feet touched the roof. He let fly.

The assassin threw her head and shoulders back, sliding on her knees and back with her feet next to her thighs as the arrow flew harmlessly over her face. She unfolded her legs and snapped them out in a crisscross motion, knocking the archer's feet from under him.

He hit the roof hard and she rolled over him, jabbing one baton into his midsection to steal his breath, then rapping him across the head with the other.

She came to her feet, sprinting away from the unconscious man and making her way to the next rooftop. She heard booted footsteps and pressed on. The front gate was close, if she could just make it before too many guards arrived ...

An arrow zipped past her head, and she darted to the side. She heard someone barking orders to flank her, and another whistle sounded. She looked ahead and saw the soldiers guarding the gate move into position.

Rayna thought to call upon her corlite beads again, but refrained. She would need to reserve her energy for the run, should she make it out.

"There he is!" she heard a man say. "Cut him off!"

Rayna finally reached the gate and went into a flurry of kicks and jabs with her batons, leaving two of the guards unconscious, and engaging a third. A fourth came against her, and she fell back, then went at them again. She dropped one man with a blow to the side of the head, then swept the feet from under another.

The pursuing guards arrived and surrounded her.

"Lay down your weapons," one soldier demanded. "You're surrounded."

Rayna took a quick measure of her opponents. Eleven in all. Half of them were green. They couldn't have seen more than a year of active duty at best. Several more were skilled, but were a bit winded from the pursuit. Only two looked to be in any condition to challenge her.

She stole a glance past them. More would be coming. This had to be fast.

She lunged at the closest soldier, closing the distance and driving her baton into his nose. It flattened under the force of the blow, and blood flowed freely through his fingers when he brought his hands up to the wound.

She shoved him away with a kick to the chest and dropped into a spinning swipe with her leg, tripping up a woman coming up behind her. The woman landed flat on her back and Rayne heard the air blast from her lungs. The assassin came around with a downward swing of her baton. She slammed it into the woman's chest with just enough force to dent the armor and cause pain, but not grievous injury.

While the woman groaned and squirmed on the ground, Rayna came back to her feet to meet the charge of three more soldiers. One brought his sword around in a fairly competent swipe, and she blocked it with her vambrace and snapped her arm down. She spun her hand around his forearm and grabbed his wrist. With a twist, she forced him to turn and kicked him in the lower back, sending him stumbling into his comrades.

Another whistle sounded. More booted footsteps running toward her. She attacked high and low, darting in every direction, using an overwhelmed adversary as a shield to hold off the others. Her hands and feet were a blur of motion that kept them off balance. The soldiers were trained well, but she was an assassin of the Khamra; trained in the ways of multiple adversary combat.

Several moments left almost all of the soldiers either unconscious, or on the ground clutching wounds. The remaining three soldiers became more conservative, and kept her on the defensive. They were stalling for time as reinforcements came.

Rayna feinted an attack to the soldier on her left, while at the same time launching one of her batons at the soldier on the right.

When the soldier on the left brought his sword up to block, she retreated and kicked the soldier on the right in the groin as he dodged the flying baton. His hands went to his groin as she dropped to the ground and slid between his legs, grabbing his ankle and yanking herself to a stop while causing him to fall at an awkward angle.

She recovered her baton and raced for the closed gate. With a corlite-enhanced leap, she was up and over.

Rayna landed in a roll and sprinted into the night, once again calling upon her beads to speed her steps.

33

NANDI AND AMIYA

For a week they traveled on foot, traversing clusters of boulders and outcroppings that seemed to have been piled together by giant hands. Nandi wondered how big something would have to be in order to stack those huge rocks in such a way.

She looked over her shoulder in the direction of the rivers and hills and valleys they'd crossed. Pursuit had been swift on those first two nights, but they hadn't seen any sign of their pursuers for several days. The man named Joga claimed that he didn't hear anything when he pressed his ear to the ground—odd as that was—and he also claimed not to smell them or their hunting dogs when he sniffed the air. Neither Nandi nor Amiya had ever smelled anything other than the fresh air of the wilds.

The Khatala man had kept close to the Ridgeline, a long snaking rift that divided the eastern lands from the western. Their father had said it was as if the Creator Himself knew that the two peoples couldn't get along and separated them. Nandi wondered if that was true.

"Daydreaming?" Amiya asked beside her. The land started uphill again. Lately it seemed like they would forever be traveling uphill.

"Why not?" she replied.

"True enough." Her sister gazed out at the open land. "You think he'll help us once we get to this New Dama place he keeps talking about?"

"I hope so. He seems like a good man."

"He can seem like a good man all the way to where he wants to get us."

"We found him, Amiya."

"After he'd broken out of prison for who knows what," Amiya countered.

Nandi couldn't argue with the logic, but she knew. She couldn't explain it, but she could see in the man's eyes all the way to his heart. They were not only in good company, but they were more likely to survive on the way to Altarra than if they were out here on their own. Just the thought of it made her shudder.

"And yeah, I know you can feel the light of the Creator shining down on his shoulders," Amiya remarked, "while the Illuminarians sing his praise."

"I never said that!" Nandi snapped. "Are you finished?"

Amiya held up her hands in surrender, chuckling. "Just teasing. Relax." She looked ahead, where the Khatala man was climbing atop yet another pile of boulders to get a better look at the land. "I think he's a good man, too. There's a kindness about him, though I think he doesn't really know what to do with us."

Nandi didn't disagree. She too, saw the indecision in the man's face. But she didn't blame him. Protecting two young girls in the middle of the wild lands was not something he'd had in mind when he'd stepped out the door of his home, wherever that was.

"Guess he got more than he counted on when he left his home," Amiya said, thinking the same as Nandi, as usual.

"Let's hope that once he finishes whatever he has to do in New Dama, he'll help us get to Altarra after."

"Do we even have time for that?" Amiya replied. "We don't know if Dad is already there, and what's going on with him. I have my doubts that 'bigbelly' went to all this trouble kidnapping us just to get Dad to deliver some package for him."

Nandi didn't know what was going on, but she agreed with Amiya's assessment.

Joga waved for them to join him. She felt Amiya attempting to delve *air*. It took her a bit of time, but finally she found the *essence* and used it to give her an enhanced jump that brought her almost to the top of the rocks.

Nandi did the same, with less effort finding the *essence*, and gave an enhanced leap of her own. Just doing that was exhilarating. She wanted to hold the *essences* all the time; use them all the time. But Joga had advised against it, saying that it was not a toy, and could be dangerous if abused. Adults seemed to be masters at taking the fun out of things.

The Khatala man looked down at them with disapproval.

"Look," Amiya said, "if we're going to learn, and not be totally helpless out here, we've got to practice."

Joga's only response was a skeptical look. "We are close," he said, pointing toward what looked like a wall of mountains frowning at them from several leagues away.

"Close to what?" Nandi and Amiya asked in unison.

Joga looked from one to the other, then shook his head and looked back at the mountain range past the rocky hills before them. "Close to New Dama," he answered.

"New Dama is in those mountains?" Amiya asked.

"Not far on the other side."

"Oh!" Amiya said in mock cheer. "So all we have to do is just skip our way over that little bump in the road and we're dancing in New Dama."

"Not as bad as it seems," Joga said. "Mountains are safer than the way around, and faster. Much better if we travel over. This is no worry."

Nandi and Amiya shared a doubtful look, but said nothing.

They heard a distant thumping sound, and Joga turned in the direction from where they had come. A cloud of dust exploded in the distance, followed by another. Then two more, each followed by a faint 'thump'.

"What's going on over there?" Nandi asked, peering into the distance.

"Something we're not gonna like, I'm sure," Amiya replied.

"Should go," Joga said in a quiet voice. "Should go now."

Nandi looked up at the man and saw alarm in his face. "What is it? What is that?"

"Don't know, but not good for us."

"Yeah, I have to agree with mountain man," Amiya said. "That's making me nervous. I don't care how far away it ..." she trailed off, staring. "Am I paranoid, or did one of those clouds of dirt just explode a little closer?"

Nandi felt dread creeping up her spine. "If so, then I'm just as paranoid, because that one was even closer." She pointed at another cloud of dust that was indeed a little closer."

"Did I just see some tiny thing bounce off the ground and fly in the air?" Amiya said. "See, look there!" she pointed at what looked like a speck in the sky. When it hit the ground, they heard a resounding 'thump', that was more powerful this time.

"Um," Nandi said, backing away. "I think those things are not far enough away for my comfort."

She looked up at Joga, who was also backing away while still staring. She slapped his arm and he looked down at her, then nodded.

"We go!" he said, and she felt him summon air and guide it under him as he hopped off the boulder.

Nandi waited while Amiya focused. It took her some time, but she managed to find *air*, and began to gather it. Nandi looked back in the distance. Whatever those bouncing things were, they were much closer now. Too close. Where they really coming for them, or was this coincidence?

Amiya hopped off the rock, and Nandi delved *air* and followed. Her descent was fast, but she slowed it just enough to land safely. She wondered how high of a fall she could make this way.

As soon as she hit the ground, they took off in a jog, navigating between the scattered boulders and the few trees that dotted the rocky, hilly landscape.

They jogged for what had to have been a league or two before taking a break in the shade of a boulder and starting again. For a while, they hadn't heard the thumping sounds, and Nandi was starting to believe whatever was causing the sound may have gone in a different direction.

The wind started to pick up and blew against them, and dark clouds rolled over the mountains to darken the sky. Nandi heard another 'thump', followed by another. She ran a little faster. "I don't think I like that." She pointed at the dark gray canopy moving toward them.

"Oh thank the Creator," Amiya said. "Otherwise, it would have been too easy to run away with the wind already in our faces. Now we can run in the rain, too."

As if to punctuate her sister's sarcasm, there was a rumble of thunder, and the distant sky flickered with lightning.

"How did it get here so fast?" Nandi asked. They hopped down a series of mounds before coming to more level ground again.

"Storms can come fast," Joga answered, putting his hand on a log and swinging his feet over. "Can blow in with no warning."

More thumping, this time four in rapid succession. Nandi's heart gave a leap of fear. "We need to run faster."

Thud thud thud thud. The sound came faster and louder, and now she felt the impact under her feet. Thud thud thud thud. *What is that?*

Thud thud thud thud.

Amiya glanced over her shoulder, then looked again and her eyes widened in fear. She screamed, "Faster!"

They ran. The thuds behind them became crashes. The sky howled at them, and another flash of lightning lit the surroundings. Four more rapid crashes.

"Amiya, what's chasing us?" Nandi shouted. A drop of water spattered against her forehead. Then another. Then a few more. Several labored breaths later the rain fell in earnest.

"Just figure it's a bunch of things that want to kill us and you've got it," Amiya huffed. She lowered her head in an all-out sprint.

Nandi did the same and tried not to look back at the sound of rapid crashing behind them. She almost slipped, and had to focus on the terrain, as the ground grew soft and wet under the bombarding rain.

Four more crashes. Several bits of rock and mud hit Nandi in the back and shoulders. Those things must be right on top of them. She chanced a glance over her shoulder and a scream tore from her throat.

She dove aside just as a something tall and heavy crashed into the ground where she'd been. She hit the wet ground and started to half slide half roll. She scrambled, trying not to roll out of control downhill while trying not to get stomped by whatever had nearly squashed her.

After some scrabbling and scraped hands and knees, she found her feet just as the ground shook again. The violent crash knocked her off her feet, and she landed bent over and stumbling into a face-first fall. She threw her hands out to break her fall, then pushed herself up into a half-run-half-stumble.

Nandi had taken no more than a handful of steps when a third crash shook the ground, followed by a fourth. That last rumble sent her in a headlong dive to the wet ground. She gritted her teeth as her body bounced painfully over the rocks.

Now she was sliding headfirst downhill. She turned her body in an attempt to get back to her feet, but that only sent her into a sideways roll. She knew she would be in trouble if she picked up speed, so she threw her arms out. She gritted her teeth through the pain of rocks and exposed roots biting into her hands and arms, and managed to slow down enough to get her bearings.

Nandi spat out a mouthful of dirt and blood, and looked around. Amiya and Joga were nowhere to be seen. She looked up and screamed again. One of those things was coming straight down on her. She instinctively curled into a ball and clamped her eyes shut.

The crash didn't come, and when she opened her eyes, she saw that the monster had been knocked into a nearby tree. It made a moaning sound, and she dared to hope it wouldn't get up.

It climbed to its feet and stared at her with malevolent orange eyes above where a nose and mouth should have been. It started to lumber toward her, swinging arms so long its hands nearly touched the ground.

Nandi shrugged off the aches from her tumble, hopped to her feet and ran. She yelled for her sister, but in the roaring deluge she didn't know whether she would have heard Amiya's response or not.

The ground was soft and slippery now, and Nandi had to focus more on not falling and sliding downhill than actually running from those things.

She looked over her shoulder and saw it just as it leaped into the air again. High into the air. In the dark gray sky, she couldn't see it for a moment, and so she ran on. Several heartbeats later she looked up over her shoulder again and saw it quickly plummeting toward her.

Nandi felt a rush of wind, not against her, but at her back, and her steps took her farther, faster. Behind her there was a loud splash. The ground didn't tremble as much as before, and Nandi looked over her shoulder to see that the monster had landed and fallen on the slippery slope.

She looked ahead just as another of the monsters landed not five feet in front of her. The impact sent her and a good portion of the ground flying away.

Nandi hit the ground in a spray of mud and rocks, but scrambled back to her feet and ran. From the corner of her eye she saw the thing crouching low to the ground, watching her. She kept a mental note that the other one was still behind somewhere, and likely had leapt into the air again. She changed directions, zigzagging her way down the hill. How long till she hit flat ground?

The ground exploded behind her, then beside her as the two monsters landed near again. The impact was so close that she bounced into the air. The downward slope steepened and now she was airborne and falling.

After several dozen feet, the ground started to level off, and she crashed into it in a forward roll, tumbling head over heels. She hit a hard surface and pain exploded in her left leg.

The world continued to spin, and then she was gliding free and over a cliff.

<hr/>

AMIYA TRIED to follow when she saw two of those tall yellow monsters go after her sister, but Joga snatched her away just before another one crashed into the ground where she would have been.

Almost dying by being splattered on the ground had a nerve-wracking effect, but she forced herself to keep up with the mountain man. They half ran half slid down the slope, trying to keep from being stomped.

Amiya thought she heard her sister calling for her off to the left, but she couldn't be sure with this Fallen cursed storm roaring in her ears.

She slipped and slid down the slope, scrambling over boulders and swinging around trees. Another one of the yellow monsters crashed into the ground beside a towering redwood tree. She heard the snapping of wood as the tree broke in two and fell toward her.

Amiya fell backward onto her rear end and slid toward the felled tree. She screamed at the sight of the giant trunk falling toward her and threw herself flat on her back. The tree crashed just inches above her, and she clamped her eyes shut against the snapping limbs that stung her face.

After a few rapid breaths, she opened her eyes and looked up. Through the rain she saw one of the things in the air, plummeting toward her. She rolled onto her stomach and pushed herself backward. The brownish yellow monster crashed into the ground and sent her flying backwards.

Amiya hit the ground and tumbled into a tree. She gritted her teeth against the pain in her back as she forced herself upright. She braced herself against the tree and willed her legs to stop shaking. She looked up to see the thing in the air again, falling toward her. "You've got to be kidding me," she groaned, and stumbled away.

The crash sent her bouncing and tumbling again, and Amiya was sure she'd swallowed a good amount of mud and other things she didn't want to think about.

She managed to reach out and grab hold of an upraised root, but her momentum was too strong, and the root was torn from her grasp. Now she was spinning sideways on her stomach, the palm of her hand stinging, and her teeth clamped shut as rain and mud and rocks pelted her face.

Amiya slid onto a flat boulder and lay there for a moment, panting. When she looked up, she saw both of the things in the air coming toward her.

She narrowed her eyes. *That's it.* She drew *fire* and *air* to her call, and sent a blast of each at the incoming monsters with a thrust of her palms.

The gust of *air* threw one of the monsters into a nearby group of boulders, while the second was engulfed in flames, its course only slightly altered.

Amiya whipped her hands around in an arc and hit the burning monster in the side. The flames were extinguished, but the monster's body looked to have been crushed on one side. It hit the ground in a heap and tumbled down the hill.

Amiya looked to where the other monster had hit, and saw it staggering back to its feet, the rain rinsing its pale green blood off of the rock. She looked around, but saw neither Nandi nor Joga. The monster let out a moaning sound, and started toward her. When she looked at it, her blood lit afire. That thing had separated her from her sister, and Nandi was hurt. She could feel it. Nandi was more than just her sister, she was part of her, as Amiya was part of Nandi. Her anger flared.

She brought *fire* to the monster. It wasn't a gentle delve, guiding the *essence* like her sister did. It wasn't delving and bending the *essence* to her will through use of corlite, like Selvetar had taught her. It was as though she had merged with the *essence*. One moment she was standing in front of the lumbering monster, the next, she was living fire.

She projected that fire at the yellow-brown monster and engulfed it in a column of flames.

Amiya narrowed her glowing red eyes, and this time a wave of living fire erupted from her; a projection of her rage. Despite the pouring rain, the monster was incinerated in but a few heartbeats. With the *essences* flowing through her, Amiya let her head fall back and reveled in the immense wave of power. She rode it like a wild horse, or a roaring rapid, and it was like nothing she could have imagined.

Nandi's scream shattered her bliss, and Amiya looked in the direction of the cry. It was useless. The rain was too heavy to see anything.

The sky rumbled again, and another flash of lightning streaked from the sky to the ground somewhere ahead.

Amiya managed to shield her eyes enough that she wasn't totally blinded. She continued down the hill until she came upon Joga on hands and knees, trying to catch his breath. In front of him was a large patch of charred earth and the body of one of those monsters. Flames licked its body like firewood. The stench of burning flesh mixed with the crackling sound of the flames made her retch.

"Nandi?" Joga asked.

Amiya shook her head. "I was hoping you'd found her."

"No," he replied.

Amiya forced down her panic and looked back in the direction she'd heard her sister's scream. "Come on." She offered a hand to the large man. "I heard her scream."

They worked their way across the hillside, slipping along the muddy ground. Amiya hoped that the lack of any more pursuit meant that Nandi had killed the other two monsters.

"You're sure?" Joga asked.

Amiya nodded. When the mountain man gave her a doubtful look, she just moved faster. "I'd know if something happened to her. She's alive."

Part of it was hope, but more of it was truth. Deep down, she knew that if Nandi had been killed, she'd know. Amiya forced her fluttering heart to slow down, and wiped the water from her face.

Luckily, her tears were mixed with the rain, so he wouldn't see her crying like a little baby.

They came to the base of a cliff and looked up as if they could see anything through the deluge. Amiya shielded her eyes with her hand, squinting up at the cliff, then down the hill. Was she up there, or further down? "Maybe we should split up."

Another scream came from further down, and they turned and raced in that direction. *Blast this Fallen cursed rain*, she thought. *We'll be lucky if we don't fall and break our necks trying to get to her in time.*

Joga lost his footing and fell on his backside, sliding nearly a dozen feet before recovering.

"Watch your step, mountain man," Amiya said. "You wouldn't want to take a tumble ..."

She lost her footing and rolled head over heels downhill. She had the presence of mind to fight to right herself, lest she open her skull on some Fallen cursed rock. After banging her knees and elbows on more than a few rocks and exposed roots, she eventually managed to stop rolling, but she was still sliding.

Cursing, Amiya managed to turn onto her back, and her eyes widened when she saw one of those yellowish, jumping monsters below, back turned away from her. She tried to summon *fire*, but she hit a bump in the slope and pitched forward.

Amiya clenched her teeth, bracing herself for the impact and hoping she wouldn't be impaled by one of those horrible spikes on its shoulders.

A thin column of fire shot past her and slammed into the monster's back. Amiya could feel the heat from the fire as it continued to stream into the dying monster. A powerful gust of air enveloped her and slowed her descent.

By the time she hit the ground, the monster was little more than a charred brick. Amiya didn't know which was worse, the throbbing pain of her bruised body, or the stench of burning monster flesh.

She climbed to her feet as Joga came down beside her. He looked around, and she had the feeling he was trying to avoid sniggering at her, considering her last comment to him. She looked around, but if Nandi had left any tracks, they were likely washed away.

"There!" Joga said, pointing to the sky.

Amiya looked up and saw one of those yellow things in the air. It was starting to fall, and Amiya was sure it was guiding its descent toward Nandi.

She started to delve *fire*, but Joga called upon it faster, and sent a blazing funnel at the monster. He missed, and it dropped out of sight into the trees below.

Amiya cursed yet again and took off. The ground was almost level now, so she took less effort at picking her steps. She heard Joga calling from behind for her to slow down and take care, but all she could think about was reaching Nandi.

Just before she came to a tree line ahead, she saw the thing shoot into the air again. She felt relief and alarm at the same time, for surely Nandi was still alive if that thing was still trying to flatten her.

Amiya skidded to a stop and her anger flared again. She grabbed hold of *fire* and sent a wave of flames at the monster. She could not have missed, for the flames were widespread, but though the monster was indeed immolated by her attack, the tops of the trees caught fire.

The tips of redwoods and oaks burned, but fortunately the rain had dampened them, and so the flames—though burning hotter than any normal occurring fire—were quick to die out. It was a lesson that could have been much more costly, Amiya realized. She could have started a forest fire with her sister caught in the middle of it.

"The last one!" Joga shouted over the storm. "Was four of them!"

"Then let's get moving and find her!" Amiya yelled back.

She nearly lost her footing again, but a strong hand caught her arm and held her upright. When she looked up to thank him, she saw that Joga's attention was fixed on the hills from where they'd just come.

Amiya followed his gaze to see small and medium-sized rocks break apart and tumble away. The ground shook again.

"Now what?" she muttered.

"Wrong," Joga said. "Something very wrong."

"You're sure?" Amiya asked. The frown on Joga's face showed he didn't appreciate the sarcasm so she shrugged. "Of course something's wrong."

"No," he said. The ground shook again, more violently this time. "Evil. Something evil in the world. Is not normal."

The ground shook again, this time dislodging several boulders. "No arguing that." Amiya turned away.

They ran into the trees, feeling and hearing the pounding of the boulders tumbling toward them. Amiya ran as fast as her legs could take her, the Khatala man right behind her. She knew his longer, stronger legs could carry him much faster through these trees, but he was probably trying to protect her. Amiya would return that protection by keeping an eye out front.

She heard cracking from behind, as if trees were being snapped like twigs, but she didn't dare look back. Joga would warn her if the thing was gaining on them.

She started to veer to the side. A quick turn might slow her too much, but if she continued to run and move off to the side, whatever was back there might not roll over them. She felt another pounding on the ground, followed by another, then another, and the ground shook yet again. She wondered if the Fallen themselves were at their backs.

A wheezing sound drowned out the roaring rain, and this time Amiya did glance over her shoulder. They had managed to move out of the path of the falling boulders, but there had been only a few of them. What continued to follow was not rock, nor another of those jumping monsters, but something bigger. Amiya's heart sank. This thing was bigger than the giant monster that had crawled out of the ground back in Vyne.

For the love of the Illuminarians. Is the world ending? She lowered her head and sprinted on, but she didn't know how much farther she could run. Her legs were starting to burn and grow heavy, and her breathing was labored.

"Getting closer," Joga said from behind.

Amiya didn't even bother to look back. "I can't run any faster." She heard his breathing getting closer. He was probably about to pass her, and she couldn't blame him. The thing chasing them was terrifying. To her surprise, he swept his arm under her legs. She cried out in surprise as her feet left the ground and her back hit his other arm. The world spun, and she was suddenly lying over his shoulder with a clear—if bouncing—view of the horror chasing them.

On four legs, it stood easily fifteen feet tall, and at least that much long. Its back and sides were littered with tiny spikes that shredded the trees it happened to brush against, and every one of its giant paws was equipped with three long thick claws that dug into the ground and left scars that a human could lay inside of.

Its flat head was protected by what looked like a plate of thick hard bone. No, Amiya realized as it lowered its head and snapped the trunk of a towering redwood. That wasn't protection, but a weapon.

The thing let out another loud wheezing sound, and a long, barbed tongue shot out toward them.

Eyes going wide, Amiya grabbed hold of *fire* and sent a small wave at the monster. It retracted its tongue and made an angry wheezing sound. It batted another tree aside with that thick head and looked at her with large red eyes. Those eyes weren't that of an animal predator. Those eyes were evil. She could see it; feel it. What was that thing?

Still holding *fire*, it was easier for her to grab the other *essences*, so she summoned *earth*. Amiya squinted her eyes shut through the effort, and managed to pull the ground up between them. The monster stumbled, but kept on, and she tried again. The ground trembled and Amiya grunted and sent a wave of *earth* crashing into the beast.

The force of the wave knocked it onto its back, and Amiya slapped Joga on the back. "It's down, do that lightning thing you do!"

The mountain man put her down, turned, and dropped into a low stance. He closed his eyes and started to hum, then balled his fists. He opened his hands and spread them wide.

Amiya felt the hairs on her arms and the back of her neck stand on end, and she felt a tingling of electricity in her body. When Joga opened his eyes, she saw that they were glowing in a color that was a blend of blue and silver.

Joga looked to the sky and it rumbled. "Step back," he said, and Amiya moved away; far away. She was still moving away when a bolt of lightning streaked down from the sky and engulfed the Khatala man.

The force of the energy lifted Amiya from her feet, and again, she fell sprawling to the ground. She lifted herself on one elbow and shielded her eyes with her arm. That much raw energy was surely the death of Joga, but when her vision cleared, she saw him standing tall amidst a shower of electricity until he was surrounded by a living bolt of lightning.

Even from this distance Amiya could feel the energy crackling in the air. In the presence of such power, she felt tiny; insignificant.

The electric bolt sped away from Joga's body and struck the monster. It spasmed and rolled on its back, wheezing through what must be an agonizing assault. When it finally ended the beast lay still on the ground, tendrils of smoke slithering from its body.

Joga fell to his knees and panted. Amiya rushed over to him, but he swallowed and held up a hand, nodding that he was alright.

She helped him to his feet and they started away, but stopped when they heard a scraping sound. Amiya's mouth fell open, and she and Joga looked over their shoulders to see the thing actually struggling to right itself.

"You've got to be kidding me," Amiya breathed.

"Run," Joga said. "Just run."

He stumbled, but she pulled him along, and they started off in a jog. She looked over her shoulder again, but the thing was still working its way off of its back and onto its side.

"What's it made of?" she asked, looking up at him. "You filled it with lighting."

"From the world below," Joga answered. "Nothing from this world could live through that."

"The world below?" Amiya replied. "You mean the underworld?"

"What your people call it," he said. "Evil from the world below is surfacing. Something happened in this world."

"Of course," Amiya replied dryly.

She heard that terrible wheezing sound, and soon the thumping of its footfalls. They navigated around the clumps of trees while the galloping monster crashed through them. Amiya hadn't realized how far they'd run, but the no longer distant mountain range was closer now.

"There's no way ... we can ... start to climb with that ... thing on our backs." She looked over her shoulder again. It was gaining ground. "We're gonna have to stop and fight."

"Yes," was all that Joga said.

Amiya tried to delve. Her legs were burning and growing heavier with each step. Her breathing grew more labored, and it was all she could do just to keep moving. She was at the limits of her endurance but still she delved, until finally she found a sliver of *essence*. It was barely a strip, but enough to grasp.

Amiya held *fire*, and sought to pull forth more of the power, but her hold on it slipped away along with her footing, and she was suddenly tumbling downhill again. Beside her, Joga had also fallen. It was a painful fall filled with more rocks and more bumps, but eventually they rolled to a stop.

The mountain man was tough, she had to credit him, for Joga was immediately on his feet. Amiya groaned, and with an effort, climbed to her feet as well. Behind them was a rather steep hill, and above was not open sky, but only a little of it surrounded by a ceiling of earth.

A pair of large red orbs appeared over the opening and glared down at them. It let out a frustrated wheezing sound, and stomped the ground.

Amiya and Joga flinched at the violence, and cast wary glances at the bits of rock and soil that dislodged overhead with each stomp. She hoped that thing didn't bring it down on them.

The monster wheezed again, and Amiya started to back away, but noticed that there was nothing but darkness behind them.

The beast backed away from the opening and they heard and saw nothing else of it for a long time. Still they waited, Amiya watching for it, while Joga kept an eye on the darkness behind. He was holding the *essences*, she could feel. She realized that she, too, was holding *fire*. How did he hold all of them at once like that? She'd seen Nandi do the same.

"You think it's gone?" she finally asked after some time had gone by. She felt Joga delve *air* more deeply than the others, and then a gust of wind swirled around them. She smelled a horrible stench that was a combination of something foul and burnt.

"You smelled that," he said. It wasn't a question. "It waits for us."

"But why?" Amiya asked. "Why was it and those other things after us in the first place?"

"What I want to know," another voice responded from the darkness.

34

EMIEL

Running again. Emiel figured they must have gotten no more than a few hours of sleep before the morgs had found them. The irony of the situation was that it wasn't Bone who had detected them, but Lief.

The tinfar had discovered the wolfish beasts far enough away that the group was able to gather their gear and get away before the ambush. Even though he didn't admit it, Emiel could tell by the young mercenary's silence that he knew he wouldn't have detected the danger as early as Lief had to give them this head start.

They came to a shallow stream and splashed across, high-stepping through the water to the other side. Until that moment, Emiel had forgotten that there was one thing worse than being cold, and that was being cold and wet.

They heard barking from behind, and Emiel looked over his shoulder. He still couldn't see the wolf-like animals, but there was no doubt they were back there.

"This way!" Lief pointed ahead and to the right, toward a steep hill. It wouldn't be the easiest climb, but there were trees along the side that would be of help.

Emiel looked at Lief with admiration and no small amount of

jealousy. How the tiny woman was able to run ahead of them when their legs were twice the length of her body was baffling.

He heard splashing and looked over his shoulder again to see five dark brown morgs galloping across the stream. The little naive part of his mind had held hope that the morgs would be put off by the water, but either they didn't care, or were too hungry.

"You keep looking backwards, you're going to run into a tree," Bone remarked from just ahead.

Emiel responded by putting his head down and running faster.

Just behind Lief, Amoura ran, her dark blue robes flapping behind her. Emiel had seen a fair number of magi in his life, and he found the woman's dexterity impressive. Most that devoted their lives to the study of the earth's power were often less physically fit; either thin, portly, or something in between, but rarely athletic.

The terrain began to incline, and their pace slowed. Emiel grabbed hold of nearby trees to boost himself, and even crawled on all fours using partially exposed boulders and roots as leverage. His burning legs screamed at him to stop, but he dare not. The barking was getting louder, closer, and Emiel forced himself not to look back.

"Keep going," he heard Lief say. "I'll slow them down."

Emiel kept climbing. When he came up beside Lief, he cast her a questioning look. She responded with a grim nod, and turned her attention back down the hill.

This time, he did glance over his shoulder, and the sight of very near snapping jaws and drooling maws sent a wave of adrenaline coursing through him, and he sprang upward, clawing his way over the rocks and bushes.

Down below, the ground exploded to a resulting chorus of whining animals, and the sound of large bodies tumbling away.

Emiel crawled to the top of the hill with Amoura and fell onto his side just as Bone came up beside him. Below, Lief was easily making her way up, with a pile of morgs writhing at the base of the hill, struggling to right themselves. They eventually did, and started back up.

"Thank the Creator for high ground," Bone sighed. "You gonna work your stuff?" he said to Amoura.

The woman closed her eyes, and when she opened them again, they were glowing dark brown. The ground shook, and then several boulders dislodged from the hill and tumbled down into the climbing morgs.

The sounds of bones snapping and horrible shrieking rent the air, and Emiel felt a pang of remorse.

Beside him, Lief gave his wrist a squeeze. "Those are not like lions, or even jarku." Emiel looked down into her childlike brown eyes as she spoke. Those eyes shown with the innocence of nature. "Morgs are creatures that reflect evil."

Emiel frowned and looked down the hill at the mass of twisted and broken bodies. He felt a shiver. "What do you mean, reflect evil?"

"Only when evil has touched the world do monsters like these surface in real numbers." Lief also looked back down the hill and her eyes hardened. It was a startling change that reminded Emiel that as innocent as nature was, it could be ruthless.

"The four-armed monsters that attacked you outside Carlayn are called drauk. They come cursing in the foul language of the under-world. With them came the appearance of a serai, leapers, and morg appearing in numbers." Lief looked up at him again. "Like bubbles of evil emerging from a cauldron."

Amoura turned away from the carnage below. "There has always been evil in the world, tinfar. There's never been a shortage of it among men."

"The reach of men is only so far," Lief replied.

Emiel shrugged off the shock of the scene below and climbed to his feet. He turned away from the carnage to see at least another league or two of trees and hills ahead. It seemed a short distance and a world away.

"Someone tell me the end of this place is on the other side of that," Emiel said. "I wouldn't even mind if it's a lie."

"No lie," Amoura said. "We've passed beyond The Triplets. That expanse will take us out of here."

"Let's move," Bone sheathed his sword and started out. "I'd like to be done with this place."

"Sounds like we actually agree on something," Emiel said.

"Yeah, don't get used to it."

Emiel hid his smirk. It almost sounded like friendly sarcasm from the mercenary.

The mood was shattered when Lief hissed through her teeth. She turned this way and that, eyes going wide.

"What is it?" Emiel asked. They looked around, but no one saw what had put the tinfar on edge.

"Soulrender!" she growled, backing away toward the edge of the hill.

"A what?" Emiel asked, not at all liking the sound of it.

"What more can come at us?" Bone said, drawing his sword again. "This whole place is evil."

"I see nothing," Amoura said.

Emiel had to give the woman credit. If she was nervous, she held it well in check. She remained still, only her eyes moving to scan their environment. He nearly fell over when a gray flame the size of his hand seeped out of the ground near his foot. It rose lazily into the air, swaying as if being gently moved by a breeze he didn't feel.

"We must be gone from here. Now." Lief continued to back away.

More gray flames floated from the ground and rose into the air around them. Bone cursed and swept his sword through a nearby flame. The blade passed through with no more effect than if it had been actual fire.

"Your weapon has no use against it," Lief said.

"They don't seem to be much of a threat," Bone replied.

At that moment the floating flames converged on them. The group moved away until they stood back to back. A flame suddenly darted forward and went into Bone's chest. The mercenary dropped to one knee, clutching his chest with curled fingers. His eyes were wide with terror, and mist puffed from his mouth with each gasp.

"It's killing him!" Emiel said.

"I said let's go!" Lief turned and fled down the hill.

"Up, on your feet," Emiel grunted, tugging on Bone's arm. "Time to go."

"I ... I can't," he said. Tears welled in his eyes. "It's eating me from inside."

Despite all of the horrors they had faced together, Emiel had never once seen fear like this from the young man. He looked around and saw the rest of the little flames floating closer.

"On your feet," Emiel repeated. "We're not done yet, kid."

"I told you to *quit* calling me that."

Despite the situation, Emiel smiled. Whatever that thing was doing to him, it wasn't strong enough to eat through the mercenary's dislike of being called a kid.

Bone squinted his eyes shut and with Emiel's help, struggled to his feet. Amoura slipped her shoulder under his other arm, and together they turned and picked their way down.

"Hurry!" Lief said from further down. "The soul flames cannot consume you, but they will slow you down so that it can get you."

"Well, it's doing its job," Bone said. "His breath was still labored, but he seemed to be recovering. His steps grew more stable with each stride.

"You mean those things aren't it?" Emiel said.

Lief didn't answer, but continued on. They'd been running from all manner of monsters for days now, but he'd never seen her so urgent to get away from something. He glanced around Bone's red haired head at Amoura. The magus didn't look like she had any answers, but she did look nervous enough to give Emiel that extra strength to get Bone moving faster.

The wind picked up, and he squinted through the gusts. A moan floated on the air like a baritone singer's lament. It made the hairs on Emiel's neck and arms stand on end. *Is there no end to this?*

"The soulrender," Lief squeaked, and now she practically defied gravity as she ran down the hill. Perhaps it was a trait of an earth tinfar.

Emiel felt something following and looked over his shoulder. A humanoid mist with glowing white eyes followed not more than two dozen paces behind.

Emiel nearly fell down the hill at the sight. "By the Creator," he breathed.

"I'm good. I'm good!" Bone said, catching Emiel's fright.

Emiel and Amoura didn't need to be told twice. They gently released him and the three practically slid down the hill.

"What's behind us?" Bone said. They sacrificed caution for speed as they stumbled and slid down.

"You don't wanna know," Emiel replied. "Let's get away first, and I'll tell you later."

More gray flames rose from the ground around them, but they pushed on. A flame rose in front of Emiel too quickly for him to avoid it, and he passed right into it, or rather, it passed right through him.

He fell backwards, gasping for air that wouldn't come. It felt like a claw sank into his chest and grabbed hold of his soul. Now he knew why that thing was called a soulrender. If it got to him, it would tear his soul from his body. The pain was like nothing he'd ever felt. His very being in the grip of the monster, and his mind in the grip of terror, strength left his body and he sprawled on his back, sliding downward.

"Get up!" Bone grabbed him under the shoulder and yanked him back to his feet. "If you make me carry you and we fall to our deaths, I'll not be forgiving you anytime soon."

Emiel barely registered the humor, instead focusing on not allowing his soul to be torn away. He clamped his eyes shut. Visions of his twin daughters came to him. They were locked away and held against their will, waiting for him, needing him to survive. What would happen to them if he gave up and died here? They would be without parents in this merciless world of monsters, both human and animal.

He clenched his teeth and fought against the assault, putting one shaky foot in front of the other. He felt the soulrender draw closer, and he forced the flame inside of him out. He fought the battle inside himself until the ethereal claw fell away as if evaporating into the air it was composed of.

"Hey magus!" Bone yelled. "It's right on top of us!"

Amoura turned and sent a wave of fire at the soulrender. It walked right through the flames as if they weren't there. She sent spears of ice that passed through it to stab into the ground behind.

"Move faster," she said. "Nothing works."

"Hurry!" Lief said from the bottom of the hill. "It can only follow so far."

"And how far is far enough?" Bone yelled down at her.

"It grows weaker with each step," the tinfar answered. "We have to keep going till it's gone."

"Great answer," he growled, stumbling again under Emiel's weight. "You think you can help out, spicetrader?"

"Getting ... better," Emiel huffed as the last of that terrible mist left his body.

"Damned horrible experience isn't it?" Bone asked.

"I'll have to search for a more powerful word to describe that, but horrible will do for now."

The last dozen feet from the end of the slope, Emiel's foot caught on a hidden rock, and he pitched forward. He landed on his stomach so hard he bounced, and the fall quickly turned into a sideways role to the base of the hill. The others made it to the bottom as he groaned and struggled onto his side. Bone hoisted him to his feet again, and with the adrenaline pumping through his veins and that awful baritone moaning on the wind, Emiel pushed through the residual pain and kept pace with the others. They dashed between trees, around low shrubbery, and over rocks until they reached a crevasse that stretched in either direction as far as he could see. Emiel leaned forward to look down. The drop was more than thirty feet.

"Keep running," Amoura shouted.

"If that fall doesn't kill us, we'll be broken all the same," Bone said.

"Trust me," Amoura replied.

Emiel found that easy to say and harder to do, but he was left with the choice of trusting her, or having his soul ripped apart.

The wind howled again, but the group backed up, lowered their heads, and ran.

"I hope you get whatever you're doing right, magus," Bone growled, his red hair whipping on top of his head.

The ground in front of them fell away, and Emiel thought his heart might just stop from fear.

"Jump!" Amoura said, and they did, hollering as they fell.

They were going to die. Emiel knew it. As the ground rushed toward them, he knew that he would not survive the impact, and even if he did, he would wish he hadn't. As gravity rushed him to his death, a fleeting thought broke through, and he wondered if the soulrender could snatch his soul away when it separated from his dead body.

The wind grew stronger, and it felt as if a blanket enveloped him. The air swirled around them, and their descent slowed. He glanced over at Amoura, and saw the magus's arms outstretched, legs together and straight, like a slowly descending cross. Her head fell back, and her glowing silver eyes looked to the heavens.

About six feet from the ground, the wind suddenly fell away. The unexpected drop sent them crashing to the ground where they lay sprawled like a pile of logs.

Emiel gritted his teeth against the sensation of what had to have been a thousand rocks bruising his bones as he'd rolled over them. When the adrenaline drained away, every ache came rushing in.

"Great show, but the finish needs work," Bone groaned, holding his head.

"The effort ... is taxing," Amoura said between breaths.

Emiel climbed to his feet and went to help her up. They looked up at the cliff behind where the soulrender had just arrived. It didn't hesitate as it reached the edge and stepped off the cliff, seemingly walking on air—or rather, down it—and came straight for them.

"Oh for the love of the Creator ..." Bone started.

"No," Lief said. "Look."

"I'd rather run," Emiel replied, but then he noticed the soulrender growing more insubstantial with each step. Several steps closer, and it started to slow. It leaned forward and reached for them, but it's body broke apart and evaporated before their eyes.

"Is it dead?" Emiel asked.

"No," Lief replied. "It reached the end of its domain."

"How can something with no physical substance have a limited domain?" Emiel asked.

"How about you find a book and read about it when we're someplace safe," Bone replied. Despite the sarcasm, Emiel couldn't disagree.

"We're nearly out of this mess of a place," Amoura said. She looked tired.

"We push on," Bone said. "I'll feel more at ease when this Fallen cursed place is behind us."

"Something doesn't want us to leave," Lief said. She had a faraway look about her.

Bone sighed. "And of course you can't tell us what that something is, I'm sure."

"I can tell you that it is a malevolent presence that's attached itself to a part of the earth like a disease." She pointed. "It's just ahead of us,"

"Then we can go around it," Amoura said.

"The mountains are too steep if we travel east," Lief said, "and you don't want to go west from here."

"Here comes that sinking feeling," Emiel said.

"Darkwood cats prowl the woods northwest of here-"

"We go straight," Amoura interrupted, her tone surprisingly nervous.

Emiel had never seen a darkwood cat, but he'd heard stories of the shapeshifting terrors. Judging by the magus's reaction, those stories weren't exaggerated.

"I'm not going anywhere near a place where even one of those things live," Bone said. "Whatever is waiting for us up ahead, I'll take my chances with that."

The clouds finally broke, and the travelers saw the first bit of sunlight in two days. Emiel let his head fall back and enjoyed the warm rays on his face. All too soon, though, the drifting clouds merged and covered the world in gloom once more.

They walked at an easy pace, each heeding an unspoken agreement that they needed to conserve their energy for whatever awaited them ahead. Emiel thought a great deal of that energy would be spent running.

The sunless gray sky continued to frown down on them as they pressed on, passing unmolested through patches of woods and over rock formations and across the last running stream. They started to top off their waterskins but Lief warned against it, saying that the water was most surely tainted.

The angry clouds finally decided to open, and the rain came. It lasted just long enough to soak their clothes through and dampen their moods further. Once the rain left, humidity took its place, and mosquitoes descended.

"I guess the good in all this is that the weather couldn't get worse," Emiel muttered.

Less than an hour later the weather grew cold and the rain returned. Then came the hail.

Bone glared at him. "Had to open your mouth, eh spicetrader?"

Emiel snorted. "If my words had that kind of power, I wouldn't be anywhere near here."

The hail grew stronger, and soon their ears were filled with the sound of ice crashing on the rocky ground. A piece half the size of a fist smacked Emiel in the back of the head. He stumbled forward, seeing stars.

"By the stinking breath of a Fallen!" Bone cursed. "Are we still in our world, or in the armpit of the underworld itself?"

More large balls of ice crashed to the ground around them, and the group started to run. The ground shook, and Emiel thought he heard a long, loud moan. "Should I even ask what that was?"

"No," Amoura answered.

"It's coming!" Lief shouted over the roaring hail.

"Really?" Bone snapped. "Are ya sure?"

The earth shook again, and ahead of them the ground broke apart and a large portion of it lifted, as if being pushed up by a mighty hand.

They veered around it and the ground shook again, but this time it didn't stop.

"What is this?" Bone yelled.

They pressed on, struggling to keep their footing on the wet and violently shaking ground. Another piece of earth broke apart and lifted on their left, while it dropped away on the right. Ahead, the ground started to glow red, as if melting.

Beside Emiel, Amoura cried out and faltered. He slipped his hand under her arm and held her up till she regained her footing.

"You can't call upon the *earth essence* here," Lief said. "It's the same as if you'd drank from that tainted stream earlier."

Waves of heat began to rise from the melting earth ahead. In front of Emiel, Lief held her hand out and closed her brown eyes. When she opened them, they were glowing.

The heating ground ahead started to cool, and by the time they reached it, the heat wasn't molten, but merely noticeable beneath their booted feet.

Emiel noticed Lief's breathing becoming more labored, and her pace started to slow. The tremors became less violent as well, though they were still pelted by hail.

Lief slowed more, and when he reached her side Emiel scooped her under his arm and lifted her to his right shoulder. She climbed over and sat facing backwards and held onto his head, her other hand outstretched behind them.

"It follows," she said.

"Can you stop it?" Amoura yelled back.

"No. But I can slow it down. You have to keep running."

"Definitely not going to stop," Bone replied.

If the earth itself could have growled at them, that would have been the sound that came from behind. Never in his life had Emiel spent more time running in fear of his life than the time since he'd been taken from Vyne, what seemed like a year ago now.

He felt Lief's grip on his head slacken, and he reached a hand up to help her stay in place.

"You alright?"

"It's too powerful." Her voice was barely above a whisper. "I'm trying to hold it back, but I can't hold on much longer."

"The trees are just ahead," Amoura said. "Will it follow us into the woods?"

"No," Lief replied. "The trees are not corrupted and their roots run strong and deep."

"Run, spicetrader!" Bone lowered his head and sprinted. "Run for all your worth."

Emiel's arms and legs, and even his lungs burned, but he kept going. If he fell here, he and Lief would perish.

The trees drew enticingly closer and the earth rumbled at them again. What looked like a giant hand made of rock came into Emiel's peripheral vision and slapped the ground several dozen paces to the left.

The impact nearly made him fall, but through luck or the grace of the Creator Himself, Emiel kept his footing.

"I can't hold it off anymore, Emiel," Lief said, her voice faltering with exhaustion.

"Just ... a little ... longer," he panted. The trees were just ahead.

Lief's body tensed against the side of his head and she let out a high-pitched grunt, then slipped from his shoulder.

He caught the tiny woman and slung her limp body over his shoulder and sprinted with the last of his endurance. The ground began to shake more violently, and Emiel felt something tunneling under the earth behind him.

The others reached the woods several heartbeats before the ground lifted under his feet. Emiel's instincts saved them, as he used the momentum and leapt forward, gliding the last bit of distance into the woods.

He landed on his feet, but stumbled and fell forward. He held the unconscious Lief over his head with both hands, taking the brunt of the fall with his chest, while consuming a fair amount of dirt.

At the angry sound rumbling behind them, Emiel opened his eyes and rolled onto his back. He stared up at the towering redwood and pine trees while he caught his breath.

"Not bad," Bone said. The panting mercenary stood doubled over with his hands on his knees. "Gotta admit, I'm impressed."

Emiel rolled onto his side and spat out a mouth full of dirt. "Thanks."

The mercenary spat on the ground. "Don't get cocky."

Emiel laughed, then coughed, as a bit of dirt went into his windpipe.

"And the heroic mood melts away," he heard Amoura say from somewhere behind him. Was that humor?

On hands and knees, Emiel hacked up the last of the dirt from his throat and mouth, and looked over at Lief. The tinfar lay unmoving on the ground a few feet from where he'd skidded to a stop.

Emiel's stomach went cold, and he rushed over to the tiny woman. He looked closely and saw that she was breathing, and sighed in relief.

Her brown eyes cracked open and she looked up at him with exhausted eyes. "You're breathing on me."

35

———

AMOURA

It had been a subdued walk since their escape from the soulrender and that evil in the ground. Amoura had read accounts of such creatures appearing during the War of the Immortals. They had supposedly preceded the coming of some greater evil that precipitated the sundering of the Bright Age.

Amoura bit her lower lip. The ever-pragmatic magus had never taken the accounts as anything more than fanciful stories of escapism.

But this. She needed to get to Altarra as quickly as possible. She had to get to the library and reference these most recent happenings. There must be an explanation beyond the fictionesque events history would present.

"How are you?" said a tiny voice.

Amoura looked down to see Lief staring up at her. The tinfar had gone into a deep slumber for more than half the day after their ordeal with the earth creature, or entity, or whatever that thing was. Emiel had carried her until she'd awoken and insisted she could walk. There was strength in those little brown eyes, but also fatigue.

"I should ask you that question," Amoura replied.

Lief tilted her head. "You wonder how I was able to fight it while you were not."

"I cannot deny my curiosity," Amoura replied. If there was such a thing as a thorn in the side of Amoura's thoughts, that would be it.

"It's the way you wield the earth's power," Lief said. "You rely on that piece of corlite on your finger."

"What other way is there?" Amoura asked. "I'm no Khatala, so how else would I access the *essences*?"

Lief gave her a doubtful look. "We're almost beyond The Triplets."

The deflection was curious, but Amoura let it go. "We are."

"What are you going to do with him?" the tinfar asked.

Amoura stole a glance at Emiel, who was preoccupied with the cliffs overhead. The spicetrader had become more wary of their surroundings by the day, bordering on paranoia. She couldn't blame him, being that he was so far out of his element. The fact that he tried so hard to remain stoic was a brave quality. Perhaps she'd underestimated him.

"Nothing." she replied.

"You're taking him to your city for a reason," Lief pressed.

"I'm escorting him to Altarra because that was the task placed upon me. Once we reach the city, my part is done."

"But you do know that he doesn't wish to go to your city, don't you?"

Amoura frowned and looked down into the small woman's sincere eyes. The question was actually genuine. "Yes, I am aware."

Now Lief frowned. "Why would you take him there if he doesn't wish to go?"

"His desire to go or not is irrelevant. His archminister and my magi master require his presence in Altarra, and that is where he will go."

"Against his will?" The tinfar seemed appalled. "You're forcing him?"

Amoura opened her mouth to respond, then hesitated. That was exactly what she was doing. There was no way around the fact; no way to dance around her actions with semantics or half-truths. She had been sent to ensure that Emiel be brought safely to Altarra so that Vladrick could study him, and the man had expressed several times that he wished nothing more than to be reunited with his daughters, who had been taken from him.

Lief's simple question was like a punch in the stomach.

They came to the end of the scattered trees to a plateau overlooking yet more hills and rocky terrain, but it would be more easygoing. The land was open and they could see far into the distance. They were vulnerable to the rain and cold winds, but no threat could get too close unseen.

Bone moved beside her. "Looks like we're finally out of that stinking place."

"I need a moment," Amoura said. "I'll meet you at the bottom of the hill."

Bone frowned. "What?"

"I must collect my thoughts and prepare for the last leg of our journey," she added. It was true enough.

She picked her way down the hill, veering to the side while the redheaded boy grumbled behind her.

Once she reached the bottom, she moved around the side of a boulder and sat gazing out at the expanse. She'd never seen so many boulders scattered across a land. Had these giant rocks been one massive one that was broken apart by rain and lightning, or were they once buried deep in the ground, only to be exposed by erosion?

Her random thoughts did little to distract her from the tinfar's questions, and the undeniable truth that she was playing a part in another person's kidnapping. When she'd left home to study to become a magus, kidnapping someone hadn't been one of her expectations.

Her steel gray eyes narrowed. Vladrick had worded it more softly, but the honey in his words was laced with venom. He wanted Emiel —whom he believed possessed some sort of hybrid abilities— brought to Altarra for the purpose of study, and it didn't matter whether or not the man wished to come. The fact that the archminister of Vyne had actually taken the man's daughters away on the condition that he travel to Altarra made it worse. And Emiel had been told he was to deliver a cargo that had long been destroyed in their fight with the leapers.

The man wasn't stupid. He'd have to be an idiot not to suspect something, given the ridiculousness of his presence on an errand that Bone would have been capable of completing without him. Had he caught on that he was the cargo to be delivered?

And here Amoura was, forcing this man to travel farther and farther from his daughters, treating him as coldly as if he was a burden to be packed up and delivered as quickly as possible so that she could be done with the bother.

Amoura tucked her knees against her chest and wrapped her arms around them. She was no different and no better than that boy mercenary who practically prodded the spicetrader forward with the tip of his sword. But what could she do?

She leaned her head back and gazed at the gray sky. She'd worked too hard to get to where she was within the Order of Magi to throw it all away now. If she refused the few tasks assigned to her, things wouldn't go well. And if she openly challenged Vladrick, he would crush her. She wasn't even sure how much of a match she was for Selvetar.

Amoura thought the situation over. If she set Emiel free, she would not only have to incapacitate or kill that mercenary boy, but also see to the spicetrader's safe return home. That prospect was undesirable, given what they had been through to get this far. And if she was to play the part of paladin through to completion, she would have to force the archminister to release those two girls.

Unappealing as all of that was, combined with the prospect of having to deal with Vladrick made the idea ludicrous.

Amoura thought of her ambitions when she'd first decided to become a magus. She'd gone to the fortress of the Order of Magi with the grand and childish aspirations of doing the greatest good and affecting positive change in the world. It hadn't taken long to learn how naive she'd been. Change from without was shallow, and change from within was slow. And when there were those as powerful as Magi Master Vladrick involved, change could be near impossible.

"Have a good quiet time?" Bone asked when she came from around the boulder. The mercenary had his arms crossed over his chest. "Think we can get moving, then?"

Amoura looked him in the eye, but kept her expression neutral. The boy snorted and walked away just as Emiel came up to her. Those eyes showed genuine concern. The dimples in his cheeks appeared when he thinned his lips.

"You alright?" he asked. "You seem troubled."

"I'm fine," she lied.

"You're fine," he repeated flatly. "Well I'm not gonna push you on it, but if you'd like to talk, I've got a pretty good ear for it." He turned and started after the mercenary, muttering about his unsociable captors.

The remark was halfhearted, but it cut a little deeper than Amoura would have liked to admit to herself.

"There's always a choice," Lief's tiny voice said from behind.

"Not always," Amoura replied. She started after the other two, still watching the spicetrader's back. He might not be a warrior or any kind of fighter, but the man was in good shape nonetheless. The days spent running and fighting to survive had further defined his physique.

"Why wouldn't there be?" Lief asked.

Amoura pinched the bridge of her nose. "It's how life is. We don't always have a choice."

"I think you humans take the choices away from yourselves," came the reply. "And then you take choices away from each other."

"Is it not the same amongst your people?"

"By the Creator, no!" came the horrified response. "I'd never heard of such a thing before leaving my home to study humans. I admit that you intrigue me, but I've never seen a more terrifying thing than someone taking someone else's life away."

"Life?" Amoura said. "Isn't that a bit dramatic in this instance?

Yes, there are bad humans who harm and kill others, but that's not what this is."

"It isn't?" the tinfar asked. "You take away that man's choice to be with his offspring in his home, and make him travel to a foreign and far away city. Is his life still his own, or have you taken it from him?"

Amoura wanted to be angry at the words. She wanted to lash out and tell the tinfar she knew nothing of what she was talking about. But she couldn't. Every word Lief had spoken was true, and that the truth was spoken in innocence and without judgement made it all the more shaming.

Lief earnestly wanted to learn about this, and why Amoura and Bone—and by extension those who employ them—would do this to another human. Lief didn't approve, but she wanted to understand. Would the tinfar try to help Emiel escape? And if she did, would Amoura try to stop her?

"I've no choice in this," she said again, but the words rang weak in her own ears.

"So, your magi master controls you? He makes you do things against your will?"

"You mean like a slave?" Amoura asked, not sure whether or not to laugh.

"I don't know that word," Lief replied.

Amoura glanced down at her again. "It means a person that is owned as property by another."

"Oh my! Lief gasped. "That's horrible! How could such a thing be?"

"In most lands it is frowned upon."

"Frowned upon?" Lief wrapped her arms around herself and shivered. "To be owned by someone as property? That's a fate worse than death."

"I agree with you," Amoura replied, "but there are some who live under such conditions."

"Why?"

Amoura's frown deepened. All these questions. Did the Creator send this little woman to show her all that was horrible about her own species?

"I don't know," she answered. "Perhaps they fear death more than living out their lives owned by another."

"But their lives are not their own, and death will come for them eventually, anyway. Why would anyone fear death when it's only a path back to the Creator?"

"I don't know," Amoura snapped, "and I'm tiring of this discussion." Lief flinched away and she sighed. "I'm sorry. Your questions are difficult, and I have much on my mind at the moment. Perhaps humans fear death because we fear the unknown, and death is the ultimate unknown."

"That's sad," Lief said after a while.

"You're people don't fear death?"

"No," Lief replied. "Among my people, fearing death would be akin to fearing the path to your own home. It's just a path. No more than that."

Amoura thought about that. She supposed it was true. There were times she didn't fear death, and other times when it terrified her.

"So sad," Lief said again. "Fearing what you don't understand, I mean. If your people are afraid of death, it means they don't know what life is."

"Maybe we fear death because it often involves pain," Amoura offered.

"But that's part of living life," Lief said. "The more I learn about humans, the more I realize that understanding you may be hopeless. Na'ta was right."

That last part sounded like a grudging admission. "Na'ta?"

"Hmph." Lief frowned. "Yes, Na'ta Corlyss."

"May I ask what a Na'ta Corlyss is?"

Lief blinked at her, then gave her head a little shake. "Oh, of course. Na'ta Corlyss is the queen of the earth tinfar. She is wise, and knows much. She also warned me against trying to study humans."

"Because it would almost certainly result in your frustration, confusion, and possible death," Amoura said.

"How would you know that?"

Amoura chuckled. Were all of Lief's kind so naive?

"Such an endeavor could easily yield the same result in a human. Your queen sounds like a wise woman."

"She is."

"And yet you disobeyed her?"

"Disobeyed?" Lief gave her a confused look.

"Went against her desire for you not to go."

"Against her desire? No. Not at all." Amoura found herself smiling at Lief's responding chuckle. The two-foot tall woman's energy was many times her body's size, and equally infectious.

"Na'ta didn't want me to leave home out of fear for my safety, but she would never forbid me my desire to do so. She'd never forbid anyone from doing what they wish."

"What of those who would do things to harm another?" Amoura said.

Lief practically flinched at that question. "That's never happened. I can't even imagine such a thing in my home."

"Never?" Amoura spared her a skeptical look. "There are none who do harmful things among your people?"

"Why would they?"

"Why does anyone do bad things? Greed, anger. I don't know."

"That's another reason I'm here," the tinfar said. "I'm curious to know."

Amoura sighed. "So everyone can do as they wish." Lief nodded. "Then why have a queen at all?"

Lief frowned at her as if she'd asked the most absurd question possible. "For guidance, of course. In her wisdom, the queen guides us when we need it. We live in harmony, but the younger of our people must learn. Who could do that without guidance?"

"Parents?"

"And who would parents go to for guidance? The queen is the

oldest of our people. Who better than her to guide us when we need it?"

Amoura massaged her temples. "Sounds organized."

"It's just what it is," the tinfar replied.

"Hey girls. Have a look."

Amoura looked to where Bone pointed. East of their position a road came into view, and in the distance she could barely make out a tower reaching toward the heavens. The tower would be composed of more than seventy floors. Every tenth floor was made of pure corlite that extended beyond the walls to balconies, that extended fifteen feet out and wrapped around the building.

Altarra.

Amoura stole a glance at Emiel and saw the man's expression harden. Her heart dropped at the feeling of guilt that washed over her. The sudden urge to wrap him in a crushing hug caught her by surprise, but she pushed it down, silently chastising herself. *What's wrong with me?*

"Our goal is in sight," she said, gazing in the direction of the sun, which had begun its descent toward the western horizon. "With a brisk pace, we can make it before nightfall."

"Lovely idea," Emiel muttered. "Wonder what's waiting for me."

"You heard the lady," Bone said. "Let's get on with it."

Emiel glared at the mercenary's back, but followed.

Anxiety, relief, guilt. So many conflicting emotions assaulted Amoura that she couldn't single any one out from the other.

Lief moved away to catch up to the solemn spicetrader. She spoke to him in hushed tones and he chuckled. Amoura allowed herself a smile.

As the group and the sun neared their respective destinations and more of the city of Altarra came into view, Emiel's dour mood gradually gave way to amazement. "Never seen a city this big before," he said. "And look at all those people lined up."

To the east people moved in a slow procession on foot, horseback, or carriage, waiting their turn for inspection before passing through the gates and over the bridge.

"One city's much the same as the next," Bone said. "Some'r just bigger than others."

"On the surface of it, yes," Emiel replied. "But every place has its own culture. The foundation of any civilization, large or small, is composed of the culture of those who've built it."

"Planning on becoming a road scholar?" Bone asked.

"You could use someone to teach you a few things," Emiel said. "Might make your personality less caustic."

Bone's expression darkened.

Amoura and Lief snorted.

"You've quite the tongue, spicetrader."

Emiel held up a hand. "I know, I know. And if I don't control it, you'll remove it for me. Just a little longer and you'll be rid of me forever."

Bone snarled "Pfft. Hardly. I'm probably going to have to babysit you all the way back to Vyne when this business is done."

"I don't think you have to worry about that," Emiel said, his tone and Amoura's heart dropping. "Whatever your part is in all this, I don't think it extends as long as my stay is likely to be."

"What are you going on about?" Bone asked. "You act like you're spending the rest of your life here."

Emiel didn't respond, but his expression spoke volumes.

Lief pointed ahead. "Who are they?"

Wrapped in her own thoughts, Amoura hadn't noticed four robed figures approaching.

"We're a good distance off the road," Bone said. "Is this a threat, Magus?"

"Not a threat at all, mercenary," a voice said.

Bone instinctively reached for his sword, but Amoura waved him off. That voice was carried on the wind, just as his words were drawn from the air and taken to their ears. It was a subtle way of invading one's privacy.

"I've never expected you to acquire manners, Agra," she said, ignoring her companions' confused expressions. "But this?"

"One can never be too careful," Agra's voice replied.

Amoura couldn't believe how foolish the *red* magus was. In his arrogance at being so adept at this particular skill, he showed his hand to everyone around him. Better to listen silently with no one the wiser. *Idiot.*

The two groups finally reached each other. Agra of the *red* sect, resplendent in his carefully creased red robes, walked in between three others that Amoura didn't know. Two were of the *air* sect, and the last was also from the *fire* sect.

"Why are you here?" she asked.

"We've been sent to see you home, Master Apprentice," Agra said.

"That's a wonderful idea that would have been more welcome had it come days earlier." Amoura tapped a finger to her cheek. "On second thought, perhaps not. I can barely tolerate your presence now. I couldn't image spending the entirety of this errand in your company."

The *red* magus glanced at the others on either side of him. Mouths smirked and eyebrows twitched.

Agra strode up to her, and she shot him a warning expression that stopped him well out of her personal space. He glanced at Bone and Emiel, then glared at her.

"I offer you respect and you spit in my hand," he hissed.

"You have an interesting concept of what respect is," Amoura replied.

"Better to know what your traveling companions intend, no?" he said.

"You think I wouldn't already know that, Agra?" she replied. "I know you're proud of your little tricks, but they're not unique to you alone."

That deflated him a bit, but he stood up straighter and waved a hand at her companions. "Magi Master Vladrick has instructed that your two companions be given the proper courtesy into the city,"

Amoura looked at Bone, then Emiel, then the empty space next to Emiel where Lief had been.

36

AMIYA

If Amiya could have rounded on the speaker with the full force of a ball of fire at her command, she would have. The voice whispering at them from the darkness down that tunnel gave her chills.

"Who's there?" Joga demanded. "Step out. Speak openly."

"Khatala male is aggressive," the voice whispered loudly from the darkness. "Khatala male should be more polite."

Great, Amiya thought. *Another person who talks weird.*

"Friend or enemy?" Joga demanded, squaring himself to the dark tunnel. Amiya could feel him delving. She did the same, struggling to grab hold of *fire*.

The voice hissed in what sounded like anger. "Stop it! The energy of Mother is not for you to take!"

"Mother?" Amiya said, glancing sidelong at Joga. To her surprise, the man relaxed, a bit.

"You are a person of the earth folk?" Joga asked. He allowed the *essences* to slip away.

"Earth folk?" Amiya looked up at him. "Mind telling me what an earth folk is?"

"Is what they say, is what they name, is how they think of those like me."

"And what I say and what I think is when you speak, you give me the creeps," Amiya replied. That actually earned a giggle from the shadows, and a girl who looked to be no older than Amiya herself emerged from the darkness.

Even as she regarded them, the girl's pupils—as black as her hair and that tunnel—began to shrink. Her skin, also as black as pitch, began to lighten. The girl went from positively frightening to somewhat normal.

"Girl is clever and honest," the strange girl hissed, and even her voice seemed to move toward normalcy. "Most pretend to be nice until there's no threat, or they get what they want. Not this girl." She was looking at Amiya the whole time she spoke.

"Others take power that isn't theirs, shape it like a weapon. Threaten with it." She turned an unfriendly stare at Joga as she said this. It was then that Amiya noticed the girl had unusually thick fingernails that were elongating as she spoke.

"The male is aggressive and unkind. Like all humans, they are of the same mind."

Joga stood his ground, and Amiya felt him delving again. The way the strange girl narrowed her black eyes at him said she'd felt it too. Oddly, she didn't seem the least bit disturbed, yet Amiya didn't feel the girl delving for any *essence*.

"Um, let's calm down," she said. "I think we're off to a bad start. Let's backtrack and put a better foot forward, okay?"

The girl hesitantly took her eyes off Joga long enough to glance down at her feet. "Feet are fine," she said. She looked back up, head turned toward Amiya, but her eyes on Joga.

Amiya couldn't help giggling at the scene. A full grown man was facing off against a girl her age, and he seemed genuinely wary of her.

"Um, I think you can let down your guard," she told the girl. "He's a friend."

The girl's eyes flicked between the two of them, still wary. Somehow, Amiya knew this girl wasn't a threat. Well, not unless they attacked her, and that wouldn't be a good idea. She kept looking at those fingernails.

"Khatala no better than the rest," the girl said.

"Tatamble living apart in judgement of us all," Joga shot back.

"Steal the Mother's power," the girl spat, her voice reverting back to a hiss.

"Steal nothing. We ask the Mother for her power and guide it."

"You take like the stone dwellers, only more sneaky."

"You do not know my people. Never try to know us."

"Don't need to know. Only need to see. Where humans go, all others flee."

"We live with the earth, not against it. Tatamble would know this if they would speak with us."

"Speak your words all you wish, but your actions are hard to miss."

"Okay," Amiya said, though she didn't dare step in between those two, still glaring at each other. "I don't know what this is about, but I think we have a misunderstanding."

The two continued their glaring contest.

"Humans take and do not give," the girl said.

"Tatamble judge without knowing," Joga shot back.

"Alright," Amiya said, holding up her hands. She faced the strange girl. "Look. I've only known this man for a short time, but I'm pretty confident he's a good guy."

"Girl is human so why should I trust?"

Amiya didn't know what to think. This girl kept referring to her and Joga as "human", as if that was something apart from herself. She was certainly strange-looking, with her odd eyes and skin, not to mention her fingernails. The girl might look unnerving, but she looked human ... more or less.

"Not all humans are evil," Amiya said, glancing between the two of them. "We aren't all the same."

"All the same," the girl hissed. "Raking, cutting, chopping, burning, building." She spat on the ground. "All the same!"

"Not all," Amiya said. "Many of us are as you describe, but not all of us."

"Cannot reason with a tatamble," Joga said.

Amiya hissed him to silence, which actually brought another giggle from the girl. "Ignore him. One thing you can say are all the same, is the stupidity of boys." The two girls shared another giggle. Joga rolled his eyes.

"My name is Amiya Dharr."

"Amya Dharr," the girl tried.

"Close enough. What is your name?"

"Amya Dharr wants to know my name." The tatamble's black eyes narrowed suspiciously. "Why does Amya Dharr want to know my name? What does girl want from me?"

"Want?" Amiya frowned. "It's how my people introduce ourselves. It's how we come to know each other."

"Why does human girl want to know me? What does she want?"

Amiya delved not for *essence*, but for an extra reserve of patience. "Maybe we can become friends," she said, sending Joga a warning look when he opened his mouth.

"Friends? Amya Dharr wants to be friends? Why?"

"Why not?" Amiya replied. The simple answer seemed to be enough.

"Given to me was the name Sama," the girl said.

"Beautiful name," Amiya said. "Do you have another name? A family name?"

The girl tilted her head, reminding Amiya of an inquisitive cat. "Why would Sama have another name? One is not enough?"

"Oh, no. I mean yes. One is fine. It's just that some people have more than one name."

"More than one name? Why?"

By the Creator I don't have time for this. I need to find Nandi. "Do you live here?" she asked. "Can you show us another way out?"

"Sama does not live in a cave," the girl said. She seemed offended.

"Tatamble live mostly in the forests and jungles," Joga said. Sama glared at him.

"Maybe you just shouldn't talk for the moment," Amiya said. She smiled at the other girl. "Do you explore this cave?"

"Not a cave," Sama replied. "Only a tunnel leading to many

places. Some places nice, some places dangerous. Some places very dangerous to ones who don't know. Other girl learn this. Girl like you."

Amiya's heart fluttered. "Other girl like me?" She tried to keep her voice calm, but Sama caught her urgency.

"Other girl, yes. Girl look just like you. Evil, girl must be, to look like you. Or evil you must be, to look like her." She tilted her head again. "Evil you are not. Nice, you seem. Other girl must be evil."

"No!" Amiya said, and Sama recoiled and hissed at her. "No, I'm sorry, Sama. I didn't mean to snap, but I'm very afraid for the other girl."

"Why afraid for evil girl who steals your face?" Sama asked.

"She didn't steal my face and she's not evil," Amiya said. "She is my sister."

"Sister?" Sama said. This time she actually looked at Joga as though the Khatala man would have an answer to that.

"Sometimes humans can be born at the same time and look exactly the same," Amiya tried to explain. "She is my twin sister and I love her very, very much. Please, please take me to her."

"Cannot be true," Sama replied, stepping away. "Evil girl must have bewitched your mind."

"They are very suspicious of what they don't understand," Joga said.

Amiya barely registered his words. All she could think of was that her sister was in danger. Tears began to well in her eyes, and she rubbed at them angrily. She hated being weak in front of others, but the tears kept coming. She sniffed.

"Why does Amya Dharr cry?" Sama asked, inching toward her. She moved in a low, hunching way, as if cautious that Amiya might make a sudden move. The girl kept her distance, but reached a hand out to touch Amiya's. She was like a skittish cat, stretching her body toward an unknown object. It would have been funny if not for the circumstances.

Amiya sniffed again. "Because my sister is away from me and in danger, and I don't know where she is." Amiya took a deep, shaky breath. She felt like a blubbering idiot. "I need to find her."

"Girl really is sister?" Sama said. She looked genuinely confused. Again, she looked at Joga, but the man remained silent.

"Yes," Amiya replied. "And I love her more than anything in the world."

Sama darted into the darkness so quickly Amiya gasped, then hiccupped.

"Wait!" She took a step forward, her hand reaching toward the darkness.

"We're better off," Joga said.

"She knows where my sister is!" Amiya shouted, rounding on the man. "She knows where Nandi is and she just bolted. Unless you can see in the dark, I don't know how we're going to find her!"

"Girl loves sister but stands here and shouts."

Amiya turned back. Sama stood just inside the darkness of the tunnel. "Sama thought Amya wanted to find sister."

"I do! I just thought you left us."

Sama looked at her as though she had just said something completely ridiculous. "Come and find sister."

Amiya felt Joga delving, and Sama hissed and crouched low to the ground, backing away. Joga held up his hand, palm facing upward, and a small flame danced above it.

Sama hissed again.

"We can't see in the dark, Sama," Amiya said. "If we don't use the fire's light we can't continue."

"Sama could guide you," she replied, staring in outrage at the flames dancing over Joga's hand. "Sama can lead you the way."

"It is too dark and too dangerous for that," Amiya pressed. "And we must move quickly to save my sister." Sama continued to glare at Joga. "We don't force anything from the Mother," Amiya said, remembering how the tatamble girl had referred to the earth. "We ask for her to lend us a small bit of her energy to aid us."

"You take!"

"We ask," Amiya corrected. "We borrow."

Sama stared at her. The girl was so skeptical.

"Many humans take and don't give," Amiya said. "But many borrow and give back."

Sama's expression softened a bit as she considered Amiya and Joga.

"Please, Sama," Amiya said. "I don't know what kind of trouble she's in, but I need to find my sister before something happens. Please, lead us to her."

Sama looked from Amiya to Joga, and then at the flame above his hand.

Amiya sighed and began to delve. It was harder for her this way, but she couldn't do it her way without scaring off the tatamble girl. After several heartbeats a tiny flame formed above Amiya's own hand.

Sama flinched, but she didn't leave them or attack.

"Lead on," Amiya said.

The tatamble disappeared into the darkness, but became faintly visible again when the light of Amiya's and Joga's flames illuminated her. The darkness was so complete that the light from the fires carried no farther than a few feet around them. If anything was waiting in the darkness, it would be on top of them before they knew it was there.

"How far does this tunnel lead?" Amiya whispered, then flinched. In the absolute quiet of the pitch darkness, even that whisper sounded like a shout.

"Sama does not know, but very far they go."

"So there's more than one? How long have you been exploring down here?"

"Years and more. Enough to know how to stay away from them."

That sent a chill down Amiya's spine, and she looked over her shoulder at Joga. The mountain man locked gazes with her and gave a silent nod. Amiya didn't need him to say the words. She saw in his expression that he was committed to helping her find Nandi and getting out of here. Amiya would never have thought such kindness existed in the world. Joga knew little about them, but had repeatedly placed his life in danger to help them.

"Who is them?" she asked Sama.

"Ones who captured her. Ones who take any they find. Ones who drain you dry."

Joga reacted to that. "Do they weave web-like substance and insert two of the strands into the person?"

Sama narrowed her eyes at him, then nodded. "Khatala is right. Web to bind, web to drain."

"Ghuza." Joga said. "Drainers."

Amiya fought down her panic. "They drain blood?"

"No." It was Joga who answered. "Non-delver would be consumed. Delver would be bound and used as conduit."

"A conduit?" Amiya said, some of the panic creeping into her voice. She looked back to Sama. "How far away are they? We need to move faster."

"Must be careful," the tatamble girl replied. "Cliffs to bottomless pits, ground that slopes toward spikes that grow from the ground like fangs."

"She is right," Joga said. "Must hope Nandi can remain strong until we find her. If they drink *essences* through her, they do it slow. Not burn her out too fast. *Essences* like delicacy to them. Will want to keep her alive as long as possible."

Amiya wanted to shout at him to stop saying that. To stop talking about her sister being killed slowly while some creatures feed off of *essence* through her till she was no more. The thought of Nandi, hanging limp and lifeless in a web surrounded by some web spinning monsters burned away her fear until only anger remained.

Nandi was alive, she knew. She could feel it. She would free her sister from whatever had captured her, and they would continue on to find their father. But first, she would turn her attention to those things that had Nandi.

And she would kill them all.

37

NANDI

Falling. She was alongside the endless drops of water that fell from the sky. She fell away from the sky to be swallowed by darkness. It carried her away and bound her. The darkness poked and prodded her, shuffled her this way and that. It clicked in her ear, clicked all around her.

Nandi's eyes fluttered open, but they might as well have remained closed. She lay upright, bound by a sticky substance that kept her aloft. Her arms were at her side, but as with her back, they too were bound to the sticky substance.

She remembered this from before she'd fallen asleep. Or had she simply passed out from fatigue? Things started to come back to her. Their flight from those jumping monsters in the pouring rain. Her fall from the cliff. She didn't remember the landing, but she supposed she was lucky to have survived it.

She tried to lift her head, but it was bound by the sticky substance as well. The only part of her body she could move was her eyes.

Nandi remembered waking to the sound of clicking all around her, and being too weak to resist whatever it was that had carried her. She'd been carefully pressed into something that felt like a giant web that had just enough give to stretch or bounce whenever she struggled to free herself.

Whenever she did that, the clicking would grow more excited, and the many painful pinpricks in her chest and abdomen would sting all the greater, and she would feel every one of the *essences* being drawn from the earth by her; through her.

She scanned the impenetrable darkness for a clue, any clue as to what the things were that held her here. She could feel that they were harnessing *essence* through her, and whenever it became too much for her to bear, they stopped. When she recovered, the process began anew, but slower.

Hands with tiny coarse hairs on their palms touched her arms and legs, checked the integrity of her bindings. It had to be some kind of web. A huge one, to hold her.

Nandi's mind raced. She didn't bother trying to speak to them. The first time she'd tried that, she had been poked and prodded by what felt like hard bony fingers. In the pitch blackness of the place, those clicking sounds and prodding appendages were enough to send her into a panicked frenzy. She took deep breaths to steady herself and her mind, lest she succumb to terror. There was a way out of this. She just had to keep her cool to find it.

Amiya was alive, she knew. The connection she shared with her twin was like half of herself that existed physically apart. They always knew what the other was feeling or thinking. Amiya knew she was alive and would find a way to get to her, but Nandi had to get out of this mess before her sister and Joga stumbled on these things and ended up in the same situation.

She shifted, then winced at the sting of the tiny pinpricks in her chest and abdomen. *What did they stick me with?*

She heard clicking in the darkness to her right, then an answer somewhere farther away. More clicking ensued. A conversation of some sort. *I barely moved and they knew it.* She braced herself for what she knew was coming.

The needles in her torso flared with heat, and her body tensed. Then she relaxed and allowed herself to enjoy the brief sensation of earth's power flowing into her. Her mind cleared for just a moment as she basked in the warmth of the *essence* flowing into her, like a comforting vapor that wrapped around her body. But before her body could absorb the vapor that she would then use as an outward projection of what she willed it to be, it drained away from her body through those needles.

Nandi clenched her teeth and squinted her eyes shut as she endured the sensation of the *essence* being sucked out of her. It felt like violation, not only of her, but of the earth's energy. These clicking things could do no more harm to the world than an ant could to an elephant, but that made it no less perverse, and Nandi was no elephant. Drawing the earth's power through her like this would eventually kill her if she didn't find a way to get free.

She felt more *essence* flowing into her body, almost more than she could withstand. When she thought she might burst from the influx of energy, they drew more out, slowly. The resulting clicks were slower, almost lethargic. *They're savoring it and keeping me alive at the same time.* Nandi instinctively shifted her eyes left and right, but they might as well have been closed, so complete was the darkness. *They're going to keep me here as a funnel to feed them* essence *until I'm dead.*

Nandi struggled against the bindings and the resulting punishment came. She felt hard bony fingers poking and pinching her again. The clicking was no longer content, but sounded loudly in her ears. She lay still and endured it in silent terror. They were eventually going to kill her, but it would be a slow and agonizing process that would leave her as nothing more than a dried out husk.

In that pitch darkness, surrounded by horrors she couldn't even see, Nandi thought of giving up. How many days had passed? One, two, ten? Had she been down here a week or a month? So many times had she passed in and out of consciousness, and in the absence of the sun's glorious light, she had no reference to time.

She couldn't stop her body from shaking as the sobs came. How long had Amiya been looking for her? She knew her sister would never give up searching, but what if they decided Nandi had made her way out? Were they still on the surface somewhere, searching the endless woods? The world was big, and they could be anywhere.

Nandi thought of surrendering. Better to die than be used in this way until her body finally gave out. She knew how to do it. The strain she felt when they forced her to draw so much *essence* gave her an idea of what would happen if she drew too much. Maybe she could willfully draw in many times more than her body could bear and burn herself up. It would be painful, but only for a short time and then she would be free of this hell.

She gasped as the draining continued. Tears streamed ran down her cheeks. She was sad and angry. Sad that she would never see Amiya and Dad again. Amiya would be enraged, and Dad would be devastated.

She was angry that she wasn't strong enough to stop these things. Angry at them for what they were doing to her. Angry that these monsters even existed in the world.

Nandi allowed her body to relax as much as possible. She thought of all the fun times their family had had. She thought of all the wonderful stories Dad told them about the mother they'd never known. She thought of all the fun and mischief she and Amiya had gotten into over the years.

She thought of the great big world that was out there, and how she and Amiya had vowed to explore every corner of it. She thought of Dad's smile and the strength behind those gentle eyes.

Nandi relaxed further, then focused on the power flowing into her. She drew in more *essence* on her own and felt the strain increase. Around her, the clicking intensified. The ones connected to her through those needles had felt it. Several bony fingers prodded her angrily, but she continued to pull in more and more.

The clicking grew more urgent, and she felt bony hands slapping at her, but still she drew in more. Pain and bliss, clarity, then confusion. Her body wanted to stop, but her mind pushed forward. She had never felt this much of the earth's power flowing into her. It was pure ecstasy and pure agony. It was beautiful and warm and comforting and power, but it was too much. Her body strained, and she began to weaken. She forced herself to draw in more.

In the darkness of her closed eyes, she saw a beautiful woman with shimmering black hair that fell below her shoulders. The woman's perfect face looked like an older version of her own, and Nandi knew this was her mother.

She smiled. *I miss you, though I've never known you.*

The slapping and prodding continued, but it was far away now. They wouldn't be able to hurt her much longer.

Thank you for coming to get me, mother. I'll miss Dad, but I will be with you.

Her mother smiled and, though her lips did not move, she spoke. Her voice was level and deliberate, and chilling.

"Get away from my sister."

38

RAYNE

Perched on a branch more than seventy feet above the ground, Rayna leaned against the trunk of a great oak. After two days of evading capture by the Nashmarese military, Rayna had spent the better part of a day resting. The Shiedra city guard had pursued her on foot, but she'd easily outpaced them and disappeared into the night. Little more than a mile out, she'd been forced to run without the aid of the corlite beads in her braided hair. Even so, she was better conditioned to outpace any one of those soldiers.

Less than an hour after Rayna had escaped the city, she'd heard the hoofbeats of riders. They were easy to hide from, but the dogs were not. As soon as she heard the barking she knew they'd caught her scent, and she'd had to push through the fatigue and continue on.

She took a deep breath of chill morning air and blew it out in a fog of relief. The dogs had been relentless, and she wouldn't have been able to outrun them even if she'd had the advantage of corlite assisted steps the whole time. That was when her training at the Treetop Khamra camp had come into play.

The dogs had trailed her through the trees into the night and into the next day and then that following night. Though her pursuers had been determined to catch the assassin, they were still human, and needed sleep. During the short naps, Rayna had also slept, and that sleep had been enough for her to take to the trees.

The dogs had found the first tree she'd scaled, but they couldn't track her through the treetops.

The assassin had moved from limb to limb, running and leaping from tree to tree until she had distanced herself from the confused dogs and frustrated soldiers. She hadn't used her corlite, since she still hadn't been fully rested. The stones were a boon to the fully refreshed body and mind, but dangerous if she was fatigued.

More than a dozen feet above any other tree, Rayna gazed out at the surrounding landscape. She'd slept for a day and a night high above the ground, where no dog would catch her scent, and no soldier would find her.

She took another deep breath and blew it out. In the treetops Rayna felt most comfortable, most safe. Up here it was easier to get a perspective on things. From so high, things on the ground seemed so much smaller and easier to handle. Easier to deal with the disappointment.

Disappointment. She had been feeling that more commonly of late. Through ridding King Alyn of the negative influence of his two warmongering advisors, she'd hoped he would listen to the more levelheaded Demarys, and the—hopefully—promoted assistant advisor, Davek. The king's mobilization to the lands near the base of Mt. Blood had soured that hope. It appeared the man was still intent on waging this foolish war against the Khatala.

Royain Dimitri had been another disappointment. When The Khamra had sent her next target, she'd thought it was a mistake. Shiedra had not been aggressive in the conflict until recently, and she'd thought that perhaps Dimitri had been ill advised and thus able to be reasoned with.

Just a few words from his mouth had dashed those hopes. Rayna could read a lie as easily as understanding the words coming from a person's mouth, but reading a person's intent when nervous easier. The royain had disappointed her.

She turned her gaze to the west, in the direction of the far away Mt. Blood. The king was already camped there, likely planning with two newly appointed advisors who were sympathetic to his desire for war.

Rayna sighed. She didn't like killing anyone. She didn't like assassinating public officials, dignitaries, or monarchs, but she would do what she must. Her life was pledged to the Khamra, and thus pledged to being a small piece of the device that maintained balance against those who were determined to destroy.

She started down, expertly picking her steps from branch to branch and all the while considering the fact that she might actually have to assassinate a king. Could she bring herself to do it if that command came?

Rayna placed no one life above another, but there was an undeniable truth that some lives affected a great many others. Even if King Alyn proved to be a burden, his death could send the entire kingdom into chaos. And chaos was the perfect environment for corruption to take root and fester.

She dropped the last few feet to the moist ground and started toward the road. She took another deep breath. The hint of warmth in the crisp air filled with pollen signaled the arrival of spring.

The road was clear on both sides, and so she started on her way, working through in her mind what she would do once she reached the nearest city or village. She'd seen chimney smoke in the distance, and so figured the nearest inhabitance to be a day away on foot. Not for the first time she regretted having to abandon her horse, but there hadn't been a chance to return to it.

No matter how much she allowed her mind to wander, it always came back to the King of Marai. Why did men wage wars with the lives of others? Why could Alyn not have waited for the situation to cool, then spoken with the Khatala leaders? Why couldn't the Khatala have tried to understand the reaction of the Marailanders? Why couldn't both groups have made an effort to understand one another? So many questions.

The hope of a passing wagon or caravan happening along her

path had barely entered her mind when she saw four men on horse-back galloping toward her. She thought first of pursuit from Shiedra, but they were coming from the opposite direction.

When they came upon her, the riders slowed their horses until they trotted to a stop. All wore dingy travel-worn riding clothes, and Rayna saw that it was not four men, but three men and one woman.

The woman had a crossbow hanging at her hip, and a dagger inside her boot. Rayna guessed that she would have at least two more hidden blades on her person.

The three men each had a sword strapped to their sides, and their loose riding clothes could easily conceal a number of daggers. All four held their reins with expert and calloused hands.

One of the men and the woman exchanged glances, while one of the others turned his horse so that his sword side was facing her.

"Ho there, milady," the rider nearest her said. "You must have traveled far to be coming from that direction." He nodded to the road behind her. "What brings you so far out in the middle of nowhere?"

"Hardly nowhere," Rayna said cheerfully. "I had to be some-where. Nobody can be nowhere, after all." She smiled up at him. "Just ran into a fair bit of bad luck is all. Pack of jarku brought down my horse, and the only reason I survived was because I ran away while they were eating it."

The man tilted his head. "And they didn't hunt you down? Jarku tend not to let prey escape without a little persistence."

"No amount of persistence will make them able to climb a tree, I assure you, kind sir. Whether it was boredom or the scent of easier prey, they left me after a while." She spread her hands. "And here I am. Would you be so kind as to tell me how far it is till the next human inhabitance? The road has been long and quite dirty."

The man and woman smirked at each other and the speaker smiled. The third rider had been circling behind her while she was talking. Her exaggerated hand gestures afforded her a quick glimpse over her shoulder at the rider at her back. His hand rested on his sword.

"It's a long walk yet," the speaker replied, still maintaining that predatory smile. "One made significantly easier when your burden has been lightened." His hand dropped to rest on the hilt of his sword, and he glanced at the man and woman to the side.

Rayna tilted her head dumbly. "I've very little burden." She spread her hands again. "Just the clothes on my back, the coin in my purse, and my foot to the road." She made a pouty gesture. "Though I would like to clean the road dirt from under my fingernails. So disgusting."

She stretched her arms out toward him as if showing him her dirty hands. She flicked her right wrist and sent one of her hidden blades shooting into his neck. Before he had begun to choke on the blade and his own blood, she sent the other blade into the second man's throat, at the same time drawing one of her daggers with her right hand. The female bandit cursed as her partner fell from his horse.

Having seen that the fourth rider had his sword on his left side, Rayna spun to the right of the horse. He took an awkward swing, but she easily avoided it and drove her dagger into his leg, then withdrew it and stabbed him in the side.

The man cried out and tried to grab at her, but she pulled the weapon free once again and slashed his hand. He recoiled and she jumped straight up and kicked him in his side. She felt several of his ribs crack, and he fell off the opposite side of the horse.

As soon as she landed, her instincts told her to drop, and an arrow sliced through the air above her head. She rolled forward and drove her dagger into the fallen bandit's throat, then rolled backward just as another arrow came for her. It found it's mark, not in the assassin's side, but the bandit who was already holding his hands against the flow of blood in his punctured neck.

The female bandit cursed again and dropped her crossbow. She drew her sword, but didn't charge. "No need to continue this," she said. "You took them three, so I'd say we're even, ya?"

"No," Rayna answered. She moved sideways, keeping the woman in view, but positioning herself close to a nearby horse.

The bandit licked her lips, eyes darting left and right. Her companions all lay dead in pools of their own blood. As Rayna had expected, the woman yanked on the reins and spun her horse about. She dug her heels into the animal's flank and the horse bounded away.

Rayna was already mounting the horse next to her as the last bandit galloped off. The woman lowered herself in the saddle and slapped the horse on the rump with the reins, urging it to run faster.

Rayna judged the woman to be a little larger and heavier than herself, and though she rode well, it wasn't enough. The assassin lowered herself in the saddle and lifted her backside, using her legs to absorb the bounce so that her mount could run as naturally as possible. Slowly she gained ground.

The bandit looked over her shoulder as Rayna came up on her right. As soon as the woman saw her, Rayna banked left, just before the bandit did the same. The woman's surprise was clear on her face when she saw the assassin now on her left, and almost right beside her.

In that instant, Rayna had slipped her feet out of the stirrups and tucked them under her. The bandit's eyes widened as the assassin leapt from her own horse and tucked her feet in. She kicked both her feet out into the woman's side, and knocked her from the saddle.

Rayna landed on her stomach across the saddle but managed to lift herself and swing her leg over. She gained control of the animal and turned in time to see the woman rolling in a cloud of dust. She tried to get up and run, but stumbled and fell over. Now she was crawling away. Irrational panic. The woman knew as well as Rayna that she couldn't outrun her even if the assassin was on foot.

She trotted the horse to a stop a dozen feet away and dismounted. She rubbed the horse on the nose and let it sniff her hand. It blew out of its nostrils with each breath, then whickered and shook its head. She gave it a pat on the neck and released the reins.

"I was against it from the start," the woman said, trying again to stand on a leg that was clearly broken. "We only rob wealthy travelers that are greedy and selfish." She wobbled and fell again.

"Of course." It wasn't Rayna who spoke, but Rayne, Khamra assassin.

The bandit saw the coldness in Rayne's eyes, heard the even tone of her voice. "I'll give you all the coins in my purse!"

Rayne nodded.

"I'm no threat," she pleaded. "I ain't had no choice in joining with them. You know what happens to a woman on the road that don't take up with a strong group?"

"A slow and terrible end."

"I ain't had no choice," the woman said again, propping herself up on one elbow and holding the side of her broken leg.

Rayne continued her slow advance. "There is always a choice. And we live and die by them."

Before the bandit could move, she snatched a dagger free from her side and sent it spinning. It took the woman in the stomach and she gritted her teeth, then coughed a mouthful of blood. After several moments of bleeding out, the woman finally went still and her hand slid free of blade in her stomach.

Rayna noted the hidden blade at the side of the dead woman's broken leg. In the exact spot where she'd been gripping the injury.

The assassin recovered her weapon and cleaned it on the woman's clothes, then took the three daggers she found hidden on the woman's body. She went to the dead bandit's horse and strapped the reins to the stirrups of her newly acquired mount.

After removing the woman's purse for the trouble of this whole incident, Rayna climbed back in the saddle and retraced her path back to the other dead bandits. The bodies had attracted carrion crows who argued over status as much as their meal.

She dismounted and went to the bodies. The large birds squawked at her, but scattered to a safe distance. Rayna took their blades and coin purses as well, ignoring the grisly work of the vultures.

She recovered her two wrist blades and clean them, then found the other two horses grazing not far away. She removed their gear and set them free.

Moments later she was back in the saddle and had both horses at a steady canter. Road bandits were a dangerous part of traveling alone or in a small group, but it proved to be a stroke of good luck. Rayna's lips tightened. Good luck laced with filth. How many lives would she end in her own lifetime? Every one of her targets was fixed permanently in her mind.

She thought back to the early days of her training with The Khamra. From the start, it had been ingrained in her that to kill was not ever an easy thing for the heart. The mind would by its very nature become hardened, but the heart was what kept the soul from darkening.

Tears threatened to spill from her eyes and she didn't fight it. Those tears reassured her that she was still human and not a monster. The tears cleansed her of the foulness. Though she'd felt no remorse for those whose lives she had ended, those who had already caused the suffering of so many, she did mourn their families and friends. How many wives and children and parents attended funerals in the wake of her actions?

In her first year as a Master Assassin, Rayna had wondered if the families of her targets had known of the horrible deeds their loved ones had committed. It took no more than that year for her to realize that it didn't matter. No amount of rationalization could pierce the grief of loss, no matter how dark the victim's soul had been.

The tears streamed down her face, washing away the filth caked upon her heart. She didn't mourn the bandits, who would certainly have robbed and killed her, or worse. She mourned for their parents, who had brought those people into the world with the best of hopes for their children.

A farm came into view, but she resisted the urge to stop. Better to put more distance between herself and what lay behind.

By midday she arrived at a village of cozy wooden homes. The stares from the locals were curiosity rather than hostility. She smiled back, aware of how out of place she must look.

"Good day to you, friend," she said, smiling down at a portly man in brown overalls and a sagging leather hat.

The round man looked up at her with a genuine smile. "Good day yourself, young lady. I'm assuming you wants a place to eat and a pillow to lay your head on. Why else would somethin' as purdy as yourself be talkin' to somebody as rotund as meself, hmm?"

Rayna made herself blush, and the man laughed. "Oh don't go givin' me the shy treatment, young lady. Been on the ground enough years to know the way of the world. Nothing to be sad about. Got too much of a taste for a good steak than attractin' a purdy face. Besides, I did all that work years ago and now me wife's stuck with me."

Rayna shared in his laughter and the man pointed her in the direction of the village's only inn and stable.

Moments later she came to the stable, which was actually attached to the inn. A stable boy came out to greet her, first admiring the horses, then looking up into her steel gray eyes. He stood fixed to the spot for several heartbeats before giving his head a shake and bowing.

"Pardon, m'lady. Lodging for your horse must be paid first, begging your pardon."

"Of course," Rayna said, smiling at him. "I would also like to speak with someone about the sale of this fine mount that accompanies me."

"Of course, m'lady. That'd be me ma."

"And pray tell me where I may find your ma?" Rayna asked.

"I'll get her if it pleases m'lady," the boy said.

"It would, thank you. And does this handsome young man have a name?" Rayna asked.

The boy blushed fiercely. "Jack, m'lady. Jack Klay at your service."

"Thank you, Jack Klay," she replied.

Rayna dismounted and rubbed her new horse's nose, then gave the second mount a few pats on the neck. She looked around the little village and felt a sense of peacefulness that made her heart less pained. People here raised their own food, built their own houses and looked out for each other. The sense of community was present and strong, here. A village this might be, but it was one big extended family.

She watched a group of children playing under the watchful gaze of a few nearby women. The larger cities were the opposite of everything she was seeing here, and it's people often looked down at country folk as though they were beneath them. Rayna knew better. All men died exactly the same.

Rayna watched an old woman who looked closer to a hundred years than ninety make her way over to where the three women sat. She hadn't realized she was still smiling until a soft voice interrupted.

"Now there's a face that's seen too much for her age."

Rayna turned to face a woman that towered over her by at least a foot, and was solidly built. She dusted off her overalls with strong, calloused hands. Her sand-colored hair hung in two thick braids draped over each shoulder. The woman regarded Rayna with kind bright blue eyes.

"Good day, young lady. I'm Horga Klay. Me boy says you wish lodging for one of your horses and a new owner for the other."

"Yes to the first," Rayna said, "but a home and family for the second." Horga regarded her curiously, so she elaborated. "It is not for me to own another life, so I ask for a small amount of compensation to adopt this animal into your family."

Horga placed her hands on her hips and tilted her head at the assassin. "Now that's an interestin' way of thinkin' about it, I must say. But if they ain't beasts of burden, what are they?"

"Sentient animals possessed of their own lives to live."

"Did you not ride 'em here?"

"After being accepted as a friend," Rayna replied. "Please excuse me. I mean not to be rude, but it's how I live."

"Don't go apologizin' little lady." Horga looked into Rayna's eyes. It was an unfamiliar experience. Most people couldn't hold her gaze for longer than a heartbeat before feeling compelled to look away.

"You've a heaviness in your heart," Horga observed. "Come. And bring your … friends."

Rayna followed the tall woman around to an immaculately tended stable. Jack was raking out one of the stalls as they entered.

"You about done, boy?" Horga called out.

"Yes ma'am," Jack replied.

"Then go get yourself some lunch."

"Yes ma'am," the boy said, nearly leaping out of the stall. He practically sprinted by the two women.

"And stay out of Miss Nebby's pies!" Horga called after him. She turned back to Rayna and chuckled. "Good boy, but got a sweet tooth that'll see him round as a cow if I leave him to it."

Rayna smirked.

"So tell me what makes such a young girl carry so much weight on her soul." Rayna's smile fell away and Horga noticed it. "Don't mean to pry. It just concerns me when young people carry the burdens of the world on their shoulders, and they ain't had a chance to live, yet."

"Some burdens must be borne," Rayna replied.

"I suppose that's true," the other woman said. "Mind an old lady gives you a little wisdom?" Rayna looked up at her and Horga took that as consent. "You tell me you made friends with them horses before you asked them to carry you? Ain't no different with people. You got the clear look of a hardworking woman from one of them big cities that works folks to death. Don't ever make yourself a tool to be used up and discarded. Ain't no way the Creator made us to live like that."

That was an odd statement that struck a little too close. "Thank you," Rayna said.

"Lodging for the horse is normally a silver mark per night, but I think ten coppers will make it square. Other currency here is work. A day in the stable or the kitchen for each night if you wish. And how much are you wanting for the other?"

Horga walked over and began inspecting the second mount. She ran her hands along the gelding's legs, running her fingers along the horse's muscles, and lifting each of its hooves. "Healthy boy, he is. Too bad his past owner didn't care much for him." She looked back to Rayna. "And I do say owner because that boy didn't think nothing of this animal; didn't care for him as much as you do."

Rayna felt a stab of alarm but kept her voice calm. "You knew his past rider?"

The woman straightened, and her soft laughter was knowing. She moved closer, and the assassin instinctively remained at ease. At ease but prepared.

Again, the perceptive Horga noticed the subtle movement and stopped short. "You've a dangerous side, girl. No, I didn't know him personally. But I do know that he was a rat that ran with a pack of three others. Dirty road rats, that group."

Rayna listened to the woman's words while considering her options. How would she handle this? Horga looked at her and laughed.

"By my guess, you happened upon them on the road and managed to, 'convince' them to entrust these fine mounts with you."

Rayna said nothing.

"Be it that, or somethin' else, the world is better for it, I'm sure. Now, your price?"

"A silver mark and a fine home for him," Rayna said.

"You could easily get ten silver marks for this strong gelding, girl," Horga said. "You rob yourself."

"It is what feels right in my heart."

The woman considered this. "Can't believe I'm arguin' a price up, but I'll give you five silver marks and a free night of lodging in my inn. Anything beyond that and it's back to coin or work."

"You're generous," Rayna said.

"I'm practically robbing you," the woman replied. "But I'll make good on it. A hot meal and a bath will wash that burden away, at least for a while."

"A bath would be most welcome, ma'am."

Horga waved a hand. "Least I can do. I don't know what place you come from, but here in Delain Village, we treats our few visitors as family. Now you head on in and tell Marlene at the bar that I said to have a room and hot bath prepared for you. Should take about an hour to get the bathwater hot, so have yourself a walk around if you like."

"My thanks, ma'am," Rayna said.

"Oh, and all this banter has me still not knowin' your name," Horga said.

"Sil," Rayna replied. "Sil Jevarin."

"Well, Sil Jevarin, be at ease and be at home," Horga said. "Just be back in an hour for that good hot soaking."

"Yes ma'am."

Rayna passed the time roaming the village, smiling and waving at those who greeted her, but mostly keeping to herself. She did listen in on the local gossip when she was able, and discovered that there had been an unusual amount of traffic passing through. She heard talk of four-armed monsters appearing out of thin air or falling from the sky. One person even said that a man had told him that these were humans that fell to some illness and transformed into the hideous four-armed creatures.

She kept the gossip in the back of her mind. Stories had a way of growing more grand with each telling, but there was always at least a grain of truth to them. Rayna had a feeling that grain of truth would be disturbing.

She looked to the western horizon, where the sun was beginning its descent. The golden and pink colors that were normal to a sunset were tinged with a red as deep as blood. It was barely visible, but she saw it.

"Bad times comin', young lady." It was the man in the brown overalls who'd first greeted her. "When the sky bleeds like that, nothin' but bad."

"What kind of bad?" Rayna asked, more to herself.

"I'm thinkin' the kind that we should avoid by holing up under a mountain and waiting it out," came the reply.

Rayna didn't respond. That colored sky was a sign. She could feel it. The Khamra would find her. They always did. A messenger would find her and deliver her task. A task she dreaded, but one that she was sure was coming. King Alyn would be marked, and she was to be the blade that stilled his heart.

Rayna thought of Horga's son, with the kind, shy eyes. Would those eyes soon close for the last time while his mother wept over his lifeless body, or the reverse? Or would those eyes harden with time?

The assassin held back her resigned sigh and glanced at the kind woman named Horga Klay. There wasn't a place in the world to hide from what was coming.

39

EMIEL

"When will you ever defrost that icy demeanor?"

Amoura stared at Agra, not bothering to favor him with an expression. "I don't know. It's a natural reaction to your presence."

"Oh I doubt that, my lovely. You don't socialize much with anyone except that withered old *blue*."

"I won't tell you again not to address me like that. And if you ever refer to Hashma Blue in that regard in my presence, I promise to remove your ability to speak."

"Such fire," Agra said, gasping the last word.

"Such annoyance."

Emiel choked back a laugh and the magus glared over his shoulder at him.

The group rounded yet another of the endless hallways of the cold and sterile fortress. Every step that took them deeper into the massive structure felt like a bit of Emiel's freedom went with it.

"I'd rather dispense with the aimless palaver and part ways, Agra." Amoura didn't bother to look at the man when she spoke, which Emiel could see grated on the other magus as much as her words. "I can escort our guests to their quarters easily enough. Find someone else to annoy."

"Can't do it, sorry."

"Yes." Amoura agreed. "You're sorry. I already know this."

Emiel felt a flare of energy. It was as if an invisible force of some kind was building. It was wafting off of that Agra guy. *What is that?*

"I implore you to set your inhibitions aside and allow your anger to take over," Amoura said. "Nothing could be more satisfying."

"You sound so confident yet you do not hold any *essence*." Agra's voice was low and even. Emiel thought he would lash out at any moment. "You'd meet an untimely end before you even began to summon the power."

"That's a logical theory," Amoura said, still not bothering to look at him. "Why not test it?"

Whether it was the woman's absolute confidence or something else, Agra seemed to doubt himself. That flare of energy fell away, and Emiel breathed again. Was this guy holding *essence*? And if so, how had Emiel felt it?

"You can almost feel the love," Bone muttered under his breath, but loud enough for everyone to hear. The other magi chuckled at that, but went quiet when Agra glared at them.

"You can keep your thoughts to yourself, mercenary," The magus snapped. "Your usefulness has come to an end. You should be honored by our continued courtesy."

Bone smirked at the magus's back. "Yeah sure. I'm so very honored."

"Your sarcasm will get you in trouble."

"Is your name actually short for aggravate?" Bone asked. "Because you have remarkably aggravating qualities."

Amoura snorted.

"You keep talking and you may find yourself a smoking husk on the ground, mercenary."

"Impossible to achieve if you've no head to command the action," Bone replied.

"Nice to see you still command such respect, Agra," Amoura said.

The magus's voice was calm, but Emiel noted his clenched fists. "You and your friend here have an interesting way of showing your gratitude for the personal escort we've provided. You could have been left to wait in the long line outside the city gates."

"Hardly," Amoura said.

They stopped at another intersection and Emiel took note of the giant columns, each carved with designs and what looked like symbols of some sort. The place was about as devoid of warmth as a mausoleum. Emiel wondered if this was the reason Amoura was so cold.

He looked at her, resplendent in her dark blue robes cinched at the waist. Despite the trials they had faced on the long road to get here, she still held herself tall and strong. He admired her beauty and strength, even if she wasn't a friend. *Is she an enemy, then?* Emiel couldn't decide.

"We can continue from here, Agra," Amoura said. "I must take him before the master and deliver my report."

"Yes, you must," Agra replied. Emiel was certain he didn't like the source of that smug smile on his face. "But you must do it without him. I am to escort him to his quarters immediately."

"You will do no such thing."

"My orders given to me by Magi Master Vladrick explicitly state that *I* am to escort our guest to his living arrangements, while you are to report directly to him. He has a good many questions for you that do not require his presence." Agra pointed a finger at Emiel. Emiel found he wanted to break that finger.

Amoura narrowed her eyes at Agra but the man smiled all the wider. "You can discuss your disapproval with the master if you wish, but you will do so alone."

Amoura's steel colored eyes narrowed further. Emiel found himself uncomfortable even though her ire was not directed at him. Even Agra seemed to feel the weight of that gaze, though he maintained his facade.

Amoura turned to Emiel, but her eyes lingered on the other magus until she had fully turned away. "I will visit you when I have information of our departure."

Emiel blinked. The words were cold. So cold. Yet he saw a flicker of affection there. It came and went so fast he wasn't sure he saw it. "Ah, sure," he responded.

Agra looked from Emiel to Amoura, and frowned. What was that about?

Emiel watched his two traveling companions move away down the hall, and his sense of loneliness deepened.

Agra turned to Emiel. "This way." He practically growled the words, and one of the magi behind Emiel gave him a shove.

"Is that really necessary?" he said over his shoulder. "What did you think I was going to do, refuse?"

"Shut up," Agra said.

"You're a mature one."

The magus stopped cold and rounded on him. Emiel nearly stumbled in an effort not to run into him. "You have a brave tongue little man," Agra said. "If you don't keep it in your mouth, I might just burn it out."

As he stared into those angry eyes, Emiel felt a tingling inside. His body was responding to the threat in a way he had never felt before. It was unnerving.

Misinterpreting Emiel's reaction, Agra smirked and turned his back. Emiel fell back in step before the man behind him could shove him again. The tingling slowly faded away. What was happening to him? Was Agra doing it, or had it been Amoura? And where had Lief gone?

He glanced around as if he would see the tinfar hiding behind a column or in a shadow somewhere. Had she abandoned him? Lief had disappeared once before, but she'd come back later.

They climbed a set of stairs, crossed an open intersection connecting yet more hallways, then climbed another long flight of stairs that led to a square platform.

A short and muscular man opened one of the side panels of the platform and they stepped in. After he closed it behind them, he went to a thick rope and gave it a yank. The rope jerked upward, and the man began to pull.

Emiel gripped the rail so hard his knuckles turned white. What manner of crazy person would want to ascend these heights on a platform pulled up by a rope?

Agra laughed at him. "Scared? I know no such things exist in your far out little town, but you needn't worry. This platform is raised by a pulley system with ropes as thick as two of your arms. A person on top pulls just as our man here does. The pulleys help ease the work.

Emiel tried not to look down. "Stairs wouldn't be a bad idea, either." Agra snorted at him.

The platform reached the top floor and they stepped out and into another hall. Agra led them out of the hall and onto a pathway outside. The pathway was a balcony wide enough for three people to walk side-by-side, and it ran the length of one side of the fortress. The view of the sprawling city was both impressive and unnerving. Altarra was a place of towering buildings as well as smaller ones, and the residential sector was no less impressive. Emiel had heard accounts of the span of Altarra, but he never imagined it could be so big.

They re-entered the fortress and Agra stopped at an iron door.

"You will remain here," he said as two of the other magi opened the door. What was with these people and iron doors? Decius had put his girls behind a similar door back in Vyne. The stray thought of his beloved daughters sent a streak of pain through his heart.

Again, Agra misinterpreted the expression. "You're a full grown man. Try not to cry on the floor because you're homesick."

Emiel didn't respond. He was confident the man wouldn't do any lasting harm to him, but he still might inflict a good deal of pain.

He entered a room with four walls, a pallet that served as a bed, and no windows. "Lucky me," he muttered.

"Food comes at dawn, midday, and dusk."

"I don't think I'm going to be here that long."

Agra's responding laughter bounced off the walls as he and the other two magi shut the door with a loud *bang*. He heard Agra's muffled voice outside. "He leaves for no reason other than by order of Magi Master Vladrick or First Magus Selvetar."

He heard several footsteps fading away, and sat down against the far wall. Never in his life had Emiel felt more alone. The love of his life was long dead, but left him with two amazing daughters who reminded him so much of her. His girls, his beloved daughters that were his reason for living, taken while he was forced to travel hundreds of miles away when they needed him.

And the only friend he had in all this mess had abandoned him. He felt as if he was the only person left in the world, sitting in that empty room. Agra's responding laughter at his claim of not remaining for long felt like an indication that his stay would be a prolonged one. But why? What did this magi master Vladrick want with him? He was a spicetrader from a city named Vyne, far to the south of this endless city.

He thought about the so-called cargo he was supposed to deliver, and how it had been destroyed early on in their journey. What use was he if there was nothing for him to deliver? And there was still that nagging question of why it was necessary that he personally deliver this thing—whatever it was—escorted by a magus and a mercenary. Either of the two were better suited to the task without Emiel to slow them down.

"Maybe it's something I know," he whispered under his breath. "Maybe they think I know something useful to them."

Emiel gripped the sides of his head. Whatever that "something" was, he had no idea. One thing he did know was that he was brought here for something this magi master thought he could offer, and not to deliver any package.

"I've been brought all this way on a mistake," he said to himself. "Whatever they think I have, I don't."

His heart nearly stopped when a tiny voice in the space next to him replied, "yes, you do."

40

AMOURA

Amoura had plenty of time to think about the current situation while waiting for Vladrick to summon her. *He wants to see me immediately upon my return, yet here I sit. Until he's ready to speak.* She tried not to clench her teeth.

Beside her, the mercenary boy fidgeted. "I mention how much I hate sitting around doing nothing?"

"Yes."

Bone looked at her. "When?"

"Several seconds ago."

The side of his mouth twitched, and he shook his head. "You really can be a block of ice when you want to."

"Depends on the company."

"Oh I doubt that," Bone sliced his hand through the air. "You're about as crisp as they come."

"I didn't realize you knew me so well," Amoura said, not really wanting to talk, but at the same time happy to break the tension of all this waiting.

"Don't need to know you well. You're icy to everybody, including your own ilk here in this dank dungeon you all lurk in. You've been frosty to me from the start, and you only recently thawed just a little bit once you got soft on your spicetrader. Wonder what they're going to do with him."

What made this fool boy think she was soft on Emiel? It was her responsibility to see him safely to Altarra, and that was what she had done. The man had been pleasant enough despite his circumstances, so why wouldn't she have warmed to him at least a little? She admitted to herself that she felt disheartened when Agra had taken him away, but that was because they'd shared this trip together for so long. A sense of camaraderie in some capacity was inevitable.

The door to Vladrick's chambers opened and an acolyte stepped out. Amoura looked at the girl and wondered if she would excel to a level that afforded her private sessions with Vladrick or his unpredictable lackey Selvetar. No, hardly a lackey. In fact, Amoura wondered if Vladrick really thought he had the first magus in hand.

"The Master will see you now," the girl said. She dipped into a curtsy and stepped aside. Amoura resisted the urge to brush past the girl, reminding herself that she too had been a hopeful doe-eyed girl fantasizing about becoming a powerful magus to help change the world for the better. Idealistic and naive. She'd been no different than any other typical youth.

They stepped into the open room where Vladrick sat at his desk. The magi master was reading over a tome that must have taken several lifetimes to fill. The scholar in her was curious about the book.

When Vladrick noticed them, he placed a marker in the book and shut it with a resounding thump. "And so my apprentice returns." He stood and came around the desk to stand before them.

"You must have met with some difficulty on your journey back. I'd expected you sooner."

Beside her, Bone snorted. "You could say that, for sure. If you can conjure an image of any monster, we likely had to deal with it."

Vladrick looked from Bone to Amoura, eyebrows raised. "That's interesting."

"That's a word for it," the mercenary responded. Amoura wished he would shut up.

"I would be interested to hear your account, Mercenary Bone. For now, I would offer the hospitality of the fortress."

"My thanks for the hospitality, Magi Master," Bone replied. "But this place puts the creeps on me. Rather explore the city, I would."

Vladrick responded with a half nod. "Very well. I can provide a guide if you wish."

"That wouldn't be necessary, but thanks all the same."

Again, Vladrick nodded. "Then enjoy the sights of Altarra. I will see to it that you have comfortable accommodations wherever you wish to stay, and your fee for services will be available to you promptly."

"Good to know. Thanks for that," Bone spared Amoura a glance, then followed the acolyte out of the room.

Vladrick returned to his desk and indicated the seat on the opposite side. "Please sit."

Amoura remained where she was. "I would prefer to stand if it pleases you."

"It would please me better not to have to look up at you as we speak," Vladrick said. A thin line of irritation floated on his tone.

She was pushing her luck. "Of course, Magi Master."

Once she sat across from him, Vladrick rested his elbows on the desk. He pressed the tips of his fingers together, tapping them to his lips as he regarded her. Amoura sat still and waited. After several long moments, the big man laughed.

"I see this little errand has not bent your will."

"Was that the intention?" Amoura framed the question in jest, though she did wonder.

"All life is a test, and whether our will is forged stronger or bent under its weight is dependent on the individual. I delivered you a task and you've completed it, albeit in a less than timely manner."

"There were complications."

"So our mercenary has so candidly indicated. I would know more."

"You sent him away."

"Because his eyes do not see things the same as yours. Everyone perceives a thing differently. I would have your account."

Amoura inclined her head. "Very well, Master Vladrick." Amoura took a deep breath and began her tale, starting with her abrupt arrival near the men as they fought off a pack of jarku. She spoke of everything that happened, but for whatever reason she could not name, she left out the presence of the tinfar. Lief had made a point of not being seen when they'd been greeted by Agra, so she wouldn't betray the tiny woman's trust.

"Quite a tale," Vladrick said. "And through all of this, did the man ever once exhibit any signs of summoning the *essences*?"

"He did not," Amoura said. It wasn't a total lie. She hadn't personally seen him summon or wield any of the *essences*, though she'd had her suspicions on a few occasions.

"Hmm." Vladrick tapped his fingers to his lips again, staring at the center of the table. His eyes found hers again. "I find that odd. Given the danger your party encountered, I would have thought he might have, at the very least, accidentally wielded a spurt of fire."

"If he did, it would have been during a time I was further occupied."

"Hmm," Vladrick said again. "No matter. I will test him anyway. If the information I've received about him is even partially true, he may be a valuable asset."

Amoura kept her features neutral. "You believe he will be cooperative in spite of his forced and continued separation from his daughters?"

Vladrick's features darkened, and Amoura wondered if she'd provoked him in some way.

"That would not have been a problem had Vyne not experienced a rather large and untimely problem."

A spike of fear stabbed her in the stomach, and the reaction surprised her. "Large problem?"

Vladrick eyed her. "Yes. Apparently a number of the same types of monsters that you encountered attacked Vyne. There was good amount of destruction and loss of life."

Amoura swallowed. "And the girls?"

"The girls?" Vladrick arched an eyebrow. "The *girls* escaped the city."

Amoura carefully released her held breath. "I see."

"As do I," the magi master said.

Amoura didn't know how to respond to that, but she took it as some form of warning.

"The girls escaped with a male wilder who was said to be complicit in the attack. The reports conflict, however, for it has also been said that he was seen fighting the creatures."

"Have they returned?"

"No. They fled the city with the wilder and have eluded pursuit. Whether they still live is in question, considering the fate of the party sent to retrieve them."

Amoura found her calm easier this time. He had seen a bit of her emotion regarding Emiel's family and was now baiting her. Perhaps he wanted to see how attached she'd grown to the situation.

"What happened?"

"A group of leapers."

Amoura went numb. "And the party?"

"Killed to a man."

"And thus no word on the fate of the girls and the Khatala man."

"Correct. Though I have a feeling those three yet survive."

Amoura realized she was beginning to lean forward in her chair, and relaxed. "What makes you believe this, if I may ask?"

Vladrick pursed his lips. "Reports have it that Decius's mansion sustained a good deal of damage. It's unlikely that two young girls could have escaped without some use of the *essences* at their disposal. I believe Selvetar indirectly facilitated their survival."

"Selvetar?" That was interesting.

Vladrick chuckled. "You think his soul as black as the Fallen themselves. Perhaps you're right, though I don't believe this to be the case."

Amoura's lips tightened, and the man chuckled again. "Whatever lies in Selvetar's heart, it shares an uncanny ability to do what is needed. He spent some time educating and training the girls in the use and understanding of the *essences*. Both have their respective strengths and weaknesses, though even he is unsure of their potential. He suspects they were hiding it from him."

Amoura almost laughed. "Two small girls were able to hide their potential from Selvetar?" She let a grin slip through her visage.

"Indeed they were. And that makes them all the more interesting. It is a shame they have been lost to me."

That offhanded remark brought the situation crashing back. "What will you do now?" she asked.

"I haven't decided yet, but I intend to see what this man is capable of. I doubt he would have sired two children so strong in summoning the *essences* without possessing some ability himself."

"The world is a big place," Amoura said. "It would be a long search that could yield no fruit."

"They're traveling on foot and we know what region they were last seen in. I've already dispatched a small number of magi and first class to search."

Amoura wanted to ask more, but she refrained. "I should speak to him about his daughters."

"I don't think that's wise."

She frowned. "He has a degree of trust in me. We've traveled a long way together."

"There's no need for him to know that his daughters aren't where he thinks they are."

Even from Vladrick this was unbelievable. "Do you not think the man has a right to know the fate of his children?"

"What good would it do him to worry about it?" Vladrick replied. "He is more useful with a clear mind. And if he does prove useful, he will be able to leave here with the abilities to aid in the search for his daughters if they have not already been found."

"They would be brought here, then?"

"That was my intention from the first," Vladrick said. "It was that malignant sow, Decius, who saw financial opportunities in the situation. I desired the entire family here together. Not only would it have been easier to deal with them without the stress of separation, but the possibilities of three hybrids to study and train would prove a boon to our efforts. Unfortunately, Decius managed to penetrate the sewage slithering through his dull brain enough to see value in the deal."

Amoura listened to it all, wondering what Vladrick was planning. "I've given you the extent of my experience during our travels. I should return to my studies."

"Oh?" Vladrick said. "And what studies would those be?"

"I must find out why these monsters have appeared. If this all means something, we should know what that something is."

"Have you forgotten your task in the northeast?" Vladrick asked. "King Alyn is almost nose to nose with the wilders and things are tense enough to spark at the slightest provocation."

"King Alyn will have his war with or without my presence, Master," Amoura said. "I believe I would be of better use arming myself with the knowledge of these strange monsters and where they come from."

"You believe the king's conflict unimportant?"

Careful. "Beside what the appearance of these underworld creatures might mean, yes. I'm not questioning the king," she was quick to add, "but I have a feeling this new problem could be more sweeping."

Vladrick thought on that. "Very well. See to your books and learn what you may. But I shan't promise that you won't be called upon to go to the king's side. He's recently had a close run with an assassin and two of his most trusted advisors were lost. He'll feel more comfortable with one as accomplished as yourself at his side, and his request is not one I can refuse."

Doubtful, she thought. The King feared Vladrick and the Order of Magi as a whole. The only reason Alyn had not already attempted to wipe them out was because he feared the effort would prove unsuccessful. And he was right.

"Of course, Magi Master."

At Vladrick's responding nod, she stood and gave a precise curtsy, then took her leave.

"I WAS BEGINNING to worry about you."

The welcomed sound of Hashma's voice brought a smile to Amoura's face.

"All right, girl. Out with it."

Amoura turned the book around and slid it across the desk. "Have you ever seen one of these?"

Hashma looked at an uncannily accurate illustration of one of the monsters Amoura and the others had fought; a monster that stood close to ten feet tall, with four arms and skin like lava rock. Hashma sucked in a breath through her teeth.

"What would make you go looking for something like this, girl?" She looked up from the book to Amoura. "What are you after?"

Amoura glanced at the book. "I encountered these on my errand to Vyne."

Hashma waved a hand and leaned back in her chair. "That thing is from the ancient stories, girl; during the time when the Illuminarians still walked earth. If they even existed, how would they come here from the underworld?"

"That's a question I was hoping to find the answer to here, or perhaps from you?"

Hashma frowned at her. "How old do you think I am?"

Amoura chuckled. "Wisdom need not be tethered to one's age, Hashma. You're wisdom transcends your few decades of life."

Hashma rolled her eyes. "Ha. Few decades indeed. I have a few decades of life beyond your parents, girl."

She looked down at the book again. "If you truly encountered one of those, I would say your accomplishments as a magus exceed most in this fortress. History is quite specific about the brutality of the these drauk monstrosities."

"There's more." Amoura flipped through the pages until she came to the nautilus-like monster they'd seen."

"By the Creator," Hashma breathed. "You've had enough adventure than most people have in several lifetimes."

"I have a feeling that's going to change soon," Amoura said. "Carlayn was attacked by both of these things, and I'm certain this is not an isolated incident."

"Why so?"

"We first encountered them on the road to Carlayn, then again in the actual city. The monsters came on in a full attack."

"A full attack?" Hashma said. "That makes no sense. The drauk are from the underworld. What would bring them here, and why now? And why in the name of the Creator would they start attacking cities?"

"I don't know," Amoura said. "But there was no mistaking what they were."

"Wait here." Hashma got up and left.

Amoura looked around at the many shelves of books lining the walls and the rows filling the room. The sun had begun to dip below the horizon, and librarians came through the halls lighting candles. She nodded her thanks to one such man as he lit her candle just as Hashma returned.

The gray-haired *blue* sat a stack of three books down and opened one simply entitled *The Underworld*. After flipping through the pages, she stopped and began to read. The words sent a chill through Amoura's body.

"... but as formidable and terrible as they are, they cannot exist upon this world without his influence. Where his gaze rests, the sickness will spread. Where his foot falls, a print of death remains."

"Who is 'he'?" Amoura asked.

"It doesn't say," Hashma replied. "But all of the books on this subject suggest that there was a great battle between the Illuminarians and a great evil."

"Of course," Amoura said, sighing. "Isn't that the crux of all stories? There is always 'a great evil' that must be vanquished."

"Your cynicism doesn't erase what is," Hashma replied.

"Perhaps not," Amoura said. "But I can't dismiss the logic that maybe this is just a few species of monster that live in the wilder parts of the world that remain unnoticed until they commit some brash action, such as attacking a human civilization."

"Oh?" Hashma said. She indicated for Amoura to continue.

Amoura knew that look. It meant she could expect the impending counter point to destroy her argument. "Think of it. We have the one who created all things, yet we also have one who destroys all things. Is this not classic fiction?"

Hashma nodded.

"And in between this great Creator and great destroyer are the minions of both sides, waging an endless war for dominance. Can we not agree that it is easier to destroy than to create? If so, the Creator would most certainly be many times more powerful than whoever this destroyer is that these texts speak of."

"True," Hashma replied.

"So why not end it all for good?" Amoura said. "Why this constant battling back and forth between lesser beings? Why wouldn't the Creator, in all His omnipresence and omnipotence, put an end to the conflict, destroy this great evil, and wipe if from the land?"

Hashma smiled affectionately, and Amoura had the feeling she was about to feel like a child. She wasn't wrong.

"And so your question makes my point for me." She held up her right hand. "One is all that is creation. The great Creator." She held up her left hand. "The other is all that is death and destruction. The destroyer. Everything has its function, and just as it is the function of evil to destroy and corrupt, it is the function of the Creator to create and nourish."

"I don't understand."

The older magus rested her hands back on the table. "The Creator is all that is good, and right, girl. The Creator is the very definition of love. It's as impossible for pure love to destroy as it is for you to sprout feathers and fly."

"If that's true," Amoura asked," how could the Creator have created this evil?"

"Who said He did?" Hashma countered.

"What?" Amoura frowned. "If the Creator created all things, surely He created the evil as well to balance the good in the world." She wrinkled her lips at Hashma's responding laughter.

"Oh, don't be so prickly," Hashma said. "I'm not laughing at you, so much as at myself and every other young person who has posed those same questions; questions that are as old as the first human who had too much free time to start thinking about everything. The answer to your question is simple. He did not create the evil."

Amoura's forehead was beginning to hurt from the deepening frowns. "Then who created it?"

"I cannot say for certain," Hashma replied, "but I have a theory."

"Yes?"

"Have you ever felt anger, or fear, or animosity, or perhaps even hatred?" the older woman asked.

"Of course," Amoura said. "Who hasn't?"

"An excellent question. The Creator. Such negative feelings cannot exist in the purest form of love."

"So what you're saying is the Creator created all things, including us, but it is the darkness in our own hearts that created the evil? If that's the case, who created the darkness in our hearts, if not the Creator? Surely we didn't create it ourselves. Why would we?"

Hashma shrugged. "You have just come to the great question, Amoura Xanna. Who indeed created the darkness that exists in all our hearts? Why are we the only living beings in this world capable of great good and evil all at once? How could a person kill another person, yet protect one they care about at the risk of their own lives? I'm sometimes led to believe even the Creator Himself must shake his head in confusion at His most unpredictable creations."

Amoura's headache was present in full. "In an attempt to bring this back to our current situation, the texts leave no doubt that these drauk are from the underworld."

Hashma raised a finger. "And, the only way they can exist in our world is through the presence of some form of evil larger than what humans are capable of."

Amoura sighed. "How typical."

"Typical of the world since we've inhabited it, unfortunately."

Amoura closed the book and leaned her elbows on the desk, resting her head in her hands. "Do you really think all this is true, Hashma? I mean everything. The Illuminarians, the Fallen, the Ruination, Final Conflict?"

There was a stretch of silence before the older woman replied, and it didn't give Amoura much hope for any decisive future.

"One thing I do know," Hashma said, "is that the historians call the battle between the Illuminarians and the Fallen, the Final Conflict. History says that this battle has happened more than once. I don't think there ever has been or ever will be a 'final' conflict."

41

NANDI

The words penetrated the haze in her mind, the pain in her body and soul. The words were a demand, spoken with such power and anger that her tormenters paused.

"I'm going to kill every last one of you," the voice said.

Amiya?

Nandi cracked open her eyes and was surprised to see two tiny flickers of light dancing in the air. One illuminated Amiya's face while the other floated in front of the Khatala man, Joga. She looked back at Amiya's enraged visage and found her twin fearsome.

All around the dark space, clicking ensued, and she could tell they were moving this way and that, perhaps calling for help.

"Nandi, get up!" Amiya said. No, not said. Commanded.

Those words penetrated her stupor, and it was as though her sister had spoken strength into her body and mind. Nandi's blood warmed, her spirit flared to life, and her eyes shot wide open. The cloudy haze of despair that had settled over her was burned away by white-hot rage.

Before she thought about what she was doing, Nandi's hands snapped up and grabbed hold of the cords that pierced her body. She felt the clicking things trying to withdraw the cords, but she held them in place. "You wanted it, have it!"

Nandi threw her head back and released every ounce of that burning rage into the cords. They lit the darkness as though aflame, and Nandi saw her captors for the first time. Horrid, twisted creatures with humanoid bodies covered in short prickly hairs with heads that looked like a cross between an ant and a spider. Their hands did not have fingers, but two sets of pincers, also covered in those coarse little hairs. They turned to each other in panic, mandibles clicking excitedly.

Those that had their cords inserted into Nandi's body received the full force of her anger mixed with every bit of the massive amount of *essence* contained in her body. They burned from the inside out and fell to the ground, glowing like the embers of a campfire, smoke drifting from their corpses.

Joga sent a stream of fire at several of the creatures, lighting them like torches while Amiya launched a wave of fire that thickened and changed its composition midair. By the time the twisted monsters were struck, it was under a blanket of lava. Their screams were thin and high-pitched, but lasted less than a heartbeat.

Nandi drew *fire* into herself and pushed it out, burning away the web that held her aloft. She dropped to her backside, but swept her hand out, sending a wave of fire into a pair of nearby creatures before scrambling to her feet. The cave flickered dark and light as the three wielded *fire* upon their enemies.

Mandibles clicking in urgency, the few survivors turned to flee, but Amiya was faster. She drew *fire* and melted a portion of the cave ceiling. The molten rock crushed and incinerated those who were not able to stop fast enough, and the others were trapped in the room.

Nandi sent water streaming into them. "You wanted *essence*, right?" The water pinned them against the cave wall, and stalagmites suddenly thrust out.

The creatures screamed their tiny screams as the stalagmites punched through their bodies. Nandi delved *air* and froze the air in their mouths, stinging their lungs even as they struggled to draw breath. She delved *fire* and melted the stalagmites that impaled them, burning her tormentors from the inside out. They sagged against the wall, held up until the stalagmites broke apart, then crumbled to the ground.

Nandi drew *fire* and sent it crashing into the dead monsters, burning them until nothing remained but blackened ash.

"Is over, girl!" she heard Joga shout.

"Nandi, stop!" Her sister's voice broke through her rage, and she released the *essence*. Darkness fell again except for the small flames that danced in front of her sister and Joga. Once her breathing slowed, Nandi drew *fire* and created her own flaming light, then almost jumped out of her skin when she saw a third form lurking near to her sister's side.

She enlarged her flame, ready to strike out at the form, but Amiya hopped in front of it. "Easy, sis! She's a friend."

"A friend?" Nandi replied, allowing the flame to shrink. "Oh. I'm sorry." When Amiya stepped from in front of the stranger, she got a better look. It was female, and looked to be around her age. But there was something definitely not human about her.

The girl hissed and looked around the room. "Not right. Not right!"

Nandi looked around the room as well, and found herself sickened at the sight of the carnage she'd wrought. Charred and smoking bodies littered the gloomy cavern while others were indistinguishable within the pools of glowing lava that had consumed them.

Nandi's stomach lurched, and just when she thought she had gotten it under control, the sound of her sister retching overpowered her will, and she also emptied her stomach on the cold cave floor.

When she thought her body would turn itself inside out from the strain, the episode subsided. She straightened and did her best not to look at the surrounding death. She had never killed a thing in her life. Dad had taught them that all life was precious. He had also taught them that it was right to defend themselves. Did that mean she and Amiya were right to have so violently destroyed these creatures? Should they have allowed them to escape when they'd tried?"

"They would have killed us, or gone for help and hunted us down to kill us," Amiya said. The flame hovering above her hand disappeared and she wrapped Nandi in a crushing hug. Nandi felt as if she'd been reunited with the other half of herself.

"How do you know that?" She asked, trying to keep her voice from shaking.

Amiya stepped away and produced her flame again. "I'll tell you while we walk. I'd like to get out of here."

They exited the cavern into the dark tunnels beyond.

"Those nasty things are called ghuza, and they only live in dark places. The reason they didn't just eat you outright was because they sensed that you could draw *essence*, so they used you for that. Once you'd died from being used as a funnel for them, that's when they would have eaten you. Disgusting things."

Nandi shivered. Ghuza.

"And as for the moral dilemma that I know you're experiencing, yes, they would have gotten help and hunted us down. They still might. There's no telling if one of them got away."

Despite her show of strength, Nandi could hear in her sister's voice that she was just as shaken. Even though the ghuza would have tortured and killed her, there was something painful about extinguishing another life. She and Amiya had destroyed so many, and all at once. How did the Khatala man deal with it? Nandi felt like her soul was tainted.

Nandi swallowed the bile in her throat. "Who's that?" She pointed at the girl skulking in the darkness ahead.

"Her name is Sama," Amiya replied. "We ran into her after almost being eaten by some big monster." She shook her head. "Dad is always talking about how horrible it would be to be eaten alive. How many times has something tried to eat us so far?"

"How did you find me?" Nandi said, still staring at the unusual girl further down the stone corridor. "Did she lead you to me?"

"Yeah," Amiya said.

"How did she know to find you?"

Amiya shrugged. "She didn't. In fact, it was by accident that we found out she'd seen you when you were captured."

"So she would have left me as a meal to those things if she hadn't run across you," Nandi said, glaring at the girl's back. "Nice."

"Don't be too hard on her," Amiya said. "From what mountain man has said, those ghuza can be pretty vicious, and there were a lot of them for one person to handle. Plus, she doesn't really think the same way we do."

"I can believe that," Nandi said, still glaring at Sama's back. Of course there was little if anything the girl could have done to help, but Nandi couldn't help being angry at being left to die. *Well, she did bring them to help me. I guess that counts for something.*

"Tatamble girl best left alone," Joga muttered from behind.

"Don't start that again," Amiya said. "We're barely to the point where you two aren't about to fight. Keep quiet if you've got nothing nice to say."

"A little girl talks like this?" Joga replied.

"Only when the mountain man acts like a little boy," Amiya shot back.

Nandi giggled at their arguing but nearly choked on it when the girl named Sama appeared out of nowhere in front of them.

"Humans talk so loud even the dark runs away."

"We're not talking that loud," Amiya replied, though she did whisper this time.

"Some things see in the dark and hear better than you," Sama hissed. "Some things have no eyes but hear all. They wait in the dark, hear from far away. You be quieter to see another day."

Nandi leaned over and whispered into her sister's ear. "Is she a poet or something?"

"Might as well be," Amiya whispered back. "She just talks that way."

"Strange."

"Girls still don't listen," they heard Sama hiss in front of them.

She's got a good pair of ears, Nandi thought, and they said no more for a long time.

Sama led them through the dark tunnels, stopping occasionally to sniff the air and listen to the silence before continuing in what Nandi assumed was a safer route around any lurking danger. They stopped once for a meal of dried meat and water. She thought Joga and Sama both would die from alarm when she and Amiya had suggested cooking the meat.

"Cooking meat smell travels far," Sama said, to which Joga agreed. Nandi didn't know if the two were more shocked at the cooking suggestion, or that they had actually agreed about something.

They continued throughout what Nandi felt must have been a full day, napping for short periods while Joga or Sama kept watch. Nandi suspected neither actually slept for wanting to keep an eye on the other.

As the hours passed, their light was often reduced to one, as Nandi and Amiya tired from prolonged use of *essence*. When Nandi felt they might never see the surface again, she caught the faint whiff of fresh air.

"You smell that?" Amiya asked. "I'd forgotten how stale the air is down her until just now."

"Yeah," Nandi replied. "The way out must not be too far away."

"Way out is close," Sama agreed, and soon they no longer needed Joga's firelight.

Eager to see the open sky again, they jogged toward the faint light. Her desperation to be above ground again fully hit her when Nandi began scrambling uphill. Dirt and soil ground under her fingernails as she clawed her way up, but she didn't care.

Moments later, they stood in the crisp open air that was devoid of the pounding rain that had soaked them during their flight from the leaping monsters. Nandi took a deep, refreshing breath.

Beside her, Amiya stretched her arms and smiled. "I can't think of the right word to say how glad I am to be out of there. That place was depressing."

"And now we move on," Nandi said, looking from Amiya to Joga. A little behind the group, Sama squatted, like a giant frog taking in the new environment.

"Should go while weather is favorable," Joga said. "Could change at any time."

"What about her?" Nandi asked, nodding at the wild girl. In the light of the day, she saw that Sama's hair was green, and right before her eyes the girl's skin was lightening.

"Goes her own way," Joga answered, "we go ours."

Nandi looked back at Sama, who stood and turned away. She watched the green-haired girl as she looked about their surroundings. Sama looked so alone. "Do you have family somewhere?" she asked.

"Once there was family, but long ago. Now there is me. Only Sama."

"Do not do what I think you will," Joga warned. "Will not find companion in a tatamble."

Nandi ignored him. "Do you have any place to go, Sama?"

"Sama has every place and no place to go. Sama will find a place."

"Do you want to come with us?"

Behind her, Joga groaned.

"Girl who looks like Amya Dharr wants Sama to come? Why?"

"Because you helped to free me from those ghuza things, and I think you would be a good friend. Do you want to be friends with us?"

"Girl who looks like Amya Dharr wants to be friends with Sama?"

"Didn't she just say so?" Amiya said. "We like you, Sama. Let's be friends and get away from that hole."

"You are Sama's friend," the girl said, pointedly eyeing Joga. "But Sama finds her own way."

Nandi held out her hands. "But we could make our way together. Watch each other's back." The tatamble girl tilted her head, clearly not understanding the figure of speech. "We can keep each other safe," she clarified.

"Sama keep you safe through the mountain, and now Sama goes."

Before Nandi could object, the tatamble hopped down the hill and was gone. Nandi ran to the spot where the girl had been, but she was nowhere in sight.

"She moves fast," Amiya said from beside her.

"Too bad," Nandi said. "Would have been nice to get to know her."

Joga turned away. "Are dangerous. Best that she left."

"She probably left because of your sourness," Amiya said. She turned to Nandi. "I know you're sad at not convincing your stray to stay with us, but we've got to keep moving."

"I'm not sad and she's not 'my stray'," Nandi snapped. "You met her before I did!"

"Yeah. I'm sure that disappointed look is because you wish we'd stayed in the cave longer."

She started off behind Joga, and after a few moments, Nandi turned away. She glanced over her shoulder at the mouth of the cave and the darkness. She'd come close to dying alone in that dark and horrible place with those creepy ghuza. What other horrors existed in the world that she didn't know about?

She hiked uphill behind the others, hoping that their father hadn't encountered anything like what they'd left behind. He didn't have the ability to delve to protect himself against things like that, and she didn't know if those he traveled with did either.

The ground started to slope downward, and she used the decline to catch up. The trees of these woods were thin and leafless, affording them better visibility as they crunched over the carpet of red, yellow, and orange leaves.

"Should not be far from New Dama," Joga said. "Will see once we clear these woods."

"Anyone ever tell you that you talk funny?" Amiya asked, and Nandi elbowed her in the ribs. "What?"

"You've said that to him before," Nandi scolded.

"Is because your language is not my first," the Khatala man answered. "Maybe you speak my language better?"

Amiya snarled. "Yeah alright I get it. So you gonna teach us some things about delving?"

Joga frowned down at her. "First you talk about talking, then you talk about delving. So fast, you change direction. And you say I talk funny?"

"Yup. Now answer the question."

"My sister is very straightforward," Nandi explained while eyeing Amiya. "Sometimes her manners suffer for it."

"Is not for me to teach," Joga said. "Am no Elder, and Khatala do not teach outsiders."

"Why not?" Nandi asked. "You don't trust other people?"

Joga glanced at her. She could tell he was choosing his words. "Khatala and Marailanders are not friends."

He must have seen the hurt on Nandi's face, for he was quick to add, "not saying that you and me are not friends. Just that Khatala people and Marai people do not like each other."

"Okay." Amiya waved a hand between them. What does that have to do with us? We're Marailanders, you're Khatala, and we've been traveling together and looking out for each other for who knows how long. If you didn't like us because we're from Marai, why did you help us get out of Vyne?"

"And why did you help kill those monsters before we left?" Nandi cut in before the man could speak.

"I ..." Joga sputtered. "Because ... it is, hard to explain. You don't understand."

"If you tell us we'll understand when we're older," Nandi warned, "I'm going to kick you in the shins."

"And I'm going to kick you in your man place," Amiya added.

Their eyes widened. They stared at her, then looked at each other. Amiya felt heat rising to her cheeks and rolled her eyes. "Look, you can let go of the adult versus child act, okay? We don't need it. Adults are always saying it, and a lot of the time it's just because they don't want to explain. We're not stupid."

Joga opened and closed his mouth over and over again, but no words escaped. Nandi managed to hold back her giggle. Amiya didn't.

"You laugh at me."

"You look like a drowning fish," Amiya said.

Joga closed his mouth, and they let him be.

Nandi lost herself in the beauty of the woods. Though it seemed like every multicolored leaf in the world coated the ground, more continued to fall. She thought of the times Dad had taken them with him when he traveled to nearby towns and villages to trade. She'd found the rolling hills and tall trees beautiful, but he'd only ever taken them during late spring or summer when it was warm and the trees were in full bloom.

The endless rows of near leafless trees were a different kind of beauty. The trunks and bare branches created slender rows of infinity that contrasted starkly with the bright and colorful ground.

"First time Khatala and Marailanders meet was not good," Joga finally said. So much time had passed that Nandi had to think for a moment before she realized what he was talking about.

"Marai King came to our land with many warriors. Despite the insult, Khatala Elders greet him with jahaka."

"Ja ... kana?" Nandi repeated. "What's that?"

"Jahaka," Joga corrected. "Is proper greeting. Warrior greeting. When leader of another land comes, hosting tribe greets with the jahaka."

"So, what happened?" Amiya asked. Nandi found herself wanting to know that answer, as well as why Dad had never told them this story.

"Marai King's warriors surround him and cut off jahaka dancers," Joga said, his face darkening.

"And I'm guessing that made your Elders angry," Amiya said.

"Was great insult," Joga said. "No bigger insult than to threaten warriors during jahaka dance."

"What happened then?" Nandi asked.

"Elders demand to know why King gives insult, while King and his close warriors shout at everyone. No one understood the language of the other. Soon everyone gets angry."

"And then there was fighting," Nandi said.

Joga nodded. "Lots of fighting. Khatala first fight with the spear and the axe, but Marai King attacked with his sorcerers. They killed many before Elders could react."

"I don't get it," Amiya said. "Your people know how to delve. Why didn't you do that from the start?"

"Honor." Joga said. "When Khatala fights non-delver, they fight with weapons of the hand."

"A fair fight," Nandi said. "Your people didn't know that there were delvers in Marai."

"Not delvers," Joga snapped. He saw them flinch and he softened. "They use precious stone from Mother *Illyu* to force *essence*. They reach in and grab hold of it, and pull it out." His tone hardened again. "They force the *essence* of Mother *Illyu*; bend it to their will."

"How is that any different from what you do?" Amiya asked. "It seems the same."

"Not the same. Khatala delve the *essence* and guide it to us; through us."

"Sounds about the same, to me."

"Not the same," Joga insisted. "To delve means unity through surrender. Must first surrender to *essence* for it to come to you."

Amiya looked skeptical, but Nandi understood. It was the way it worked for her. When she'd delved through Selvetar's ring, it felt wrong. It felt just as Joga had described; reaching in and grabbing hold of the *essence*, and bending it to her will. It was mostly how Amiya did it.

"I don't know about that," Amiya said. "I don't know if I could 'surrender' to anything. I don't like feeling vulnerable."

"Before the power of Mother *Illyu*, all are vulnerable," Joga replied.

"Maybe," Amiya said. "But since she's got this power that you suggest, maybe it doesn't hurt one way or the other."

The Khatala man seemed to think on that a moment. "Your Ba gives you bread and smiles, and tells you to have some. Or he stands over you, push bread at you and shouts "eat!" Neither words hurt you on the outside, and either way, you will eat bread."

Nandi watched as her sister contemplated Joga's analogy. It wasn't often someone was able to splash water into her sister's spicy mouth.

"I never thought of it that way," Amiya said, and for a long time, they contemplated his words in silence.

Joga suddenly stopped and turned around.

"What?" Nandi asked. Just the sight of his alarmed expression set her heart racing.

"Not here!" Joga whispered. His eyes darted left and right, and he dropped into a crouch.

Nandi and Amiya dropped to the ground with him. "*What?*" They hissed at him in unison.

"Darkwood cats not live in this part of the world," Joga said. "Should not be here."

"Darkwood cats," Amiya said dryly. "And I'm sure they're not the friendly sort that rub up against you or run away when they don't know you."

"As big as you are," Joga replied. "Best hunters."

"Then why are we whispering here and not running?"

"Not know where we are. We run, they find us faster."

"How do you know they're here?" Amiya asked, but then she froze, as did Nandi when she heard it.

A mewling sound came from somewhere in the woods, but they couldn't tell which direction. It was soft and welcoming; almost playful. It made the hairs on the back of Nandi's neck stand. "Why does such a cute sound make my skin crawl?" she whispered.

"The call of the cat," Joga said, eyes still darting around. He looked up at the treetops as well.

"They can't be up in the trees," Amiya said, also keeping her voice down. Despite her words, she also looked up. "If they are, it's not like they can jump down on us from way up there."

"Can hunt from ground or tree," Joga replied. "Must get out of these woods."

"But you don't know where they are," Nandi said.

"Must be quiet," Joga said. "Move forward but keep watch and be ready.

Nandi and Amiya crept slowly behind him, scanning the surrounding woods and trees for any signs of the mysterious cats. They saw nothing, but still heard the occasional mewling.

"Can't we just make a run for it?" Amiya asked.

"Would only excite them," Joga replied. "Like to hunt prey that runs away."

"Sport hunters," Nandi said dryly. "Of course."

They heard more mewling, this time closer. "I think they're hunting us even though we're not running," Amiya said.

"More fun to stalk," Joga replied. "We run, they pounce."

"Definitely sounds like a cat," Amiya remarked.

The mewling grew closer and Nandi thought she saw movement in the corner of her eye, but when she looked, there was nothing there. She opened herself and after a few heartbeats, felt the sweetness of the earth's power flow into her.

She felt Joga doing the same, and felt her sister straining to draw upon the *essences* as well. "Just open yourself to it, Amiya," she said.

"What do you think I'm trying to do?" Amiya snapped. "It's not as easy for me this way."

Nandi knew better than to push it. Amiya was more aggressive by nature, and opening herself up to anything was a challenge.

There was a rustling in the trees, but again, when she looked in the direction of the disturbance there was nothing there. Nandi split her concentration, focusing on moving forward and deciding which *essences* to combine. She was so engrossed that she didn't notice a protruding root on the leafy ground and tripped over it. Her head rattled from the impact of the fall and she lost her grip on the *essences*.

The mewling grew more excited, and she heard Amiya growl a curse that would have had Dad's eyes ready to pop out of his head.

She was quick to get back to her feet, but Joga and Amiya were standing back to back, scanning the woods.

Nandi turned to see several sets of green eyes staring at them from the distant trees. They flickered in her vision. Perhaps the animals were blinking, or moving about. Either way, it was unnerving.

She began to delve again just as the first cat stepped into view. It stalked forward, body lowered, lean corded muscles moving beneath black fur with wavy white stripes running the length of its body. It didn't snarl or growl, but simply regarded them with bright green eyes that angled upward at the corners.

Nandi glanced at Amiya who glanced at Joga. "It doesn't look like it wants to attack us," her sister said. "It just looks curious."

The large cat mewled and blinked at them. To Nandi, the sound should have come from something smaller and looking to be cuddled. It was hard to feel threatened by the animal. It bared no teeth and didn't looked in any way threatening.

"Maybe you're wrong, Joga," she said. "It doesn't look ..."

The cat stood up fully on its hind paws. It didn't sit upright like any other four-legged animal would, but actually stood fully upright on its hind paws. Nandi's mouth dropped open at the sight. The giant cat stood with its muscled forelegs hanging at its sides, long tail twitching behind it, and stared across the distance at them. On its hind legs it was taller than Joga.

Nandi unconsciously took a step back, then another. Those green eyes found hers and bore into them. It was like the animal looked right through her with that penetrating gaze. She felt like a rabbit transfixed by the predator that was about to pounce on it.

"I really don't like the look of that thing," she heard Amiya say from what seemed far away. "Let's get out of these Fallen cursed woods."

The big cat took a step forward, which made it even more unnerving. It still kept its eyes locked with Nandi, who felt fixed to the spot. Those angled green eyes narrowed into slits, and she heard a throaty growl even though the thing hadn't opened its maw.

The giant black striped cat took another step forward and Nandi and the others took another step back. She felt Joga drawing in what felt like a large amount of *essence*, and she opened herself up more. Though still struggling, Amiya had managed to grab hold of *fire*, and held it ready. Was she planning to burn the entire woods down? At the sight of the monster in front of them, she couldn't find much concern at the moment.

More mewling sounded from all around, then from above. She

heard Amiya gasp, but Nandi still couldn't tear her gaze away from those piercing green slits. The cat took another step, then another.

"Must run," Joga breathed. "Everywhere. Must not let them get in front of us."

"You really think we can outrun those things?" Amiya asked.

"Must try," Joga replied.

"Nandi?"

Somewhere in the back of her mind, she heard Amiya call her name, but so transfixed by that stare was she, that Nandi couldn't will herself to speak.

"Nandi? NANDI!"

A pair of hands grabbed her arms and gave her a rough shake. Nandi blinked, then looked into Amiya's concerned face. She frowned. "What's wrong with you?"

"Don't look it in the eyes," was all Nandi could manage.

"I don't plan on—"

"It comes!" Joga shouted.

Nandi and Amiya looked back to see the darkwood cat crouch, then leap what must have been twenty feet in one bound.

They turned and ran, but Nandi knew they couldn't outrun such an animal. She stole a glance over her shoulder and saw the animal closing in. "We can't outrun it!" She looked ahead and up at the trees to see dark forms darting through the branches. Impossible!

"We've got to stand our ground," Amiya said.

"Too many," Joga replied.

Amiya skidded to a stop. "Well it's going to have to take a bite out of me from the front, not my back!" She drew *fire* and sent a spear of flame racing at the large cat.

It dug its claws into the ground and bounded to the side, avoiding the fire. The flames struck a nearby tree and instantly consumed it.

"Amiya watch what you're doing!" Nandi said.

Amiya didn't respond, but when she struck again with a more controlled burst that was more of a wave in the air.

The cat tried to dodge again, but the wave was too wide, and the flames caught it. It burst through the dissipating wall of fire, fur singed but otherwise unaffected. It leaped the last dozen feet, and Nandi cried out and sent a spear of ice at the animal.

The huge cat let out a bloodcurdling cry and hit the ground with a heavy thud. It struggled to rise despite the spear of ice lodged in its left shoulder, but then the ground beneath it exploded and sent it hurtling away. They didn't wait to see the effect, for more of the things were closing in around them.

"Cannot get away," Joga said. "Too many and too fast."

"You giving up, mountain man?" Amiya said.

Nandi could tell her sister was getting angry. That was how she dealt with fear. Even when they were small children, she would get angry when she was afraid; angry at herself for being afraid, and angry at the thing that made her afraid.

"Not giving up!" Joga replied, a hint of irritation in his voice.

"Good, then," Amiya replied, and the air around them stirred.

The trees suddenly rained giant black forms all around them. They landed and crouched, staring at them with those same neutral, almost inquisitive eyes.

"Not this time," Nandi said under her breath, and drew in more *essence*. She released it in a burst of freezing cold air that pushed the giant cats back. This time, there was no soft mewling, but growling of predators closing on their prey.

Nandi delved *water* and filled the freezing air with moisture. In seconds, the icy wind was filled with balls of hail that flew sideways toward the surrounding animals.

Joga and Amiya faced opposite directions, forming a triangle. The ground quaked as Joga delved *earth*, and sent a large chunk of the ground splashing toward the darkwood cats. Several were scattered, but one leapt through the debris.

Joga threw his hands up and several stalagmites punched though the ground and impaled the beast.

Amiya brought her hands over her head and threw them down. A curved column of fire followed her motion and crashed down on the backs of two unlucky darkwood cats. The column pounded the animals into the ground where they lay still and burning.

They were wasting energy, Nandi knew, for every one of these predators they killed, there were more to replace them. "We've got to run."

"Must run and fight," Joga said. "Only way we survive this."

"Then let's move," Amiya said.

They ran, launching *air, fire, water, and earth* at any of the striped black cats that came too close.

"Will you try to be careful with that?" Nandi said as Amiya sent another column of flame racing at a dodging cat.

"I'm not trying to, Nandi," Amiya growled, "but if I have to burn these woods down to survive, I will!"

"There's three other *essences* to use," Nandi said, hopping over a tree that Joga had felled. "Use them."

Her sister grunted, but she did as Nandi asked. The effort was less powerful, as Amiya had a strong affinity for *fire*.

The cats pursued them through the woods, darting between the trees and lunging whenever there was an opening. One cat hopped from a low branch and dealt Joga a glancing blow to the shoulder and the side of the head. The impact knocked him sideways.

Nandi felt a stab of panic, for the Khatala man had been knocked away from them and was now alone and surrounded.

"Joga!" she shouted, slapping Amiya on the arm. He shook his head and struggled to rise on wobbly legs.

Amiya grunted, and a split in the ground caused several of the cats to stumble away while one caught its leg in the rift.

Nandi sent a barrage of ice shards flying into the cats, but it was only partially effective.

"Put more power into than that, Nandi."

Nandi snarled. "You think I wouldn't if I could? He's in the middle of those things and I can't control it that well.

Some of the cats turned their attention on the twins while others remained focused on Joga, who managed to send a wave of flame at several who crept in close.

I'm getting tired, Nandi thought. The *essences* were becoming more and more difficult to draw upon.

She threw her hand out and sent another wave of icy shards racing into two pursuing cats. The barrage dealt enough injury that the giant cats yelped and skidded to a stop. The cats stared at Nandi and Amiya for several tense heartbeats before turning and bounding away into the woods.

When she turned back, Amiya had reached Joga and was helping him to stand. Joga thrust his hand out and sent a wave of *earth* crashing into the darkwood cats.

Nandi reached them and together they helped Joga to his feet. Amiya used her free hand to send a wave of fire at three approaching cats, but they avoided it. *Are they adjusting to us?*

"C'mon, you lug," Amiya groaned. "You're too heavy for us to carry. If there's biscuits in your land, you need to cut back."

Joga was still dazed from his partial impact of what must have been more than three hundred pounds of striped cat. Still, he managed to send a weak burst of *earth* at another approaching animal. As they were turning, he cried out and fell forward.

Nandi and Amiya couldn't have held him up even if they were not fatigued by the exertion of so much delving. When the Khatala man fell, Nandi and Amiya saw four bloody slash marks across his back, and when they turned, it was to face a darkwood cat bigger than any they'd seen so far. The black cat stood on its hind legs, and they skittered backward.

Emboldened, more of the cats stalked forward, some rising on two legs, others moving in on four.

"I don't think I've got enough left in me to fight," Nandi said. She could feel the *essences* slipping away.

"NO!" Amiya shouted, and a wall of flames encircled them and burst outward. Several of the surrounding darkwood cats fell or ran this way and that as they burned. The biggest cat actually leaped over the flames and landed between them. It's massive size was several times the girls' weight, and they were simply knocked away, like scattered twigs.

Amiya hit the ground hard, and Nandi was sent into a sideways roll. She came to her feet intending to send the last of her energy into what she hoped would kill or at least wound the great cat, but a huge paw slapped her in the side of her arm and sent her spinning to the ground.

She squirmed at the explosion of pain in her arm, and when she clamped her hand around it, blood trickled through her fingers.

Amiya's circle of fire winked out, and another of the animals stalked in. Its lips curled back in a snarl, revealing a set of fangs as long as an adult finger and twice as thick.

Nandi fought against her fear and strained to access an *essence*; any *essence*. It wouldn't come, and without it, she was helpless. She glanced over at Amiya, who still lay on the ground, shaken. The big one was moving toward Joga while two others looked on the verge of devouring her sister.

The anger and fear she felt at seeing what was about to befall Amiya gave Nandi a surge of adrenaline, but it was only enough for her to regain her feet. The cat in front of her bounded forward, and Nandi clamped her eyes shut.

She was tackled from the side, and though it was pointless to fight the more powerful animal, panic sent her into a fit of blind kicking and punching. To her surprise, she heard a cry of surprise which preceded a slap to her face.

Nandi's eyes popped open just in time to see long green locks flashing away from her. She leaned up on her elbows to see Sama tackling the darkwood cat and delivering a punch to its ribs. The cat yelped and hopped sideways.

The tatamble girl was far from done. She sprinted past Nandi and skidded to a stop in front of the biggest darkwood cat who was poised to disembowel Joga. Down on four legs again, the cat growled and swiped a giant paw at her head.

Sama ducked the attack and punched it in the nose. The cat made a surprised sound and backed away a few steps, then stood to its full height and bared its claws.

Sama said something in a language Nandi didn't understand, and spread her arms out wide. She spoke again, and her tone was more forceful.

The darkwood cat seemed to consider her for a few long heart-beats, then responded with a series of grunts. The cats that had surrounded Amiya backed away, and the one nearest Nandi stopped its approach. The cats still hidden in the distance receded back into the woods.

The giant alpha—for surely it must be—and the tatamble girl faced each other in what would have seemed a comical scene if not for the circumstances. Finally, it dropped back to four legs and issued another deep growl, then walked right past Sama, even brushing against her. The girl actually giggled!

Nandi ran to kneel beside her sister. She rolled her over and Amiya's pained yelp sent a wave of relief through her.

"That hurt a lot," her twin groaned.

"Stop being a baby," Nandi replied, brushing away a few stray tears. She stood and made her way to Joga, who was now sitting up with his hand pressed to his lower back.

"You alright?" Nandi asked. She moved behind him and her breath caught at the sight of all the blood on his back. There were four angry slashes from where the alpha had struck him. She sucked air through her teeth. "This looks bad."

"Will be fine," he said.

"Don't be stupid," Nandi said. "The Creator only knows how your insides are still inside you, but we've got to clean and bandage this."

"Claws of darkwood cat kills," Sama said. "Kava root heals."

"Do you have any kava roots?" Nandi tried to ask, but the girl bounded away.

"Should not expect from her," Joga said. "Tatamble will not help."

"Tatamble saved your life," Nandi replied.

Joga tried to stand, but his eyes widened and he fell back on his backside, breathing in short gasps. "Cannot ... cannot walk. Must rest."

Nandi gingerly felt the area around the wound. The skin felt like it was on fire. She looked back at Joga, who saw the concern in her face.

"Do not worry," he said. "Will live to fulfill bloodmark or leave this place to join with Creator *Amyadali*."

"Who?" Nandi tried to keep her voice firm as she stared at the angry slashes across his back. "Don't talk like that. You'll be fine." She tried not to let the tears fill her eyes as his breaths came in short labored gasps.

"What are we gonna do?" Amiya said, limping toward them. "I can't move that fast. Maybe you could find this kava root the wild girl mentioned."

"I would if I knew what it looked like," Nandi said, scanning the once again empty woods. There was a thump from behind, and she spun around to see Sama crouched behind a pile of roots.

"Kava root," the green-haired girl said. "Chew the root, spit on the wound."

"What?" Amiya said, wrinkling her nose. "That's disgusting."

Nandi grabbed a root and bit into it. It was soft, and she bit down harder and tore a chunk away. Amiya mumbled under her breath as she too grabbed a piece of root and began to chew.

"Come on, mountain man," her sister said in a muffled voice. They eased him over onto his stomach and lifted his bloody furs.

With an unobstructed view of his muscled back, Nandi nearly choked at the sight of those four horrible slashes that glared back at her.

"Spit into cut, spread over wound," Sama said.

They complied, spitting saliva mixed with chewed kava root into the long cuts and spreading it across. Joga groaned, but held still.

"Lovely," Amiya said once they'd finished.

"If it saves him, I don't care," Nandi said. She looked at Sama. "How long will it take to heal?"

"Wound this deep, one or two days to sleep," Sama replied.

"One or two days?" Nandi and Amiya replied in unison. The tatamble girl gave them a nervous look and backpedaled a few steps.

"Can you help us protect him until he can move again?" Nandi asked.

Sama looked from her to Amiya to Joga several times. "Will stay.

Will help." She looked down at Joga, who had already fallen into a deep sleep with half his face buried in leaves. "Will stand again in day or two if you do not move."

"Not that we're strong enough to move him anyway," Amiya muttered.

"Thank you for helping us again," Nandi said. "Can I call you friend?"

The girl stared at her. "Friend like family. Friend helps each other. Friends give life for each other. Friends keep you warm in the wind and rain."

"Rain?" Nandi replied, just as the first few drops spattered on her nose.

42

JOGA

Joga awoke in a cold sweat, escaping dreams of glowing green eyes and snapping jaws. He sat upright too quickly, and had to hold his head to keep it from spinning. After the throbbing dulled, he opened his eyes to see the tatamble girl staring at him from a shadowy corner. She crouched like a frog on the floor next to the room's only chair, staring at him with very little kindness.

Careful not to move his eyes too quickly and bring on another headache, Joga scanned the room, taking note of the solitary table—the room's only other furnishing—beside the chair. The curtains were partially drawn to allow in a bit of sunlight. He took a deep breath, inhaling a mouthful of the smell of leather and stale riding clothes, and coughed.

He glanced back at Sama, but when the girl made eye contact, he looked away. "Amiya and Nandi?" he croaked through a dry throat.

"Rooms with tiny ponds made by man," the tatamble girl said in that whispering voice of hers. "Rooms where water sits hot with bubbles not made by waterfall."

"Called baths," Joga replied, wishing they hadn't left the wild girl in the room alone with him. Though Sama had saved his life, his first reaction was still that the tatamble might have done something to him in his sleep.

"Why does humans make things already provided?" Sama asked. She looked to the window as she spoke, and Joga understood her sentiment. He didn't care much for easterners' affinity for giant manmade structures and enormous cities where they all seemed to pile in together. From what the Ancients had told him, the city of Vyne was considered small by Marai standards, and Joga had found it stifling.

"Not all humans build like this," he replied, longing to be out of the confining walls. How could people stand it?

"Glad you finally wake," Sama said, looking at him with fatigued eyes. "Two days you sleep and keep us trapped in giant box." She looked around the room and at the ceiling, giving a little shiver. "Had to leave at night to breathe air."

Joga nodded. He could only imagine the reaction these easterners would have had, seeing a girl with green hair and eyes so dark they could be black, walking amongst them. Her skin was a light brown complexion now, given the tone of the room. He wondered if she consciously changed her hue to suit her environment, or if it was a natural bodily reaction.

"Did not want to come to this place of boxes," Sama complained, looking back at the window. "Shelter is good, but not prison box. You heal better and faster outside box than inside. Not smart, girls think you need box to heal."

"Is how many humans live," Joga replied. "They do what they think best. Girls are still young."

"Must leave," Sama said, wrapping her arms around her knees. "Will be crushed if stay here."

That was one thing they had in common. The walls felt as if they were closing in on Joga as well. "Yes. When they come, we go."

"So many humans live in boxes. You do not. Why?"

"Same reason you do not," Joga said, carefully sliding his legs over the side of the bed. "My people do not like giant square boxes anymore than you."

"Build things too," Sama replied, looking back at him again. "I see your people. They build things."

"Build things provided by Mother *Illyu*," Joga said.

"Mother?" Sama tilted her head.

"*Illyu*," Joga repeated, speaking the word slowly. "Easterners call her the Earth, and call one of Her four aspects, the *essences*, by the same name."

The mention of one of the earth's aspects drew a frown from the tatamble, and Joga immediately regretted it. But to his surprise, she softened.

"All things provided by Mother," Sama said. "Why Khatala build? Why take Mother's stream of life?"

"Do not take it," Joga replied, choosing his words carefully. "Direct it when we need it. Never taken away. When we need it no longer, goes back to Mother *Illyu*. My people build because ... because, we are not good at living on Mother *Illyu* like tatamble." That drew a smile from the girl, and he returned it.

The door creaked open to admit Nandi and Amiya. They looked from Joga to Sama and grinned.

"There's a cozy sight." That sharp tongue had to belong to the one named Amiya. It was the only way he could tell them apart. "You two actually getting on without wanting to throttle each other. I wasn't sure it was possible." She elbowed her sister, who frowned at her. "Guess you know some things after all."

"I know I don't like your elbow at my ribs," Nandi snapped.

"Oh don't be a baby," Amiya shot back.

"Sisters always fight?" Sama asked.

"Fight?" the girls responded in unison. "No!" Also in unison.

Sama turned a questioning look on Joga, but he shrugged. It seemed like they always fought to him, too.

"I would never fight my sister," Amiya said, giving Nandi an exaggerated hug while her sister moaned and tried to push her away. "Though I probably should knock her senseless from time to time." She feigned a punch at Nandi, who giggled and grabbed her fist, and the two started wrestling in front of a very confused Joga and Sama.

They looked at each other again, then back at the twins, who were still apparently having a good time of whatever joke they shared. Joga had never seen siblings behave in such a way. It seemed like they were always snapping at each other, especially Amiya toward Nandi. But to them, it didn't seem that way. And to actually throw a punch at a friend or member of family? Even in jest, was that not offense? Joga shook his head. Easterners.

"We go now?" Sama jumped to her feet.

"Eager to get back out into the hot day and cold night?" Nandi asked, disentangling herself from her sister. "It's warmer and comfortable in here."

Sama made a disgusted face. "Walls fall in and air hard to breathe."

Amiya took a deep breath, then coughed. "Okay," she grunted. "It does smell like saddles, boots, and stinking boy in here, but it's still warm at night, and cooler in the day. And it's dry."

Joga snarled. *Stinking boy?*

"No rain falls from sky here," Sama replied.

"Still more comfortable," Amiya said.

"You stay and not breathe," Sama said, making her way to the door. "Must have air. Walls too close."

"Somebody's claustrophobic," Nandi remarked.

"Does not like being shut in your boxes," Joga said. "Neither do I."

"My boxes?" Nandi sighed and looked at her sister. "I guess we'd better get moving before they go crazy in here." She looked back to Joga. "Can we at least eat first?"

Sama took the scarf the girls had bought her and wrapped her hair in it the way they had taught her. Joga held back a snigger at the sight of a tatamble wearing such headdress. Sama glared at him.

"Food in the world outside," she snapped.

"We'll grab a meat pie or something," Nandi said to Amiya, whose eyes lit up.

"Ooh, those looked good and smelled even better! I was hoping to try one before we leave."

Joga wondered how they would pay for such things. He'd

embarked with little money, not planning to stay in any eastern establishments on his way to New Dama. The thought made his heart drop at the reminder that they were standing in the room of an inn. How had they paid for this?

The aggressive girl read his expression and grinned again. "Don't choke on your tongue, mountain man. We took odd jobs in the stable and kitchen to help pay for the room and meals. No one will be seeing you out the door at spearpoint."

A wave of gratitude settled over him. These two, and even Sama, had cared for him when they could have easily left him to die in those woods. Maybe all easterners and tatamble weren't so bad.

"Thank you," he said. "For my life you saved. Thank you. I owe you debt."

Amiya snorted and waved it away. "We've been saving each other's skin for days now. But you're welcome. And you're heavier than you look. Are all mountain men as solid as you?"

Joga raised his hands and let them drop. "Not from the mountains." How many times had he told her that?

"Yeah, yeah, Frostlands and Sandlands or something like that." She slapped him on the arm, and he tensed, but reminded himself it was their way. "You look like you're from the mountains, though."

They moved down the creaky wooden stairs and the girls maneuvered toward the bar where they engaged in a conversation with a woman with a stern yet kind face. She dried her hands on her apron and came around the counter to sweep the girls in a crushing hug, then looked up at Joga.

"You gave your little companions here quite a scare," she said in an accent he didn't recognize. "Can't help but wonder what business you have traveling with three young girls who obviously aren't your daughters, but they look well enough, though they could stand a pound or two on those little bones."

She favored the three girls with a motherly smile. Joga kept his laughter firmly in his mind at the thought of that woman regarding a tatamble girl with such warmth. He wondered what her reaction would be if she knew the truth of the wild girl.

"Thank you," he said.

"Thank them," she replied, indicating the three girls. "I only played a small part in letting them work to house your sick body. I have to admit that even in the borderlands, two Marailanders and this child," she indicated Sama, "dragging in a sickly Khatala man is not a sight I've seen before. How could I not help?"

She straightened her already straight apron. "Have to admit I'm still wondering what kind of food you feed that quiet one there." She looked at Sama. "They struggled you in the door to be sure, and received a couple adult hands to get you up the stairs, but my eyes never seen a girl strong as that one there. Held your left side up by herself while the other two struggled together to hold up your right."

"My thanks for your hospitality," Joga said, not wanting to answer too many questions.

The lady smiled and straightened her apron again. "Think nothing about it. Those two identicals there helped me out somethin' nice to pay for your food and room. Didn't myself think it proper for three girls to be sharing a room with a grown man, even if you were their father, but you was in no condition to be alone. And I nearly forgot, what with yappin' with you."

She went back behind the counter and returned with some travel sacks. "Don't take much to see you four had a long and tough road here. Not that any road leading to this place is easy, but you all looked like you had trouble breathing down your necks."

She handed each of them a sack. "Not much in those, I admit. Just some dried meat and fruit, and some cloths for whatever you can use them for. You'll have to share the two waterskins or buy a third one. They're a little expensive out here in the desert. New Dama ain't exactly sitting next to any place else, so just about everything is overpriced."

"Thanks again, Mrs. Slada," Amiya said. "We would have been out in the cold if not for you."

"Oh nonsense." Mrs. Slada straightened her apron again. "You all would've just holed up in somebody's barn or something. You've the mischievous looks about you." She winked. "Judging by those accents of yours, I'm placing you somewhere really far south. Maybe Carlayn, but my ears are telling me even farther. Have to say I can't imagine what would drive you all the way here from someplace that far."

There was a brief silence where the kindly innkeeper fussed over her apron some more before gently ushering them toward the door. "Do be careful out there. I don't know what brought you all this way, but don't nobody come through my doors looking that haggard," she glanced at Joga, "and near death, if there wasn't trouble at your back. I must be crazy helping you in the first place. You watch yourselves." She leaned down and spoke softly to the girls, but Joga managed to hear.

"Keep your feet moving fast. The world's getting dangerous these days. Been talk of four-armed monsters running around, and giant things bursting out of the ground. Even heard talk of folks foul to the eye walking around. There one second, gone the next, and the ground cracked and parched wherever they walk."

She waved a dismissive hand. "Bunch of nonsense, I tell you. But bad things are happening no doubt. Local volcano blew its top not long ago, and it's been slumbering for longer than I been alive, though don't you go guessin' at my age, mind you."

Joga felt a chill settle over his body. Figures appearing one place, then the next, and leaving dead land wherever they walked?

"You alright, young man?" Mrs. Slada asked. "You lost some of that color you finally got back to your face. I can't have you walking out of here and falling on one of these girls, now. No, I'm not having that."

"I'm fine, thank you, Dashan." He placed his right hand over his heart and bowed.

"Oh now don't go on with that formal Khatala behavior with me, young man," Mrs. Slada replied, though she smiled through it all. "Mrs. Slada is just fine, but thank you. Your parents and your tribe surely raised you right."

Joga bowed again, hand over heart, and smiled back.

Once outside, the twin girls wrapped their woolen cloaks about themselves, while Sama seemed unbothered by spring's chill bite.

"How is this a desert, yet it's so chilly?" Nandi asked, blowing out a cloud of air.

"Ancients in my tribe say New Dama desert still cold in the nights and mornings," Joga said. "All year long."

"I guess it's easier to sleep at night," Amiya replied. "Nothing worse than trying to sleep in what feels like an oven."

Joga adjusted his furs and looked around. The borderland city of New Dama was the most unique place Joga had ever visited. The sandy stone streets teemed with people from every corner of the world.

A woman with the nose ring, long eyelashes, olive-colored skin, and graceful step native to a Nashmarese glided by, while a group of Marailanders in what looked like several layers of died furs huffed past. Joga chuckled. With all those furs they wore, one would think they were in the deepest parts of the Frostlands.

Several groups of tribeswomen and tribesmen from varying parts of Khatal also moved comfortably about the streets. They nodded to Joga as they passed, and he returned the gesture, staring after the group. If ever there was a place he would live if outside the lands of Khatal, it would be New Dama, where all peoples commingled without conflict.

"Anyone know what our kind innkeeper lady was going on about with the things people saw?" Amiya asked.

"What is there to say?" Nandi replied. "We've seen all that."

"Not all of it," Amiya said. "I distinctly remember something terrifying about someone walking around leaving parched ground in his footsteps."

"You also heard her say it was probably rumor," Nandi said, but Joga could tell she didn't believe her own words. Both girls were smart, but that one spent more time thinking things through.

"What about you?" Amiya asked Sama. "You haven't said anything."

The tatamble girl looked distracted, but she heard the question. "Where their feet falls, ground becomes dust. They bring trouble too big for us."

Amiya responded with a confused grin. "What's that supposed to mean?" She looked at Joga. "You have an interpretation of our traveling poet's words, here?"

"Dazra," Joga whispered. "Your people call them Droughtlord." Just speaking the word made him nervous. "Where they go, there is death."

"Of course!" Amiya said brightly. "This would have been far too boring if all we had to deal with was everything we've already dealt with, *and* finding Dad. Now we've got to hope we don't run into whatever this Droughtlord thing is."

Joga hissed through his teeth. "Do not speak of them so openly."

"Why?" Nandi asked. "I don't see anyone fitting that description around here?"

"Nothing good by speaking of them. Can be anywhere."

"So what now?" Amiya asked.

Silence answered that question. Joga stared to the north. Beyond the brown and white adobe-made homes and businesses, the volcano sat quiet, as if it hadn't recently spewed evil creatures upon the world. Despite New Dama's stroke of luck at being spared from the recent events, people still glanced warily at the distant figure.

Joga thought of his bloodmark. It had been a mystery to him before he'd first set out, but after the events of these past weeks, he thought he might be coming to an answer.

"You daydreaming, mountain man?"

Amiya's voice snapped Joga out of his thoughts and he looked down at three expectant faces. Even Sama seemed to be interested in what he had to say. Their little talk alone in the room seemed to have eased the tension between them. A bit, at least.

"To the volcano," he said. "Must fulfill my bloodmark."

"Your bloodmark is sending you to that?" Nandi asked, frowning at the volcano. "What's in there?"

Another word Joga didn't want to say. He started walking, and the girls fell in step with him. "Mulgin," he finally answered. The Marai-lander girls gave him blank stares while Sama hissed in fright.

"Know this word," the tatamble said. Her eyes darted wildly

around as though she was afraid the beast would appear at any moment. "Terrible beast. Should not awaken."

"Already awake," Joga said.

"Beast?" Amiya and Nandi echoed in unison.

"What does it look like?" Nandi asked.

"Great lizard," Joga answered. "Plate scales as red and hot as the lava it lives in. Smart and dangerous, and very big."

"I've read about something like that," Nandi said. "It sounds like you're talking about a lavakhan. You're crazy."

"Wait," Amiya said. "It lives *in* lava? *In* it? How could anything live in lava?"

"You sure about this, Joga?" Nandi said. "How are you supposed to deal with something like that if you can't get to it or touch it?"

Joga's jaw clenched. "Must find a way."

"You're people sent you to do something like this without any help?" Amiya asked.

"Must do this without the help of my people," the Khatala man answered.

"Alone?" Nandi asked, and Joga nodded.

"We're helping," Amiya said. "We're not leaving you alone so this thing can fry you extra crispy."

Joga shook his head. "No. Must do this thing alone." Even if he could accept help, how could he ask it of such young girls? Admittedly they had surprised him with their resilience, but they were children.

Nandi, looked at him as though he were slow-witted. "Do you know what those things look like?" she asked. "I've seen a few drawings, and all of them are terrifying."

"Does not matter. Bloodmark was given to me by Creator *Amyadali,* and I must fulfill. If task is given to me, She will give me what is needed to complete it."

"Does that mean you're guaranteed to succeed at this, then?" Amiya asked.

"No," Joga said. "No promise. Creator gives me what I need, but still up to me to succeed or fail."

Amiya blinked. "Just to be clear, if you fail, you're dead."

"Then there will be another."

"Sounds like your Creator is a harsh one."

"*Amyadali* uses Her people hard, but world is hard. She gives us what we need. Up to us."

"Whatever you say," Amiya replied. "I still think it's stupid to go it alone."

"I agree with my honey-tongued sister," Nandi said. "Don't you think you're misinterpreting what your *Amada* … I'm not even going to try to pronounce that. But don't you think you might be thinking about this wrong?"

Again Joga shook his head. "This is clear. Must do it alone." He smiled at them. "And you must find father, no?" The conflicted look that crossed their features told him that he had them in a bind. "Go now. Find father. Maybe one day we meet again."

"Because the world is such a small place," Amiya remarked dryly. "You know just like we do that once we say goodbye, it's goodbye."

Despite her sarcasm, Joga saw concern in her eyes. He had two friends here, and they had a friend in him. Even the tatamble girl, who they had only recently met, had grown on him. A little.

"World is big, but small to Creator *Amyadali*. If it is Her will, we meet again."

Amiya rushed forward and wrapped him in a crushing hug. "Will you shut up with that?" She rammed her head into his abdomen, nearly blasting the air out of him. "You're already being stupid," she said, voice muffled in his stomach. "Try not to be more stupid."

"Will do my best," Joga said, hugging her back.

"Oh move out of the way," Nandi snapped, peeling her sister free and then wrapping him in a hug just as tight, though not as painful. "Just watch out for yourself, okay? Boys always go for the hero bit, but usually get themselves hurt because they're stupid. Don't go being stupid and getting eaten or burned alive, or anything."

"Will do my best," Joga repeated, knowing that in all likelihood, he would not survive this.

"Yeah right," the girl replied. Was it even possible at all to lie to these two?

She released him, and he looked up to see Sama staring at him. "Khatala human's destiny kills him, but still he fulfills. Goes to death to help his people." She looked on him with a respect that caught him off guard. "Some humans can be good? Maybe you show Sama this."

"Know that I, and by extension my people, name you all friends of the Frostland Khatala. Is my hope that we meet again, in this life or next."

"I wish we had 'people' to declare as friends to you," Nandi replied, "but we're your friends," Joga. Good luck and be careful."

"And to you," Joga said. "Find father. Am sure he worries about you but will be proud of how strong you are. Luck to you on your journey, friends."

He waved as he turned away, forcing himself not to look back lest he lose his nerve. How he wished to have his three unlikely companions with him. He didn't know what he was more ashamed of; his fear of what lay waiting for him, or that he wanted three young girls to accompany him into the fiery lair of a mulgin.

He could feel the girls' eyes on his back and lengthened his stride until he came to an intersection. He rounded the corner and continued on until finally stopping to lean against a wall. For the first time since his capture in Vyne, he was once again alone. He thought about the many times he and his companions had saved each other's lives over the course of their adventure together. Now there was no one to save him if he faltered. This time, failure meant certain death.

The weight of that realization fell over him like a heavy blanket. He took a few deep breaths and pushed away from the wall. People went about their business along the rough stone streets. The sandy streets of New Dama were everything the stories had said, and everything Joga wished the world could be. Shetara, Nashmarese, Marailanders, and Khatala mingling together without hostility.

Joga wondered if these people feared that the volcano might

erupt again, and that this beloved desert city might not be as lucky next time.

At the city limit, he looked out at the short expanse between himself and the volcano. It occurred to him how odd it was that a long dormant volcano existed in the middle of a desert, when usually such a thing would be surrounded by vegetation.

He adjusted the pack on his shoulders and set out into the desert. Every step grew heavier. Every breath grew thicker. But his resolve grew stronger. He actually smiled. Perhaps this was freedom. Knowingly walking into what would likely be his death had a liberating effect. Perhaps it was knowing one's destiny and living without the uncertainty.

The sun was well into its descent to the west when he reached the base of the volcano. He sighed with a sense of calm resolve. Whatever befell him, he would succeed. "I come, mulgin," he said. "I come for you."

His words were soft, but the responding tremors were violent. The volcano rumbled, and he thought he heard a hiss.

43

EMIEL

Three days. For three days this magi master Vladrick had ground Emiel through exercise after exercise, determined to wring out the tiniest bit of whatever it was he thought Emiel was capable of.

He dropped to his hands and knees, winded. This man was so certain, so confident that Emiel could do what he called summoning the *essences*. Apparently that was what these magi people did when they wielded their terrible power. He couldn't ever think of one of them without thinking of the trouble tampering with the earth's power brought. He'd seen what these people could do, and they could go straight to the underworld if they thought to drag him into their world.

"What do you want from me?" Emiel asked for what must have been the twentieth time. "I've told you over and over again that I can't do what you do. I've never summoned anything in my life and I've never had the desire to."

"Your lack of experience or desire is irrelevant, my friend," the tall man said.

He towered over Emiel whether he was on hands and knees, or standing fully upright. This Vladrick was the tallest man Emiel had ever met, and solidly built. There must be a hundred pounds between them.

"Funny way to treat a friend," Emiel replied.

Vladrick shrugged as if it didn't matter. "Some are able to tap their abilities through verbal guidance, some physical. And there are some who are able to tap their ability through more unconventional means."

"You mean beating the subject senseless?" Emiel asked.

"I've not touched you," came the amused response.

"Why would you need to?" He climbed to his feet on wobbly legs. "You've been hurling your power at me enough that I feel like I've soaked it into my skin." The magi master arched an eyebrow, and Emiel thought he possibly shouldn't have said that. As disturbing as that thought was, it did feel somewhat like his body was absorbing what the man was throwing at him. That was impossible, though, no matter what Lief had said to him.

That stray thought brought him back to the first day when the tinfar had somehow slipped into his room undetected. She'd told him that he did in fact have within him the very thing Vladrick sought.

Emiel didn't believe it; wouldn't believe it. Not one time in his life had he ever done anything resembling what Amoura, or Vladrick or any other of these Fallen cursed magi did. He didn't have it and he didn't want it.

"Your face betrays you," Vladrick said. "There is something within you. You know it is there but you deny it either to me or to yourself."

"I'd say neither."

"I would say both."

Emiel took a deep breath. That helped at least a little. "All I can do is tell you, yet again, that I have never in my life done anything like what you suggest, nor do I have any desire to do so. I was sent here on some trumped up task as an unnecessary delivery boy only to have the cargo destroyed on the way. Now you've got me here as a *guest*, and insist that I undergo this testing every day. I've failed every test you've set to me, yet you insist to keep trying."

He realized he was growing more angry with each word and settled himself. This man was not only physically bigger and stronger, but he could crush Emiel without laying a hand on him.

"I barely have a concept about this summoning thing you do, and that's fine with me. I'd also be fine to get back to my family."

"You have within you the ability to better protect your family from what has already befallen them," Vladrick said. "Is that not an attractive possibility?"

Emiel couldn't think of a worse possibility. He had to get away from this man and this place, but doing that with no help other than a two-foot tall tinfar seemed impossible. He thought of Amoura and felt a fresh wave of betrayal.

He had been a little disappointed in Bone, but the boy was a mercenary, no matter the bond they'd forged over the weeks. Amoura, he'd thought, was made of more integrity. He was sure there was some kind of loyalty or honor in those eyes. And the way she'd looked at him from time to time he'd thought maybe ...

Emiel sighed, feeling quite the fool. Amoura had been sent to escort him to this man, who was intent to use him as some tool. Nothing more. But he was a tool only if he could provide the necessary function. And if after all this testing Emiel proved to be a failure, would he be allowed to leave? Would this magi master actually let Emiel walk freely out of this horribly cold fortress and set out back home to his girls?

Emiel didn't think so, and that made his situation all the more desperate. There was nothing else for it but to ask and get the reaction. "You're not planning to ever let me leave here, are you?"

The man was good, he had to admit. If there was one thing Emiel had the knack for, it was judging a person's reaction to a straightforward question. In his line of work you had to know how to read people. Magi Master Vladrick did a good job of quickly readjusting his reaction, but Emiel caught it.

"I suspect you think less of your accommodations than what they are," came the response. "You are no prisoner here, but it's my job to see that if you possess the potential to summon, you are provided the proper guidance. Otherwise you could be a danger to yourself and others."

Surely now, Emiel thought. Whatever his words or intent behind them, Emiel was certain from his eyes that this man had no intention of allowing him to leave. "Well you've been punishing me through this process quite a bit and have managed to squeeze nothing but pain out of me. Is that not enough?"

"Sometimes the things we are capable of are buried deep."

"I'm not a child learning how to run, Mr. Vladrick." Emiel reined in his irritation. "Look. I'm not trying to be short on manners, and you've made my *arrangements* comfortable enough. But I've got nothing to give you and I'd like to get home to my family ..."

He trailed off at the sight of air swirling next to him. Emiel sighed, expecting some other painful lash meant to force him into reacting by wielding one of these *essences*. He'd seen what Amoura did with it and couldn't imagine himself doing anything of the sort. He berated himself for thinking of the woman again. Best to erase her from his thoughts.

No lash came, however, nor was he buffeted by cold air and bombarded by nearly vertical hail. No icy shards cut at his skin either. The air swirled, then began to take shape. His eyes widened when the air took the shape of a girl about the height of his shoulder with hair braided into rows that extended from the front of her head to below the nape of her neck.

"What?" Emiel's blinked at the image. It wasn't one of his girls, he knew. It couldn't be. This was some sort of trick. He continued to stare in disbelief at the transparent, but perfect, figure standing just above the ground beside him. The figure noticed him and turned with a smile. Emiel's heart leapt at that expression and he smiled back. "Amiya?" he said, reaching a hand toward her. "Nandi?"

His transparent daughter opened her mouth, though no sound came forth. She reached her hand out to him, then quickly looked to the side and cringed. She dropped to the floor, flinging her arms in front of her face.

Emiel turned to where the frightened girl had looked to see a ball of fire forming in the air. "What are you doing?" he yelled. Vladrick didn't answer. The man just stood passively, staring at the ball of fire and rock.

"Stop it!" Emiel shouted.

The flaming rock flared to life and hurtled toward his daughter.

"VLADRICK!" Emiel flung himself in front of his daughter, and what felt like an explosion of energy burst from his body and shattered the fiery rock. He shielded his eyes from the flaming debris, but soon realized there was no need, as a protective dome of air shielded himself and his daughter from the shrapnel.

Emiel didn't know how long he stayed crouched over his little girl before he realized the truth of everything. Though he didn't want to, he looked into the face of his triumphantly smiling daughter. Not his daughter, but the image of his daughter. She winked at him, then dissipated.

Even though he knew it wasn't his real daughter, he felt a sense of loss when she was gone. He also knew that her self-satisfied smirk mirrored the man he wished he didn't have to look at.

"Fascinating," he heard over his shoulder.

Emiel continued to stare at the space where the image had been. "I supposed I don't need to ask what you're talking about."

"Fascinating that I did not think of this sooner," Vladrick replied. "And fascinating just how decisive was your reaction."

Now Emiel did look at him. "And that means what?"

"There are four year students who would dream of drawing forth the level of power you have."

"I'll wager if you threaten their families they might surprise you."

Vladrick chuckled, and Emiel wished he could conjure up some of that power again and do something horrible to the man. He didn't feel the slightest guilt at the thought, and that made him dislike the man all the more.

"You hate me." It wasn't a question.

"I try not to hate," Emiel said.

"Severely dislike, then."

"Now you're on course." The man arched that eyebrow again.

"Think one level below hate," Emiel clarified, wanting to snatch that eyebrow off of the man's face. The thought made him snigger.

"You find humor in the most interesting things," Vladrick said.

"What now?" Emiel stood. "You've managed to pull this awful thing out of me that I didn't know was there. What now?"

"You must be taught control."

"I don't need to be taught anything, sir," Emiel said, struggling to control his rising temper. "The only thing I need is to get home to my daughters."

"There are alternatives," Vladrick offered.

Emiel looked straight into those calculating eyes. "Magi Master Vladrick. I wouldn't have my girls within a thousand leagues of this place."

"They would be safer here," Vladrick replied.

"According to whom?" Emiel almost laughed. "You? With respect, I've been doing a fair job of it on my own."

"Yet here you are, so far from them."

"Yet here I am," Emiel shot back. "Far from them at the behest of the tip of a sword."

"Perhaps if you were better trained to defend yourself and your family?"

"Should I have to?"

The man chuckled. It was a deep and foreboding sound that reminded Emiel of the man's power.

"It isn't often I encounter such idealism in an adult," Vladrick said. "Were this world perfect, we would be in agreement. Sadly it is not, and a man must supply himself with the means to ensure his and his family's safety."

"I'd like to avoid a philosophical conversation regarding the necessity for violence as a means to any end," Emiel said. "But in our history, has there ever been a situation where swords and bows yielded a result that didn't leave at least one side crippled or broken?"

"There are some who will only allow peace at the, 'tip of a sword', as you put it."

"Every side has a perspective," Emiel said. He held his hands up and let them drop. "So you've got your confirmation. As much as I hate it, I have this thing I can do, and you obviously want it. So are you going to hold me here and force me to—"

"The ability passes on to each generation," the magi master interrupted.

The words were idly spoken, but the intent was clear as polished glass. He believed Amiya and Nandi could do what he did, and thus had every intention of bringing them here.

"Well," he said. "I suppose that's where things lie."

Vladrick moved closer and Emiel took a step away. The man, head and shoulders taller than Emiel, placed a large hand on his shoulder. "I understand your sentiment, given the circumstances, but I assure you I am no enemy."

Emiel said nothing. He didn't know whether his mouth had gotten him into deeper trouble, or revealed just how much trouble he and his girls had been in from the start, but numerous questions swirled around in his mind.

"I admit that my actions have been impolite, but they were necessary. Left untrained, there was a very strong possibility you may have summoned by pure reaction and not known what you were doing. Judging by what I've just witnessed, I doubt you haven't already done it."

Emiel wanted to deny it. He wanted to tell the man he was completely wrong, but he couldn't. He thought back to several instances when he had nearly been killed only for some unseen intervention to save him. He'd thought it was Amoura or Lief, but both had denied it every time. And why would they have lied? They had saved him on plenty of other occasions, so what would it have mattered?

The more he thought about it the more foolish Emiel felt. He'd ignored the signs and allowed himself to be led by the nose straight to the stable to be broken and saddled. If he'd not been so busy denying the things obvious in front of him, he might have somehow avoided all of this.

"I see you're coming to the truth of my words," Vladrick said.

"Take heart, Emiel Dharr. You aren't at all into the development of your abilities. You and your daughters can be properly trained to at the very least, know what you are doing and control it."

"And become one of your magi?" Emiel said, wishing the man would take his hand off his shoulder. He glanced down at it, and Vladrick smirked and removed it.

"That would be my preference, but it's not a requirement. The Order of Magi was not created for the subjugation of those who possess the ability to summon, but to guide them into the ability safely. Of course, most do aspire to join our ranks, and all who do, do so of their own volition."

"This is making my head hurt," Emiel replied. "I'd appreciate some time to think on all this."

"Of course," Vladrick said in what sounded like an effort at compassion. To Emiel, it had the same effect as a hyena trying to pass its smile off as friendly.

"I appreciate it," he said.

Vladrick escorted him to the door. "You are free to roam the structure, but I must insist you remain on the grounds for now."

"I'm sure my kind escorts will ensure that I do," Emiel said, and immediately cursed his quick tongue.

If he'd taken offense to the comment, Vladrick didn't show it. "I urge you not to think of yourself as a prisoner here. You are not, but there are steps that must be taken."

"Yes of course," Emiel said. "I'm just exhausted and frustrated."

"Understandable." Vladrick nodded to the two magi standing on either side of the door. One was wearing blue robes, the other brown.

Once back in his room, Emiel dropped to the floor and held his head in his hands. Though she'd briefly visited him several times, Lief was nowhere in sight. Sitting alone in that pragmatically furnished room made the sense of loneliness return.

Think! He thumped himself on the forehead. There had to be a way out. There might be a way Lief could help him. But how? According to her, earth tinfar could only manipulate the corresponding *essence.*

He slammed his palm on the ground and ignored the stinging pain. How had he let this happen, and what could he do about it? So many questions. How did Vladrick know so much about him? Were his girls still in Vyne, or had the magi master already sent for them? Were they being carted here even as he sat in this room?

The thought of his girls locked in the back of some wagon, or on horseback possibly facing the dangers he'd barely survived threatened to send him into a panic.

Pull it together, he told himself. *Gotta be strong for Amiya and Nandi.* He sat straight and took a few deep breaths to steady his nerves, then began to list the facts of his situation one by one.

He'd barely begun when he heard talking outside his room. Several moments later the door opened to admit the magus who was stationed outside his door, and Amoura Xanna.

44

SELVETAR

Selvetar pressed a knuckle to his lips as he digested Brother Amerus Layun's words. Vyne, Carlayn, several of the bordering towns to Shiedra, and even the far away Shetar. "It seems the underworld is selective in its hostility," he said.

"Or random," Amerus replied.

"Mmm." Selvetar looked down at the map on his desk. After another moment of consideration, he leaned back in his chair and stared at the monk as he thought about the situation. "There are more appealing targets," he said. "Why not Altarra, or Shiedra, instead of its surrounding towns?"

"Why not New Dama?" the monk offered. "The place sits directly under the glare of that awful volcano from whence the evil came forth."

"So poetic, Brother Amerus," Selvetar said. The monk glared. Selvetar sighed. "Need we regard each other with such hostility, Brother? If we are to discern the nature of these happenings and deal with them properly, we must be united."

"And I am here," Amerus said, "despite your frequent barbs."

"My apologies, Brother Amerus," Selvetar replied. The monk nodded. Selvetar considered the man during the stretched silence.

The Senior Monk was prideful to a fault, but he was also a practical man, and no fool. More than once had Selvetar wondered how powerful a magus Amerus could be.

No. Everyone had their part to play in life, and all had their respective talents and pieces of the puzzle to fill. Amerus may or may not have been a great magus, but he was already a great senior Monk to the Brotherhood of the Source. Monasteries around the world knew of the Vyne branch of the Brotherhood, and it was due in no small part to the efforts of this man.

"Despite the looming threat of the underworld sitting in front of us, is First Magus Selvetar still searching for an argument to convince me to join his Order?"

Selvetar chuckled. "I confess, I would find your addition to our ranks beneficial, but I have long given up that endeavor, Brother Amerus." He looked back at the map.

"There is other news," Amerus said, and Selvetar looked up again. The monk looked past him, but his thoughts were farther away still. "I think The Khamra are active."

A tiny frown creased Selvetar's forehead. "Hmm. Are they not always?"

"In some way, yes." Amerus wrinkled his lips. "But when they are active enough to take note, that is cause for ... attention."

"Do continue," Selvetar said.

"Two of King Alyn's advisors were murdered during a meeting," Amerus said.

"Not necessarily the work of the Assassins," Selvetar countered.

"The third advisor, the lady Demarys, was spared. According to her account, she was told to continue to walk the right path. She's been flinching away from shadows ever since."

"I would imagine witnessing two peers cut down in front of you would do that to the nerves," Selvetar responded. "That is interesting considering two of Alyn's three advisors are in favor of the war. I believe Demarys was the outlier."

"And so she remains breathing," Amerus agreed. "Ever have The

Khamra operated under political motives while holding to an otherwise philosophy."

Selvetar made a noncommittal sound. That was both true and not. The Khamra were feared by every person who held power, but they only acted aggressively when there was a larger threat. Economies had risen and crumbled without a hint of activity from the assassins. But stretch too far, make threats too broad, and it was certain to illicit a visit from one of The Khamra's legendary assassins. The first magus had heard it said that one could never lie to a Khamra assassin. Only absolute sincerity of your cause could save your life, and that, only if you were truly misguided in your efforts. Selvetar wondered what such a visit from one of the feared assassins would be like. Certainly not pleasant.

"I also received word from my messenger in Shetar," Amerus said, interrupting Selvetar's thoughts. "The Royain apparently had somewhat unwholesome intentions."

Now that was unexpected. "Royain Dimitri has been eliminated?" The monk nodded. "That's interesting," Selvetar said at length.

Amerus frowned. "That is one way to describe it. Royain Dimitri was not a bad man, and has ever been an ally to the king."

Which was precisely why he was not a good man. Until Selvetar had paid a personal visit to the king, it remained to be seen what Alyn's intentions were. Dimitri, on the other hand, stood to gain plenty from a shared effort against the Khatala. The man understood the value of corlite and knew that the Khatala had it in excess, though why the people never used it was a mystery.

"Would you share your thoughts, Selvetar, or will I continue to sit in silent speculation of your true reaction?"

Selvetar refocused on the man. "If The Khamra disapproved of Dimitri's decisions, they disagree with the king's."

"And yet Alyn is still among the living," Amerus said.

"He may have been too well guarded."

Amerus gave him a look that said he didn't believe that line of thought any more than Selvetar did. In a straight fight, one Khamra assassin could kill a handful of guards efficiently.

"They may be unsure of him," Selvetar offered. "Those who take even a small amount of time to assess the beginning of this conflict know that it was simple misunderstanding."

"As is the root of many wars," Amerus said.

"As is the source of many a gain by a smart opportunist who would bolster the pawn's efforts."

"You do not suggest Royain Dimitri was using King Alyn as a pawn," Amerus said, incredulous.

"Not in a direct sense," Selvetar replied. "But if the king's efforts would yield such a healthy bounty, why not? Dimitri had ever been the opportunist."

"And so The Khamra came calling," Amerus spat. "For the good of the people."

"I suspect that is exactly their intention, my good Senior Monk."

"Compliance to their ideals by force," Amerus said.

"That would seem to be the case," Selvetar said.

"And what does the first magus feel about such heavy-handed methods?"

"I see them as what they are," Selvetar answered. "And they've made their choices. Is the conflict with the wilders any different?"

"Is it any better?" Amerus said. "I don't suggest one side is more right than the other."

"And yet, your monks are among the most feared of the Brotherhood."

"I might not desire to fight the fool who would accost me, but that does not mean I will allow him to murder me in the street," Amerus said.

"And it could be that our king felt he was about to be, as you put it, murdered in the street."

"In the moment, perhaps." Amerus stood. "As always, this discussion has been a pleasurable exercise of my giving you far more information than I've received. I must take my leave now."

"Have you spoken to Decius?"

Amerus looked as though he had bitten into a lemon at the mention of the archminister. "He talks of fortifying our defense for the possibility of another attack, but there is 'pack up and flee' look in his eyes. If an opportunity were to present itself, I wouldn't be surprised to see the whole of his wealth and a dusty trail of pack-horses in his wake to an island somewhere on the other side of the world."

Selvetar smirked at that. "And where does Senior Brother Amerus stand?"

"I stand for the good of Vyne," Amerus said. "As you well know. If it means I must travel beside the viper, then I will do as I must." He held up a finger. "But make no mistake, First Magus. I no more count you as a friend than you do me. But it is my hope that our interests are aligned at least in some way, and we can prevent a larger atrocity from befalling our beloved city."

If only the monk knew the extent of it. "Of course, Brother Amerus."

The monk stared at him, then turned on his heel and departed. After the door to his office closed behind the irritated monk, the first magus extinguished all but one of the candles in his office and sat in the dim, flickering light. He watched the shadows dance on the walls, considering what to do next.

The Vyne branch of the Order of Magi and the Brotherhood of the Source would work together to ensure the safety of the city. Bolstered by the efforts of the city guard, Selvetar was confident that Vyne would remain safe while he continued his work between here and Altarra.

Magi from various parts of the world were traveling to his call, and soon he would have a sizable force at hand. He would need to work fast. The king was poised to assault the Khatala at Mount Blood, which would only unite the Khatala from every land against him. The Khamra might well assassinate the man, which would send the kingdom and the surrounding territories into chaos, and the ruling class and monarchs of every land into paranoia.

Selvetar hummed under his breath at the thought. Had any such event ever happened in history? Surely even The Khamra would balk at the idea of dispatching such powerful figures as a king.

And what of the spicetrader? Vladrick had yet to share his intentions with his little hybrid pet project, and Selvetar didn't doubt that the magi master saw the same distrust in Amoura's eyes as he did. Selvetar didn't blame the woman, but she was shortsighted.

Little insignificant Vyne was not a noticeable presence, which was exactly why it was the perfect place.

He needed to move quickly.

45

EMIEL

"I have to say I'm surprised to see you," Emiel said. "I can't think of a single reason why you're standing in here with me."

"You're relieved," Amoura said to the other magus. He looked at her doubtfully, but Amoura never looked in his direction. He glanced at Emiel, and he gave the man a shrug. The magus looked one more time at Amoura, then turned away, his red robes swishing behind him as he went out the door.

Amoura started to approach him and Emiel instinctively took a step away. She didn't seem surprised by his reaction more than hurt, and stopped short. "We don't have much time," she said hesitantly.

"Time?" Emiel said. "For what? For your boss to do whatever it is he wants to do to me before bringing my kidnapped daughters here for the same?"

"I can talk to you about this after we—"

"What do we have to talk about, Amoura?" he snapped. She could fry him on the spot, or rip him to shreds with a storm of ice shards, but at that moment he pressed on anyway. "You brought me here knowing it was me that Vladrick really wanted. This was nothing more than kidnapping my daughters and forcing me to come here on a lie. Now I'm stuck, and apparently he might be having my girls brought here as well."

He forced himself to calm down. "What could you possibly want with me? I've been a burden to you from the start."

"Your daughters are not in Vyne," Amoura said.

The edges of Emiel's vision went dark, and a coldness settled over him. "What did you say?"

She started toward him again, but there was no strength in Emiel's legs other than to keep him upright. "Your daughters are no longer in Vyne."

"So he already has them coming here," Emiel said. "He had them sent here, didn't he?"

"There ... was an attack on your city," she said. "The same monsters we battled on the path here also attacked Vyne."

"No." Emiel's legs finally gave out and he dropped to his knees. Tears welled up in his eyes, but then the despair gave way to panic. He looked left and right. This had to be a dream. A nightmare.

"They're alive." Those two simple words broke through Emiel's desperation and he looked up at her. Those steel gray eyes were determined, focused. Unsure.

"You're not telling me the truth," Emiel said, forcing himself to stand. He would not let her see him vulnerable, no matter how much his heart was breaking at the moment. "What happened to them?"

Amoura stared at him for several tense moments before responding. "They escaped the archminister's mansion and were last seen fleeing with a man from Khatal who had been imprisoned."

Emiel almost dropped to the floor again. "A prisoner? My girls fled the city with a prisoner?"

"Please," Amoura said. It was the first time he could recall her using a tone that even approached softness. "We don't have time to talk about this now. We have to get out of here first."

"Out?" Emiel said as she grabbed him by the elbow.

"They were last seen fleeing the city with a small hunting band after them. The hunters failed."

She led him down the halls, stopping to peek around corners

before continuing. "The hunters followed them well into the wild, but never caught up."

"Into the wild?" Emiel gasped. "My girls are out in the wild somewhere?" His heart felt like it would drop into his stomach. "This can't be happening." He wiped his suddenly clammy hands on his shirt.

"I think you have every reason to be confident they're alive," the woman said.

"They've never been farther from home than an hour or two ride to a neighboring village," Emiel said.

"They also never had the first magus as a mentor."

Emiel stopped. "What?"

Amoura rushed back and grabbed him by the arm. "Come on. We can discuss this away from here, or in a cell. And I might not be in the mood to talk to you if the latter happens."

A quick retort came to Emiel's lips but he held it back when it finally sank in that she had taken a great risk in getting him out of that room. "Why?" he asked.

"Why what?" Amoura replied as she tugged him on.

"First, why are we sneaking? Your magi master said I was free to roam the grounds. Second, why are you helping me out of here?"

She glanced back at him. "For the first question, you must truly be naive. For the second, I'm not sure myself." At least she was honest.

"It feels wrong, what he's doing. You're a good man and don't deserve ..." she scowled. "What does it matter? I'm helping you out of here to try to find your daughters. Must there be some conditions attached? Do you suspect I want some payment in return? Have my actions earned that much contempt?"

"Woah, woah," Emiel said, patting his hand in the air. "Calm yourself, woman. I think it's a fair question, since you delivered me here. I'm not insinuating anything."

She turned her piercing gaze on him again. Those grey eyes had seemed so cold to him, but now that he looked closer, there was more there. He saw a hint of compassion buried in that frosty exterior.

"Stop staring at me," she said.

"I'm sorry," he replied.

"I just don't like people staring at me," she said.

Emiel decided to try his luck. "Why?"

"A question better suited near the warmth of a campfire, or better yet, a hearth, don't you think?"

Emiel looked down at his side to see Lief trotting beside him. "What? How? I haven't seen you since that first day in my room. I thought you had—"

"Abandoned you?" The tiny woman sniffed. "No. I was really just spying on her," she said, and Amoura's face tightened.

"Be silent," the magus said. She peeked around another corner, then signaled for them to follow. Halfway down the hallway three magi rounded the far corner. "Keep walking," she said.

"Amoura Xanna," one of the magi greeted as they closed the distance. The man wore red robes and had the kind of smile that looked as if it hid a poison-tipped dart. "I've heard about your adventures playing delivery girl." He leaned around her to look at Emiel. As was typical, Lief was nowhere in sight.

"I confess that I'm surprised to see you escorting him this way. Should he not be in attendance with Master Vladrick?"

"Should you not be attending to matters that do not concern my business, Nial?" Amoura replied. Ever diplomatic.

Nial narrowed his eyes. "Have you ever wondered why you have so few friends?"

"No." The cold, mater-of-fact tone of Amoura's voice set them on their heels.

Nial's mouth bobbed several times before he finally found his voice again. "Perhaps you should at least attempt—"

Amoura started walking. "I've no time or inclination to expend any more time or energy with you than I already have, Nial. I'll be on my way."

"Why the rush?" he said, moving to block her path.

Emiel watched them. The man named Nial tilted his slick black haired head and smirked at her. He practically had no lips, and the tips of his eyebrows were so sharp, they looked lethal. His long pointed chin begged to be met with a fist.

The other two magi fanned out to either side of Nial. *Great*, Emiel thought. *Nothing like a confrontation when you're in a hurry.*

"Step aside," Amoura said, and Emiel was surprised at her warning tone despite being outnumbered three to one. He would help in any way he could, but he doubted there was much he could do. Perhaps Lief was hiding somewhere waiting to help? Could she?

"Oh, my dear woman. Your arrogance is this potent? That you actually think even you could forcibly remove three magi is rather amusing."

"That is not my wish, but you're about to make it my intention," Amoura replied.

The ring on the finger of Nial's right hand glowed the same color as his robes. The rings of the other two red-clad magi also glowed red. Emiel looked at the ring on Amoura's finger. It remained passive. Did she plan on punching her way through?

Nial noticed her ring as well. "So confident. It is my belief that you have ill intentions, Master Apprentice Amoura Xanna, and I demand that you and your charge accompany me to Magi Master Vladrick."

Amoura's ring flared blue, then immediately green, and she sent a blast of *air* that knocked all three magi off their feet. She summoned *water*, and sent a stream speeding toward them.

All three magi came to their feet and their rings flared silver. The stream of water slammed into an invisible shield. The three magi struggled against the assault as Amoura strode toward them. She held her hands out in front of her and to her sides, and the streaming water surrounded the magi.

Her ring flared red, and the hallway grew hot. The water streaming at the magi started to evaporate in the sweltering heat, and Emiel thought he might evaporate with it.

Nial grunted and his ring flared blue. He swung his arms out wide, and the heat lessened.

The other two magi sent columns of fire at Amoura, but the

columns bent in either direction away from her and returned to their senders. Both men cried out in surprise and their rings flared blue again. Amoura's ring flared silver, and the three men were pushed backward by an invisible force.

She swept her hand left, then right, and the trio lifted into the air and slammed into the wall on the left, then the wall on the right. They dropped to the floor in a tangled heap, and Amoura leaned against the wall.

Emiel rushed to her side and helped her to straighten. "Now I think you're definitely right. We need to get out of here fast." He draped one of her arms over his shoulder and half carried her down the hall.

"I can run ... now," she said. She was still breathing heavy, but Emiel released her arm.

Amoura took the lead, and they navigated the halls at a full run. Luck was with them and they encountered no one else.

"Where are we going?" Emiel asked.

"Still doesn't know when to be quiet," a young man's voice said from around a corner further down the hall. They rounded the corner to see Bone leaning against the wall. "You need to learn how to be quiet, spicetrader. I heard you all the way down here."

"You?" Emiel could hardly believe his eyes.

"That's a nice greeting," the mercenary said. "Let's get out of here. This place gives me the shivers."

"That was amazing, back there," Emiel whispered as they jogged down the endless winding hallways of the magi fortress. "You could probably take on that Vladrick guy."

"We don't want that," Amoura said.

The response stopped them dead.

"And why not, my young apprentice?"

46

JOGA

Joga had never felt such heat in his life. The first few hours of his journey into the volcano were dark, but not overly uncomfortable. But as he traveled ever downward, light came with the presence of the lava. And along with light, the lava brought heat. Horrible, intense heat.

Joga stopped and took off his pack. He pulled free some rope, and took off his furs and tied them to the back of his pack. Wiping sweat from his brow, he took a long draw from his waterskin, and replaced it to the pack and shouldered it once more.

He took a step forward, then glanced back the way he'd come. Something was following him. After the first hour or so into his journey down here, he'd had the unmistakable feeling that something had taken an interest and was trailing him through the rocky tunnels.

He turned back and continued on his way, hoping that the ever-increasing temperature would make whatever was following him decide that the stuffy heat wasn't worth its curiosity.

The minutes became hours, and as the hours passed, Joga found the heat becoming unbearable, but he pushed forward. He hoped he could find his way to the lair of the mulgin before he was forced to delve *air* to cool himself. He needed as much of his strength as possible for whatever the confrontation might bring.

The path started upward, then began to shrink as he climbed. Soon he was sliding on his stomach through the tight corridor, very much aware of his vulnerability. He sighed in relief when he finally came to the end of the narrow tunnel and swung his legs over the side and dropped down.

After a few dozen feet, the new pathway widened on either side. Little streams of lava flowed across the ground, like tiny glowing veins. He stepped carefully across them while keeping a wary eye on his surroundings. Whatever was following him was still there.

The ground rumbled and he froze and waited it out. After a few moments the tremor subsided and he continued. He passed intersections to tunnels leading in various directions, but followed his instincts. The ritual that led to Joga receiving his bloodmark had infused him with a sort of inner map. Perhaps it was a connection created between himself and the mulgin? Joga didn't have the answer, but it didn't matter. Once he'd gotten inside the volcano, he knew which direction to go.

The tremors started again, and again he stopped and waited them out. A few feet away the ground split and a burst of steam hissed from the opening. Joga stumbled forward, not wanting to be anywhere near that skin melting steam.

The shaking continued for some time, and it was all he could do to keep from falling or tripping over his own feet. He stumbled to the side and placed his hand on the wall to steady himself. The wall was burning hot, and he cried out and snatched his blistered hand free.

Joga looked further down the path and saw the tunnel bend to the right where a bright light glowed. He carefully picked his way down, cradling his hand while summoning *air* to cool and sooth it.

He peeked around the corner expecting to see a bed of lava as the source of the light. To his dismay, it was a tunnel whose walls no doubt housed flowing lava just beyond. The stone walls and floor glowed red, and the heat they emitted was more than he could bear. He backed away a few steps and considered another route. But there was no other route. Deep inside he knew there was only one way to the mulgin, and it was through that molten corridor.

As he delved *air*, he first thought to try and cool the corridor, but dismissed the thought immediately. It would take an impossible amount of stamina to draw enough of *essence* to accomplish that. He also couldn't use water to cool the ground, as the steam would kill him as surely as stepping in that corridor would.

He delved *air*, then *water*. The two *essences* came readily to his call, and a funnel of water swirled before him, growing colder by the moment. He moved as close to the tunnel as he could bear, then focused on the water flowing in the air around him. It grew so cold that it nearly burned his skin. Joga huffed. The irony might have been humorous, were the circumstances different.

He sent the swirling water into the tunnel and focused on freezing it. Steam rose from the ground, but he continued, remaining just out of the way. Soon the steam thinned to reveal a rapidly melting coat of ice as tall as his waist on the floor.

Joga wasted no time and rushed in. He slipped and slid, but focused on keeping his footing as he made his way over the ice. He ignored his fear and tried to ignore the melting ice around him. He was almost to the corridor's end, but the frozen path was nearly melted. Joga scrambled for the end of the path, then slipped and fell on his back.

He ignored the stars in his vision and arched his neck to look behind him. Several tiny streams of lava slithered through the ice toward him, and the heat of the lava on his back as the ice continued to melt into the hot floor.

Still sliding forward, Joga fought his way to his feet and half stumbled half crawled. The long sheet of ice cracked and broke apart as it thinned, and Joga leapt across a gap to the next chunk just as it split apart. He landed and slipped again, but turned onto his stomach and tucked his feet under himself, then hopped over the next gap.

He half-ran half-slid the last several feet, then jumped just as the ice melted away. The end of the corridor was not straight, however, and Joga partially collided with the stone wall. The extremely hot rocky wall burned his right arm as he rolled and fell to the ground.

Joga gritted his teeth through the searing pain while he squirmed on the ground holding his arm. After several ragged breaths, he looked at his arm. It was burned, but not horribly so. Luckily the impact had been at an angle, and quick.

He stood and looked back at the tunnel. The thick sheet of ice he had created on the ground might as well never have been.

He turned away and continued. The corridors started to grow wider, and he began to see scars on the walls, as if something had raked long nails along the rock. Those scars were a hand deep, and Joga had no desire to meet the animal that did that, though it was doubtful they were anything as formidable as what awaited him.

The ground shook, and this time he heard what sounded like a breathy growl. It continued through the duration of the tremor. Joga took a deep breath, another sip from his waterskin and pushed forward, wiping the constant running sweat from his face.

He came around another bend to see an enormous bed of lava rippling like a lazy ocean wave. Joga wished it was a wave in the ocean instead of that deathly pool.

In this open space the heat was unbearable, and Joga was forced to delve *air,* and wrap himself in a cool constantly flowing breeze. He couldn't do it indefinitely, so he had to be quick about this. He moved into the open area and saw a huge plateau of rock that extended partially over the lava pool.

Joga leaned to look around it, but there was no way to see if there was a cave beyond.

"Creator *Amyadali* give me strength," he said, closing his eyes to offer a prayer. He then prayed to Mother *Illyu.*

He delved three of the four *essences*, bringing *air, water,* and *earth* ready for his call. Joga took another deep breath and settled himself, then formed a spear of ice many times larger than his body and sent it flying straight into the lava.

The result was instant. The cavern shook and the lava pool rose and fell, and Joga dove aside as a wave splashed over the place where he'd been standing. Joga forced his rapidly beating heart to slow, and looked over his shoulder. That magma would have burned him to nothing in an instant.

He remained focused and kept the freezing field of air around him. He sent another spear of ice into the lava, and this time used a powerful blast of *air* to repel the responding wave of lava that again splashed at the place he was standing. He sent another spear, and this time the cavern shook violently. A red plate scale more than twice the size of his body rose from the lava, then sank again.

"By Creator *Amyadali* herself," he breathed. If that scale was any indication, the thing was massive. What could he do against that?

Joga steeled himself. He would do what he must. Even if it meant his own demise. If Creator *Amyadali* placed this upon his shoulders, She believed he could succeed.

He delved *air* and *water* again and sent several giant spears of ice into the lava. One stopped only halfway into the lava before it broke in half and melted. The cavern rumbled violently and lava spewed from the pool like a geyser.

Joga's eyes widened in shock, but his training and instincts saved him. He threw his focus into drawing *air,* and pushed it outward around his body. The lava splashed against the invisible barrier and slid away as though falling along the sides of a dome.

The tremors continued, bubbles rose and popped from the pool of magma, and Joga saw a ripple moving toward him. He steadied himself and started combining the *essences.* As soon as the beast revealed itself, he would ...

The impact came from beneath the surface of the lava, and the rocky platform crumbled beneath him. At the same time, he was tackled from the side and saved from what would have been an instant death.

The impact sent him rolling, but he managed to stop himself. He rose to his hands and knees, dazed. "Fool girls!" he shouted. How could he not have known it was them who had been following him all the way down here. He held his head, still shaken. "Told you I must do this on my own."

When he looked up, it was not the twin girls and Sama that he saw, but a creature that stood on four legs with gray, leathery skin that seemed to glow from the inside. It stared at him with tiny red eyes above a mouth that stretched nearly to the back of its head. That mouth hung open in what looked like a smile to reveal two rows of yellow teeth.

"Tryeck," Joga whispered. The stories he'd been told as a child spoke of these volcano dwellers as aggressive, but not very smart.

Joga straightened and faced the beast. "I would have preferred my friends." He delved *earth* at the same time the monster crouched and its body suddenly erupted in flame. It charged and he released a blast of freezing water.

The assault slowed the monster, and Joga continued to freeze the air and water until it became a horizontal deluge of ice shards. The ice did little damage to the tryeck, though the flames on its skin were extinguished.

The tryeck powered through the icy assault, and Joga barely dove aside in time. He rolled back to his feet, doing his best to ignore the pain that exploded through his burned arm and hand, and focused another blast of icy air at the monster.

The tryeck was less affected this time, and barreled right through the assault. It rammed its head into Joga and sent him flying back into the wall where he crumpled to the ground. The monster's head was as hard as stone, and the impact left Joga winded. Still he managed to lift his hand and send another blast of ice and wind, but it was weak.

The tryeck stomped wildly and Joga roared in defiance as that huge maw opened and swallowed the world around him.

Joga kept his eyes open in a last show of defiance. He would not flinch away from his death, but face it. But death never came, and he was not swallowed in darkness. In fact, the only thing that attacked him was the horrid breath of the tryeck when it grunted from being knocked sideways by a chunk of rock the size of Joga's body.

Joga turned in the direction of this new threat to see a figure standing near the opening he had come through. Then its mirror image stepped out. Even though the heat waves blurred his vision,

Joga didn't need to see clearly to know it was the twin Marailander girls.

"Watch your back, mountain man!" one of them shouted. Only Amiya called him that.

He turned back to see that the tryeck had rolled and bounced to a stop, and was struggling to right itself. A wave of soreness went through him as Joga struggled to catch his breath, but managed only a loud wheeze.

"All Khatala people so foolish?" a voice said as a figure with reddish skin darted past him in a rush of cold air.

"I can't keep you cool that far away, stupid girl!" Amiya shouted, running toward Joga, then past him.

Nandi came to Joga and knelt next to him. "You're stupid too, you know?"

Joga was still too winded to offer any response, so Nandi stood and moved toward the other two.

Joga looked after her and saw Sama, dancing in and out of the tryeck's reach. He winced. One bite would snap the tatamble in half. He needn't worry, however, for the girl was a blur of motion, scoring slice after slice either with the belt knife she carried, or the sharp nails of her own fingers.

The tryeck bled from more than a dozen wounds that it ignored as it tried to get a hold of the troublesome tatamble. It charged, and Sama did a somersault out of the way, scoring a slash to the monster's leg as she moved. It stumbled and slid into the wall, but came back to its feet and spat at her.

Sama dodged and again Joga winced when he saw the ground sizzling where the tryeck's hot spittle landed.

"Oh that's disgusting," Nandi said. She leaned forward and Joga could tell she was focusing. A piece of the wall behind the tryeck broke apart and slammed it to the ground.

The cavern shook again, and they all stumbled. Even the tryeck lost its footing as it dug itself free of the rubble.

Joga looked at the pool of lava and his heart nearly stopped. A claw large enough to crush an elephant rose from the pool of magma.

The molten liquid slid from the claw and down a thick, scaly leg. Another claw appeared from the pool and dug into the stone wall on the far side of the cavern.

Black nails dug deeply into the stone as the mulgin climbed out of the huge molten pool. Joga forced himself to stand and face the beast. "By Creator *Amyadali*," he said in his native tongue. "Only a teliak could be larger than this behemoth."

"We need to get out of here!" he heard Amiya shout from somewhere to the side.

"Let's not forget about this flaming hyena thing either," Nandi yelled back.

Joga heard the words, but his eyes were locked on the monstrosity climbing out of that molten bed of lava. Rock crumbled as it clawed its way upward, and before he realized it, Joga had backed into the wall.

The mulgin arched its neck and let out a hissing roar that made his bones vibrate. Its forked tongue flicked in and out several times and then it turned its scaled head in Joga's direction. Those black eyes locked with his, and Joga almost lost his grip on *air*, and hopped forward when the heat from the wall burned his back.

The mulgin climbed higher, then flicked its tongue out again. It looked to the side, and Joga followed its gaze. The three girls still battled the tryeck, who was bleeding profusely but showing no signs of slowing. Sama was backing away with a hand clamped to the front of her leg, and Nandi buffeted the monster from left to right with blasts of *air*. The tryeck stumbled under the assault but continued forward.

Joga started toward them, but that hissing roar stopped him dead. They needed to get out of this place. *If I fail to fulfill my bloodmark, so be it, but I'll not let them die here with me.*

Joga gathered himself and delved. The girls were already backing toward him while taking turns assaulting the tryeck. Smart. They realized they weren't hurting it, so they were trying to slow it down while making a steady retreat.

A heavy thud shook the ground, followed by another. Joga

looked back to the mulgin. It was glaring at him with those black beads for eyes. There was something wrong about those eyes. Mulgin normally had green eyes, not those seemingly endless black pits.

The mulgin climbed sideways around the circular cavern wall, making its way toward the tryeck. In but a few long strides the massive beast stopped, and its tongue flicked out and knocked the tryeck into the wall.

The smaller beast grunted and spat at the mulgin's eyes, then charged toward Joga and the others. Joga shouted for the girls to move aside, as the beast was now more interested in the only exit to the cavern than the four of them.

The mulgin ignored the burning spittle and flicked its tongue out again. This time, that long forked tongue wrapped around the fleeing tryeck. It snatched the beast off the ground as a frog might snatch an insect, and the tryeck disappeared into the mulgin's mouth with a sickening crunch.

Sama and the twins wasted no time watching the spectacle and were in a full run toward Joga, who was backing away while keeping his eyes on the mulgin.

Its head whipped around at him and it roared its angry hissing roar again. It planted its claws into the wall and inhaled till its stomach bulged.

Joga drew as much of *air* as he could channel through his body and created a wall between them. The mulgin convulsed and vomited a molten substance at them that splashed into the invisible wall.

"Disgusting!" Nandi said, but they were still running for the exit.

The mulgin stomped its claw into the wall and the cavern shook.

The girls stumbled and slid and tripped over one another. Joga backed closer to them as the mulgin advanced. It stopped and rotated its body until its back was to them.

"Puking at us was disgusting enough," Amiya said. "I really hope it's not about to do what I think it is."

The mulgin whipped the tip of its long tail into the wall above the exit to the cavern, and the ceiling collapsed over it.

Nandi screamed and shielded her eyes with her arm. "I didn't know lavakhans were that smart!"

"Do not," Joga replied, positioning himself between the girls and the giant lizard. Molten liquid still dripped from its armor-plated body. "Is inhabited."

"Inhabited?" Nandi said. "What's that supposed to mean?"

"Something controls," Joga explained. "Something evil."

The mulgin narrowed its black eyes at him as he spoke, and he realized it understood them.

"I don't see any other way out of here," Amiya said.

"Death is only way out," Sama replied. "Time to wake from this life."

"Maybe for you," Amiya replied, and Joga felt her delving. "I'm not planning to stand here and be crunched on like a snack."

Joga glanced back at the girl, the angry girl. Though her twin sister looked terrified, but determined, Amiya looked furious. Her eyes glowed red, but she must have realized fire would do nothing to the monster. The red faded away and, and her eyes shone blue, then silver, then brown. The colors of the three *essences* pulsated in Amiya's eyes, and Joga felt the power building around her.

Nandi glanced at her sister. "Amiya?"

"I'm not going to die here, Nandi," the feisty girl said. "And neither are you."

A light shown in the other twin's eyes, and Nandi turned to face the mulgin. Joga felt her delving as well, and in seconds she had three of the four *essences* swirling around her. There was more power flowing through those two than any ten children should have been capable of.

Sama looked as if she wanted to bolt, but there was nowhere to run. She backed away and settled into a defensive crouch.

Joga turned his attention back to the mulgin. Adrenaline pumped through his body at the sight of his young companions. The girls were strong, but not enough to destroy this monster. "Must stand together." Joga clenched his fists. He would give everything he had, down to his last breath, to see that his friends survived this and that Nandi and Amiya had a chance to find their father.

He delved *air, water,* and *earth*, and filled himself with the three *essences*. The power leapt to his call, and he could barely contain the wild tempest of Mother *Illyu's* power swirling inside him.

The mulgin curled its body around and swiped its tail at them. Joga jumped and used *air* to aid his ascent. He took a quick glance over his shoulder and saw that the girls had ducked under the tail.

Joga turned and sent a stream of ice shards speeding at the lizard. The shards shattered on impact, and when Joga landed he had to dive forward to avoid being impaled by the tip of its tail. It left a hole wider than his body in the ground where he'd stood just an instant before.

A chunk of the cavern ceiling broke away and crashed on top of the mulgin's head. The lizard nearly lost its grip, and sent rock tumbling into the lava bed as it struggled to regain its balance.

"Good one," he heard one of the girls congratulate the other.

Joga summoned *air* and *water*, forming an icicle twice as wide around than his body, and sent it flying.

The mulgin tried to move out of the way, but it was still dazed by the blow to the head. His aim was true, and the giant icicle struck the lizard in a vulnerable spot under its shoulder. The giant spear of ice punched through the tough hide and out the other side of its shoulder, pinning it to the wall.

The mulgin hissed and squirmed, and a storm of ice shards flew past Joga and straight into its open maw. As it choked on the ice, the air around its mouth began to freeze.

Joga looked to the side at Nandi and Amiya. *They improve every day.* He sent another storm of ice shards at the mulgin, this time focusing them into its eyes.

The lizard shuddered and thrashed, and the icicle snapped. Despite its painful injuries, it still held onto the wall.

The twins delved *earth* again and dislodged another giant chunk of rock detached from the wall and hit the mulgin in its side. It swayed and nearly lost its grip.

"Of course," Joga said, and delved *earth*. He dislodged two pieces of the wall where the mulgin held on, and the massive lizard gave a great hiss of anger as it slipped away.

Joga yelled a curse and ran toward the twins. "*Air!*" he shouted, and the three of them delved the *essence* and produced an invisible dome around themselves and Sama, who was still crouched nearby.

The mulgin fell back into the lava and sent a wave of magma splashing over them. The heat was almost unbearable, but the dome of air held. For several nervous heartbeats they waited as the lava slid down the invisible dome.

"You think that did it?" Amiya asked.

"It's injured and blind," Nandi said.

"And angry," Joga added. "Hold *air*. Not over."

Joga wished he was wrong, but the second splash of molten rock and lava that washed over their protective dome confirmed his words. They moved as far back as they could, and a giant claw shot out of the pool and slammed onto ground. A second claw emerged, and then that flicking tongue.

Beside him, Joga felt the girls preparing, as was he. The lizard's head appeared from over the side, larger than all of them combined. Its eyes were a ruined mess, and it had only its tongue to smell the air for them.

Amiya sent a stream of water at the ground where the mulgin was pulling itself up, then froze it. The beast had nearly climbed out by then, and the ice caused it to slip and fall onto its belly. The ice cracked apart and started to melt.

Nandi sent a chunk of rock from flying from the wall to crash into its nose just as its tongue flicked out. There was a splash of blood, and the lizard made a coughing sound around its ruined tongue.

It reached out a claw and Nandi dove out of the way just as it clawed the ground where she had been. It tried to flatten her again, but the girl was fast. This time, she dove out of the way and at the same time delved *earth* and pulled a stalagmite from the ground.

The mulgin's mouth opened in agony as the stalagmite impaled its claw, and it whipped its tail around at the girl.

Joga sent a blast of air that knocked Nandi safely away, then ran toward the lizard. He knocked the mulgin's head to the side with an *air*-enhanced punch, and the beast returned his attack with a backward swat of its claw that nearly sent him into the bed of lava.

The shield of *air* he'd been holding saved his life, but he was still knocked senseless, and the *essences* fell away. When the lethal heat assaulted him, he had just enough presence of mind to delve *air* again to stay alive.

In the fog of his mind he heard the muffled sound of Amiya swearing an oath no girl should let cross her lips, and three stalagmites shot up from the ground and impaled the mulgin in one of its legs and its neck.

It thrashed and swept its claw out. The girls tried to dodge, but were hit and knocked from view. The sound of their screams snapped Joga back to his senses, and he forced himself to stand. The mulgin kicked and slapped at the stalagmites until they finally broke.

It slipped in a pool of its own blood and turned to face him. Its lips drew back to reveal teeth as long as his forearm as it stalked toward him. Its steps were labored, but it continued on as if unaware of the blood spilling from its neck.

Before Joga could formulate a plan, the giant lizard charged him. It swept a claw at him and he dove to the side, then sent a stream of ice shards into its face. The area where its eyes had been was still sensitive, and it flinched away from the impact. Joga swept his hand at the monster and sent a wave of rock filled with smaller stalagmites crashing into it.

He delved *air* and *water* again and sent another blast of the razor sharp ice into its face, then froze the air inside its opened mouth. It coughed and half turned its body.

Joga knew what was coming and quickly formed a sheet of ice as narrow and sharp as a blade. He formed the razor-like sheet of ice vertically between himself and the sweeping tail just before it reached him. The thick tail sliced right into the blade of ice and half of it fell away.

The wiggling piece of tail hit the ground not far from Joga while the mulgin hissed and thrashed. He lifted his hand in the direction of the space above the lizard's head and formed another giant icicle.

When the beast slowed enough for him to time it, he used every bit of strength left to him and swept his hand down. The icicle crashed into its skull, through its brain, and out of its chin with such force, it pinned the mulgin's scaly head to the ground. The muscles in its neck bulged as it squirmed to lift its head, but soon it ceased struggling and lay still.

Joga didn't stop to revel in his victory, for the girls had been knocked out of his line of sight. Joga prayed to Creator *Amyadali* that they hadn't been killed by the giant claw, or burned alive in that molten pool.

To his relief, they lay scattered on the ground, moaning, but alive. He rushed over and inspected each of them. "So strong," he said, and smiled at them.

"Urgh, tell me that when I don't feel like I've been hit by an elephant," Amiya said.

"Two elephants," Nandi added, and Joga chuckled as he helped them up.

"I'm sure I can do better than that," a voice said from behind.

47

NANDI AND AMIYA

Ironically, the promise of more pain by that chilling voice actually made Nandi forget her pain. She looked past Joga to see a man with skin that looked like it was made from the stuff in that lava pool. Actually, she realized, he looked to be made of the same thing as those four-armed cursing things that had attacked Vyne.

Joga positioned himself between the magma man and the three of them. She felt him delving *air, water,* and *earth,* and did the same. Beside her, Amiya delved as well.

"Ah, cute," the man-thing said. "Little children one and all, playing at things they don't understand." His voice was smooth and confident, in contrast with his glowing black and red body. Those pulsating red eyes saw them as insignificant. "I'll educate you."

An unseen force smacked Nandi in the side of the head and sent her spinning. She heard Amiya cry out as she too went spinning to the ground.

Joga staggered sideways but held his feet. "You strike a child?" the outraged Khatala man shouted.

"Apply a bit of intellect, Khatala, and you will realize that I don't care."

Nandi remained on the ground, only moving her eyes as she

looked first to ensure that her sister was alright, then looking for Sama. The tatamble girl was nowhere in sight. Nandi started to feel the heat from the ground under her and realized her focus was slipping. She summoned as little of *air* as possible, and cooled the area beneath her, then lifted her head just enough to see Joga and that thing still talking.

"No fight with you," Joga was saying. "Come to stop problems coming from here."

The lava rock man laughed at him. "You come here with children to stop the 'problems' that come from here?" His laughter lowered to a condescending chuckle. "Don't be so slow-witted. You come here and destroy my pet, then seek to undo all the fun I've created?"

Nandi felt Joga delving again, and judging by the lava man's amused look, he felt it too.

"Still summoning up all that power to smite the mighty adversary, hmm?" He spread his arms. "Do your worst, wild man. Your absolute worst."

Joga struck. A sudden formation and explosion of the most powerful blast of ice shards and flying rock Nandi had ever seen enveloped the man made of molten rock.

"Woah," Amiya said from somewhere to the side. "Never seen him do anything like that before."

Nandi shielded her eyes with her hand. "Fine for me. Better to blast him to nothing and be done with it."

"How long's he going to keep that up?" Amiya said, squinting against the storming power. Pieces of the stone wall broke apart and fell on the platform as well as splashed into the lava pool. From the corner of her eye, Nandi saw a bit of hair whipping against the wall. She focused more closely, but Amiya frantically waved her off. What was her sister up to?

Joga delved deeper and funneled more of the *essences* through him, guiding them to form a tempest of destruction. Freezing air mixed with ice shards blew from the front, while head-sized rocks struck from the sides and below, and in the span of a dozen heartbeats, a horizontal column of water formed and blasted into the man with enough force to strip his skin away.

Nandi and Amiya gritted their teeth at the sight. Joga seemed intent on utterly destroying this man. Nandi was glad for it, but it was still frightening to see.

Through the wild display of power, she saw the shape of the man materialize. He walked right out of the storm, smiling the whole way. Nandi thought her blood would freeze at the sight.

The man waved a black and red arm, and the storm simply winked out. Nandi felt him delving, no, not delving, commanding. The *essences* were snatched from the natural flow and brought to him.

With his other hand, he curled his fingers. Joga gasped and gripped his throat as he knelt. His eyes bulged and it looked to Nandi as if he was suffocating.

"You have a good grasp of the power, boy," the lava man said. "But you are like a baby, swinging a sword. You swing it well, but there is no strength behind it. You have no idea what it's like to have to watch so many children playing with power they cannot understand."

Nandi wanted to delve, wanted to attack this man and help Joga. But he would know. She wasn't as strong as the Khatala man. She couldn't approach what he'd just done, and this man, this thing, had walked through it laughing. She nearly jumped when she heard Amiya's voice next to her ear.

"We gonna help out mountain man or wait for him to die first?"

"What can we do against that thing?" she asked.

Amiya shrugged. "Die fighting, or just die."

Nandi was afraid. She didn't want to die. Not here. Not like this. She'd never felt so helpless in her life, and that was the most terrifying thing of all.

The man looked directly at her and winked. It was as if he'd heard that last thought. "I can feel all that fear, little girl. Calm your nerves. When I have finished with this," he looked down at the kneeling Joga, and the Khatala man convulsed again, clawing at his chest. "I can provide you with a chance to be what I am, invulnerable and power personified, or a quick death.

"I'm surprised you offer a humane option," Nandi forced herself to say.

The man gave her a half smile. "I wouldn't say that. It's more a matter of boredom. Torturing children isn't as much fun because you're more fragile. There's usually no more than a minute or two of enjoyment before those little hearts wink out. Not worth the effort."

He looked down at Joga again, and again, Joga convulsed. Again and again he struggled to rise, until finally he fell over on his side.

"You said something about becoming like you?" Nandi said. "What do you mean by that?"

"And why would we want to do that if it means looking like you?" Amiya asked, catching Nandi's intent. As always, her twin had read her mind, but she wished Amiya would mince her words.

"Hmm. That's a surprise," the man said. He half turned toward them, and Joga relaxed, just a tiny bit, but it was something. "I sense great potential in you. With my guidance, you could be two of the most powerful girls the world has ever seen."

"We could?" Amiya said, sounding skeptical.

The man turned a malicious smile on her. "Not really," he replied. "But I thought I'd indulge your little pedestrian attempts to distract me."

Behind him, Joga cried out in anguish, and in that instant, Amiya delved and grabbed hold of more *essence* than Nandi thought her sister capable of. Even the lava rock man seemed surprised. "Impressive," he said. "I wonder if your more docile mirror image can summon up half of what you're doing."

Nandi's temper flared. "Docile?"

"Watch your mouth, molten man ... *ah!*" Amiya doubled over, and most of the *essences* left her.

Nandi cried out and wrapped her sister in *air*. Surprisingly, Amiya hadn't fully let go of the power, but why wasn't she focusing it on keeping herself cool?

"Oh the love of a sister," the man mocked.

Seeing Amiya curled up on the ground set Nandi's temper aflame. She opened herself to the *essences* and they flooded through her.

"Woah, look at that," the man said, and she felt what seemed like a presence attempting to tear the *essences* away from her. She fought it, and then she felt Amiya delving again.

"You're gonna pay for that," her sister said. Nandi felt Amiya's rage, and the power connected to it. It was such a surprise that Nandi nearly lost her focus. She surrendered to the earth's power and let it flow through her in a torrent of bliss and terrible destructive force. Through the raging storm fighting to release itself through her, she heard the man growl, and she felt him focus on them.

When she could contain the force no longer, Nandi released it in an explosion of water, ice, and air. Ice shards and icicles flew into her enemy, while freezing air pushed him back. Nandi drew upon *earth* and a piece of the stone wall broke free and fell over the molten man-creature.

He grasped *air* and swatted the chunk of rock away as Amiya sent more freezing air at him. For a moment, it looked as if his body was beginning to freeze, but then the tiny rivulets of lava that flowed across his body grew brighter, and the ice melted away.

Nandi attacked again, launching icicles as large around as her body. Amiya did the same, sending balls of hail the size of a man's fist crashing into him.

"I'm impressed," the man growled through the assault.

Joga came to his feet, and Nandi felt him delving again. How he had managed to hold on to enough of *air* to keep from dying in the heat while being tortured like that, Nandi couldn't imagine.

Joga attacked, sending *earth*, *air*, and *water* crashing into the lava man. Through it all, Nandi still felt him resisting. He moved forward, eyes glowing with hatred. He looked to the left, and a wave of lava rose up from the pool.

AMIYA SAW the wave of lava rising up to wash over them and focused her efforts on it. She drew *air* and created a barrier between them and the towering magma, then pushed back. The molten wave splashed against the barrier and Amiya spread her arms up and around, creating a dome around them.

The lava slid down the invisible dome to collect on the ground around it Beside her, Nandi grunted, and Amiya felt her sister send another horizontal storm of ice spears at the molten man. Amiya looked back at that smug expression and grew angrier. She sent ice and water, freezing air and large chunks of rock crashing into him.

Further up, the mountain man also attacked. Despite all their efforts, the man-thing still held them off, and Amiya was beginning to think he might be waiting until they tired. Even now, despite allowing her anger to give her more strength, her stamina was waning. There was only so much of the *essences* she could channel, and what she'd just done was more than Amiya would have thought possible for herself.

The cavern rumbled, and the lava man stretched his arms out. He whipped his left arm toward the trio, and a huge chunk of the cavern wall broke apart and fell toward them.

Joga punched his fist in that direction and the rock broke apart. Amiya focused on the now smaller but still large pieces of rock and threw her arm forward. The rocks raced at the surprised lava man and crashed into him.

What must be a ton of rock crashed into the man-creature and knocked him into the wall. Tiny pieces of molten skin chipped and fell away.

Nandi dropped her hands to her sides, palms facing up, and curled her fingers. She threw hands up, and several stalagmites punched through the ground, two impaling the lava man and causing more of his lava rock skin to break apart.

He screamed and a funnel of lava more than twice his height formed in front of him, and raced straight at the group.

That thing's huge! Amiya focused *air*, and jumped to her sister's side. Together they threw their shoulders forward as if pushing against an unseen wall.

The lava funnel crashed into the invisible wall and began to drill through it. Nandi clamped her eyes shut and gritted her teeth.

Amiya thought her teeth would crack as well, so hard were they clenched.

Joga broke off a bit of his assault and focused *water*, sending the *essence's* namesake into the molten funnel. He followed with a blast of freezing air, and the funnel gradually began to freeze.

After several tense heartbeats, Amiya started feel relief from the intense heat, but she knew it would be short lived. *Urgh,* she thought, then glanced at Sama, still crouched defensively to the side of the conflict. *Will you get yourself together and do something, already?* She felt her strength slipping away, little by little. *Come on, Sama. We can't hold this ugly thing off much longer.*

As if hearing Amiya's silent plea, Sama lowered herself even more, and moved away from the wall where she'd been camouflaged and hopped into the freezing funnel. Amiya wished she could make her skin do that. It was the perfect disguise, well, except for when her cotton-headed sister nearly gave it all away by staring at Sama's hair earlier.

Sama raced through the funnel. The girl was fast, and by the time the funnel of lava had fully frozen and crashed to the ground the tatamble had just managed to leap free and slash her knife across the lava man's face.

He cried out and staggered away, but Sama wasn't done. The now red-skinned girl slashed him across the stomach, and when she saw only a few bits of rocky skin fall away, she reversed her grip and stabbed it into his chest.

The lava man stumbled under the assault, but then swept his arm out and backhanded the tatamble girl.

Amiya flinched at the heavy blow that knocked Sama off her feet and toward the lava pool. The tatamble girl hit the ground hard and tumbled. Somehow, she managed to right herself and scratched and clawed the ground on her way to the ledge. With one last scrabble at the hard stone, Sama fell over the side.

"Sama!" Amiya and Nandi cried out, and Amiya felt her body grow hot. Flames lit around her and she sent them at the man in a storm of fire.

A storm of icy wind flew from Nandi and enveloped the fire, freezing it in the air. The frozen jagged flames crashed into the man and threw him back against the far wall.

Nandi threw her hands forward left, right, left, as if throwing stones, and large chunks of rock tore free from the opposite wall and flew across the cavern, pounding into the impaled man who hung suspended to the wall, unable to fend them off.

Somehow, the lava man shattered the frozen flames and dropped back to the platform, but an enraged Joga roared and charged him. The Khatala man's bellow made Amiya's chest rattle, and he slammed into the other man and lifted him by the neck with both hands.

Freezing air flowed from Joga into his enemy, and in a few heartbeats he hung completely frozen in Joga's grasp.

Amiya felt him delving a powerful buildup of *air*, and the frozen lava man exploded into thousands of icy chards.

He dropped to his knees and started sobbing. Amiya felt her own stomach twisting as the tears came. A pained grunt broke through the grief and she looked to where Sama had fallen. They raced to the edge, and Joga made it there first, already delving *air*. He dove to the side and threw his arm over.

Nandi made it to the edge just before Amiya, and they dropped to their hands and knees and looked over the side.

Sama hung on to a protrusion on the no doubt extremely hot rocky wall above the lava bed. How was that possible?

Joga extended his protective bubble of *air* to Sama and reached down. She swung a hand up and grabbed him. "Hold on!" Joga shouted. "Don't have a good grip on your hand."

Amiya felt helpless kneeling there, but there was nothing they could do but watch. From the corner of her eye she saw Nandi move closer, watching intently. She began delving air.

"What are you doing?" Amiya asked, but Nandi appeared not to have heard her. Maybe she thought to help lift Sama with a pocket of air beneath her. Amiya delved as well, not sure how she would do it, but determined to try. She would follow Nandi's lead.

"Hold!" Joga yelled just as he lost his grip on Sama's hand.

Amiya dropped to her knees and Nandi screamed.

"NO!" Joga bellowed.

Amiya felt a massive amount of *air* flow into and through Nandi, and her twin sister reached out toward Sama and fell over the side.

"NANDI!" Amiya screamed. She scrambled over to the side just in time to see her sister disappear into the molten pool.

"NANDI! NO!" Amiya started to dive in after her sister, but Joga's strong arms wrapped around her and pulled her back. "Get off me!" She shouted. "Let me go! I can freeze the lava! Help me do it!"

She kicked and squirmed and pulled at his hands, but his grip was like iron. Her adrenaline played out, she started to shake as sorrow washed over her. The loss of Sama hurt, but the loss of her twin sister, the other part of herself, was more than she could bear. How could she live in this world without Nandi? They had entered the world only seconds apart, and they had planned to leave the world the same. But not like this. Not now.

Grief overwhelmed her, and for the first time in her twelve years of life, Amiya cried. Her sister and best friend, gone. Her father lost to her. Her new friend who had helped save Nandi's life, gone. The world suddenly lost meaning, and she didn't care what happened to it.

"Ssh," Joga cooed, rocking her in his arms. Amiya had completely lost her focus on *air*, but Joga had them wrapped in a cool pocket. "Did not hurt," he said. "Happened fast." The words were not comforting, though she knew he meant them to be. She wanted to punch him in the face.

"Yes it does!" a voice said from over the side.

Amiya dropped to the ground when Joga suddenly released her. She scrambled to the edge and looked over the side to see Nandi and Sama, arms wrapped around each other, slowly rising out of the pool of lava.

"What?" Joga breathed.

Amiya grasped *air*. She could see the strain on Nandi's face, feel her struggling to pull as much of the *essence* as she could to rise out of the lava while maintaining the bubble of freezing air around them.

As hot as that pool was, she would have had to be constantly flowing air cold enough to freeze them both solid.

Amiya felt what her sister was doing and imitated it. "Keep them cool!" she yelled at Joga, and the Khatala man complied. He wrapped the two girls in a pocket of freezing air, and the relief was visible on Nandi's face. They rose a bit more, but she was still struggling.

Amiya threw all of her strength into *air*, and sent it down. The lava around Nandi and Sama began to draw back from the sides first, then from below.

The strain threatened to overwhelm her, but Amiya held her focus and her will. She thought she'd watched her sister die. She'd kill herself before letting it truly happen. She dropped to her knees but held her focus. Below, Nandi panted.

"I don't know ... how much longer ... I can hold on, Amiya."

"You better not let go!" Amiya shouted at her. "You shut up and focus. You hear me? You shut your mouth and throw in everything you have!"

"Amiya—"

"SHUT UP!" Amiya screamed, and the ground shook beneath them.

The lava receded further, and Nandi and Sama flew out of it with such force they hit the wall behind Joga and fell in a heap.

Amiya screamed, and her body erupted in flames. Decius had taken their father away. Their home was destroyed by the monsters that molten man created, and he had nearly killed Nandi and Sama. And now they were trapped in this Fallen cursed volcano! Amiya wished the lava man was alive again so she could kill him. She wanted him to suffer tenfold all the suffering he had caused. She was angry. Angry at Decius. Angry at the molten man. Angry that they were trapped here. Angry at everything that had happened to lead them to this fiery tomb.

A tomb for someone else.

She felt *fire* flowing into her, through her. From someplace far away, she heard Nandi screaming her name.

No. They would not die here. They would not die in the middle of a volcano while that fat archminister laughed at their demise. She would find him and bring the whole of creation down on his head ...

"Amiya!"

The fire spread, and it was as if the world itself was aflame. A column of fire erupted from her and shot into the roof of the cavern. The flames cut through the rock like a knife through butter.

"Amiya!"

She hated this volcano. That thing had lived here before Joga had killed it. That lava man had lived here before Joga had killed him. She looked down at the lava and wished she could destroy it for what it had almost done to her sister.

"Amiya!"

The flames around her began to diminish as if something was fighting against them. Amiya pushed, but it was like pushing against a strong bubble. It gave way every time Amiya pushed against it, then contracted tighter the instant she eased up. Each time, it drew in a little closer.

Cool, soothing air wrapped around the flames and gently extinguished them. Her rage played out, Amiya collapsed and the world went dark.

48

JOGA

Never had air smelled so sweet.

Joga drew in another deep breath and blew out a cloud in front of his face. He looked down at the girl cradled in his arms. He still couldn't believe what he'd witnessed. So much power wrapped in a little package of skinny arms and legs only four feet tall.

So much power, but so much rage. By all accounts, the girls were well raised and well loved, but this girl had a fire within her that needed to be controlled.

"You're sure she's fine?" Nandi asked.

Joga smiled down at her. "Will be fine. Exhausted herself."

Nandi nodded and looked at her sister, sleeping soundly in Joga's arms. She almost looked sad. "I don't know where all that anger comes from."

Joga thought he had an idea. His parents had been killed when he was a boy, younger than these two. He understood that anger, but Khatala tribes raised children as a community. Adults and their children had helped, but his adopted sister, Mikuna, had been the biggest influence aside from the Ancients.

"Can help," Joga said. After all they'd been through together, he knew that his tribe would welcome these girls, and even Sama, as family.

He looked at the tatamble girl who stood on Nandi's other side. The girl had been resourceful. She might not have been able to delve the *essences*, but she'd found her place in the fight. It was amazing how she was able to change her skin color to blend with her surroundings so well. She fussed over her bandaged hands until Nandi gently grabbed her wrists.

"You're gonna tear those off and the air is gonna blow over that burned skin. It'll hurt a lot, I'm telling you."

Nandi had been a surprise as well. How the girl had managed to keep Sama from being burned alive from that distance, Joga couldn't say. Even when they thought she'd fallen into the lava, Nandi hadn't given up. Joga glanced at the little girl and shook his head. She was just as powerful as her sister. Might she even be more powerful? He thought about how Nandi had maintained a freezing bubble of *air* around Sama after she'd gone over the side, while still hurling powerful attacks against their enemy in those final moments. Was she more powerful, or more versatile?

"Sama doesn't like hands being wrapped," the green-haired girl said. "But Sama likes pain in hands less. Will try not to tear."

Nandi turned back to Joga. "Thanks for the offer to help, but we've still got to find our dad."

"Yes," Joga replied.

"Thanks for agreeing to help us get back to New Dama," she continued. "I'm sure once Amiya is back to normal we can find a ride to Altarra from there."

"Will find a way," Joga said. "And will find your father."

Nandi frowned up at him. "Through your weird accent it sounds like you're including yourself."

Joga frowned at her. "Think I would leave you after save my life. Before, I counted you friend. Now, you are family." He deepened his frown, then bounced his eyebrows. "Even though disobey and help me. Told you I could not have help."

"Um, no," the girl said. "You told us you couldn't have help from your people. We're not your people."

Joga thought about that. He remembered Mikuna's dream of a fiery rock splitting in two perfect halves, one aflame. She'd said the split rock would help him in some way. He laughed and winked at the Marailander girl. "So it is. Girl is right."

He drew in another sweet breath of brisk spring air. "Thank you," he said. "Help fulfill my bloodmark. You are family." He looked at Sama. "My sisters."

Sama hadn't seemed to be paying attention, but she looked up at him with an unreadable expression. "Sisters?" she said in that somewhat husky voice. "How can tatamble and Khatala be brother and sister?"

"Here," Joga said, pointing at the center of his chest.

Sama looked at him skeptically. "You ... Sama's brother?"

"Would give my life for you, sister Sama," he replied.

A flash of emotion came and went across the girl's face.

"Not think Khatala would be friend. Never think Khatala would be brother." She looked back to the fields beyond, then back into Joga's eyes. Reading him. "Sama would be sister to Joga Khatala. Sama would give life for him."

She already had, or near enough. Joga owed these three girls a debt he could never repay, but he would start by helping them find their father, then maybe finding a way to make peace between the Khatala and the tatamble. It was the only thing he could think to do.

He turned and gazed back at the volcano behind. He had fulfilled his bloodmark and the threat of the mulgin was no more. He didn't know what that man was, but he hoped there were no more like him. Joga had never felt such terrible power.

A feeling came over him, and his smile fell away. He peered at the top of the volcano, and though of course it was too high for him to make anything out, he couldn't shake the feeling that something was watching them.

"We go," he said, still staring. "Can still make New Dama before night."

"Good idea," Nandi said. "I don't want to be anywhere outside at night anymore."

At that moment Joga couldn't agree more.

49

EMIEL

They skidded to a stop and looked around, but the hallway was empty. "This is creeping me out," Emiel said under his breath. Beside him, Bone unsheathed his sword.

"No response?" the voice said.

"What would I respond?" Amoura replied. She stood facing forward while Emiel and Bone watched the other direction.

"A proper question."

The voice came from behind them, and Emiel and Bone turned to see a swirling column of wind, and the magi master stepped out of it.

"Now that's a nice trick," Bone said.

"I wouldn't call attention to myself were I you, mercenary." Vladrick's ring flared silver, and Bone lifted into the air. He hit the ceiling twenty feet above, and Emiel dove out of the way to avoid the falling sword. Bone dropped from the ceiling and Amoura's ring flared silver as well, and the mercenary's body slowed until he dropped safely to the floor.

A blast of air pounded into them, and Emiel was swept off his feet. He hit the ground in a backward roll, but forced himself into a crouch. Amoura still stood, and leaned against the blast, her dark blue robes flapping behind her. Amoura's ring was glowing steadily silver, and it looked to Emiel as if she was throwing everything she had into fighting against the magi master's assault. At the other end of the hallway, Vladrick's robes swirled gently around him.

Vladrick made an appreciative expression. "Not bad." As if hit by an invisible force, Amoura stumbled backward. "This is a shame, Amoura. Such potential wasted on a girl so hesitant to fully immerse herself in what she could become under my tutelage."

"You would fashion me in your image," Amoura grunted. "I have my own mind."

"You are willful in all the wrong ways."

"You are uncomfortable with my possession of morals."

Vladrick frowned and Amoura lifted off her feet and flew backward. She stopped midair and floated above the floor.

Vladrick's eyebrows rose. "You surprise me, young lady. I hadn't expected such strength."

Amoura dropped to the floor and she fell to her knees, but scrambled back to her feet.

Her ring flared silver.

Vladrick's ring flared red.

A column of fire the width of the entire hallway extended toward Amoura, and the woman leaned back, then threw her shoulder forward, and the flames slammed into a wall of air. Her face beaded with perspiration, but she gritted her teeth and pushed back.

"Very good..." Vladrick started to say, but the flames suddenly split in four smaller columns and arched back toward him. The magi master crossed his arms, and just before the flames reached him, they burst into a cloud of smoke.

Emiel heard footsteps running away from him, and he heard a grunt, followed by the sound of a sword slicing through air. He heard it again, and again, followed by Vladrick's soft laughter.

"Brave fool boy," Vladrick said from somewhere in that thick cloud, and Emiel heard armor shuffling and Bone cry out.

Amoura ran through the smoke, and Emiel saw a flash of blue, then silver, then red. He crept forward and squinted against the smoke. *I have no idea what I'm doing. How could I possibly help with this?*

With no weapon, and his enemy nearly twice his size, Emiel felt helpless.

Amoura screamed, followed by another holler from Bone.

"Such a waste of resources," Vladrick said from somewhere in the cloud.

As the smoke started to thin, Emiel caught sight of Bone pressed against the wall, holding the naked blade of his sword in a reverse grip, the tip of which was pressed into his stomach. Blood dribbled from both of his gloved hands.

A gasp from overhead drew his attention to the ceiling, where Amoura was pinned, her face was blue and her mouth was open. *He's choking her with* air, *somehow.*

Emiel thought fast. The magi master had his back to him, but he still wasn't sure what to do. The sound of Vladrick's voice threatened to send him into a panic.

"Wait there but a moment longer, Emiel Dharr, and I will attend to you. There will soon be a vacancy in the position of master apprentice. An opportunity for you, perhaps?"

Amoura's body gave a shudder, and Bone arched his neck and cried out as a tiny stream of blood fell from his stomach, where the tip of his sword pierced him. Emiel licked his lips. *We all live or we all die.*

As quietly as he could manage, he ran toward the big man. He was but a few feet away when he was buffeted by a blast of air that sent him tumbling backwards.

"Idiocy," Vladrick said. "It's unfortunate I must look elsewhere for ... *auck!*"

The magi master stumbled sideways, and clamped a hand to his left eye. Amoura dropped from the ceiling and plummeted to the floor.

Emiel hopped to his feet and sprinted toward her. He dove the last few feet with his arms outstretched. He felt a rush of the *air essence* flow through his body, through his arms, his hands, and it rushed upwards to wrap around Amoura. Her descent slowed until she was gently deposited on the ground. Body still extended in midair, Emiel landed flat on his chest with a winded gasp.

Amoura's eyes glowed silver, and Emiel felt her delving *air*. A rush of precious oxygen swirled into her mouth, and she inhaled deeply and started coughing.

Bone grunted and pushed his sword away so forcefully it flew from his bloodied hands and clanged to the ground beside Vladrick, who was still holding his eye.

"Very well," the magi master said. "I will end this now…"

His head snapped back, and he grunted. His ring glowed silver but somehow, a fist-sized rock passed through the protective column of *air*, and struck him in the same eye again.

Vladrick roared, and Emiel didn't know if it was pain or anger. Giggling echoed from further down the hall. Lief!

The tinfar remained out of sight, but the rocks continued to assault Vladrick, who had now taken to guarding his face with his arm.

Emiel rushed to Bone first, since Amoura was already climbing to her feet. "You alright?"

"Aah whaddya think, spicetrader?" the boy groaned.

Emiel groaned as he helped the armored young man to his feet. "Well enough, apparently. Let's move."

The words had barely left his mouth, when Emiel's feet locked to the floor. He looked at Bone, who wore a similarly confused expression that bordered on alarm.

"Only in death, will you leave this place," Vladrick said. A heavy force dropped on them and pressed Emiel and the mercenary down to the floor.

"Oh shut up," said Lief's tiny voice from farther down the hall. A storm of rocks assaulted Vladrick that had him growling as he fended off the stinging projectiles while trying to find the source.

Emiel glanced further down the hall. *Where did she find rocks in this place?* He turned to Amoura. "You good to run?"

"I will do my best," she replied. She turned to face Vladrick, and held her hand out. Emiel's mouth dropped open when her ring and her eyes flared red, and the magus sent a column of fire racing at Vladrick. Her ring stayed red, but the red in her eyes shifted to silver. The fire column wrapped around Vladrick, and *air* send it swirling in several directions at once. When Amoura dropped her hand, the fire continued to swirl around the magi master despite her eyes and ring having reverted back to normal.

They sprinted down the hall, Bone holding his sword in one hand and his stomach in the other. "Path ... to the left," he panted. "Horses ... just outside.

"We must hurry." Amoura said. "He'll break through."

She barely uttered that last word when Vladrick's enraged bellow shook the hallway with a burst of red light. Amoura's eyes flared silver just as a ball of fire came racing toward their backs. The fireball hit a barrier of *air* and exploded in a shower of flaming pebbles. The group stumbled, but continued forward.

"Oof!" Bone grabbed the back of his neck. "That burned."

"Better a burned neck than being immolated," Amoura responded.

"Not complaining," the mercenary said.

"This way!" Lief finally appeared in front of them. She hopped and landed on Emiel's shoulder. "Just around the corner." She pointed, and Emiel saw the end of the corridor, enticingly close.

As they ran down the hall toward freedom, a figure in a purple cloak cinched at the waist appeared out of nowhere and smiled at them. His eyes—also purple—glittered, and before they could react, he winked and the space just in front of them bubbled.

Amoura tried to stop, but they crashed into her back and the group stumbled through the bubble and crashed to the floor.

"Urgh," Bone groaned through clenched teeth.

Amoura looked up, and her mouth fell open. "Oh no."

"What now?" Emiel climbed to his feet and looked around. They stood on a path of rock that was no more than eight feet wide. On either side of the path was endless darkness.

"Wouldn't want to fall in there," Bone said, peeking over the side. "Where in the cursed names of all the Fallen are we?"

"Somewhere I'm guessing we really don't want to be," Emiel said.

Lief looked around. "I don't like this place." The concerned expression on the tinfar's face sent a chill down Emiel's spine.

"The Maze," Amoura said. She sounded on the verge of hopelessness. "We've been sent to The Maze."

"What's The Maze?" Bone asked, looking around.

"The Maze of Khell," Amoura said. "The worst place we could possibly be. Every path leads to a different horror, but some paths lead to places you would rather die than enter."

EPILOGUE

"That was interesting."

Hands clasped behind his back, Devrin stared across the distance from his place atop the volcano at the unlikely group. A Khatala, a tatamble, and two Marailanders traveling together. Three members of three groups that have no love for each other, yet they enter the lair of Layik's lavakhan and not only kill it, but kill him as well.

"So many years it took to groom him," Devrin said, though he hardly cared. Training a droughtlord did take work and a good amount of time. Sometimes more than a century. He shrugged. It mattered little, for what was a century or two when one lived forever?

Devrin looked to the southeast. He could feel Shurza even from this distance. Of all the Fallen, he had been the sole voice of uncertainty with creating the thing. Millennia after millennia they had suffered humiliating defeat to the hated Illuminarians until Mordayne had devised the idea. *A good option at the time. A mistake for the future.* Devrin had always been the one to see things more clearly. He'd warned of the potential for disaster at creating a being of absolute hatred, a void of light and life itself.

He'd been overruled to a person. Not a single one of the other Fallen had so much as entertained his words, so focused were they on their hatred of the Illuminarians.

Devrin narrowed his glowing red eyes. They rarely listened, and when Shurza had so decisively beaten the Illuminarians and trapped them in a void of absolute darkness, they'd believed their victory complete.

But somehow, one last Illuminarian had escaped their attention, and managed to trap Shurza and defeat every last one of them.

A tiny bubble of anger rose in Devrin, and the ground beneath him cracked and died. How he hated Malkiem, the most powerful of the Illuminarians. The coward had hidden himself while Devrin and the other Fallen had defeated his brethren, then come with his trickery and beaten them when they had finally achieved victory after so long.

Devrin released his anger. This time was different. There were no longer any Illuminarians to in the way, only a bunch of children playing at wielding the *essences*. The fact that Shurza was free again was a sword that cut both ways. It was unpredictable and wanted nothing more than to destroy everything. But it was now the source of power for the Fallen, and their ability to walk this world in their whole form. Another unforeseen and unfortunate side effect of creating the thing.

"You were a fool, Mordayne," Devrin said under his breath. "But once we finally have this world in hand, I'll clean up your mess, as always."

He turned away and descended back into the volcano. The others would have awakened by now, and soon a council would be called. Until the call came, Devrin would plan. He'd tried to instruct Layik against unleashing the drauk and other creatures of the underworld, but the fool had been too hungry to show his power; too eager.

Devrin wrinkled his lips at the thought of a droughtlord, *his* droughtlord, falling at the hands of three little girls and a Khatala man.

He sank into the pool of lava and closed his eyes, enjoying the soothing warmth of the thick magma flowing around him.

* * *

Dan Petrie sifted through his notes, then pulled a stack of books closer. He grabbed a thin book and thumbed through it, then referred back to a tome that must have weighed as much as he did.

He was close, he knew it. *No better place for this research than the Kingdom of Jietar.* The library was older than anyone could remember, and had survived two wars, and the gentrification of an entire section of the city. Some of the books in this library were older than man of the cities of Marai.

"There has to be something." Dan ran a hand through his silky black hair as he sifted through the pages. "Something."

A librarian came by with a pitcher of water and refilled his mug. Dan smiled in thanks and returned to the book.

"Hmm. The War of the Immortals." It was only reference he'd found to any type of ancient conflict that resulted in the casting down of the Fallen by the Illuminarians. Every book he'd found on the subject had detailed the war with armies of men from every region fighting against the minions of the Fallen, while the immortals fought the great battle to determine the fate of every living thing in the world.

Though each book's description varied, the end was essentially the same; the Fallen were defeated and cast into a lifeless void where they remained for time eternal until the hearts of men grew too dark.

Dan carefully turned the delicate pages of the tome, then stopped on a faded page. "Never seen this before." He skimmed the typical depictions of the War of the Immortals until he came to a section where the war was covered in more detail. Names were even given to certain events of note. Dan wiped his sweating palms on his pants and read on. The Light. The Song. The Sundering. The Incursion. The War of the Immortals. The Dark Creation. Unleashed.

Dan felt a great weight pressing down on him as he read the last two words. He repeated the words over and over again, hoping to find some other way to interpret them, but there wasn't. Jack and Mick were dead, but he had to find a way to right the wrong they had created; the wrong they had let loose on the world.

Dan read those two words again, his heart sinking each time. He had to find a way to stop this. He had to find some way to stop The Ruination.

ALSO BY RAMÓN TERRELL

<u>World of a Broken Age:</u>

Echoes of a Shattered Age

Legends of a Shattered Age

Heroes of a Broken Age (forthcoming)

<u>Hunter's Moon:</u>

Running from the Night

Hunter's Moon

Darkness of Day

Revenire (Forthcoming)

<u>The Fairies:</u>

Out of Ordure

<u>Saga of Ruination:</u>

Emergence (Forthcoming)

ACKNOWLEDGMENTS

A lot happened between the beginning and end of this book, and my usual tidily met deadline was shattered. Through delays and some rough challenges, this book was finally completed, and I cannot thank Rick Rhodes and Paula Howard enough for your help in beta reading and editing this work. The two of you worked hard and quickly to help me get this one done, and I am every appreciative of it.

Also, I'd like to thank my ever patient wife, Tanya, for understanding my need to burrow away in the cave to get the work done. Although there were many Canucks games that helped with this, I am thankful nonetheless.

Last, and most certainly not least, thank you to all of the fans who have read every book I've written. I am truly blessed to have you all, and thank you a million times over.

Ramón Terrell
February 16, 2014

ABOUT THE AUTHOR

Ramón Terrell is an author and actor who instantly fell in love with fantasy the day he opened R. A. Salvatore's: The Crystal Shard. Years (and many devoured books) later he decided to put pen to paper for his first novel. After a bout with aching carpals, he decided to try the keyboard instead, and the words began to flow.

As an actor, he has appeared in the hit television shows Supernatural, izombie, Arrow, and Minority Report, as well as the hit comedy web series Single and Dating in Vancouver. He also appears as one of Robin Hood's Merry Men in Once Upon a Time, as well as an Ark Guard on the hit TV show The 100. When not writing, or acting, he enjoys reading, video games, hiking, and long walks with his wife around Stanley Park in Vancouver BC.